AMONG
THE
ASHES

GRAHAM ELIOT NOVELS

The Well of the Soul
Among the Ashes
The Place of Descent
The Invisible Thread

A GRAHAM ELIOT NOVEL

AMONG
THE
ASHES

DOUG POWELL

BRENTWOOD
PRESS

AMONG THE ASHES

This is a work of fiction. All characters and events portrayed in this novel
are either fictitious or used fictitiously.

First Edition: 2022 White Fire Press
Second Edition: 2025 Brentwood Press, LLC
P.O. Box 132
Arrington, TN 37014
BrentwoodPress.net

ISBN: 979-8-89689-488-9 (print)
979-8-89689-492-6 (digital)

10 9 8 7 6 5 4 3 2 1

ONE

Amber light tinted the small room, casting a fragile ambience like an ember that could just as easily flame up as extinguish. Graham Eliot allowed himself a moment to appreciate the equivocal light and how appropriate it was given that—in a way—it illuminated the future and the past simultaneously. The future was found in a complex assembly of black metal supports that yawned upward to form a large mechanical V-shape standing on one side of the room. A network of cables ran along the frame like muscles and tendons connecting bones. The wires were collected into a single thick electrical snake serpentining across the tiled floor to the base of a wooden table where the cables split into capillaries connecting to a control unit. A large monitor sat on the desk displaying the software interface that controlled the fifty-megapixel digital camera mounted to a conservation copy stand. Most of the screen was devoted to a window framing the item it documented. The past was found in the form of a 1,500-year-old codex sitting in the jaws of the stand.

Graham looked from the manuscript to its image on the monitor. The page had roughly the same dimensions of a small paperback, but the image on the screen was twice its actual size. The camera zoomed out, fitting not only the full folio on the screen, but also grayscale and color scale bars so the images could be calibrated for color accuracy.

"Looks good to me, Dr. Eliot."

Graham leaned over the shoulder of the graduate student operating the camera, double-checked the settings, and made a final adjustment to the light temperature.

Alexander Pearl had become his grad assistant only a few months earlier, but they quickly developed a good rapport after discovering a common love of what Alexander called *Classic Rock*, but what Graham simply called *music*. In the first week of working together, Graham had been showing him how to use the image processing software and asked if he preferred to be called Alexander, or if he went by Alex or Al. Alexander responded by saying, "Only if I can call you Betty." Graham had guffawed at the reference to Paul Simon's "You Can Call Me Al," and they had talked music ever since.

"What do you think?" Alexander asked. "Is what you see what you get?"

"Sometimes it's hard to tell," Graham said. "It's going to take us a while to sort through it all. But I always love discovering the unseen."

Collecting the data required twenty-four images taken under various narrow wavelengths of light from across the spectrum, from infrared to ultraviolet. The images would then be compiled, enabling the final image to be enhanced using many of the same techniques that astronomers used to create pictures of galaxies and stars too distant to be examined any other way. This process of multi-spectral imaging had produced a number of surprising results, including the recovery of palimpsests—texts that had been erased and written over.

"Take it," Graham said, tapping Alexander's shoulder.

Alexander clicked a button and saved the image as an uncompressed RAW file that was then converted to TIFF and JPG formats before being uploaded to a database that scholars from all over the world could access. In Los Angeles, other students on the team from Calbi University would create an additional tape backup for storage as insurance that would allow the images to be recovered in the event of a catastrophic failure of the database server.

In the past, scholars had to travel to wherever the manuscripts were—libraries, museums, monasteries, private collections—and ask permission to study the copies. Sometimes a scholar would arrive at a remote monastery after weeks of travel only to be denied access to the material. That changed when Graham's good friend and colleague Andrew Singer began an ambitious program aimed at digitizing every extant New Testament manuscript in the original Greek—over 5,800 copies. It had been wildly successful and expanded its scope to include early translations, commentaries, and writings of early Church Fathers.

But the program was threatened a year ago with the murder of Singer after he discovered a copy of an expanded version of the Copper Scroll, an unsolved treasure map found among the Dead Sea Scrolls. The map had contained enough additional detail about the locations of priceless items from the second Jewish Temple that he had been killed for it. After following the map's newly identified locations to prevent the murderer from damaging sites of profound biblical importance—including the Temple Mount—Graham assumed the work left undone by Singer.

"I still can't believe I get to do this," Alexander mused. "This camera is amazing. The next best thing to hydrosulfurate of ammonia."

Graham laughed as he shook his head, thinking of how the chemical used in the 1800s as a reagent to enhance fading texts just as often destroyed them.

"And now look at us. Think about how far we've come. In the middle of the Sinai Peninsula, in the world's oldest monastery, in the world's oldest operating library, surrounded by a laptop more sophisticated than the computer used in the moon landing."

As if to prove the point, Alexander transferred the image to the MacBook Pro sitting next to the monitor. He checked to make sure it was copying to the backup server in the cloud as Graham started tuning the LED lights, programming the wavelength for the next shot.

Alexander had recently graduated with a master's degree in Ancient Near East Studies from the University of Michigan and had come to Calbi University to do his doctoral studies under Graham. Alexander's upper Midwest accent sounded harsh and barbed among the laid-back delivery of the southern California natives. His dark complexion, stubbled beard, thin frame, and long, wild hair made him appear equal parts hipster and ascetic to the undergrads he taught. Graham thought he favored a young Chris Cornell, but when he said as much, he found none of his students had any idea who the singer or the band Soundgarden was, making him feel old.

What surprised Graham most about Alexander Pearl— aside from the stately name that seemed, on him, stolen from another time and place—was that his eccentric look encased a quick-witted, thoughtful young man who was both welcoming to and welcomed by everyone. And that had led him to a desert on the other side of the world, to the Sacred and Imperial Monastery of the God-trodden Mount of Sinai, better known as Saint Catherine's.

"So if Saint Catherine's has its own camera to digitize this stuff, why are we here?"

Graham kept his eyes on the screen as he adjusted the settings for the lights. "Look at all these books. There are 4,500 manuscripts—sermons, liturgies, histories, biographies of saints—all kinds of stuff. Only the Vatican Library has more manuscripts. A lot of it was shot on microfilm sixty or seventy years ago. They've been working on digitizing it for several years, and the rate they're going, it would take another 300 years to finish. Nothing happens quickly here. They need all the help they can get."

"It's kind of funny if you think about it," Alexander said. "This is where God spoke from the Burning Bush, right?"

"Yes…" Graham said quizzically.

"Words came from the fire. Well, the fire in the monastery gave us all these texts. Words came from the fire again."

"Yeah, I guess you're right." Graham smiled as he thought about how the manuscripts they were working on had been discovered. "I was in grade school when that fire happened—1975—and they still haven't finished inventorying all of the manuscripts."

"So that was like right after Moses was here, right?"

Graham laughed. "I might be old, but I grew up with all the good music."

"No argument from me," Alexander said, throwing his hands up. "But it does make me wonder how many other forgotten rooms there are in the monastery. And if it'll take a fire to discover them as well."

"It'd be great if there were ancient manuscripts in all the debris we sorted through," Graham said. "But even without the New Finds from the fire, there was already more work here than we could do. The New Finds added another 50,000 fragments from more than a thousand different manuscripts."

"Not to mention the icons," Alexander said. "Some of the oldest to survive."

"Exactly. A massive haul. Prince Charles may have donated the money for the camera rig they have, but he couldn't give them more time in the day for the work or more monks to do it. And that camera costs more than the car you drive."

"That's not saying much."

A knock at the door made both of them look up from their tasks.

"Enter," Graham answered.

White light spilled into the room as the librarian entered. Father Nikolaos divided the jamb with a tall, almost skeletal figure draped in a black robe. A long, graying beard hung from his gaunt face, atop which sat the kalpaki hat of Greek Orthodox clerics, the traits accumulating to create the effect of elongation. Dark, melancholy eyes were shielded by wire-rimmed glasses that looked anachronistic on his otherwise ancient appearance. He carried an air of stillness about him, and seemed to move only when necessary, a discipline exemplified as he nodded a greeting to both men in a single, tilt of his head.

"I'm sorry to disturb your work, Dr. Eliot, but may I have a moment to speak to you? In private?" His gentle tenor voice floated into the dim room, matching the delicate atmosphere. Father Nikolaos's English was almost without accent, and though Graham always imagined an exotic quality to the inflection, he knew it was actually Canadian and that Father Nikolaos was one of the first monks allowed at the monastery who was not from Greece.

"Of course."

Graham left Alexander with some instructions for continuing the work. As he closed the door, he could hear the first bars of the Genesis song "Behind the Lines" bleeding through Alexander's headphones.

TWO

Father Nikolaos guided Graham through the main room of the narrow library, hands clasped behind his back as he walked. Even in motion, the monk projected stillness, an illusion enhanced by the floor-length robe hiding the movement of his legs. As they passed a sign reading no photos or videos, Graham resisted the urge to make a joke, given the work he was there to do. Instead, he scanned the shelves of ancient books, and tried to make small talk out of the monastery's most famous manuscript.

"The history here is almost overwhelming. I remember as a student I would try to picture what this place was like when Codex Sinaiticus was found."

"Stolen." Father Nikolaos stopped and turned to look at Graham. "Surely you mean *stolen*."

The reaction made Graham wonder if his innocent banter had just provoked a quarrel about the story of the discovery of the oldest known complete New Testament.

"My apologies, Father. I meant no disrespect."

"I understand." Father Nikolaos gave another of his humble bows to acknowledge the contrition. He turned to lead them to a desk at the far end of the empty room. "Unfortunately, it is a tale told far too often. And like most such tales, its tellers fail to investigate the facts. Indulge me. Tell me the story as you know it."

Graham paused, suddenly uncertain about what he had never questioned. "Constantin von Tischendorf visited here in the 1840s, searching for ancient copies of the Bible. He was one of the first scholars to do anything like that. He found pages of ancient parchment in a basket that was going to be burned for heat. When he took a closer look, he recognized the text was the Septuagint, the Greek translation of the Old Testament. He found about forty-five pages and published them after he returned to Germany.

"In the following years, he came back two more times looking for the rest of the Bible. The second time he found the remainder of the Bible in the cell of one of the monks. Altogether, the codex contained the complete New Testament as well as a lot of the Old Testament. Pages were clearly missing, most from the beginning of the book, but some from the end. The codex was so old—mid-fourth century—that it was created before the end of the canonization process. Tischendorf then convinced the monks to send the manuscript to Saint Petersburg as a gift to the czar, who was the monastery's source of funding. As a result, the world's oldest Bible was put on display in a Russian museum. Sixty years later, the Soviet Union sold it to the British Museum. I've seen it there many times."

Father Nikolaos showed no emotion as he patiently listened to the account that had become one of the most well-known stories in biblical archaeology. When he spoke, his voice was utterly reasonable. "Consider this: have you ever burned parchment? It gives off very little heat. Not to mention the stench is unbearable. And surely I do not need to point out the irrationality of burning books to heat a library."

Graham knitted his brow in thought, but before he could respond, the monk continued.

"Consider also that Tischendorf did not speak modern

Greek well. Yet modern Greek was the only language spoken by the librarian at that time. How could the librarian convey to Tischendorf he was burning the manuscripts? That's who he claimed told him what was happening."

"I had no idea," Graham admitted.

"No. Then consider this." Father Nikolaos gestured to Graham to take a seat in the chair opposite him, and opened the lid of a MacBook Pro. After several mouse clicks, he spun the laptop around to reveal the screen and let it speak for itself.

Graham stared at the document for several seconds before picking his way through the handwritten modern Greek.

> *I, the undersigned, Constantin Tischendorf,*
> *attest that the holy confraternity of Mount Sinai*
> *has delivered to me as a loan an ancient manu-*
> *script of both testaments. Being the property of*
> *aforesaid monastery and containing 346 leaves*
> *and a small fragment. These I shall take with me*
> *to Saint Petersburg in order that I may collate*
> *the copy previously made by me with the original*
> *at the time of the publication of the manuscript.*
> *This manuscript I promise to return undamaged*
> *and in a good state of preservation to the holy*
> *confraternity of Sinai at its earliest request.*

Graham realized it was the note surprisingly discovered in 1960—some said a little too conveniently—and matched Tischendorf's handwriting.

"As you can see," Father Nikolaos said, pushing the computer aside, "we are still waiting for Tischendorf to honor his promise."

"Again, I did not mean to offend you, Father. Please forgive me. At least The New Finds returned some of Sinaiticus to you," Graham said, referring to the twelve folios and fourteen fragments of the legendary Bible that had been discovered in the debris of the forgotten storeroom.

Father Nikolaos formed a small, kind smile, which—on his normally passive face—looked almost radiant. "There is no need to keep apologizing, Dr. Eliot. I merely thought you would appreciate knowing the truth."

"I do," Graham said. "It's fascinating."

"Actually, that appreciation is why I wanted to speak with you," Father Nikolaos paused, apparently carefully choosing the words to say next as he kept his eyes on Graham. "I have been in contact with Chaim Yaniv at the Israel Antiquities Authority. He tells me you can be trusted. That you helped him in a sensitive matter."

Graham recalled the events of a year earlier in the wake of Singer's murder, the explosion that killed a friend and almost killed him, the discovery—and loss—of one of history's greatest treasures. It had been Yaniv, the director of the IAA's Robbery Prevention Division, who had entrusted him with the mission. Although it sounded like a life-threatening quest, Graham looked back on it for what it was: the tool God used to restore his faith just when he had abandoned it.

"That's true," Graham said, guarding himself with a short answer until he knew what they were talking about.

"Good." Father Nikolaos tilted his head down slightly and arched his eyebrows. "What I am sharing with you must remain confidential."

"Yes, of course. What is this about?"

"I'm afraid it is far more serious than a stolen book." Father Nikolaos raised his head, resetting his expression to its usual state. "It is about murder."

THREE

"Murder?" Graham flinched in surprise. "In a monastery with a legendary library? Sounds like *The Name of the Rose*," he said, citing the Umberto Eco novel.

Father Nikolaos rocked in a single, almost silent chuckle. "I promise there will be no inquisition," he said, adding his own reference to the book. "And not to worry—it is not a recent murder."

"I'm intrigued," Graham said, lacing his fingers together on the table.

"In the winter of 1938, a Palestinian Arab came to this monastery," Father Nikolaos said, nodding once toward the room they had crossed. "He asked to speak to the skevophylax, the keeper of the sacred vessels here. The man claimed to be the driver for James L. Starkey on the day he was murdered."

"I read all about Starkey's murder," Graham said. "Very strange circumstances."

"Indeed." Father Nikolaos rested his elbows on the desk, tenting his fingers. "Tell me what you remember about them."

Graham took a deep breath as he collected the major points. "He spent several years excavating Lachish, about forty miles southwest of Jerusalem. He was traveling from there to Jerusalem to attend a preview of the Rockefeller Museum before the grand opening. Some of the artifacts he had un-covered made up one of the featured exhibits. But he never arrived. The car was stopped outside of Hebron by Arab ban-dits. This was odd because Starkey was well-known in the area and the Palestinian locals liked him because he hired them at the site. But he had recently grown a long beard, and that kept the bandits from recognizing him. They thought he was a Zionist, so they shot him."

"And do you recall the artifacts that were exhibited at the Rockefeller Museum?" Father Nikolaos asked.

"They were ostraca—pottery shards that contained writ-ing. They were from 588 BC, if I remember correctly. That was when Lachish was sacked by Nebuchadnezzar, two years before he conquered Jerusalem, destroyed the Temple, and exiled the Jews to Babylon. As Nebuchadnezzar's army had approached, Jewish military outposts needed a way to report information to the commanders at Lachish. But because Nebuchadnezzar was at war with Egypt, papyrus—which was made there—was scarce, so pottery shards were used for the communiqués. Starkey found eighteen ostraca, and three more were found in the months following his death."

"That was the account published in the newspapers." A spark lit Father Nikolaos's eyes. "Here is the part of the story you don't know. The driver told the skevophylax that Starkey was killed because of an ostracon he had just unearthed."

"I'm not sure I understand," Graham said. "He discovered almost twenty ostraca."

"But Starkey kept the last ostracon secret." Father Niko-laos paused, emphasizing the words with silence. "The excava-tors in the camp knew he had discovered it, but he refused to show it to anyone."

"Why not?"

"The driver did not know. But there were rumors in the camp before he died. Apparently, it mentioned something about Mount Sinai."

Graham squinted in bewilderment. "Why would a military communiqué concerning a battle at Lachish mention Mount Sinai?"

Father Nikolaos fanned his hands, showing his palms empty in an almost liturgical gesture. "Like you, I am at a loss. I was told the driver did not know why the mention would be a secret or controversial. What shocked him was that there were Arabs who would kill because of it and wanted to destroy it. But what seemed to bother this man the most was that Starkey knew his killers. He had befriended them earlier in the dig."

"That doesn't make sense from the stories I read. If they knew who Starkey was, why did the reports say it was because they thought he was Jewish?"

"According to the driver, after they were stopped at gunpoint, he kept yelling that his passenger was Starkey. He insisted that they knew precisely who he was."

"That means that someone besides Starkey had to know what was written on it if others were willing to kill for it." He looked up in thought then focused on Father Nikolaos again. "There must have been a leak on the team."

"I agree. Especially given what happened to the bandits."

"I forget," Graham said. "What *did* happen to the bandits?"

"They were silenced." Father Nikolaos raised his brows meaningfully. "Two of the men were captured, tried, convicted, sentenced to death, and executed within twelve days of Starkey's murder."

"Sounds more like vigilante justice than a territory under British control."

The monk extended a finger, adding a point. "And four months later the leader of the bandits was killed in a gunfight with police near the place where Starkey died."

Graham shook his head. "And nobody thought that was suspicious?"

"As I said: it seems they were silenced."

Graham thought he detected a layer of dark humor buried in the euphemism.

"But there was another problem," Father Nikolaos continued. "The killers did not find the ostracon on Starkey. The driver thought that if Starkey had given it to them, he may have been allowed to live since it hadn't been published, let alone announced. Without the ostracon, the only way to insure it remained unknown was to intimidate anyone who knew about it by murdering its finder."

"Wait," Graham said, holding up a hand. "I don't understand why the driver cared so much about all this."

"Because this man—the driver—had the ostracon." Father Nikolaos paused again. "Starkey apparently handed it to him when they were being stopped by the bandits.

"Why would he do that?"

"The driver wondered the same thing, but he said he thought they didn't search him because he was an Arab. They pulled Starkey from the car and told the driver to keep going. Actually, they forced him to drive away at gunpoint."

"And they didn't say what they wanted?"

"The driver heard the bandits demand the ostracon as he left. But he watched what happened next in his mirrors. They made Starkey follow the car, then the leader raised his gun and shot him in the back twice. They left him for dead. The driver sped to Hebron, brought the police back, and found the body still lying where it had fallen. All his pockets had been turned out. The driver thought if anyone discovered he had the ostracon, he would be in danger as well, so he kept it a secret. But he never knew why it was important. To the few people who knew it existed, the ostracon simply disappeared."

"No one at the Rockefeller Museum knew anything about

it?" Graham asked. "Maybe he was going to announce it at the opening and add another item to the collection."

Father Nikolaos shrugged. "Perhaps. But if that was the case, it seems he did not tell anyone. There is no indication anyone at the museum knew it was missing. All I can tell you is that after the murder, the Arabs looted the excavation site. The driver thought they were looking for something specific. And when they didn't find it, he thought they might start to look for him. He wanted to rid himself of it, but he knew it was important. So he brought it to the safest place he could think of—Saint Catherine's. It is, after all, at Mount Sinai. He thought if there was anything to the rumor then the monks here would recognize its significance. And it would be safe from the Arabs because an order of protection had been placed on the monastery by the Prophet Muhammad himself."

FOUR

Graham had to think a moment. "You mean the Ashtiname?"

"Yes, the Patent of Muhammad."

Father Nikolaos reached for his laptop again and opened an image of a tattered sheet of parchment. The edges had blackened and cracked with age and bore the wounds of repeated rolling. A rough drawing of the chapel on the peak of Sinai sat in the top right corner, stairs zigzagging down from it. Below the steps, a mosque was squeezed into the space between the text and the right edge of the folio. Two handprints—one gilt, one black—sat below the body of text.

"I have seen the copies in the monastery museum, but I never took the time to study it."

Father Nikolaos motioned toward the screen. "According to tradition, Muhammad had been treated with kindness by the monks of the monastery. Some evidence suggests Muhammad became familiar with the monastery during the time when he led trade caravans, before he became the Prophet. In return for their hospitality, he issued the Ashtiname. The covenant protected the monks and exempted them from the usual obligations of non-Muslims in Muslim territory. Look at what it says." Father Nikolaos zoomed in on the image, pointed to a passage near the top of the text, and read aloud as he moved his finger across the Arabic letters.

"Whenever Christian monks, devotees, and pilgrims gather together, whether in a mountain or valley, or den, or frequented place, or plain, or church, or in houses of worship, truly we are behind them and shall protect them...for they are of my subjects and under my protection.

"I shall exempt them from that which may disturb them; of the burdens which are paid by others as an oath of allegiance. They must not give anything of their income but that which pleases them—they must not be offended, or disturbed, or coerced or compelled. Their judges should not be changed or prevented from accomplishing their offices, nor the monks disturbed in exercising their religious order, or the people of seclusion be stopped from dwelling in their cells."

Father Nikolaos leaned back from the screen. "This protection is, in fact, probably the reason this monastery still exists."

"What do you mean?"

"Just before the time of the first Crusade, a Caliph came to power, an evil man—al-Hakim, I believe his name was. He destroyed the Church of the Holy Sepulchre, then decided to destroy Saint Catherine's. But while he was on his way, he suddenly changed his mind."

"I remembered the Church of the Holy Sepulchre being damaged," Graham said, "but I had forgotten what he planned to destroy next. Sounds like a road-to-Damascus conversion."

"Hardly," Father Nikolaos said flatly. "One story is that the monks here repurposed a building as a mosque and added a minaret that he'd see as he grew near, hoping he'd show mercy. More likely, al-Hakim was shown the Ashtiname and ordered the mosque to be built. That is one of the things that most surprises our visitors—the mosque within the monastery. This covenant not only saved the lives of the monks, but also the library we are in right now. Remember, that was a time of iconoclasm when much of the heritage of the church was destroyed. This protection is how we came to have the largest collection of Byzantine icons in the world."

"Forgive me for asking," Graham said, "but what is your opinion that the Ashtiname was forged by the monks out of self-preservation?"

"Its authenticity would be hard to prove definitively," Father Nikolaos admitted. "However, despite the skepticism of some Orientalists, the Ashtiname has historically been viewed as authentic by most Islamic scholars, as well as by the Greek Orthodox Church."

Graham studied the image.

"What you see is not the original document, but a copy. The original was taken by Sultan Selim I to his palace in Istanbul in 1517, after the Ottomans took control of Egypt. The golden hand is his seal and vouches for its authenticity. The black handprint is Muhammad's signature. The patent is still there in the Topkapi Palace Museum. With very few exceptions, Muslim leaders have faithfully kept this covenant with the monastery. It is also why the Ashtiname is used as an example of the tolerance of Islam, and a model for how Christians and Muslims can coexist peacefully."

"And yet ISIS has attacked this place twice in recent years." Graham had had to consider this fact before his previous trip to Saint Catherine's.

"The monks have consistently met the requirements of the patent. And despite the exceptions you mention—which are rare—the Muslim rulers have kept Muhammad's promise for him."

"Actually, Sultan Selim broke the covenant just by removing the document," Graham said. "And every ruler since has been complicit."

"What do you mean?" Father Nikolaos looked more curious than concerned as the roles reversed and Graham pointed to the text and read aloud.

"Look at the next two sentences."

> *"No one is allowed to plunder these Christians, or destroy or spoil any of their churches, or houses of worship, or take any of the things contained within these houses and bring it to the houses of Islam. And he who takes away anything therefrom, will be one who has corrupted the oath of God, and, in truth, disobeyed his messenger."*

"Sultan Selim took something contained within this house—the Ashtiname—and brought it to the house of Islam."

Father Nikolaos released a puff of amusement. "I had never thought of it that way."

"Looks like he pulled a Tischendorf before Tischendorf did."

"I think you may be right." Father Nikolaos offered a small smile and nodded once. "Nevertheless, the protection granted by the patent is why Starkey's Arabic driver thought the ostracon would be safe here."

"But why doesn't anyone know this story? Why haven't you published a translation? I still don't understand."

Father Nikolaos folded his hands across his lap. "Given it has already cost several lives, surely you can see how it might be dangerous were it to become known. Also, to be candid, the ostracon's ownership is unclear. It was found in Lachish when it was still a part of Jordan, which itself was under

British control. There was no state of Israel at the time. Jews, Muslims, and Christians have each ruled this area at different times between then and now. The previous librarians had other things to occupy them as the whole region destabilized and shifted politically.

"That does make sense," Graham admitted. "The Ottoman Empire fell, Israel was formed, the kingdom of Saudi Arabia was formed, Israel captured the Sinai Peninsula, then returned it to Egypt years later—no one could be bothered by a shard of pottery."

"It is also why we still don't even know exactly what it says." Father Nikolaos held up a professorial finger. "No one with the proper training has seen it since Starkey handed it to his driver the day he died. I think it is time to change that."

"Are you asking me to translate it?"

Graham felt himself being evaluated by Father Nikolaos's unblinking stare.

"I am entrusting you with something of great value, and because the trust of the monastery has been violated so greatly in the past, it is hard for me to ask for your help. Yes, I am asking you to translate it."

"It seems my visit has developed a motif," Graham said.

"How so?"

"Lachish was destroyed by fire after a siege. Starkey discovered the ostraca in a layer of ash, just like the New Finds here."

Father Nikolaos allowed another modest smile, then turned serious as he tapped the desk with his finger for emphasis. "However, there is one condition: there must not be another Tischendorf incident."

Graham raised his right hand and touched the nearest bookcase with his left. "When I was a kid we used to say, 'I swear on a stack of Bibles.' But this is the first time I've made a promise where that was literally true." He patted his left hand on the manuscripts. "I promise you, I have no intention of stealing the ostracon."

Father Nikolaos seemed to evaluate Graham's sincerity, weighing the vow in the silence that followed. After several seconds, he reached into a leather satchel sitting on the floor behind the desk and pulled out an 8-by-10-inch photograph. He placed it face up, rotated it on the table to orient it for Graham, and pushed it toward him.

The ostracon in the image was triangular and covered in lines of text written to fit the odd shape. It sat on a canvas cloth, and something about the print gave the impression that it was old.

Graham glanced at the picture without touching it, then looked back to the monk. "If I'm going to do a proper translation, I want to see the actual ostracon."

"Please, indulge me. I will explain." Father Nikolaos pressed his palms together as if he were praying and bobbed them once. "Begin with the photograph. It was taken just after the driver brought it here. Do an initial translation. Then I will tell you the rest of the story."

FIVE

Graham retrieved his laptop, then opened a paleographic chart of Paleo-Hebrew letters. The characters on the ostracon in the photograph bore little resemblance to modern Hebrew, although they did look the same as on the other Lachish Letters. The squared form that made Hebrew so distinct had not yet developed when the letters were written. Instead, the Hebrew of 588 BC basically used Phoenician characters to write Hebrew words. The paleographic chart contained variant ways of forming characters that would help Graham date and read the text.

On his first full reading, he didn't try to grasp the nuance and detail of the text, just a broad understanding to orient himself. On the second pass he went more slowly, typing a literal, word-for-word translation as he went. The result was too formal and stiff, and it would take at least one more pass to refine the text before he was satisfied with how it read.

Translating languages was never a matter of simply substituting one word for another. Languages often had differing syntaxes, requiring the word order of the original language to be changed to compose a sentence in the receptor language that conveyed the same meaning and texture. Occasionally, the original language used verb tenses that did not exist in the receptor language. Original languages included idioms, idiosyncratic expressions with connotations that could not be inferred from the words themselves, and therefore would result in meaningless phrases in the receptor language if they were translated word-for-word.

Also, words in one language did not always have an exact equivalent word in the receptor language, forcing the translator to be somewhat creative in word selection. Sometimes the syntax of the receptor language required a word that did not exist in the original language, a situation that could easily damage the text in unskillful hands.

Graham remembered being baffled to learn in his first class in Koine Greek, the Greek of the New Testament, that the language had no indefinite article—there was no word *a*, only the definite article *the*. The word *a* was implied in Greek only when a particular syntactical form occurred. Although it seemed trivial, the professor then demonstrated how a misunderstanding of the rule could result in heresy. The professor had the students read along in the Greek New Testament as he read aloud from a translation of the first verse of the first chapter of the Gospel of John. "In the beginning was the Word, and the Word was with God, and the Word was a God." Every student's head shot up in confusion as they heard the word *a* inserted where it was not justified, a single letter that transformed Jesus from being a person of the triune God into an entirely separate being from God. It was the heresy of Arius that had been condemned at the Council of Nicea in AD 325, and it had been repeated in the New World Translation of the Jehovah's Witnesses.

All of these issues wove themselves into an ever-present aphorism that sat on the fringe of Graham's consciousness as he worked: Translation *is* interpretation.

The characters were slanted, almost italic, giving them a visual urgency Graham would soon find reflected in the message. The black carbon ink used to write them was faint and had worn almost completely away in several places. He hoped he would be allowed to make his own photograph of the ostracon using multi-spectral imaging to make sure all the text was recovered with certainty.

Father Nikolaos returned just as Graham finished up a third pass through the text, massaging the translation to make it flow more naturally. He was almost startled to see Father Nikolaos back so soon, then realized that over half an hour had passed in what felt like five minutes. Somehow the monk seemed more peaceful than Graham had ever seen him, and for a moment Graham stared at him in envy, wondering what it would take to feel the way Father Nikolaos looked.

"My apologies, Dr. Eliot. I didn't mean to startle you."

"No, no, I was just finishing. I didn't hear you come in."

"You were successful, then?" Father Nikolaos raised a hopeful brow. "You were able to make a translation?"

"Yes, but...I'm not sure if..." Graham stuttered, then paused, unsure of his own words.

"Something is wrong?" Father Nikolaos asked.

"Maybe," Graham said, cautiously. "It's just that I don't want to appear disrespectful or upset you."

Father Nikolaos closed his eyes as he gave a slight, benevolent bow. "I have just come from the charnel house. It always puts things in perspective."

Graham pictured the small building where the bones of the monks were kept, separated into piles of skulls, legs, arms, and other parts. He knew the monks visited it regularly, but the thought of it still struck him as macabre.

"The thought of death," the monk continued, "like all other graces, is a gift from God. Are you familiar with *The Ladder of Divine Ascent?*"

"I remember the name," Graham said, placing it somewhere in the Middle Ages, "but I've never read it."

Father Nikolaos nodded regretfully. "John Climacus, an

abbot here, wrote it in the seventh century. He taught that it is not possible to spend the day piously without regarding it as the last day of our life. The charnel house reminds me how little time the Lord has given me to do the work He prepared me for. We must make the most of what we have been entrusted with. That is, in fact, what you and I are doing right now."

"I confess, I forget that far too often." Graham shrugged apologetically. "Life gets lost in the living somehow."

"Exactly. It also reminds me that I am part of a rich tradition, a link in a chain that is tethered to a spot chosen by God to be the place where He made a people for Himself."

"Well, Father, that is actually what is making me hesitate."

"I don't understand."

Graham paused, trying to find diplomatic words to cushion his findings for his host. But something in the eyes of Father Nikolaos said he would prefer frankness. "According to the message on the ostracon, Saint Catherine's is not at Mount Sinai."

SIX

Father Nikolaos glanced at the photograph, but otherwise remained unfazed. "Surely there must be a mistake," he said. "Perhaps if you had more time?"

"No, that's not the issue, Father. Let me show you." Graham positioned his computer so they could both see the translation as Graham read.

> Your servant Hoshaiah, sent to inform my Lord, Yaush. The signal-station of Azekah has not been seen in three days. Hear these, the words of your servant and scout: The army of Nebuchadnezzar is like a sea flooding into Judah. Pharaoh's army waits at the river of Egypt to the west. There is safety only to the south, on the path of deliverance. Look to the route of Elijah's fleeing, beyond Timna and Ezion-Geber, to Midian. Safety points to the Mountain of the Law. Surely YHWH will protect and fight for His people as He did at Sinai. For it was YHWH who brought us here from there. May YHWH let my Lord see the present season in good health.

"According to the ostracon, Midian is beyond Timna and Ezion-Gezer, to the south," Graham said, looking sidelong at the monk. "The Mountain of the Law is south of there, as is Midian itself. Although Saint Catherine's is south of Ebion-Gezer, it is just as far west. Father, this mountain we are on is not in the location the message describes."

"Dr. Eliot, you make too much of this." Father Nikolaos gave a gentle, reprimanding frown while still appearing peaceful. "Obviously this letter was not meant to be used for navigation."

"Take it at face value." Graham motioned toward the shard. "Why would the Arabs kill because of it?"

"It is a valuable artifact," Father Nikolaos said. "James Starkey may have been murdered purely for the value the ostracon could bring on the black market. Its content might well be completely irrelevant."

"Possibly," Graham said, leaning back in his chair. "But why was no one hurt when the first eighteen ostraca were found? Or when the other three were found later that year, after his death?"

Father Nikolaos sat for a moment, then punctuated the silence with a sigh. "I had not considered that."

"So, what was so important to the Arabs in 1935 about the communiqué of a military scout from Lachish just before it was sacked?" Graham asked. "There is nothing about the troop movements of the Babylonian army that would hold any relevance for Arab bandits 2,500 years later. It must be about the geography. What's important is the location of Sinai."

"Not necessarily. It is only important that Sinai actually existed, not to know exactly where it was."

Graham searched the monk's face for irony. "That's a strange thing to say, coming from a monk at the monastery built at the foot of Mount Sinai."

"I am quite aware that there has been much debate among scholars about where Sinai was, but I accept the tradition of

Helena."

"Even though she identified this location because of a dream? I wish all my work was that easy." Graham hoped the humor would keep the conversation friendly. "The only reason the claim was ever taken seriously is simply because she was the mother of Constantine. Who's going to argue with the emperor's mother?"

Father Nikolaos broke into a rare full smile. "Indeed. But what you fail to appreciate is that this place has been venerated as the Mountain of God for almost 2,000 years. That alone makes it sacred in an important way, even if not in a historical way."

"I don't deny the rich tradition here," Graham said, looking around the room. "And Saint Catherine's is historically important whether or not this is the actual place Moses met God. But the fact is that almost no scholar accepts this site as the actual biblical location. More than a dozen other places have been suggested as Sinai, all with better logic to justify them than this location."

"And yet here is where the tradition took root," Father Nikolaos said, appearing more peaceful with each challenge. "There must be something to be said for that. God is sovereign, after all. Even before Helena's designation, it is said that angels delivered the body of Saint Catherine of Alexandria here after being martyred on the wheel."

"Again, I acknowledge the importance of this monastery. I also know there were ascetics in this area a hundred years before Helena had her vision. But the ostracon was already almost a thousand years old when the first hermit staked out a cave. Lachish was sacked at a time when the Jews still knew where Sinai was. And what we now call the Sinai Peninsula has always been a part of Egypt—the country Moses *fled* before arriving at Sinai."

"That is debated." The monk raised a finger to make his

point.

"Surely you don't deny it has been Egyptian territory. Even before the Exodus they had fortresses here to protect the mines and trade routes they had established."

"Yes, that is true," Father Nikolaos conceded.

"The border of Egypt is mentioned by God when He gives the boundaries of the Promised Land." Graham opened his Bible app and found the passage. "Here it is. Genesis 15:18, when God makes the covenant with Abraham. The southern border is the river of Egypt. That's mentioned in the ostracon. Numbers 34:5 also gives the boundaries and calls it the brook of Egypt, which is the wadi not far from Kadesh-Barnea. That's 150 miles northeast of here."

"More north than east," Father Nikolaos said. "As in the ostracon."

"And when Elijah ran for his life from Ahab after defeating the prophets of Ba'al..." Graham snapped his fingers several times as if to wake the memory that could recall the outline of the different books of the Hebrew Bible. "First Kings, eighteen or nineteen. He went to hide in a cave at Horeb, at Mount Sinai."

"Ah, but that passage does not say *where* Sinai was located." Father Nikolaos opened his hands in a futile gesture. "It merely talks about it as a real place, which is my point. That is what is important."

"It means the Jews in the middle of the ninth century BC remembered where the mountain was. They didn't have to be told." Graham got the feeling that Father Nikolaos was enjoying the sparring, that he didn't get to exercise his mind in this way often. "It was only during the Babylonian captivity three hundred years later that the knowledge of the location was lost. This ostracon is an indication of where Sinai actually is and, therefore, where it isn't. And it was written during the time when there was still a collective memory among the

Jews."

"But you forget, this mountain has the support of the Egyptian Archaeological Service. And you are neglecting to consider the Ashtiname."

"The real question," Graham said, "is why Muhammad would grant an exception to Islamic law for a Christian monastery, of all things. If Muhammad really wanted peace and coexistence with Christians, he could have made it the law of the land, not a privilege for a specific place. Not only that, but neither Muslims nor Jews even believe that this is the location, only Christians. So why would he exempt Saint Catherine's?" He paused to give the question more force. "Could it be that Muhammad knew where the real location of Sinai was and endorsed a site he knew was wrong in order to keep Jewish and Christian pilgrims from visiting the site where the prophet Musa met with Allah, to protect it from the blasphemy of infidels? Or is there something more, something of value there that he wanted to keep hidden?"

Father Nikolaos raised a skeptical brow. "You are saying that Muhammad moved the mountain? You are being too fanciful, my friend. Entirely speculative."

"Not at all. Muslims have a history of destroying evidence that is contrary to Islam's historical claims or is against their beliefs. Sometimes one Muslim sect even does it to another. Preventing Sinai from being correctly identified is a way of keeping the Bible from being authenticated, which would affirm Jewish history. Without evidence, all that is left is tradition and legend."

"I fear you are making this more complicated than it has to be." Father Nikolaos's calm voice sounded designed to dampen Graham's theory.

Graham got the feeling he had pushed his point far enough and chose to end the debate graciously. "You're right, of course, about it being speculation. There may be something on the ostracon that isn't clear in the photo and could change the reading. Can I see the real thing now?"

"Ah, yes." Father Nikolaos planted his elbows on the table and steepled his fingers. "That brings me to the reason I have shared this with you. Earlier you promised not to steal the ostracon. I'm afraid you have misunderstood. That is precisely what I am asking you to do."

SEVEN

Graham squinted in confusion. "I don't understand."

"The ostracon is not here." Father Nikolaos remained utterly still, apparently evaluating Graham again.

"What happened to it?" Graham said, feeling a twinge of loss despite having just learned of its existence. "Where is it?"

"The skevophylax wanted to add a layer of protection in case the driver was found out. If the bandits discovered what he did with the ostracon, then it might bring trouble to the monastery. The skevophylax didn't know if the Ashtiname would be honored by men who would brutally murder a man who was a friend to them."

"That makes sense," Graham said. "So he hid it somewhere else."

"In Istanbul." Father Nikolaos's mouth curled slightly upward on one side. "He did not think the bandits would suspect it any more than you did, judging by the look on your face."

"The patriarchate?" Graham pictured the headquarters of the Eastern Orthodox Church and residence of its spiritual leader.

"No," Father Nikolaos said, "but nearby, in the metochion."

"I'm afraid I don't know what that is."

Father Nikolaos nodded gently. "A dependency. As you know, the Eastern Orthodox Church is really a family of autocephalous orthodox churches, each with their own diocese and archbishop. When a diocese wishes to be represented outside its territory, it establishes a metochion. Think of it as a cell from this monastery placed in another location. The Church of Sinai is actually its own diocese. It is the only monastery with its own archbishop, though he primarily resides at the metochion in Cairo. In the 1800s, there were nearly a hundred dependencies. Now there are only a handful. The Church of Sinai used to have a metochion in Istanbul."

"What do you mean 'used to'?" Graham asked.

"The Turkish government confiscated it in 1967. But they did nothing with the building. It has sat abandoned since then. In its time, it was an elegant mansion, on the bluff overlooking the Golden Horn."

"I'm sure I must've driven past it before," Graham said. "How do you know the ostracon is still there?"

"I do not," Father Nikolaos said, smiling sadly. "But since the archimandrite—the representative priest—who was evicted returned without it, I think there is a very good chance that it still rests in its hiding spot."

"And you know where that is?"

Father Nikolaos opened his hands in an apologetic shrug. "Not exactly. The skevophylax hid the ostracon in the throne room, the place where the archimandrite received visitors. That room was damaged by a fire in 1955, but during the renovation it was not discovered. No serious search was made for it because the priest did not want to raise suspicions among the workers since many of them were Muslim. And the priest didn't want to damage the restoration by opening up a wall or floor when he left. He thought it would be seen as vandalism. We prayed the eviction was temporary and wanted to maintain good relations with the Turkish government if possible. But now the metochion has fallen to ruin. With all the development in Istanbul, I'm sure it will soon be razed or restored—either way the ostracon will be lost if we do not take action."

"And by *we* you mean *me*," Graham said.

"I have pressing responsibilities here," Father Nikolaos said, "overseeing the work being done to modernize the library. Yes, I am asking you to retrieve it."

Graham sifted his thoughts, which ranged from the opportunity to be part of a historic discovery to logistical questions to research and publication rights. "And if I am able to find it, what do you plan to do with it?"

"I would prefer it be housed here, though given its—shall we say—unusual provenance, I am under no illusions that it would be free of controversy. Announcing its existence and publishing on it will invite such speculation."

"I'm not sure what you're saying, Father. This is a very important find and it has already sat silent for eighty years. It needs to be published."

"I agree." The monk nodded. "All the more reason for you to be the one to do it—at least as lead author. I would play only a supporting role. If we co-published then you would provide the legitimacy of the find, and I would provide the claim of Saint Catherine's as its custodian. That would go a long way to bridging the question of ownership. Especially if the monastery came into possession of it through theft. I refer to Starkey's driver, of course, not what I am asking of you. You would simply be returning an item to its caretaker—something left behind when the metochion was closed. You are not claiming ownership, and therefore your interest is purely academic. I have no interest in the academic glory—if there is any to be had. I simply want the ostracon safely back here."

Graham smiled questioningly. "Is that true even if it turns

out that the historical Sinai is in a different location than here?"

"I am not concerned about that." Father Nikolaos remained unflappable. "It is doubtful that any evidence could conclusively prove the location of the true Sinai. What needs to be investigated is if people are still willing to kill over that location—if, indeed, that is what happened in the first place. These are unknowns that would delay that announcement of the ostracon, but they are irrelevant concerns if we cannot recover it first."

Graham inventoried his obligations and—given that the summer break was only half over—decided none of them couldn't be put off for a week or so. "Okay. I'll go to Istanbul and see what I can find out."

"Excellent." Father Nikolaos rewarded the news with a smile that almost wrinkled his face.

Graham tapped the photo. "I know you need to keep this, but I'd like to make a copy. I need to have some way of knowing that what I find is the same one brought to the monastery."

"Yes, of course." The monk dipped his head. "But we are trusting each other now."

"No Tischendorf, I promise."

Father Nikolaos ignored Graham's light response and raised a finger in warning. "Even the photo is valuable and may still pose a threat."

"I understand," Graham said. "I have always thought it was curious that one of the most important sites in world history is not known with certainty."

"To some," Father Nikolaos equivocated.

"But at the same time," Graham continued, his thoughts snowballing, "why would Muhammad endorse a site that he may have known was the wrong place? And if that *is* what happened, then what was he hiding that is still worth hiding now? Is that why Starkey died? If so, is it still worth killing for now?"

Father Nikolaos responded with a motion that looked as if he were consecrating the questions. "These are exactly the things I would like answers to."

EIGHT

Graham found Alexander with his back to the door, bent over the desk, staring at the computer monitor—the same position Graham had left him in. Tinny music bled from the earbuds, and Graham immediately recognized the shuffle beat of the Genesis song "Misunderstanding." He gently placed a hand on Alexander's shoulder, causing him to jerk in surprise.

"Sorry. Didn't mean to scare you." Graham chuckled as he patted Alexander's shoulder.

"I was totally in the zone," Alexander said, blinking himself present.

"I could tell. *Duke* is a great record."

Alexander set his headphones on the table and paused the music. "On my second time through in a row."

"I'm impressed," Graham said. "Most people your age don't know how to listen to albums anymore."

"Most of my favorite songs are the deep cuts," Alexander said, running his fingers through is hair. "And sometimes listening to a song by itself is like watching a scene separated from a movie, or a chapter without the book. It's just like archaeology: it's all about context."

It was a mini-lecture Graham had given countless times, and he smiled as he heard it repeated back to him. "Ah, I have trained you well."

"So, I was thinking about something," Alexander said. "I saw Father Nikolaos has a MacBook Pro. Think he sees the irony?"

Graham glanced at his own MacBook Pro. "What do you mean?"

"The logo on the lid." Alexander pointed to the symbol. "It's an apple with a bite taken out of it—a picture of original sin."

A laugh escaped Graham before he remembered he was in a monastery library and stifled it. "I never thought of that! There's a problem, though. There is only one bite. Original sin is the fall of Adam, not Eve. Sin entered the world through Adam, so that must be Eve's bite mark. It's a picture of the apple before Adam took it, otherwise there'd be two bites."

"Got me there," Alexander said. "But either way, it came from the Tree of the Knowledge of Good and Evil. And now Father Nikolaos is the keeper of knowledge at the world's oldest functioning library."

Graham stifled another laugh. "And you've become that library's DJ, doing Genesis theology while listening to Genesis. That'll look good on your resumé." Graham took a seat at the workstation. "Okay, back to business. I have a quick research project I need you to knock out."

"Roger that," Alexander said, instantly serious. "What do you got?"

"I need you to look up every mention of Mount Sinai in the Bible. That includes any mentions of Mount Horeb, its other name. Make a list of every feature you find. Where is it? What's there and what's around it?"

"You mean stuff like the altar of the golden calf and Elijah's cave?"

"Exactly."

"What's it for?"

"I can't really say at this point," Graham said. "But I

would like you to go ahead and work on it now. I can finish up the rest of the photography today."

"Sure thing."

Graham waited until Alexander left, then slipped out the photograph of the ostracon, put it in the copy stand, and took a high-resolution image of it. As he stared at the ostracon on the screen, he wondered if the message would do the same kind of work the multi-spectral light did on the manuscripts and make the invisible Sinai visible.

NINE

Graham awoke as the first light of day leaked through the arched window, dissolving the night. Bare walls emerged from the darkness, delineating a generic environment whose main characteristic was its lack of character. He felt the rough blanket scratch through the bedsheet as he sat up in the twin-sized bed, wondering if anyone ever felt comfortable in such austere utility. Then he remembered the room was designed by monks and guessed the room's size and private bathroom were luxurious by their standards.

The monastery had recently built the guesthouse just outside its walls to accommodate the relative explosion of visitors resulting from modern transportation. Prior to Tischendorf's discovery of Sinaiticus, Saint Catherine's was almost completely unknown. Even after the birth of its fame, the monastery was too remote to reach easily and remained unvisited except by the most determined and resourceful pilgrims. Now the resort city of Sharm el-Sheik, on the tip of the peninsula, hosted an airport where travelers could rent a car, hire a taxi, or ride a bus across paved roads to arrive in less than five hours. There were several hotels at the village of Saint Catherine, two miles away, but for Graham the convenience of the guesthouse outweighed the austerity of the accommodations.

He found Alexander sitting at a plastic patio table in the

courtyard outside the dining room plucking a travel guitar. The miniature body had fit surprisingly well in Alexander's backpack, and the end of the short-scale neck barely speared through the top. Graham heard a Mediterranean melody and thought Alexander was merely noodling around at first. Then he recognized the muted plunks from a David Bowie song as he took a seat across from him.

"'Yassassin'?"

Alexander lit up. "Good call, Dr. E."

"Pretty deep cut. That song was twenty-years-old when you were born."

"Most of the best music was." Alexander smiled sadly, as if apologizing for the music of his own generation. "I guess I woke up in a Bowie mood."

"Yeah, that happens to me, too," Graham said. "Muting those strings actually makes it sound a lot like the record. I'm impressed you know the song at all, let alone can play it. You could start a whole new field: guitarchaeology."

"Ha!" Alexander bucked backward, rocking the front legs of his chair off the ground. "I guess some people are old souls, and some are just old."

"That hurts. But, as you say, at least I grew up—"

"With the best music," Alexander finished for him. "Yeah, yeah, yeah. No contest."

As Alexander stowed the guitar, Graham stared at the embroidered patch sewn onto the black backpack. It showed a beam of light refracting as it passed through a prism, recreating the cover of the Pink Floyd album *Dark Side of the Moon*.

Alexander followed Graham's eyes. "Great record."

"One of the greatest."

They made their way to the dining hall, and after finding places at the end of one of the long tables, looked at their breakfasts in amusement.

"I think the food here is an amenity only in the academic

sense," Alexander said, nodding in resignation.

"Yes, somehow they are able to come up with the culinary equivalent of the room decor." Graham studied the eggs on his fork before continuing. "In other news, I won't be able to leave with you today. I've had some work come up here and I need to stay a few more days."

"Need me to help? I can stay if you want me to."

"No, thanks," Graham said. "It doesn't have anything to do with the digitization work. And I don't want to keep you from your research in Manchester. Not everyone gets to do work on their dissertation at the John Rylands Library. You'll be in ancient manuscript heaven."

"I'll definitely have plenty to keep me busy," Alexander said. "Actually, I'm going to go to London for a couple of days as well. My aunt is there. She's going to show me around the British Museum."

"Talk about heaven. It's like biblical archaeology's greatest hits. But I need to confess something to you." Graham rearranged his face to become serious. "The first time I went to the British Museum, when I went into the manuscript area, I got totally distracted. I was in the presence of the Codex Sinaiticus and Magna Carta, but the only thing I could focus on was a glass case displaying the handwritten lyrics of the Beatles."

Alexander guffawed, causing several guests to look up from their meals.

"I mean, these were the actual pieces of paper they used when they wrote the songs!" Graham continued. "There were words that got crossed out and verses that went unused. I couldn't look away. So I totally blew it the first time I was there, as far as ancient documents go."

"Thanks for the cautionary tale, Dr. E. I'll try not to fall into the same trap. At least you got to see Sinaiticus. Amazing how it got there from here. It's fascinating to think how

Tischendorf recognized it belonged in a museum and saved it from being burned for heat. Then Russia turned communist, fell into depression, and sold off Sinaiticus for the money."

Graham remembered how Father Nikolaos had bristled at the story but decided not to pursue the topic for fear of being overheard by the monks and appearing disrespectful. "Your aunt in London on vacation?"

"Sort of," Alexander said. "She's a philologist at USC. She's doing some research at the Museum, trying to decipher something. Can't remember what it is. We realized we'd be in England at the same time, so we worked it out to travel back together." Alexander sat up suddenly. "Hey, I finished the project you gave me yesterday. I emailed it to you. I really got into it and added some other material."

Graham opened his phone and retrieved an email with a PDF attachment. He scanned the document and smiled. Not only had Alexander compiled a list of criteria, but he also included references from ancient historians, rabbis, and early Church Fathers. Another category listed European explorers of the nineteenth and early twentieth centuries, as well as a list of mountains that various scholars and explorers had proposed as the true location of Sinai.

"This is excellent work," Graham said. "I'm impressed. Very helpful, Alexander. Thank you. You may have to change your dissertation."

"I thought about it," Alexander said in mock seriousness.

"You better get going if you're going to catch the bus to Sharm el-Sheik."

After watching Alexander cram into the minibus with half a dozen tourists, Graham spent the rest of the day taking the final images, uploading them, and packing the camera. But he worked in distraction, his mind partly devoted to parsing Alexander's PDF, wondering if the answer to Sinai was there. And if it was, Graham wondered if he would recognize it.

TEN

This is the LORD'S gate—the godly enter through it.

Graham translated the quote from Greek and identified it as a verse from Psalm 118. The inscription above the entrance to the Katholikon seemed to have a weight that settled on him as he walked through the world's oldest functioning doors into the oldest functioning church. The Church of Saint Catherine was built at the same time as the compound's massive fortification walls in the middle of the sixth century. The church enclosed the building Helena erected on the spot of the Burning Bush, turning it into a chapel behind the altar. Like Moses, Graham had been required to remove his shoes, though now the holy ground was tiled in Byzantine patterns. Eight other chapels dedicated to various saints stood on either side of the sanctuary. Its three aisles were formed by two rows of six pillars, one for each month, each displaying the saint venerated that month.

Graham shuffled along behind Father Nikolaos, then took a place standing in the rear of the church as Saint Catherine's two dozen monks assembled for worship before him. A coffered wooden ceiling—painted blue and accented with gold stars—acted as a firmament from which hung lamps suspended from chains. Graham got the impression of an inverted grove of brass trees blooming with light. A spectacular mosaic of the transfiguration adorned the apse, transcendent above the altar. The altar itself was veiled by the iconostasis—a wall of icons dividing the nave from the chancel. The images acted as a kind of incarnation, a visual theology to accompany and enhance the Divine Liturgy.

The scene evoked a mysticism that touched Graham's spirit in a way his home church did not, and he understood why Eastern Orthodoxy was growing so quickly among younger Christians in America. Many of them had grown up in churches that emphasized Jesus as a friend, and though that was certainly true, somehow the transcendence of God was lost. The utterly holy, self-existent, omniscient, omnipotent God of the universe was—by definition—completely unique, wholly other. The design of the church was a reminder of how the Hebrew word for glory came from the word weight, and what he saw on display was an architectural expression of theological truth. Graham found a balance in the comparison that allowed him to enter into worship.

Being invited to the service was a rare privilege. Protestants were not usually permitted to join the monks, and the gesture was a testament to the friendship that had developed between the two scholars. Father Nikolaos even teased that he promised not to hold Graham's Presbyterianism against him.

Graham watched Father Nikolaos and was impressed by the man's unflagging devotion. Even though it was just after breakfast, he knew that this was not the first service of the day, nor would it be the last. The monks gathered several times a day for worship, the first being at four a.m. Father Nikolaos had almost laughed when Graham sarcastically thanked him for not asking him to the early service.

After worship, Graham stepped out into a monastery devoid of visitors, since none were admitted on Sundays or Fridays. On the mornings when visitors were allowed, about a thousand people would tour the four-acre abbey. But rather than take advantage of having the place to himself, he planned to hike to the top of Sinai and see how many things he could find on Alexander's list.

He had turned his phone off before entering the church, keeping a promise he gave Father Nikolaos not to take pictures of the interior. As it powered back up, he received two emails from Alexander, the first with the subject Golden Calf, a caption to an image he'd attached.

> *About a mile north of the monastery, at the foot of the mountain on the left as you leave, where the road jogs left.*

Graham scrolled down and saw a group of rocks worn smooth by wind and whatever water flowed through the wadi. Behind it, the north side of the cluster of mountains that included Sinai began their rise from the desert floor. At first, he wondered what he was looking at. It wasn't until he zoomed in to the center of the picture that he saw it. The profile of an animal facing left, extruded from a scarp of tan rock. The large feet and long tail looked more like a Chihuahua to Graham. Yet he had to admit that the shape of the head and the divot that formed the black shadow-eye looked like a calf.

He knew it couldn't have been the actual idol made by Aaron since it was stone, not gold. But it made him think about the mechanics of how the idol may have been made, and it *did* look like one-half of what would be used to make a mold. However, he supposed it could also have been carved by a pilgrim or monk. Then again, there were many shapes in the smooth rocks around it, and although none were obviously figurative, the calf could be nothing more than seeing what you want to see rather than what is actually there. Maybe he was finding a shape in the rock like he used to find shapes in the clouds with his daughter, Aly. Graham decided to give the rock the benefit of the doubt for the purpose of seeing how many possible things he could find.

The subject of the second email read *Campsite*, another caption, this time for an image of the hotels along the highway in Saint Catherine's Village. Below, Alexander wrote, "2 million, easy." Graham studied the vast space of the valley the hotels sat in and agreed.

He turned south, away from the monastery and away from the golden calf. There were two paths to the summit. The Camel Path was the easier climb, but it was longer, wrapping around the south side of the mountain in its ascent. The other option was a trail that led straight up the mountain, the Steps of Penitence. The hewn granite stairs were said to follow the same route Moses used and had been built by a monk as a show of repentance for his sins, creating 3,750 contrite steps that delivered people to and from the summit.

Graham looked at a map of the two trails—which most people hiked as a loop, taking the long way up and the short way down—and saw there was nothing on the list that could be seen only on the Camel Path. According to Father Nikolaos, the Steps of Penitence could take as little as forty-five minutes. Graham decided to follow the way of contrition.

ELEVEN

Graham entered the shade collected by the tall, narrow walls of a slot canyon and stopped for a quick rest, already realizing the hike would take longer than he'd thought. Although he didn't sweat easily, he could tell his body was close to its threshold and guessed the temperature would near a hundred degrees before he reached the peak. He looked back at the valley through the V-shaped frame formed by the deep shadow of the canyon and recognized the view as the perspective from which the monastery had so often been photographed.

The initial ascent allowed him to see down into the walls of Saint Catherine—a city-block-sized Byzantine island in the desert. The guesthouse sat on the far side of the walls, looking much smaller than it felt when he was there. To the left of the monastery, against the wall that faced arriving visitors, he could see the small charnel house and the layout of the garden surrounding it. The oasis of trees and flowers had been engineered through the ingenuity of some of the first monks. They not only dug cisterns to catch rainwater and snowmelt from Sinai to be used for irrigation, they imported the very soil from which the garden grew. And they had done their work so well that 1,500 years later their spiritual descendants still ate the olives and other fruit the trees produced.

Graham turned to face the steep slope and began to climb

again. The first hikers ascended before dawn, hoping to reach the summit to watch the sunrise. Another wave would make the journey in the mid-afternoon in order to watch the sunset. For some reason, he thought the trail would be lonely at this time of day, but instead discovered a constant stream of tourists.

The repetitive churning of the steps became mechanical, reminding him of a stair-climbing machine, an exercise he'd always hated. But where the stair-climber was a tedious torture to him, the hike had purpose accompanied by scenery that looked like a barren planet.

Graham lost track of time—and he certainly hadn't marked progress by counting steps—but he knew he had reached the halfway point as the Chapel of Our Lady of the Steward came into view. The chapel was built at the base of a cliff, its rock walls covered in faded whitewash. Large white crosses were graffitied on the cliff face above the roof. He glanced at it without slowing, given that it wasn't relevant to the criteria he had so little time to investigate.

After the chapel fell away behind him, the canyon walls shrank and narrowed. A granite arch had been built across the gap. The width was just enough for a single person to pass through comfortably, forming a gate into a section of the mountain that was set apart. He heard a tourist with a German accent identify it as the Gate of Confession, asserting it had been built by Moses himself. Graham was certain not even Father Nikolaos would defend that claim but kept on in silence.

A second arch eventually appeared, spanning the space between the rock wall on the left and the side of a boulder that had fallen into the gulley on the right. A legend said the arch had been built by Elijah when he took refuge here. However, an inscription from the sixth or seventh century AD was found on the keystone that hinted it might have been built in honor of John Climacus.

The pitch finally relented, and Graham found himself on the edge of a relatively flat, open area identified by a stone marker as Elijah's Basin. A path branched to the right, leading to several ancient chapels where hermits had lived, part of the tradition of asceticism that predated the monastery. He kept walking the main trail toward a rock-walled garden containing a few cypress trees in the center of the plateau. Between Graham and the buildings, a thick stone wall created a dam that held a pool of rainwater and snowmelt, keeping it from flooding the path to the monastery and Saint Catherine's itself. Above it sat the well of Elijah. But it was another building that immediately held his attention. Starbucks Coffee.

The ramshackle stand was like dozens of other Bedouin booths littering the trails on and around the mountain. Swaths of cloth and blankets were draped over different parts of the shack, giving it the feel of a boxy patchwork tent. Water bottles in different sizes sat on a rough wooden shelf between a rack of postcards and various food bars. A taller shelf formed a counter, and behind it a Bedouin in a red and white keffiyeh headscarf stood serving coffee and tea as a cigarette dangled from his mouth. A hand-painted cardboard sign reading Starbucks Coffee had been tacked to part of the wood frame. Graham bought a bottle of water from the man as he wondered vaguely if the server considered himself a barista.

He took a long pull from the plastic bottle, then saw the next item on his list on the far side of the area. The cave of Elijah. Actually, he didn't see the cave, only the building that contained it, the Double Church of the Prophets. The left half of the structure was a yard bounded by a stone wall. The right side was the church proper and had smooth whitewashed plaster walls. Alexander's notes said the building had been mentioned by Egeria, a pilgrim who visited here in the fourth century and kept a journal of the visit. According to Father

Nikolaos, the entry was to the Church of Elisha. Once inside, it connected to the Church of Elijah.

The Church of Elijah was smaller than a one-car garage, and the walls wore the same whitewash as the exterior. An altar draped in red cloth sat along the right wall, and a censer hung from the wall on the left, between two shallow alcoves. The wall at the far side of the room was the area around the mouth of a small cave that looked more like a fireplace. A candle lit the interior, and smoke damage had worn away the center of the fresco that framed the opening.

Graham felt underwhelmed, and he realized that although he hadn't tried very hard to picture Elijah's cave, he expected to find something more substantial than a niche in the rock. He took a couple of pictures with his phone, then stepped out of the church and took a few of the exterior. This spot had also been identified as the possible plateau where Moses and the seventy elders came to ratify the covenant God made with the people.

Graham added mental checkmarks to the list, giving them the same benefit of the doubt as the golden calf for the sake of argument.

He rejoined the path, followed it up and behind the Double Church, then lost sight of the building after a hard-right turn. Almost immediately, the number of hikers walking toward him increased, and he realized he had reached the intersection of the Camel Path and the final ascent. He joined the pilgrims and funneled into a passage that had been carved through the rock called—appropriately enough—the Cutting. From there, 750 steps remained, but Graham quickly discovered that although he was close, progress was slow. The severe angle of the slope made it the most treacherous part of the trek, and many of the tourists had their commitment tested as they struggled to reach the top.

Graham again fell into a rhythm, pounding his feet into

the mountain. He felt the sensation of emerging from stone as his surroundings suddenly felt expansive. Two-and-a-half hours after leaving the monastery, he had reached the summit, the place where God descended to speak with Moses.

TWELVE

The peak formed a point almost like a child's drawing of a mountain. As Graham pushed himself up the last hundred yards, the profile of a church emerged from the boulder field, balanced at the apex. The sight was like a magnet, pulling him onward at the moment when he felt completely spent.

He trudged on, absorbed in the panorama of harsh, barren mountains tearing through the floor of the wilderness to construct the most inhospitable environment he had ever seen. And yet—according to tradition—this is where God played host to his people for the first time since the Garden of Eden. Interestingly, a sense of God's sovereignty and power settled over Graham, and he discovered a majesty in the view which brought with it an impulse to worship the one true God. The words of Paul's letter to the Romans filtered into his thoughts, shaping them like a lens.

> *Since the creation of the world his invisible attributes—his eternal power and divine nature—have been clearly seen, because they are understood through what has been made.*

Graham agreed with the theologians of the church who taught that God had revealed Himself in two books; the Bible, where He revealed Himself specifically, and creation, where He revealed Himself generally. Between the service where Graham's day began and the sight before him, he was more convinced than ever that this was true. They both proclaimed the same message. And even if this was not the actual God-trodden mountain, everything belongs to God and His presence was everywhere. Graham could imagine Father Nikolaos using the insight as justification: "In that light, what mountain isn't God-trodden?"

He leaned on a rock wall and finished off his water as he looked at the small, modest chapel dedicated to the Trinity. It had been built on the ruins of a larger church erected at the same time as the monastery. An even older chapel had stood here prior to that. Remnants from the foundation of the second church formed tiers near the current chapel. According to Father Nikolaos, the stone beneath the chapel provided the tablets for the Ten Commandments. And some monks claimed there were prints in the stone left by Moses's knees.

A modest cross rose from the roof above the wooden doors, a symbol allowed by the fact that Jews had never venerated this mountain as Sinai. The left wall was built against a boulder with a cavity along its base. God—again, according to Father Nikolaos—had stood on the rock as He spoke to Moses, and the cavity was the cleft where Moses had taken shelter as God passed by. To the right, just down the slope, a tiny mosque stood, enclosing the cave where Moses fasted for forty days. It was a reminder that Islam, too, considered Moses a prophet and called the site *Jebel Musa*—Mountain of Moses.

Graham staked out a relatively vacant spot, pulled out his phone, and opened the PDF containing Alexander's list.

- Golden calf altar
- Campsite while Moses was on mountain
- Boundary markers around the mountain

- Altar of uncut stone
- Wadi next to altar
- 12 standing stones or pillars
- Elijah's cave
- Plateau for 74
- Split Rock
- Campsite near Split Rock
- 11-day journey to Kadesh-Barnea
- 40-day journey to Mount Carmel
- In Midian

Once again, he mentally checked off the golden calf altar, Elijah's Cave, the Plateau where the elders met God with Moses and Aaron, and the campsite for when Moses was on the mountain.

God had told Moses to put markers around the mountain to keep people from entering the holy area. Anyone—or any animal—who passed the boundary and touched the mountain would die. Graham joked to himself that the fact that he was on top of the mountain either meant the punishment was no longer in place or that he was on the wrong mountain. Or both. Either way, there were no markers or boundary stones that he saw at the foot of Sinai.

The next item was the altar of Moses. Alexander's notes mentioned that Egeria, a fourth century pilgrim who recorded one of the earliest explorations of biblical lands, was shown a stone purported to be the altar, but it didn't seem to match the biblical description. Graham tried to picture what it might have looked like and didn't think it would have been able to survive 3,500 years intact since it was stacked stone that could easily fall apart or be repurposed. And without the altar, the wadi next to it could not be found, either, although Egeria also claimed to have seen that as well.

The other feature was the group of twelve standing stones

or pillars next to the altar, each representing a tribe of Israel. Egeria made no mention of them, and there was no tradition for them near the mountain.

The most recognizable landmark to find besides the golden calf altar would be the rock that Moses split to bring forth water for the people. Although the event happened at Sinai, it occurred as the Hebrews made their way to the main campsite and was therefore on the opposite side of the mountain from the golden calf site.

Sure enough, there was a location for it. An alternate route up the mountain left from the village of Saint Catherine and followed a wadi on the west side of the cluster of peaks. Halfway between the town and the south side of the mountain where the ascent began, a small Greek chapel marked the traditional Rephidim. Graham opened the images of the site he had found online and studied them. The alleged rock Moses struck was about ten feet tall, round, and—like the Cave of Elijah—unimpressive. A column of twelve horizontal slits indented the stone. Again, for the sake of the argument, he checked it off the list. He opened the satellite image of the wadi, decided that it would be highly impractical for two million people to camp there, but not impossible, and ticked that item off the list as well.

The next two criteria were the eleven-day journey to Kadesh-Barnea and the forty-day journey to Mount Carmel. The first was a stop on the itinerary of the Israelites in their wandering through the desert, and the distance was mentioned in Deuteronomy. The second was where Elijah had fled from when he took refuge on Sinai, and the distance was noted in 1 Kings. Graham had no way of judging their accuracy off the top of his head, so he discounted both from the list.

Graham added up the score and found six of the items on the list, eight if he included Egeria's testimony. Three were unaccounted for, and two could not be known. By count, the traditional site did better than he thought it would. But one item carried more weight than all the others: In Midian. Whatever else this site might have going for it, there was no evidence it was ever considered a part of Midian. If this site wasn't in the right country, then it could not be the place no matter how many other items might be found. It was a defeater that took down the whole case for the traditional location of Sinai.

Less than an hour later, Graham stepped off the bottom stair of the trail. His knees were so weak he thought they might buckle him into an involuntary posture of prayer, and his legs felt like they were vibrating now that the strain of the hike was over.

As he wound his way around Saint Catherine's to the gate, he studied the wall surrounding the monastery. It was 10-to-20 meters tall. Although construction from the fifth century still made up the majority of the fortress, there were obvious newer patches—repairs made by Napoleon. In fact, after conquering Egypt in 1797, it was the emperor's interest in the area that was one of the factors that gave rise to the discipline of archaeology itself. One of the repairs was near a shed jutting from the wall on cantilevers thirty feet off the ground. Graham thought it resembled an outhouse, but knew that until 1861, it was actually the only entrance the monastery used, and wasn't fully retired until the 1920s. It housed a windlass used to raise and lower visitors through the floor by a rope and harness—a welcome ritual Graham was thankful he did not have to endure.

He entered the monastery, passed between the mosque on his left and the archives on his right, and walked down the right side of the Katholikon, taking him to the corner of the abbey. A tall, rounded retaining wall was built in the corner of two buildings. Branches spilled over the top of it like an enormous green wig. According to tradition, this was the Burning

Bush itself.

Father Nikolaos admitted that it had been moved to different places as the buildings in the monastery were erected, but to the pilgrims who visited here, this was the spot. Another wall curved toward the bush and cramped the space. It was the chapel at the end of the Katholikon that enclosed the holy ground where Moses stood as he spoke with Yahweh for the first time. Graham looked around the court and laughed aloud, then caught himself when he saw a fire extinguisher sitting next to the retaining wall. Apparently, the monks didn't want the Burning Bush to catch on fire.

It was the one item Alexander had left off the list, and he wasn't sure why. Maybe it was because he couldn't think of how such a claim could be proven. But Graham thought the same could be said about almost everything on the list. Except one: *Midian*.

In Father Nikolaos's view, it didn't matter if this was the Burning Bush or not. It represented the bush, and the historical event had long been venerated at the location. Whether or not these were the geographical coordinates where the historical event actually took place was not of great importance.

But Graham wasn't satisfied with that answer. He didn't want a symbol of history, he wanted the history itself, and—if possible—to peel back the layers of tradition.

Graham found Father Nikolaos in the library and shuffled in exhaustion toward his desk. The monk looked up from his work, raising his brow.

"The Steps of Penitence might've lifted my spiritual burden, but I feel like I got paid back double in gravity. I can see why you only do that climb once a month. It might take me that long to recover." Graham collapsed into a chair across the table from the monk. "I remember reading something about plans for a cable car to the top. I can see why."

Father Nikolaos gave a forbearing blink, and Graham

wondered if the monk was blotting out the image or grudgingly picturing it. "Mercifully, God protected the abbey and the plan failed. Think of it: a machine intended to bypass the work of repentance while reaping the benefits of it. Could there be a better illustration of sin?"

Graham chuckled. "Good point. Plus, 'The Funicular of Penitence' doesn't really carry the same spiritual weight, does it?"

"Indeed," Father Nikolaos said, allowing a brief smile. "You are leaving tomorrow?"

"Yes," Graham said, "and I wanted to thank you for being so hospitable. You have been very gracious."

"We are working toward the same end, my friend," Father Nikolaos said, sounding as if he were giving a benediction. "Have you given any more thought to what Starkey found?"

"It's all I've been thinking about, actually," Graham said. "I changed my plans and am going to see what I can find in Istanbul. If I can get into the metochion, I'll look around and see what I can find. After that, I'll go to Jerusalem and talk to Yaniv. I also want to look at the other ostraca in the Rockefeller Museum." Graham paused as he saw concern cloud Father Nikolaos's face. "We can trust Yaniv. I'll keep you informed every step of the way. And I promise: No Tischendorf."

THIRTEEN

The hypnotic staccato groove of Peter Gabriel's "Digging in the Dirt" excavated Graham from sleep at 3:30 the next morning, the alarm a corny archaeological joke he hoped would help him wake up. His body protested as he tried to stand, and he could feel the cost of every one of the penitent steps to the top of the mountain. Voices of sunrise hikers bled through the walls, rallying each other to start their trip to the summit, and he silently wished them well.

Thirty minutes later, he was in a taxi he had arranged the day before, the fastest way to get to the airport in Sharm el-Sheik. The highway took him straight east to the coast, then followed it south, circumventing the mountains. Just after 7:30, the taxi pulled up to the terminal. Even though the same amount of driving would have taken him to Israel—his final destination—the border crossing was closed because of a recent terrorist attack. And because of the long-standing tension between Israel and the Muslim countries surrounding it, there were no flights from Egypt to Israel, which meant taking a circuitous route that made the journey almost ten times longer than the distance he actually needed to travel. Providentially, one of the cities that flew to Tel Aviv was Istanbul, and he had booked a flight that gave him a day-long layover. He needed the time to search the metochion and see if there was anything to Father Nikolaos's story.

As the Turkish Air flight lifted him over the Straits of Tiran, he studied the swirl of coral and land just below the surface of the water, giving the islands marbled turquoise haloes. Graham recalled that the straits had been suggested as the place Moses parted the Red Sea and tried to imagine the corridor of land cutting through the water. The distance from Egypt to Saudi Arabia was only fifteen miles at this point, and there were islands in-between the mainlands. The theory did have the virtue of leading to Midian, but if the geography and geology were the same now as they were then, it would mean walking fifteen miles on sharp coral—an implausibility that was somehow harder for Graham to believe than the miraculous parting of the sea itself.

He nodded off for the rest of the hour-long flight to Cairo. When he stepped off the plane, he suddenly realized how hungry he was, and had a craving for any food not prepared by monks. He decided to spend his four-hour layover working over a decent meal. Although he was mildly curious what the Egyptian versions of Burger King, McDonald's, and Cinnabon tasted like, he resisted the urge to find out and found a spot at a café with room for his laptop. Graham put in an order of Shish Tawook and a Coke Light, then did an image search for the Metochion of Sinai.

A matrix of images tiled his browser window, but immediately he knew the vast majority of them didn't have anything to do with what he was looking for. He supposed he was looking at other metochions or buildings named after Mount Sinai, and there were also several dozen pictures of the monastery itself. Scattered among them were less than a dozen images of what he wanted to see.

The three-story stone building was darkened with grime and pollution, giving it a charred look. On the facade, each story was slightly larger than the one beneath it, jutting out on stone corbels. Shrubs plumed over the roof from unlikely beds of unseen dirt, creating an accidental garden. Graham thought it looked like the earth was pulling the building down into the ground, reclaiming the plot of land. The sinking effect was enhanced by the fact that three quarters of the ground floor was below street level since the paving of the road had lifted the surface after the mansion had been completed in the seventeenth century. To adapt to the rising street, steps had been cut into the road in front of each of the doors, like stairs into a basement. As if to further mar its opulence, an iron grille barred each of the windows, turning the cells of the monks into something more like jail cells. The metochion was abandoned more than fifty years ago, yet Graham would have believed it had been falling into disarray for twice that long.

He picked up the skewer of chicken, dipped it in the raita sauce, and pulled the cube off the stick with his teeth. The yogurt mixed with spices carried more flavors than all the food he'd had at the monastery in a week, and his tongue was immediately revived by the ambrosial flavor. Graham wondered if the monks would consider it a culinary heresy to savor the taste.

A sepia tone photo caught his eye and he realized it was the only image of the interior returned in the search. A domed ceiling rose in the center of the room and was bound with an ornate cornice. Two pillars on each side supported the dome and were connected to each other by arches to form an arcade. The far side of the arcade connected to a small ante-chamber with a door that allowed access to the room. The furnishings gave the space the same cluttered elegance Graham had seen in the sanctuary of the monastery. According to the caption printed at the bottom of the scan, the photo was taken in 1920 and documented where the representative of Saint Catherine's—the archimandrite—formally received visitors. And according to Father Nikolaos, this was where the ostracon was hidden, the room that had been destroyed by fire in 1955.

Graham pulled more food into his mouth as he downloaded the images and saved them into the folder with the scan of the ostracon photo. When he was done, he selected all the images at once and opened them into a slideshow he could easily scroll through. As he reviewed them, he tried to remember what Father Nikolaos had told him about the place. Other than its address, he hadn't taken notes because it didn't seem important at the time. But now that he saw the strange building, he found he was intrigued by it.

The metochion was located along the shore of the Golden Horn, an inlet of the Bosphorus River, which divided Istanbul. A number of mansions had been built in the so-called Fener district around the same time as the metochion by wealthy foreign merchants who had dealings with the Ottoman government and formed a kind of embassy row. All but one were now abandoned. Archimandrites from the monastery had lived here from 1686 until they were evicted after the mansion was confiscated by the Turkish government in 1967.

Graham finished off the last of the Coke Light and headed for the gate. He used the two-hour flight to Istanbul to plan the next day. Even if the ostracon was still in the metochion—which he thought was unlikely—he might not be able to actually get in the building or find it if he did get inside. But his flight to Tel Aviv wasn't until the day after tomorrow, giving him all of the next day to see what he could find.

As he looked at a map of the area, he saw the Topkapi Palace Museum—the place where the Ashtiname was archived—was on the same road, three miles south. He supposed if his mission was a bust, he could redeem the rest of the day there.

By the time he got to his hotel near Hagia Sophia it was almost eight o'clock and the day's early start caught up to him. He lay back on the bed, melted into the mattress, and started to say a prayer of thanks that monks had not furnished the room. But before he finished, he was asleep.

FOURTEEN

As the morning prayers finished, Graham crossed the plaza in front of Hagia Sophia and walked to the Sultan Ahmet Mosque, better known in the West as the Blue Mosque. As magnificent as it was, he wished Constantine's palace hadn't been razed by the Ottomans to make room for it. He found a taxi next to the site of the ancient circus and sank into the back seat, lost in thought. Underneath the possibilities of what lay ahead at the metochion, he found himself absently humming "Istanbul (Not Constantinople)," the 1950s novelty song covered by They Might Be Giants in the early 90s. He was absently staring across the estuary of the Golden Horn as the tongue-twister lyrics resolved into the refrain: *Why did Constantinople get the works? That's nobody's business but the Turks.* He smiled privately, as he considered Constantinople had not only gotten the works, it had given it as well; at the time the ostracon had been written, the city was known as Byzantium.

"Why do you want to go there?"

It took Graham a moment to realize the cabbie was talking to him, and he stuttered as he discovered he wasn't sure how to reply.

"I do not take many Americans there." The cabbie mercifully kept him from having to contrive an answer. "Too many people without homes. They try to stay there. There are many empty buildings in the neighborhood they stay in."

Graham was still wondering what implications that news might have as the taxi turned into a break in the median separating the direction of traffic. The median widened into a park on his right, and the cabbie gestured to the door, ushering Graham onto the curb. The opposite direction of traffic was lined with colorful three-story row houses hosting shops on the bottom floor. Dilapidated buildings were interspersed along the road, evidence that the area was in the process of being revitalized. The greenery of the small park was blemished by several ancient structures, one of which he knew was the Metochion of Sinai.

Less than a minute later, Graham studied the derelict mansion from across the street. The front of the dirty gray stone structure was now veiled by corrugated metal sheets that reached to the third-story windows. The rest of the building showed the decay of four hundred years of wear combined with fifty years of neglect to create the most unwelcoming house he'd ever seen. The surreal sinking impression of the metochion given by the photographs was obscured by the membrane of sheet metal. Tufts of plants squeezed through the cracks in the rock walls and along the joint between the building and the sidewalk, making the structure look like a dam about to burst with wild greenery. He crossed the street and followed the narrow sidewalk to the metal barrier, looking for a loose panel, but there was no place to slip through to access the front door.

A café had been built to the right of the building, abutting the south side of the metochion, leaving no alley between them. To the left of the building, a low wall of ancient stone about thirty-feet-long connected the metochion to a square, corbeled, two-story building that was in as much disrepair as the rest of the complex. Without the corrugated fence, the sinking appearance was striking. A doorway had been constructed in the wall, and a well of steps cut into the sidewalk. The opening was framed in elements of Greek architecture, with columns extruded from the stone on either side, supporting a triangular entablature.

In contrast to the Greek aesthetic, the passage had been sealed shut with a pair of heavy iron doors, streaked with corrosion, each ornamented with a cross. Given that at least half the wall was below street level, Graham thought the easiest thing to do would be to climb over. But after considering the heavy traffic and the shops across the street, he thought it would call attention to himself. And he didn't know if he could get back over to the street side if he got in. He restrained the impulse in favor of walking around to the back of the café to see if there was an easier, less conspicuous way in.

Graham was surprised to find the back of the metochion completely open and accessible by a narrow flagstone path running along the side of the neighboring café's back patio. He stopped at the end of the walkway and looked to his right, into a derelict courtyard. Broken, rotted plywood was scattered among more corrugated panels—the remains of a collapsed, makeshift wall isolating the courtyard.

Squatters had claimed the second, lower building, evidenced by drying laundry and cups of herbs. Some of the windows and doors had been repaired with scraps of tarp, and an ad hoc network of pipes formed a rudimentary plumbing system. But despite the evidence of inhabitants, he didn't see or hear anyone inside.

The opposite side of the courtyard from the street was occupied by an eighteenth-century chapel dedicated to John the Baptist. Although it wasn't in good shape, the modest pink, green, and white plaster walls and terra cotta roof looked almost modern next to the dilapidated metochion.

The back of the metochion was exposed and unshielded,

revealing the extent of the dilapidation of the edifice. The tall, arched windows were glassless, their panes replaced with grids of iron bars. A patchwork of fatigued masonry had given way to foliage in places. An arched entry into the ground floor was sealed with a solid iron door, similar to the gate in the wall. Another entrance was open on a landing on the second floor, blocked only by a loose corrugated panel leaning against the threshold. Graham climbed the stairs to what looked like a loading dock, then slid the panel aside.

It wasn't until he faced the dark hallway that he realized how unprepared he was for the practical part of his search. He rebuked himself for not thinking to bring a flashlight as he pulled out his phone and turned on the flash. The stench hit him as soon as he crossed the threshold. Fifty years of decay mingled with the refuse of squatters to create a viscous miasma that made him squint. He pulled the collar of his shirt up over his nose and mouth, hunching reflexively, knowing it was a useless gesture. A well of stairs opened to his right, and he took the flight leading upward, testing each step as he went. The photo of the receiving room showed a domed ceiling, and he assumed that meant it was on the top floor.

The scratch of grit under each step gave the darkness a tangible quality, as if he were scraping across it. At the top of the second flight, a pair of slim doors stood below an arched lintel. Dignitaries and vagrants had both passed through the doors, and now Graham would add treasure hunter to their company. He pressed the seam between the doors, and they groaned in resistance as they opened.

Spears of light needled through cracks in the wood that boarded up the windows on three sides of the room. Thick dust floated languidly, making the air look almost liquid. The once-extravagant chamber was in such shambles, that Graham wondered if anything had ever been done to restore it after the fire. Shelves lined the small antechamber, but instead of the mementos and treasured items that had been displayed there, they now held debris. Two pallets of worn, dirty blankets lay on either side of the doors, their filth a testament to desperation. Even though he had made it to the room, the mess was so overwhelming that he felt no closer to finding the ostracon. He let out a long, hopeless sigh, then started rifling through the shelves. After finding nothing, he stirred each blanket with his foot, trying to search them without really touching them.

Graham stepped into the main room and stood beneath the center of the dome. As he pivoted around, he looked for anything that could be a hiding place. His eyes kept being drawn back to the dome's elaborate molding, and he wondered if there were any cavities hidden behind them. And if the ostracon was hidden in the molding, would there be some kind of symbol to mark the spot? He suddenly thought of the symbol of the monastery: an s leaning against a stylized k— for the Greek spelling of Katherine—beneath a small, square cross whose arms flared from the center. The image gave him a jolt of inspiration and he began scanning the room with purpose.

But almost as soon as he started, he remembered that for all its elegance, this was still a home for monks. He tried to picture Father Nikolaos making a secret compartment here and marking it with the sign of the monastery, and instantly realized how foolish the idea was. This was a place for clerics and diplomats, not spies.

Chastened, he conjured the image of Father Nikolaos again, but this time instead of directing the monk, he tried to let the imagined monk direct him. He envisioned the ostracon in his hand, then looked around the room with fresh eyes, putting himself in the place of the monk. Where would someone who was resourceful and practical, and whose character abhorred deceit, find a hiding place? The picture of the ostracon brought its history to mind as well. The artifact had been found in the ruins of the gate of Lachish which had suffered from massive fire damage. Just like this room. *Where would be the best place to hide something that had survived fire?* He asked himself the question, then realized the answer stood in front of him. The fireplace.

A large stone hearth was built against one of the walls, beneath a conical hood that had funneled smoke into the chimney. Blackened pieces of scrap wood indicated it had been used recently, and smears of soot on the outside of the hood hinted the flue was at least partially clogged. Graham kneeled and pointed his phone's light up into the hood to see it there were any places to conceal the ostracon, but quickly found nothing.

He started to push himself out of the firebox and felt a groove under his hand on the floor of the hearth. Ashes and unburned wood obscured a rectangular metal panel, about eight-by-four inches, resting flush inside a lip. After wiping it clean, he took his driver's license from his wallet, slid it into the groove, and used it to pry up the plate. Graham shined his light down the hole and realized it was an ash dump—a perfect place to hide the ostracon. He leaned back and searched the room, quickly finding a broken dowel in the debris. He stuck the rod into the ash dump and began to stir and prod the cinders, feeling for any kind of solid form. The ash had hardened some with age but was easily loosened.

Then he felt it. A tap. He blindly tried to retrace the movement of the dowel, and after several tries he felt it again. He pulled the rod out and mentally marked the spot since the hole was too small to reach through and look through at the same time. He peered in where he thought the contact had been made, then reached his hand into the ash dump. His fingers searched the powder and finally brushed across the edges of something hard, possibly ceramic, but was just out of reach. He maneuvered himself into an awkward position in order to force his arm deeper and grunted with effort as he stretched farther into the ash. After several attempts, he was able to scissor the object between his first and middle fingers, then he extracted himself carefully from the hole.

He rocked back from the fireplace and dropped the item into the palm of his hand. It was a shard of pottery coated in ash, and Graham recognized its outline from the photograph. He blew on it several times, then wiped it gently to reveal the Phoenician letters of ancient Hebrew. He had done it. He had found the missing ostracon, the one James Starkey had apparently been killed for.

The thrill of discovery absorbed him, making him so unaware of his surroundings that he was completely unprepared for the shock of pain that exploded across his back. He watched the ostracon drop from his hand with an odd detachment as every ounce of breath spewed out of him, almost taking his consciousness with it, smothered in pain.

FIFTEEN

Graham caught himself on the hood of the chimney, clinging to consciousness as much as the fireplace. The blackness that threatened to envelop him receded, leaving a residual daze that gave the assault a surreal quality. Pain was his hold on reality. Someone was really trying to hurt him.

He gulped air like a drowning man, forcing it into his lungs, then turned his head to see his attacker. What details the shadows didn't hide were blurred by motion as the figure raised the scrap-wood weapon. Graham slid off the chimney hood, dropping to the floor as the arc of the second swing crashed into what had been his refuge a split second earlier. He landed on his hands and knees next to the dowel he had used to explore the ash dump. Instinctively, he snatched the two-foot-long rod and used both hands to jab it hard into his assailant's abdomen.

The lance produced a primal howl that transformed into an angry growl. The man stumbled backward, clutching his stomach. As Graham pushed himself into a stand, the man charged forward, propelled by a primal scream. Graham swung the dowel at the man's head, but misjudged the blow, ineffectually striking the man's shoulder just before the man tackled him. The collision sent them backward into the low, decorative railing separating the main room from the ante-chamber. They crashed into the shelves, releasing a shower of dust and debris as they collapsed onto one of the pallets.

Again, Graham had the wind knocked out of him, but this time the weight of the other man's body pressing on his chest made him feel smothered. He grabbed at the thick, black hair on either side of the man's head and twisted his neck until the man screamed and rolled into the center of the room. Graham staggered to a stand, then kicked the man's stomach twice as hard as he could.

He scrambled back to the fireplace and recovered the ostracon. A groan came from behind him, and he spun around to see the man still on his side, doubled up. Graham hopped over the body, planting his right foot just outside the threshold of the entrance. His mind was already visualizing himself several steps down the stairs when he felt a hand clutch his left ankle. The grip was weak, but it was enough to trip him up. He jerked his leg with more force than was necessary to free himself, and tumbled into the hallway, down the first few stairs.

Graham flew out the back of the building, looped around the café to the road, and ran across the busy street through a narrow gap in traffic, incurring several angry honks. The stream of cars and delivery trucks gave him some cover as he quickly walked away, moving as fast as he could without drawing attention to himself as he stole backward glances. As it became clear that the narrow street had few intersections, he realized how easy he would be to follow, especially since there were no other pedestrians. The opposite side of the street contained the rest of the park, and the open space would have exposed him to view, leaving no choice but to continue moving south, down the road.

The Topkapi Palace Museum sat on this road, but although it was where he had planned on going next, it was three miles away. He had to get out of here fast, before the man caught up to him.

Several taxis passed, but they all had fares and ignored his signals. As the one-way section of road rejoined its opposite direction, a side road created an intersection. He ran for the corner and followed it as it angled into a claustrophobic strip of shops and cafés. Two blocks in, he found himself at the edge of a cluster of tourists outside a walled compound. It took him a moment to register the place. He had been here before—the ecumenical patriarchate, residence of the spiritual leader of the Eastern Orthodox Church.

Although the interior of the Church of Saint George was beautiful, the compound as a whole was extremely modest compared to the headquarters it had occupied for over a thousand years—Hagia Sophia. The Ottomans had evicted the patriarchate 600 years earlier, and given the lack of Eastern Orthodox followers left in Turkey, Graham thought the patriarchate was probably thankful to remain in its ancestral city.

He started toward the entrance, hoping to disappear in the crowd, but stopped when he saw the security checkpoint. A standard X-ray screener scanned the contents of visitors, manned by taciturn guards. But it was enough to make Graham realize he couldn't explain the ostracon.

As he abandoned the idea of the patriarchate, a taxi deposited its fare, and he leaped into the back of the cab before the previous passenger could shut the door.

SIXTEEN

As the taxi merged into traffic, Graham looked out the back window, kneading his wounds as he searched for any sign of the man who had attacked him. The feeling of being pursued continued to push him onward, and he was comforted by the acceleration of the car.

"Is there something wrong?"

The driver's voice spun Graham forward in his seat, and he was suddenly aware of how hard he was breathing. "No. Thank you. Everything's okay."

The driver stole several glances into the rearview mirror, appearing as unconvinced as Graham had sounded to himself. He tried to calm down, but the deliberate effort to act naturally made him self-conscious.

He looked down at his right hand, at his fingers tightly wrapped around the ostracon, indenting the flesh of his palm. Seeing the shard suddenly gave it weight, as if the lost letter had materialized the instant he saw it. The thrill of the recovery started to return, diluting the anxiety of the attack, and he wished Father Nikolaos was there with him.

What would he do with it? How was he supposed to walk into the Topkapi Palace Museum with this priceless treasure of antiquity? How could he possibly explain his possession of a 2,500-year-old piece of pottery? If he changed course and took it back to the hotel, he would still have to figure out how to get it through airport security the next day. The last thing he wanted was to go to all this trouble only to have it confiscated and put in a museum that had no real claim to it. Or worse—confiscated and *not* put in a museum at all, but simply hidden or even destroyed because it didn't conform to Islamic history. He had to find a way to get the ostracon out of Turkey and back to Saint Catherine's. And to do it, he had to find a way of making the shard invisible, or at least inconspicuous.

Traffic slowed the taxi, growing more congested as they neared the New Mosque. Two minarets towered like rockets waiting to launch on either side of the enormous seventeenth-century edifice. The main building was a collection of over two dozen domes of various sizes, making the gray stone building look like it was bubbling up toward heaven. A plaza opened to the right, filled with worshippers, tourists, and shoppers, giving Graham an idea.

"Let me off here, please."

Graham gave the driver a generous tip as an apology and quickly walked into the square. Within seconds, he was certain that anyone following him would have lost him in the crowd, yet he couldn't shake the feeling of being watched. He angled his way to the structure adjacent to the mosque—the Egyptian Bazaar.

The L-shaped building was constructed at the same time as the mosque, and the profits it generated had been used to maintain the place of worship for 400 years. Almost a hundred shops were strung along the main corridor, each inside its own arched entrance, identified by vertical neon signs. The market had earned its name in the eighteenth century when most of its offerings came from Egypt. Now tourists called it the Spice Bazaar, after what filled most of the stalls. Teas, nuts, candies, jewelry, fabric, clothes, and souvenirs added variety to the shops, but spices were obviously the main draw. Most of the shops turned their bins of spices and teas into artful displays, organizing them by color like paints. Each booth became a different abstract pointillistic composition, and together they comprised a riot of color and smell.

Graham melded into the current of shoppers and let himself be carried through the stalls anonymously as he looked for something he could use to hide the ostracon. He floated past the spice vendors and stepped into the first booth he saw that sold ceramics. Elaborately painted plates and pottery crowded into shelves along the walls, and a sign hung above the cash register that read *Aladdin*, written in the same font as the Disney movie.

"Hello. American?" A nearly bald middle-aged man in blue jeans, running shoes, and a polo shirt greeted him with a wide smile.

"Yes, hello," Graham said. "I want to buy a jar or pot."

"Yes, we have many to choose from." The man looked up into the shelves as a show of the inventory.

"No, I need something unpainted."

The man knitted his brows. "I do not understand."

Graham searched his Turkish for the right word. "No decoration...*Ghyr masbugh*?"

"Yes, I see." The man smiled. "No. Only what you see here. We have no...unpaint pots here."

Graham thanked the man with a nod and rejoined the stream of shoppers.

After two more failed attempts, it became clear that the pottery sold here was not painted at the bazaar. He stood at the side of the corridor and tried to adapt to what was available around him. As he slowly scanned both sides of the market, an image of spices in unpainted ceramic pots came into his mind, though he was unsure if it was memory or imagination. He joined the shoppers flowing against the way he came, this time looking at how the spices were displayed in each store. After passing more than a dozen displays of plastic, glass, wood, metal, and lined baskets, he saw the jars he had pictured.

A three-tiered riser held an array of jars containing saffron, curry powder, sumac, paprika, nutmeg, cinnamon, and a variety of peppers. Each was the size of a large soup pot with a rounded belly and a flared lip.

Before he even stopped, a shopkeeper who looked like he could have been one of Graham's students had spotted him.

"You like spices. I make you a good deal. Sell them all to you. Matching set!" The shopkeeper waved his arm over the display with a prompting, expectant look.

Graham laughed. "Very tempting. But what I'm really looking for is one of *these*." He tapped the closest jar with his index finger.

"You want a whole jar?" The young man's eyes went wide in surprise. "Which spice?"

"No, no. I want to buy just the jar. Do you have an empty one?"

"You do not want that jar," the man said. "It is plain. I have beautiful bowls over here. Come look." He feinted a move deeper into the store, trying to take Graham with him.

"I'm sure the bowls are very beautiful, but I need a plain one like these."

"They are for display only, not for sale."

"Will you really turn down a sale?" Graham asked, opening his hands in a question. "I'll just buy one from someone else."

"No! Please! I will look in the back. Wait here. Please."

Almost as soon as he disappeared, he returned with an identical jar.

"Perfect," Graham said, inspecting it. "How much?"

Five minutes later, Graham walked out to the sidewalk on

the far side of the bazaar carrying the empty jar in a plastic bag. Graham hadn't even tried to haggle the price, and was certain he overpaid horribly for the pot, but he had what he needed. He wove his way through the crowded street to a small table at an outdoor café. After ordering a Coke Light and a döner kabab of lamb stuffed into a pita, Graham put his plan into action.

He lifted the plastic bag knee-high off the cement, then let it drop. The sound of breaking pottery was covered by the sounds of the busy street. When he looked in the bag, the jar he had purchased was in pieces—just as he intended. He reached into his jacket, pulled out the ostracon from one of the pockets, and gently set it into the bag of shards. The size and color matched surprisingly well. To anyone glancing into the bag—a security guard at a museum or customs agent at an airport—it looked like the pieces of an unfortunate accident, the result of poor packing. Exactly what he was after.

He opened the map app on his phone and confirmed that the Topkapi Palace was less than a mile away. After he finished his food, he followed the route to Hagia Sophia, which stood between him and the palace. The expansive plaza was filled with tourists, and he camouflaged himself in visitors milling between Hagia Sophia and the Blue Mosque.

As he made his way along the perimeter of Hagia Sophia, Graham marveled at the spectacular architecture and the history that had shaped it. In 532, Emperor Justinian erected the magnificent edifice on the ashes of two prior versions of the church, which had been destroyed in riots a hundred years apart. After the conquest of 1453, the Ottomans converted it to a mosque. In 1935 it had become a museum with the founding of modern Turkey, but the rising tide of conservative Islam reconverted it to a mosque in 2020.

Graham smiled as he remembered his first visit to Istanbul. He had built a day-long visit into a trip during grad school, hoping to check Hagia Sophia off his bucket list. Unfortunately, he didn't plan well enough and discovered the hard way that the museum was closed on Mondays.

SEVENTEEN

After Constantinople fell to the Ottomans, construction began on the palace that became the headquarters for the sultan's empire and was now a museum preserving the heritage of their 500-year reign. Graham walked through the Imperial Gate and onto the grounds of the first of four courtyards around which the palace was organized. The park-like expanse contained the Istanbul Archaeological Museum and Hagia Irene, the church that served as the patriarchate while Hagia Sophia was under construction.

He passed through another gate—this one flanked by towers—into the interior of the palace grounds and paid the admission. The second courtyard was divided by paths that splayed out from the gate, segmenting the lawn as they guided tourists to different features such as the armory, the stables, the kitchens, and the Imperial Council Hall. One path led to the entrance of the harem, a separate living area with more than a hundred rooms reserved for the sultan's concubines. After consulting the map of the grounds that came with his ticket, Graham walked to the far side of the courtyard.

The Gate of Felicity led him into the third courtyard, which contained the sultan's audience chamber, as well as the library and the treasury. Most importantly, it was the location of the Chamber of Holy Relics of Islam.

Graham skirted past Asian tourists photographing flowers in the garden and joined the line that snaked from the entrance and ran under the marble colonnade. The crowd around him gave him a sense of safety that kept him from growing impatient as the line shuffled toward the door. Elaborate Iznik tiles of stylized blue tulips accented in purple, teal, and gold surrounded a marble arch that framed a green door trimmed in gold. But the adornments were merely a foreshadowing of the rooms it led to.

The backside of the doors to what was also called the Privy Chamber—the sultan's personal living quarters—were covered in a pattern of mother-of-pearl set into gold. The walls of the rooms were covered in the same style of tile as the outside, though even more ornate. Sculpted wood, gilded, trimmed each room as a visual reminder of the sacredness of the objects on display.

The first room was the Destimal Chamber, which contained several glass display cases. Graham studied an exhibit alleged to be the sword of King David. He squinted in concentration at the engraved flourishes and determined they were suspiciously—anachronistically—Arabic. Presumably, it was the sword David took from Goliath, then used to behead the giant. Graham couldn't help raising his brow skeptically as he moved on.

The next glass case was illuminated with a soft, delicate light revealing a staff of wood. Half a dozen knots bulged from the shaft, and the stub of a branch several inches long served as a handle. He frowned in disbelief as he read the description claiming it was the staff of Moses. He leaned closer to the glass, scrutinizing the wood, trying to imagine it becoming a snake when Moses threw it down before the Burning Bush, or the Red Sea parting as Moses lifted it over his head, or striking the rock at Rephidim to bring forth water.

The flow of people pushed him onward to the next case,

containing a rusty metal pot and a turban. Again, he had to check himself as he read the claim that the pot had belonged to Abraham, and the turban was the headgear of Joseph. Another case purported to contain the forearm and hand of John the Baptist, as well as a piece of his skull. And a rectangle of stone held an impression of a footprint left by Muhammad at the site of the Dome of the Rock in Jerusalem as he ascended to heaven.

The chain of tourists pulled him into the next room, leaving behind the most outlandish claims of the museum. Instead, the room displayed mostly items from the Kaaba in Mecca, the most holy place in Islam, and the place at the center of the *qibla*, the direction faced during prayer. Items on display included the Kaaba's gutters, a door, keys, and a casing that once held the Black Stone that Muhammad mounted in its wall. Swords that had belonged to the first four caliphs were also on display.

A third room, the Audience Chamber, featured a pair of swords and a bow that belonged to Muhammad. Another display exhibited hairs from his beard, a reliquary containing his tooth, and a box of soil from his tomb. A mufti read aloud from what was said to be the oldest extant Qur'an, a duty performed by a rotating group of readers twenty-four hours a day.

Finally, he entered the viewing area for the Chamber of the Blessed Mantle. Rather than a plate glass case, one corner of the room was sectioned off by silver screens fitted into an engraved silver frame that stood almost as high as the ceiling, making a sacred cupboard or vault. Arabic phrases were worked into the filigree of the screen, which itself was an artistic achievement worthy of display. But it was what was behind the screen that people had lined up to see. A gilded table held a golden chest in which was kept the cloak of Muhammad. Supposedly. It could be empty, for all he knew. According to tradition, the sultan used to open the box only once a year. Graham didn't know the last time anyone had actually seen the mantle. Another chest held the standard Muhammad carried into battle. However, it was also kept closed.

But among all the treasures, there was no Ashtiname. Graham assumed this was where Selim I would have saved all of the artifacts of Muhammad, including the covenant made with Saint Catherine's Monastery. Yet, it wasn't here. He opened the map and scanned it to find the Ağalar Mosque. Although the man marked a building in front of him as the library, he knew that what had been the sultan's collection was no longer there and only the decorative room itself was on display. The books and documents had been moved to the Ağalar Mosque, to his right.

The mosque had been built at an odd angle to the wall in order to orient the pulpit inside to face Mecca. But since its restoration in 1928, it had been the central archive of the palace. The collection held over 13,000 manuscripts from across the Ottoman Empire. Graham hoped that one of them was the Ashtiname.

He walked through the door and found a sanctuary from the tourists outside. Apparently, Muhammad's tooth and the harem were bigger draws than the priceless documents kept here. He half-expected the Ashtiname to be displayed prominently, as an attraction for visitors—like the Declaration of Independence or the Magna Carta—especially since it had become such a commonly cited document by Muslim apologists after the 9-11 terrorist attacks. But the entry hall had no displays. The last mention Graham could find of anyone claiming to see the covenant was a non-Muslim scholar who translated directly from the original in 1898.

Graham made his way to the reception desk—the only furniture in the small lobby—but before he could prepare something to say, the guard addressed him.

"May I help you, sir?"

"Hello. Yes. My name is Dr. Graham Eliot. I'm a research professor in Ancient Near East studies at Calbi University in California. I wanted to examine a document I think you have here."

"Have you submitted an application?"

"Unfortunately, no. I didn't know I would actually be in Istanbul when I started my trip, so I didn't have time to submit any research application forms. But once I found myself here, I thought I would see if I could apply in person." Graham hoped he didn't appear as inept as he felt.

"I am sorry, Dr. Eliot, but I'm afraid you must have a permission letter. All requests have to be made to the Turkish Ministry of Culture and Tourism. Then it must be approved by the General Directorate for Cultural Heritage and Museums, as well as the Department of Museums."

"Yes, I understand. I just thought since this was a special circumstance, an exception might be made and I could talk to the head librarian."

Graham looked at the guard and found himself held by a strange expression, paused, then wondered if some silent message was being conveyed. He took a business card from his wallet, wrote down his cell number on the back, then folded five American twenties around the card.

"Here's my information. Do you think you could pass it on to the directorate?"

The guard looked pleased that his message had been received and took the money. "I will be happy to let him know your request."

"Thank you. I'll be on the grounds the rest of the day. Please have him call."

Graham stepped out into the courtyard and checked his phone to make sure he had reception. He was surprised to see it was only one p.m. The museum didn't close until 6:45, and he hoped his bribe would work quickly. Until then, he decided to pass the time at the Istanbul Archaeological Museum.

EIGHTEEN

Like the Lachish Letters, the inscription on display was written in Hebrew using the Phoenician alphabet. The description card detailed how Sennacherib—a hundred years before Nebuchadnezzar—laid siege to Jerusalem after sacking Lachish. However, King Hezekiah had built a tunnel to route the water to the Pool of Siloam, bringing the city's only natural water supply within the city walls. The inscription was carved into the tunnel wall after work was completed but wasn't discovered until boys playing in the water found it in 1880. It was one of the most important archaeological corroborations of Old Testament history.

But Graham had a connection to it for a different reason. The treasure map the IAA had commissioned him to follow a year earlier had taken him to Hezekiah's Tunnel, where he had been attacked and almost drowned. Although he didn't find a hint of the treasure in the tunnel, his disappointment was outweighed by his survival.

Now the Siloam Inscription had a new relevance for him. He recalled that a few years earlier the mayor of Jerusalem had asked the Turkish government to return the inscription to Jerusalem. The Turks refused, saying it had been discovered in Ottoman territory and was part of their cultural history. Graham felt the weight of the ostracon in the bag and was determined not to let the same thing happen to it.

His silenced phone vibrated, and despite not recognizing the number, he answered. The librarian informed him that the director would see him at 2:30. Graham thanked the man, then gave a quick prayer of thanks to God. The baksheesh—he didn't like to think of it as a bribe, but as an acquiescence to the culture—had dissolved the red tape in only forty-five minutes.

After a cursory tour of the remainder of the museum, Graham once again passed through the courtyards to the archives. He took a seat on a bench just inside the door, not expecting to be there long. But it was another thirty minutes before the door opened and a large, ovate man presented himself. His white Oxford shirt was tucked into light khaki pants, which—given his frame—created an egg-like appearance. A stubble of dark hair made a permanent shadow on his scalp, and Graham had to suppress the thought of him as a swarthy Humpty Dumpty.

"Dr. Eliot? Sadik el-Muzayni. Very good to meet you, sir."

Graham took the offered hand, and el-Muzayni shook it warmly. "Thank you so much for allowing me to barge in. I assure you this is not my normal practice."

"Do not say another word about it." He waved away the apology as he spoke. "I understand completely. Now please, what is it that you would like to examine?"

"The Ashtiname of Sinai." Graham studied the man's reaction, but the director seemed unfazed.

"The Ashtiname." He nodded appreciatively. "Please, come this way."

The director opened the door he had emerged from and shepherded Graham into the archives, a mishmash of old wooden bookcases mingled with metal storage racks.

"Please sit. I will bring you the Ashtiname."

Graham took a chair at one of the two plain wooden

tables in the middle of the room and looked at the material surrounding him. Cardboard bankers boxes—several without lids—filled more than half the space on the shelves. He was shocked to see they were cheap cardboard rather than archival quality alkaline buffered document boxes that protected paper contents from the acids present in common storage boxes. The rest of the space contained books, and a number of those were stacked horizontally on top of the boxes. Graham couldn't discern any order or system, and it looked to him more like his attic storage area than a preservation of world heritage and culture. He didn't see any manuscripts and assumed they were stored in another room—hopefully cared for more thoughtfully than whatever was in this area.

He felt a sudden kinship with Constantin von Tischendorf, who—by his own account—felt much of the same worry over the conservation of the treasures he found himself among. All Graham needed were some muftis or imams burning manuscripts for heat.

A few minutes later, el-Muzayni returned with an oversized cardboard envelope. He opened the flap and Graham felt a measure of relief when he saw an archival quality clear polyester sleeve sheathed the document inside.

"The Covenant of the Prophet Muhammad with the monks of Mount Sinai," el-Muzayni said, as if introducing a dignitary.

Graham took the document, careful to handle it so it didn't bend in any way, laid it flat on the table, and stared at it. It was not only bigger than he expected, but it was formatted differently. The text was the same Father Nikolaos had shown him, but it was formatted as a block in the upper two-thirds of the sheet. A black handprint sat below it next to a line drawing of a minaret and two mountains, one of which had a path ascending it.

"There is something wrong?" el-Muzayni asked, apparently watching Graham's reaction.

"This is the Ashtiname?" Graham could feel the lines of confusion on his face as he looked up. "The covenant made with Saint Catherine's Monastery?"

"Yes. Absolutely."

"The original?" Graham asked.

El-Muzayni looked surprised. "No, it is a copy. Copies were made to renew the promise each year until the end of the Ottoman rule. Is that a problem? I can assure you the text is identical to every other copy. The differences you see are only in the ornamentation and various notes made by the copyists."

"I don't doubt you, but I would like to examine the original brought here by Selim I, if I could please."

"Well…yes," El-Muzayni stammered. "I suppose that would be fine. Please be patient with me as I bring it to you."

"Of course. Thank you. I very much appreciate all the trouble you are going to."

"No trouble. Please wait."

Despite the director's words, Graham sensed some hesitation. It was almost an hour later when el-Muzayni returned with a different storage container.

"Please forgive me. I hope you appreciate how many ancient manuscripts we care for here. Sometimes it is difficult to find exactly what we are looking for."

Graham wondered why something as important as a letter of Muhammad was lumped in with the rest of the collection as if it were simply one more item, but he tried to be gracious. "Not at all. I am the one imposing on you."

The director slid out a document different from either of the copies Graham had seen before. The top third of the sheet was devoted to a stylized colored landscape bordered with Islamic ornaments. The text of the covenant filled the rest of the page, along with the black handprint vouching for the authenticity of the document.

"This is the original?" Graham asked.

"Unfortunately, no. I must apologize, Dr. Eliot, but I am afraid I cannot locate the original at this time. But this is a very ancient copy. Most trustworthy."

"It is a beautiful manuscript, and no doubt quite valuable. But for the purpose of my research, I would need to see the original. I am a little surprised that something of such importance has been lost."

"No, no. Not lost." El-Muzayni lifted both index fingers as if making parallel points. "I did not say it was lost, only that it cannot be located at this time. I assure you, it is here."

"Do you know the last time it was seen?"

"Yes!" The director seemed proud to be able to give a solid answer after the embarrassment. "In 1904. Sultan Abdul Hamid II renewed it that year. I know it is not what you hoped to see, but I assure you the text is identical. You have a saying in English: A needle in a haystack, yes? What you are asking is more like looking for a particular piaster in the treasury of a rich man." He froze in a shrug with upturned hands. "Please do not think too harshly of us, Dr. Eliot. After all, the Jews themselves lost the Ark of the Covenant." El-Muzayni laughed at his own joke.

As Graham walked out of the courtyards in the late-afternoon sun, he once again thought of Tischendorf and wondered if he had actually been justified.

NINETEEN

Although Graham was not afraid of flying, something about it always put him in a prayerful state of mind. In fact, it was on a plane a year earlier that he had re-embraced his faith after the spiritually dark wilderness period that began with his five-year-old-daughter's death from cancer followed by his wife's accidental drowning in the bathtub. He had not seen God in those things—at least at the time.

It was in the middle of the night on a plane above the Mediterranean Sea that he realized God had always been there, had never stopped being good or in control. It was above the endless black water that he realized where God had been: He had been hanging on a cross to pay for the sin that had brought a curse on the world, that manifested itself in Alyson's cancer and Olivia's accident. God had taken sin on Himself and died so they might live. And the bodily resurrection of Jesus was the promise and the proof that Aly and Olivia would not only be healed, but never suffer for the rest of their eternal lives. God, he realized, not only loved Aly and Olivia even more than Graham did, God hated death and disease infinitely more as well.

Now, Graham looked out at the same sea in the light of morning from his window seat. As the plane passed the Hagia Sophia—the church of Holy Wisdom—he stared into the grounds of the Topkapi Palace next to it. The sight of the two together inspired Graham to pray for wisdom for what to do with his discovery. He prayed for the wisdom to understand the implication of the ostracon's message, and for the wisdom to make sense of the Ashtiname.

The flight path gave him an excellent view of the half of the city on the Asian side of the Bosphorus. In the distance he could just see Lake Iznik, and he thought about the other church named Hagia Sophia that stood in the town on the far shore. It was there that Constantine called the first church council, inviting bishops from all over the world to settle a theological dispute dividing the church. A pastor named Arius from Alexandria, Egypt, had taught that Jesus was created by God, and that Jesus made the rest of creation. Although Arius wasn't in a position of great authority, his teaching neverthe-less spread throughout the church for one simple reason: he was an excellent songwriter.

At a time when most Christians did not own private copies of scripture, they articulated and remembered their theology through hymns and creeds. Arius put his teaching into music that was so catchy, it became popular around the Christian world. But his theology did not share the excellence of the music he set it to, and the result was a rift in the church that threatened to split it in two. Constantine wanted unity in the newly legalized religion and called a council to settle the issue.

Although the majority of bishops with an opinion on the matter arrived supporting Arius, the argument against him made by Bishop Alexander and his protégé Athanasius was so firmly grounded in scripture that Arius was condemned as a heretic. And to protect the church against future heresy, the council composed a creed that became the standard of orthodoxy. The creed became known by the name of the town on the lake the council met in, which at that time was called

Nicea.

Graham thought about the power of music and how the influence of Arius was still at work in cults who repeated his errors such as the Jehovah's Witnesses. Then he smiled inwardly at the thought of Martin Luther, himself a musician who, like Arius, wrote songs to teach Christians their faith, but unlike Arius, was a relentlessly biblical theologian. One of Graham's favorite Lutherisms made its way to the forefront of his thoughts: "Next after theology I give to music the highest place and the greatest honor." He thanked God for the wisdom that came from deliberating with other learned people. It was for this very reason he was on a flight to Tel Aviv en route to Jerusalem, to meet with Chaim Yaniv, a man who could help him think through these things.

As soon as the Turkish Air flight landed in Tel Aviv, Graham took his phone off airplane mode and a ding announced a text from Alexander. He was surprised to see that the only content was a link to a Spotify playlist named *Sign Eye*. He clicked the link and found it contained six David Bowie songs. Graham knew the songs—most of which he loved—but it was a strange collection of obscure tracks from records spanning Bowie's long career. He usually enjoyed sharing in Alexander's musical discoveries, but he was too preoccupied to listen and put his phone back in his pocket.

Two hours later, Graham had driven his rental car to Jerusalem and checked into the Promised Land Hotel. Although it was not the most luxurious place to stay, it had the virtue of being less than a block from the Old City's northern wall and had a spectacular rooftop view. It was also on the other side of the block from the Rockefeller Archaeological Museum, which housed the headquarters of the Israel Antiquities Authority.

Graham walked the block to the Rockefeller along Sultan Suleiman Street. The sultan had earned the title "Suleiman the

Magnificent" for his many building projects in the empire, including rebuilding the city wall which paralleled the street.

Graham stepped through the doors of the building that not only resembled a fortress but had actually been used as one by Israeli troops during the Six-Day War of 1967. Scars from bullets could still be seen in the stonework of one of the galleries. He made his way past the exhibits of the North Gallery, then turned into a door leading out of the public area of the museum and into the offices of the IAA.

Chaim Yaniv sat behind his desk, hunched over a scattering of photographs. Graham had never seen him in anything but a navy polo shirt that was one size too large and embroidered with the logo of the IAA over the left breast. His short black hair had become thinner in the year since he had seen him, foretelling his future baldness. Wire-frame glasses too small for his kind, intelligent eyes tilted up at the sound of Graham's entrance, transforming his expression.

"Graham! It is good to see you, my friend." Yaniv navigated around the desk as he spoke.

Graham returned his embrace, then sank into the same chair he had spent so many hours in when they had planned their excavations looking for the treasures of the Copper Scroll. The chair beside him was suddenly conspicuously empty, and he was unexpectedly stung by a pang of grief.

"I miss Daniel as well," Yaniv said. "He was a good man."

Graham thought about Daniel Harel, the friend he had made and lost during his work the previous year. Harel had retired from the Mossad and come to the IAA's Robbery Prevention Division, fulfilling a childhood dream of working at archaeological digs. But his assignment with Graham proved more dangerous than any of them expected. Graham had watched Daniel die, murdered by a black market treasure hunter in one of the cisterns hidden beneath the Temple Mount.

"So, what is it that brings you here this time? Your message was a bit mysterious. You are not on another treasure hunt, are you?"

Graham held Yaniv's eyes, then nodded. "Actually, yes."

TWENTY

"James L. Starkey was murdered over an ostracon he found that went missing." Yaniv repeated the main points of the story back to Graham, making sure he understood it correctly. "But before he died, he gave it to the driver, who took it to the librarian at Saint Catherine's, who took it to the…what did you call it?"

"The metochion."

"Who took it to the metochion in Istanbul. Fascinating." Yaniv put his elbows on his desk and rested his chin in his hands. "And what happened when you went to the metochion?"

"I was attacked. It was like someone had been waiting in the room where it was hidden, like they were guarding it."

"And you are unharmed?"

"Bruised, but yes. Once I made it outside, I went as fast as I could to the Egyptian Bazaar."

"Very clever. But it is unfortunate that you could not find Starkey's ostracon."

"I didn't say that." Graham smiled conspiratorially as he set his plastic bag on the desk. "Please understand, this does not exist. At least, not yet."

Yaniv stared at the bag for a moment before spreading the top and looking inside.

"One of those shards is not like the others," Graham said.

"Just so." Yaniv reached in, then retracted his hand, holding the edges of the triangular ostracon, careful not to handle its face. "Extraordinary. Absolutely extraordinary."

"Chaim, I hope you understand that I cannot let you keep it. I have promised Father Nikolaos. I need to return it to Saint Catherine's. Then the authorities can sort out the ownership."

"I *am* the authorities. It really is my duty to confiscate it, you understand." Yaniv kept his head tilted down toward the artifact as he raised his eyes to Graham, affecting a slightly chastising look. "Its brothers and sisters are here. Some of them, anyway. In the North Gallery. But I do understand the situation, I will speak with Father Nikolaos about how to best handle things. And I promise to help you keep your promise in any way I can."

"Something isn't quite right about all this, though."

"How so?" Yaniv gently set the ostracon on the desk.

"I don't think Starkey was killed because of the ostracon itself. I think he was killed because of something mentioned in the writing."

"Go on."

"The message alludes to the location of Mount Sinai. At least the general area. But it is not where Saint Catherine's is. It is not even close."

"And that is a surprise to you?" Yaniv said. "The Jews have never venerated the location where Saint Catherine's is. That is an entirely Christian invention."

"Yes, I agree," Graham said.

"What does Father Nikolaos think about the message?"

"That I am making too much of figurative language not meant to be read as a map."

Yaniv shrugged. "So what is the issue?"

"While I was at the monastery, I saw the Ashtiname, the

covenant Muhammad made with Saint Catherine's."

"I am familiar with it." Yaniv cocked his head slightly at the turn in the conversation.

"Does it make any sense to you? Why would Muhammad issue a decree of protection for a group of infidels, people who believe Islam is a lie? Especially when it was an exemption given only to them. It's not a manifesto declaring religious freedom."

Yaniv's eyes glazed over in thought, then refocused. "It is an interesting question, but what does it have to do with Starkey?"

"The newspaper reports said Starkey was murdered because they thought he was a Zionist. But the driver said the Arab bandits knew exactly who he was. They didn't rob him, though they did loot the dig site at Lachish, and they got no benefit from his death. So why kill him?"

Yaniv gestured to Graham to answer his own question.

"Because of something on the ostracon they wanted kept secret for the sake of Islam. Especially since this was a time when the Zionist passion to reestablish the land for the Jews was gaining momentum. And the only thing in the message that could be relevant to modern times is the apparent location of the true Sinai. Starkey's murder and the Ashtiname make sense if the goal was to hide the true location of Sinai.

"By issuing the Ashtiname, Muhammad gave the appearance of legitimizing the claim of the monastery to be at the actual site. But if Sinai is really where the ostracon points to—in Saudi Arabia—then it starts to make sense why Muhammad would send people in the wrong direction. They both take away any legitimate claim of the Jews to one of the most important historical locations of their heritage. And that prevents the history of Jewish scripture from being corroborated."

Yaniv rocked gently, processing the theory. "Very compelling. Well, I hope that whatever it was that got James Starkey killed is no longer there. A fourth excavation of Lachish is currently underway. I know they found a toilet in the same gate complex where the ostraca were found, but apparently the toilet was not worth killing for." Yaniv paused, checking himself. "Forgive me. I do not mean to be disrespectful. Starkey was a great man. And you could have been seriously injured. Or worse. What I am getting at is this: Do you think the ostracon is the only incident?"

"What do you mean?"

"If, as you say, Starkey was murdered because of the ostracon, and you were attacked when you found the place it had been hidden, then it may not be the only thing like that. There may be other artifacts that refer to the true Sinai or give clues about it. There may be other incidents that are connected but have gone unrecognized."

Graham put his chin in his hand, as he weighed the idea. "I hadn't considered that. Are you thinking of anything in particular?"

"No, but give me some time. Perhaps if we visit the other Lachish ostraca, we will discover another clue."

Yaniv led the way to the North Gallery of the museum. Graham had always loved the feel of museums after they had closed for the day. Though he had devoted his life to recovering items from the past to share with the world, he also loved the after-hours when he had history all to himself.

A wood and glass display case held six of the ostraca found by Starkey. They varied in shapes and size, but the writing was similar. Graham held the new ostracon flat in his palm, compared it to the others, and saw no reason to think it was not from the same group of finds.

"Looks like a reunion to me," Yaniv said.

"Me too. It's funny how time can transform garbage into treasure. If I took one of the other pieces of broken pottery in that bag and used it to write a letter to you, it would still be considered worthless garbage. Anyone who found it would throw it in the trash can."

Yaniv snapped his head around to face Graham. "What did you say? Throw it where?"

Graham frowned in confusion, rethinking his words. "The trash can. You know, the rubbish bin."

Yaniv looked amused. "I heard you incorrectly. When you said *trash can*, I thought you said *Ashkelon*."

"And…"

"Think about it," Yaniv said. "What is the first thing you think of when you hear *Ashkelon*?"

"Lady Hester Stanhope?" Graham said the name as if testing the answer.

"Just so!"

TWENTY-ONE

"What do you remember about Lady Stanhope and Ashkelon?"

Graham scrambled to shift into the unexpected topic. "Well…that's where she carried out the first archaeological excavation ever done in the Holy Land. But it was really a treasure hunt."

Yaniv smiled skeptically. "Is that all you recall?"

"If I remember correctly, she was secretly given a manuscript that described where ancient caches of money had been buried in several cities along the coast of Palestine. The manuscript came from a monk, who claimed to have copied it from the original he found in a monastery in Syria."

"Just so," Yaniv said. "Found among the possessions of the monk after he died, in fact. She was living outside of Sidon as a British expatriate. Anything else?"

Graham continued, still trying to make the connection as he remembered aloud. "She had apparently moved there for her health, but there was some suspicion about that since there were many more comfortable places in the region a person of her rank could live. I think at first she thought the manuscript was some kind of test to see if she was actually there as a spy or for hunting treasure. That was at a time when Egypt and other parts of the Mediterranean and Middle East were allowing their antiquities to be taken back to Europe and put in museums. It was just old, broken junk to them, and they couldn't understand why anyone would want the stuff. But they started to feel like they were being used and were growing resentful. Lady Stanhope thought the manuscript might have been given to her as a way of revealing her motives and true character."

"Understandable, is it not?" Yaniv motioned to the display cases. "Some would say we are in the company of thieves, you and I."

"But Lady Stanhope didn't take advantage of it," Graham said, ignoring the comment as his recall unpacked itself, each detail extracting others with it. "She did recognize its potential importance, though, and got permission from the Ottoman government to search for the treasure. However, to do so she swore she was not looking for antiquities, just the money. I think they agreed to share whatever money she found."

"A more generous offer than we get from black marketeers today," Yaniv said with a wry smile, drawing a chortle from Graham.

"So Lady Stanhope went to Ashkelon, the place where the biggest horde was supposed to be. It was in the ruins of a mosque that had originally been a church. She had her workers start digging, and after a couple of days clearing the site, they found an underground vault. The manuscript said they would find something like three million pieces of gold. But the site had already been looted. All she found was a huge statue. I can't remember who it represented."

"Bacchus," Yaniv said. "And what happened to the statue?"

Graham's face bloomed in realization, finally connecting the dots. "She destroyed it. She had it broken up and thrown into the sea."

"And why would she do a thing like that?" Yaniv prompted again.

"She said it was so that no one could accuse her of coming to look for statues to take back to England. She said she had no choice but to destroy it in order to keep her integrity."

"And do you believe that such a cultured woman who recognized the historical importance of such a find would shatter a priceless antiquity simply to protect her reputation?"

"I hadn't really thought about it before," Graham admitted. "But, no, not really."

"Not at all," Yaniv said. "In point of fact, it sounds almost as if she were being threatened to keep something hidden, does it not?"

"And you think the statue had something to do with Sinai? Like an inscription on it somewhere?"

Yaniv turned his palms up. "The story does not make sense as it has been told. And remember, the Ottoman government sent an official representative from Istanbul to accompany her. He oversaw everything she did. Who knows what she would have done with the statue had he not been there."

"Maybe," Graham said. "But it's an awfully big stretch to connect it with Sinai. Besides, she found a torso from a second statue. There was a rumor that she smashed it and discovered that the gold had been hidden inside. Then she gave half to the official and kept the rest."

"Merely a rumor." Yaniv gave a dismissive wave. "She died with almost nothing. She paid for the expedition herself and it broke her. There is no evidence she ever found the gold."

"Well, it sounds just as plausible to me as your conspiracy theory. It's certainly a bizarre incident. But if there are other incidents like Starkey's, then they'll need to have a more direct tie-in to Sinai. We can't just plug Sinai into gaps in the stories."

Yaniv nodded. "Just so. But at the same time, Sinai may

be like a puzzle piece that fits into holes that need explanation."

"I admit it works in Starkey's case. And there may be others. I just don't want to force it where it does not belong."

"Agreed. Let us talk of it more tomorrow. I know you
must be very tired."

TWENTY-TWO

Graham's laptop provided the only light in the hotel room as he sat up in bed, breaking a state of limbo. His mind was too awake to let his exhausted body rest, and after failing to will himself to sleep, he decided to use what energy he had to review Alexander's notes.

In the list of mountains that had been proposed as the true Sinai, Alexander had gone to the trouble of including the GPS coordinates for each of the twelve locations. Graham opened Google Maps, entered the coordinates of each candidate, and dropped pins to mark their spots. He shrank the window to make room for another image he could put next to it, then opened the map of Midian made by Richard Burton.

For four months in 1877 and 1878, Burton traveled throughout northwest Arabia to make a survey of what he referred to as the "wild and mysterious Midian." The expedition was the first documentation of the area. He had made a brief expedition earlier in 1877 to determine the mineralogical value of the region. And he had passed through parts of it twenty-five years earlier when he traveled to Mecca and Medina. That adventure—in which he had disguised himself as a Muslim—had made him famous. According to Burton's map, Midian comprised the land on the east side of the Gulf of Aqaba and ran down the coast of the Red Sea nearly to Medina. Burton's scholarship, his reverence for local traditions, and his ability to assimilate—including learning an entire language in a few weeks—left little doubt as to the map's trustworthiness in Graham's mind.

Of the twelve alternate locations of Sinai in Alexander's list, seven were in the Sinai Peninsula and one was in Israel. Only four were within the boundaries of Burton's map of Midian. Graham clicked on the option to view the Google map with satellite imagery, then zoomed in on the traditional Mount Sinai. Where would two million people be able to camp near the mountain? He wasn't good at estimating the space needed but remembered looking at the monastery from the mountain and thinking they could fit into the wadi. He also remembered thinking they could fit into the space on the other side of the cluster of mountains near the supposed Rephidim, where the Split Rock stood, but now he questioned if there was enough space. Also, the route from the Split Rock to the spot of the monastery would have easily taken less than a day, which didn't correspond with the biblical narrative. As due diligence, Graham made the same estimation on each of the locations and decided ten of the mountains had a place that could hold two million people, and that seven had places for two camps on opposing sides of the mountain. He noted that all four Midian locations had places for two camps.

Graham looked at Burton's map again and saw that one of the candidates was off course from the ostracon's directions, erring too far east. If the ostracon was correct, then he could eliminate this candidate as well. He opened a document and began to make notes on the remaining three.

The northern most location was Jebel al-Baqir. It stood in Jordan, ten miles inland from the tip of the Gulf of Aqaba and the resort town of Eilat, Israel, twenty miles north of the border of Saudi Arabia. According to Alexander's notes, it was identified as Sinai by Charles Beke in the 1870s. Graham made a note to read Beke's account of the exploration.

Jebel al-Lawz, the next location, was about halfway down the coast of Aqaba, thirty miles inland. It had been proposed by Ron Wyatt in the early 1980s. Graham remembered Wyatt was an amateur archaeologist who was some kind of medical doctor or nurse, and Graham had never paid much attention to the claims. As far as he knew, no trained archaeologist had ever visited the site to do a proper investigation. Graham added a note to do a search of Burton's writings to see if the place was mentioned, and to look into Wyatt's claims more closely.

The third mountain was Zuhd, also known as al-Mani-fa. It stood twenty-five miles south of al-Lawz, thirty miles inland from the Gulf of Aqaba, and twenty miles from the Red Sea proper. Saint John Philby, a British advisor to the first king of Saudi Arabia, and an explorer who mapped more of the Arabian Peninsula than any other European, had identi-fied it as Sinai. He made a note to check Philby's rationale.

Graham closed his laptop, his head finally heavy, and was asleep almost as soon as his head sank into the pillow.

The image of Moses picking his way down the mountain appeared in a dream that seemed to be waiting for him. Moses held a tablet in each arm, each with all Ten Commandments written on them by the very finger of God. Graham's dream eye watched Moses's face become a mask of anger, and Gra-ham turned to see the celebration around the golden calf. His perspective pivoted back to Moses just as the prophet raised the tablets of stone and smashed them against the rocks, breaking them into pieces. When he looked up from the fragments, Moses was at the altar of the golden calf, pounding at it, turning it to dust. Graham's voice sounded in his head: *Moses himself destroyed priceless artifacts of great importance.* As the prophet pounded the idol, he transformed into a Bedouin and began building a fire under a monument shaped like a tombstone. Graham not only heard his own voice but felt its resonance in his chest as he screamed *NO!*

The desert disappeared, replaced with his hotel room like a bad edit in a film. He was awake and breathing heavy, unsure if he had actually screamed or not. But even though the room sat before his eyes, the image he saw was of the fire. Or rather the monument the fire was built beneath.

The Moabite Stone had been a source of fascination for Graham since his undergraduate days. He'd even written a research paper on it as part of his master's program.

In 1868, Frederick Klein, a medical missionary from Germany, was at a Bedouin camp east of the Dead Sea, near Dibon, Jordan. The Bedouin told him about an ancient stone nearby that had an inscription on it. He found the four-foot-tall basalt block lying face up in the sand, not far away. Klein couldn't read the writing, but he knew it was a stele, an ancient marker and valuable archaeological find. The Bedouin agreed to sell it for 100 Napoléons—francs minted in gold coins. Klein returned to Jerusalem and persuaded the Prussian Consulate to send the money and planned for the monument to be placed in the Berlin Museum. But when Klein tried to make arrangements to get the stele, the Bedouin broke the agreement and demanded 1,000 Napoléons. Klein decided to negotiate with the Ottoman government, but the Bedouin resented being ruled by the Ottomans, and they buried the stone.

The situation grew more complicated after word of the discovery leaked out and made its way to Charles Warren and Charles Clermont-Ganneau, each of whom contributed some of the most important archaeological work done in the Holy Land. Clermont-Ganneau in particular became a legend in the field and trained many influential archaeologists who came after him, including James L. Starkey. Both Warren and Clermont-Ganneau sent men to make squeezes of the stone, copies made by laying wet paper across the inscription and pressing it into the grooves of the inscription, then letting it dry. The result would leave an impression of the writing, preserving the content. But the political atmosphere surrounding the stele had become so poisonous that even taking a squeeze was dangerous. As Clermont-Ganneau's man was waiting for his squeeze to dry, a fight erupted among the Bedouin, and somehow the man was stabbed in the leg. During the chaos, one of the guides who brought the man ripped the wet paper from the stele, jumped on his horse, and galloped away. The squeeze had been torn into pieces, but it was dry enough to retain some of the inscription.

The Bedouin decided that rather than letting the Ottomans dictate what should be done, they would solve the problem by destroying the stone, spiting everyone involved. They built a fire under the monument, heated the stone, then poured cold water on it, shattering it. The smaller pieces were given to members of the clan as talismans. The larger pieces were buried.

After ten years of searching for as many pieces as they could, Warren and Clermont-Ganneau had collected about two-thirds of the stele. Clermont-Ganneau reconstructed what he could, then used the squeezes he and Warren had made to recreate the missing pieces. Graham had seen the result on display in the Louvre.

When it was translated, it was found to be a declaration of King Mesha of Moab, and mentions the names *Israel* and *YHWH*, the personal name of the Hebrew God. Even more importantly, it possibly mentions the House of David. Although disputed, it was the first potential evidence of the biblical king ever found outside of the Bible. Only recently had one other inscription been found that offered corroboration of David as a historical figure.

But now Graham thought about what the Moabite Stone didn't say. Strangely, when Klein saw the reconstruction, he said it was the wrong shape and that some of the text was missing. Those parts of the squeeze had either not survived the process or had been lost. And that meant there was text that was unknown, that would probably never be known. Like the death of Starkey, the promise of the Ashtiname, and the treasure of Lady Stanhope, the story was as much a mystery as it was a discovery.

Graham quickly shook his head several times, clearing his head of conspiracy and reordering his thoughts. He chastised himself for entertaining a theory no better than Yaniv with Ashkelon. The only thing Lady Stanhope and the Moabite Stone proved was that sometimes monuments were destroyed, and sometimes the reason was lost with them.

TWENTY-THREE

Early morning was Graham's favorite time of day in the Old City, the time when the past was most exposed, unobscured by tourists and trinkets. The narrow streets became intimate arteries he alone flowed through, carried on its ancient pulse.

After entering through Herod's Gate and making his way to the Antonia Fortress, he followed the Via Dolorosa, the route Jesus was said to have walked from His sentencing to the cross. The voice of Father Nikolaos entered his thoughts, and Graham realized that—like Sinai and the Burning Bush—whether or not this was the actual route had become almost irrelevant. What was important was that the traditional spot commemorated the historical location—wherever it actually was.

Graham followed Via Dolorosa Street as it zigzagged toward the Church of the Holy Sepulchre, then stopped in front of one of the many antiquities shops.

Avraham Antiquities didn't open for another fifteen minutes, but Graham could see Gideon Ravid behind the counter, preparing for the day. Ravid had been a reliable source not only of interesting artifacts, but of information about other finds that were available. Ironically, his excellent reputation for integrity brought a steady stream of black marketeers hoping to entice him with their latest plunder. In the antiquities business there was no better way to sell illegal goods than from behind a mask of respectability. Ravid paid enough interest to keep within their orbits despite the fact that he had never actually bought anything from them and never sold anything that had been stolen. The result gave him a window into a secret world.

At a time when the antiquities business was becoming more difficult because of the ever-decreasing inventory of authentic items to sell, he occasionally used his insight to help the IAA, who returned the favor by turning a blind eye to the worthless facsimiles of items he sometimes sold to unsuspecting tourists who were not serious collectors. Ravid reasoned that a fake oil lamp held the same sentimental value as a genuine one—both were mementos of the Holy Land, which was what they were really purchasing.

Graham tapped the window with his knuckles. Ravid's annoyed expression broke into a wide smile of recognition as he started for the door. Ravid always conducted himself in a formal manner and emanated an understated elegance, his thin hair in place and his slender body tastefully dressed.

"Shalom, Dr. Eliot! Such a nice surprise to see you again."

It had been a year since Graham had last entered the shop, a span of time that felt simultaneously like a decade and a day.

"An unexpected detour. But a happy one."

They stepped through the small shop lined with wood and glass shelves crowded with excellent pieces mostly from the Roman era.

"What is it I can help you with, my friend?"

Graham faltered as he wondered how to approach the subject. "I have a question that may not be for legal ears, exactly."

A veil of concern drew across Ravid's face. "You may ask me anything you wish. But I make no promises to be able to answer." He added a look that conveyed he might not be able to share information even if he did know the answer.

"Have you ever heard of anyone looking for or selling ostraca from Lachish?"

"No…" Ravid inflected the word as if it were a question. "Has there been a new discovery there?"

"Not that I know of. Have you ever been offered anything that was supposed to be from Mount Sinai?" Graham felt almost silly asking the question and screwed up his nose like he smelled something foul.

"Yes, actually I have!" Ravid seemed more amused than curious. "On occasion, a Bedouin will claim to know of the true Sinai and bring rocks with inscriptions or petroglyphs to sell."

"But you don't think any of them are authentic."

"Of course not. None of them are real. The rocks might be from a mountain they think is Sinai, but the inscriptions are quite obviously faked. Letters are formed incorrectly. Words are misspelled."

"And yet there seems to be some kind of market for them," Graham said regretfully.

"Too true," Ravid said. "Fortunately for the forgers, there are always buyers who are blinded by what they want to see rather than what is in their hands. They have no discernment. And unfortunately, there are dealers who willingly prey on that self-delusion."

"But not you," Graham said, testing Ravid's sincerity, hoping not to offend him.

"Not me," Ravid said, shaking his head. "I refuse to buy such things or to take advantage of such people. But they merely find somewhere else to be deceived."

Graham wondered how he justified selling reproductions of oil lamps as originals in his shop but ignored the contradiction. "Have they ever said what mountain the rocks are from?"

"Not always." Intrigue crept into Ravid's face. "But I have heard they are supposed to be from Saudi Arabia. A place called…what was it? A mountain. Something about almonds? It does not matter. It is just another flying goat."

"I don't understand," Graham said. "A flying goat?"

"Ah. You do not know the story?" Ravid smiled. "It is an old Arab fable. Two men were walking together and saw an animal far across a field. The first man said, 'Look at the crow.' The second man said, 'That is a goat, not a crow.' As they got nearer the first man said, 'See, it is black like a crow.' But the second man said, 'Even if it is black, it is a goat.' As they got close enough to see the details of the animal, the first man said, 'It has wings and feathers. It is obviously a crow.' But the second man said, 'Those are not feathers or wings. It is the hair of the goat.' Then the animal started to move away from them. The first man said, 'See how it hops? It is a crow.' But the second man said, 'No, the goat is limping. It must have injured its foot.' Finally, they came so close that the animal flew into the air. 'See how it flies? I told you it was a crow!' said the first man. But the second man said, 'It is a goat, even if it flies.'" Ravid loosed a contemptuous snort. "Fools always see what they want to see."

TWENTY-FOUR

Graham turned right out of the shop and continued down Via Dolorosa Street. Most of the shops had awakened, their merchandise congesting the already claustrophobic alleys. He negotiated the maze of streets until the lane opened into a plaza with a tall, three-tiered fountain at its center.

He entered a wedge-shaped building that held the Panorama, a café featuring seating on the roof. He was fortunate enough to find a small table near the edge that was within the shade cast by a blue tarp tied to the posts of the railing. The table gave him a perfect view of the Church of the Holy Sepulchre only fifty yards away, its gunmetal gray domes rising above the other side of a building between them.

He was one of the first people in the restaurant and it took long enough for a server to come to the table that he wondered if it was open yet. But he wasn't there mainly for the food. It was a place to open his laptop and do some work while enjoying a fabulous view in the midst of the ambiance of the Old City. The shakshouka and Diet Coke he ordered were merely the price of renting the table.

He opened his laptop and connected to the internet through the hotspot of his cell phone. The canyon of the Old City made cell reception difficult at best, which was another reason he liked this café. He navigated to a cloud storage site where he kept a digital library of reference books for research. The first mountain he had made notes of the night before was Jebel al-Baqir, so he scanned the list of books in the library to find a PDF of Charles Beke's Sinai in Arabia.

The book was a travelogue of Beke's expedition to the mountain to verify that it was the true Sinai, and to confirm his theory that it was a volcano. By the time Beke made the journey, however, he was elderly and in poor health, which deteriorated even more during the trip. He died only months after returning to England, and the book was published four years after his death. Graham found the chapters detailing the discovery, copied the most relevant passages out of the PDF, and pasted them into his notes.

During the trip, Beke also wrote several letters to the paper in London, documenting his progress in the Times. One letter announced his mission had been successful and that he had found the actual location of Sinai. Graham combined this letter with excerpts from the more detailed account in Beke's book, putting the passages from the letter in brackets so he could recognize the source of the text. When he was finished, he read back through the compiled account as he picked at his poached eggs in tomatoes, olive oil, peppers, and garlic.

Jan 30 ,1874

[We left Aqaba under the personal escort of Sheikh Mahommed ibn Iját, the chief of the Alauwin Tribe of Bedouin and proceeded north-eastward up the Wady-el-Ithem (the "Eth-am" of the Exodus) and encamped in the evening at the foot of Jebel al-Baqir.]

One of the results of our alliance is that he has been telling me the story of Jebel al-Baqir, which, he says, is a holy mountain; on the summit of which is the tomb of a wely or saint and at the foot of it is a mosque; and every time the Hadj returns from Mecca to Cairo, sounds are heard in the mountain like the firing of a canon. This, he solemnly assures me, he has himself heard with his own ears.

I am writing now at 8.30 p.m. and I have just heard thunder, or something which must surely come from Jebel al-Baqir!

Jan 31, 1874

I

have found my "Mount Sinai," which turns out not to be a volcano. [From its manifest physical character, it appears that my favourite hypothesis that Mount Sinai was a volcano must be abandoned as untenable.] This will surely please both parties, I hope: the anti-traditionists, who will have seen a deathblow given to the traditional Mount Sinai; and the traditionists, who do not like the Scripture History to be deprived of its miraculous character. The prayer that the Hadjis say when they first come in sight of this mountain is the fátha, or first chapter of the Qur'an.

A sheikh of this neighborhood has come into the camp, who tells me that Jebel al-Baqir has always been known as the "Mountain of Light."
…At the very summit of this mountain is a place of sacrifice surrounded with stones, where may be seen the horns (and bones?) of sheep and goats sacrificed there.

Mount Sinai (Jebel al-Baqir) would have been visible to thousands or hundreds of thousands of people encamped in the "plain" here below.

[As the climbing part of my expedition necessarily devolves on my young companion, Mr. Milne] he went to the very summit, and found the horns and heads of the animals slaughtered there, just as I had been told...he was able to distinguish a large "plain" to the northeast of this, into which, in fact, this valley opens.

He has found and copied some "Sinaitic Inscriptions" of our own.

But I will relate the particulars of the ascent...in Milne's own words:

"On the way we passed a stone on which were cut the words, 'Ya Allah!' Something else had been written, but it was defaced, in Cufic, or old Arabic characters. In the gorge we stopped to admire a large stone near which the Bedouin come and say their prayers. This stone...is about five feet long and two feet square and is made of granite. It originally stood upright on the ground. It is now fallen over, and rests between its pedestal and the side of the gorge.

"On reaching the summit of the mountain, we found numerous skulls and horns, and a few bones of animals—it being the custom of the Bedouin to come up here to pray, bringing with them a lamb, which they kill and eat on the spot....
We came to a low wall across the gorge, which was filled with large boulders; and close above the wall on the right-hand side is a well about three feet across, and about the same to the water in it, which may be two feet of water. On the ridge on the left-hand side of the gorge, about a hundred

*and fifty yards distant from the well, we came to
a pile of large, rounded boulders of granite, on
several of which were inscriptions, which I copied
as well as my cold fingers would allow me to do.
The stones, which were much weathered, were ex-
ternally of a dark-brown color, against which the
inscriptions stood out and made themselves visible
from their being of a somewhat lighter color.*

"On the side of the mountain are many large

*so much disintegrated on their under sides as to
form small caverns. One in which I entered was
as much as about twenty feet high at the entrance,
sloping down toward the back, the roof being
dome-shaped and the sides curved."*

Graham made a note that this is where the quote from
Beke's companion ended and Beke resumed in his own words.

*[As the existence of a cave or caves on Mount
Sinai is essential in order to meet the requirements of the texts (Exodus xxxiii.22, and I Kings
xix.9), the fact that such caves do actually exist is
most pertinent and important.]*

*[Jebel al-Baqir is one of the loftiest peaks of
the range of mountains. It will be sufficient to say
here that it consists of a mass of pink or reddish
granite, which, in places, where it is weathered,
assumes a dark-brown hue.]*

*[Not less significant is the fact that this majes-
tic mountain is visible in all directions, and that
round its base toward the east and south there is
camping ground for hundreds of thousands of per-
sons.]*

*I am content with the discoveries I have made.
And the best of it is that the sheikh says he has giv-
en orders to all the Bedouin to discontinue the use
of the name Baqir.... So that in a few years the
"tradition" will be that it has always been known
by that name, as the true "Mount Sinai" by people
who have never heard of Dr. Beke...and my views
will doubtless soon be adopted by many both at
home and abroad.*

Graham smiled as he read the last lines, thinking about
how Beke over-estimated the acceptance and influence of his
discovery—if, in fact, it was a discovery. At the same time, he
had to admit that Beke's observations were more compelling
than he expected them to be. Based on what he read, he had
to keep Jebel al-Baqir as a legitimate possible location.

TWENTY-FIVE

Graham looked away from his laptop to the dark gray domes of the Church of the Holy Sepulchre. It occurred to him that he was looking at the bookend of Sinai. The smaller dome hovered above Golgotha, the place where Jesus paid the penalty for the sins of all who believe in Him. And sin was revealed by the Law given to Moses on Sinai. It was that same Law that Jesus kept perfectly on Earth, and His obedience was credited to believers, making them righteous before God.

He realized that both locations had also been lost. Sinai had been mostly forgotten during the Babylonian Captivity. And the tomb of Jesus—including nearby Golgotha—had been buried by Hadrian in AD 135 in an attempt to erase it from memory. The Temple where the ceremonial law had been kept had also been lost, destroyed when the Romans attacked the city to put down the Jewish insurrection in AD 70.

But the ironies of history had convinced Graham that God had a sense of humor. As part of his plan to eliminate sites holy to the Jews and Christians, Hadrian filled in the quarry where Jesus had been buried, then erected a temple to Venus above the spot. When Constantine's mother, Helena, made a pilgrimage to Jerusalem two hundred years later, she asked where the tomb was. After learning it was beneath the temple of Venus, she ordered the temple torn down. And when the fill had been removed from the quarry beneath it, they discovered the tomb that was venerated to this day. Hadrian hadn't erased the location at all. Instead, he had preserved it. Other tombs were found in the area, but the one directly beneath the temple was a less common form of tomb used by the wealthy, which corresponded with the accounts in the gospels.

Constantine chipped away the rock around the tomb until it was a free-standing monument, then had an open-air rotunda built around it and a church in front of it. During the following centuries, the rotunda was enclosed, and the church expanded to become a complex covering the entire area, including Golgotha. During its history, the building and the tomb itself had been damaged by fire, earthquake, and war. Yet remains from Constantine's rotunda could still be seen. And a recent restoration of the tomb showed the burial bench and lower half of the back wall were probably part of the original burial chamber.

But although Helena was a Christian, she still carried with her some of the superstitious pagan tendencies she had been saved from. She claimed to have discovered the cross of Jesus in a cave near the tomb, as well as the nails that held Him to it. Helena put some pieces of the cross in a chest for pilgrims to see when they came to the church and sent the rest to Constantine in Constantinople. Before long, there were so many pieces of the one true cross displayed throughout the empire that a ship could have been made from all the wood, as well as a pier to moor it to. Then—just as now—false artifacts were latched onto by the superstitious and uninformed. And there were always unethical people willing to supply them.

As a case in point, Graham thought about how so many pilgrims dropped to their knees just inside the entrance to the Church of the Holy Sepulchre to kiss the Stone of Anointing, where Jesus was prepared for burial. Graham knew the stone dated to 1810 and had no legitimate claim to be the place Jesus was prepared. The church didn't even try to hide that fact, but that didn't stop the pilgrims from bizarre displays of emotion they equated with faith. Sometimes it made Graham feel conflicted about his work. If he recovered authentic artifacts, he ran the risk of them being venerated. Even the ancient Israelites—once in the Promised Land—had started to worship the bronze serpent Moses had made for them, the image of which was a remedy for poisonous snake bites suffered during the wandering in the desert. King Hezekiah's solution was to demolish the artifact that had been turned into an idol—a measure Graham couldn't imagine himself taking. On the other hand, if an authentic item could not be found, often fakes would stand in their place. He didn't know which was worse.

And there were always shepherds tending the flying goats.

TWENTY-SIX

The crisp *ding* of a text alert interrupted his thoughts, pulling Graham's eyes away from the Church of the Holy Sepulchre. The message was an invitation from Yaniv to work from his secretary's desk since she was out today.

Graham paid his bill and threaded his way through the streets of a different Old City than the one he had entered—crowded, busy, and loud. Jerusalem felt like a distracted host whose attention he was jealous of. The Rockefeller Museum, on the other hand, seemed abandoned. Yaniv was not in the office when he arrived, and he quickly got to work.

Although his sense of order told him to investigate the second mountain on the list next, the name Philby caught his eye from the notes on the third mountain and he decided it sounded more interesting. Al-Manifa—also called Mount Zuhd—had been the Sinai advocated by Saint John Philby. Graham opened the library on the cloud drive and was searching for Philby's *Land of Midian* when Yaniv entered the office.

"Shalom. I see you got my text."

"Yes, thank you. Very kind of you to offer."

"What is it you are looking at?" Yaniv nodded once toward the laptop. "Can I be of help in any way?"

"I've narrowed down the list of possible Sinai locations to three places. I'm going through each of the three and learning what I can about them."

"Excellent!" Yaniv said, craning his neck to see the screen. "And what are the three?"

"I was reading up on Jebel al-Baqir when you texted."

"Ah, Beke's mountain."

"It has more merit than I thought it would," Graham said. "It's definitely a viable candidate. I'm just starting to dig in on al-Manifa."

Yaniv squinted. "I do not recall that mountain."

"Philby thought it was the biblical Sinai."

"Philby!" Yaniv's face soured. "Traitor!"

"Wrong Philby," Graham said, taken aback by the reaction. "Not Kim Philby, the spy." Graham remembered that the explorer's son was one of the most infamous double agents in history. The British spy had risen through the ranks at MI6 with such distinction that he had received the Order of the British Empire, an honor he held for nineteen years. What British intelligence hadn't known was that Philby was a KGB agent. After finally being outed, Philby defected to the Soviet Union and received the Order of Lenin.

"I mean his father, Saint John Philby," Yaniv said. "As you say: the apple does not fall far from the tree. Saint John was anything but a saint. He was a traitor, like his son. A traitor to the British Empire and Mandatory Palestine, which was under its authority. Did you know he was made head of the secret service in the mandate even though he was an anti-Zionist?"

"I never read a lot about Philby's politics," Graham said. "I only knew him as an explorer and Arabist."

"I agree his work on that front is quite interesting." Yaniv nodded. "I remember reading how he went looking for some mythical lost city in the middle of Arabia. Like Atlantis, only in the desert. But he was only there because he was forced to resign in light of his position against a Jewish state," Yaniv said, raising his index finger to make the point. "Then he revealed his true self and converted to Islam. He changed his name to Sheikh Abdullah and helped establish the first king of Saudi Arabia. He even became the king's advisor on relations with the West, but he mostly used that power to undermine the British. When it was discovered how much oil there was to be had, he cut the British out of negotiations for the rights. It was his idea for Standard Oil to form a partnership with the Saudis."

"Aramco was Philby's doing?" Graham asked, surprised. "That's one of the most valuable companies in the world."

"Just so." Yaniv's eyes became unfocused, lost in thought. "In fact, all of this was happening about the same time that James Starkey was murdered…"

"You're not saying Philby had anything to do with Starkey, are you?" Graham said skeptically. "That they are connected somehow?"

"It would explain a lot," Yaniv said. "Philby would have still had contacts in Palestine. Maybe he ran agents that were told to put down the Zionists. Remember: Starkey's finds at Lachish were fortifying the historical claim on the land by the Jews, which would give legitimacy to their quest for a state."

"I think the connection is a bit too far-fetched. I admit it is an intriguing story, but it is beyond the facts."

"Yes, it is circumstantial," Yaniv admitted. "But this is how I must think to be effective in my work."

The phone in Yaniv's office rang with an electronic gobble and he excused himself.

Graham opened a PDF of Philby's Land of Midian and began to copy relevant parts into his notes. Given the importance of the site, he was surprised to find how little space Philby devoted to it. When Graham finished the section, he read back over his notes.

*From here, my guide and I climbed up the cliff
to visit the "circles of Jethro" on the summit of
Musalla Ridge, from which we climbed down
quite easily to our camp on the far side.... A
cairn marked the spot where Jethro is supposed
to have prayed, and all round it are numerous
circles. From here I had a magnificent view of
the whole of the Midian mountain range, with
Lawz and its sister peaks in the northeast and
al-Maqla very little north of east, with the valley
of al-Numair separating the latter from the
low ridge of al-Marra, extending from east to
southeast, where the two peaks of Hurab stood
out in front of the great range of Zuhd, which
runs down to a point not far from the sea to our
southward.... The spot that held my imagination
was the smooth, double-headed, granite boss of
Hurab, an obvious candidate for identification
with the Mount Horeb of the Exodus...the only
candidate for the honor which can claim to have
preserved the name.... According to Hasballah,
the name Hurab applies primarily to the wadi,
while he calls the mountain itself al-Manifa
(which simply means lofty.) The main peak of
Lawz, partly in cloud, rose to the southeast of our
position.... The upper part of the valley varied
from 500 to 1,500 yards in width, with occa-
sional wider basins, allowing splendid views of
the great mountains, including the Lawz summit
on which there seemed to be a patch of snow.
The guide confirmed that it was snow; and, if
so, it was the first and only time that I have ever
seen snow in Saudi Arabia.... Burton had never*

examined the gullies of Lawz or the other moun-
tains in the Midian chain, and it is not unlikely
that they may contain minerals of various kinds.
The basalt pyramid of al-Maqla looked climb-
able, but the sheer granite of the Lawz peaks
would have needed more time and energy than
I now had at my disposal. So far as I know, they
have never been climbed by any human being.

Graham opened the satellite map of Sinai candidates and zoomed in on al-Manifa. A vast plain to the southwest could easily hold a camp of two million people. When he had studied the location before, he hadn't thought there was space for a second camp. But as he looked again, he reconsidered the question, then reversed himself, picturing a long strung-out camp set up within the contours of the wadi.

Yaniv walked back in the room, starting to talk to Graham as soon as he hung up. "That Cave of Skulls just won't give me any peace."

Graham pictured the cave that had been discovered in the fury of exploration sparked by the unearthing of the Dead Sea Scrolls. Seven skulls had been found at the back of the cave, giving it its name. It had been excavated by archaeologists three times, and each time when they finished, Bedouin treasure hunters were able to find more artifacts buried inside.

"Are you excavating the cave yet again?"

"Yes!" Yaniv said in exasperation. "After that Bedouin tried to sell a fragment of parchment on the black market. Fortunately, the Bedouin had the bad luck of picking one of the scrupulous dealers to offer it to." Yaniv formed a mischievous smile. "But as irritating as it is that the cave keeps giving its treasure to the wrong people, I must say that mounting the sting to arrest the Bedouin and recover the parchment was rather exciting. Of course, that also meant opening another excavation, which is what is happening now. I go out when I can. Actually, you were lucky to find me in the office instead of on site." Yaniv motioned to the office. "Do you have everything you need?"

"I have one more location to look at, but to tell you the truth, I'm dragging my feet a little bit."

"And why is that?"

"Well, it's kind of like the Cave of Skulls—a place where amateurs keep claiming to find things. The difference is the site has never been properly investigated."

"Really? What mountain is it?"

"Jebel al-Lawz."

Yaniv smirked. "I understand the problem. Follow me. I have something you should see." ly hearing?"

TWENTY-SEVEN

Yaniv led the way to a storeroom within the museum warehouse. He unlocked an anonymous door, and they entered a room the size of a large office. Floor-to-ceiling shelves stood against the walls, and a free-standing rack bisected the center of the room. Gray archival boxes of varying sizes filled almost every available space, crammed but orderly.

A small workstation was positioned next to the door, and Yaniv bent over the chair to type on the keyboard. He hit *return* then mumbled a reference number to himself several times as he moved along the shelves.

"Ah. Here you are."

Yaniv slid a box from the shelf, carried it back to the workstation, and set it down next to the computer monitor. Like the other boxes, it was made of acid-free barrier board with reinforced metal corners. The clamshell lid opened like jaws, and he lifted a dark red stone from its mouth, then offered it to Graham.

"No gloves?" Graham didn't want to take the artifact without protecting it from the oils of his skin.

"No need," Yaniv said. "It is a fake. Everything in this room is. It is where we keep the best examples of forgeries that we confiscate."

Graham looked around at the walls of boxes with renewed

interest. "I know where you can find the Staff of Moses to add to your collection."

Yaniv laughed. "I, too, have visited Topkapi Palace." He nodded once, prompting Graham to take the rock.

It had the dimensions of an iPad but was several inches thick. Each side featured a design that had been carved into the surface, revealing a lighter stone underneath. One side showed two ovals that formed eyes, and an elongated U dropped between them to form a nose. Another oval about the same size as the eyes represented a mouth. A set of lines radiating out in an arc of grooves created a stylized beard. The left cheek was inscribed with a figure that resembled a cross between a trident and a football goalpost. The right cheek featured what looked like the lowercase form of the Greek letter *Theta*. He rotated the stone to reveal that the other side was blank except for two characters. One looked similar to a magnifying glass, the other like the fork on the front side, except the descending middle line had a zigzag.

"So what is this a fake of?"

"This was being offered by a dealer on the black market who claimed it had been found at Jebel al-Lawz. He claimed it proved the mountain was the true biblical Sinai."

"Really," Graham said, intentionally incredulous. "Ravid was telling me about something like this just this morning."

"Ravid had too much knowledge to fall for this." Yaniv reached for the stone and turned it face up in Graham's hands. "That mask is the face of Moses. And—according to the dealer—those characters spell *YHWH*, the personal name of God given to Moses at the Burning Bush."

The idea of it was so monumental that even the suggestion seemed to make it feel heavier in Graham's hands. "It would be astounding if this were actually real."

"Just so. But unfortunately, that is not what the characters spell. The forger made an error. It does not say *YHWH*. It says

WHHY."

Graham laughed at the irony of the unintentional word. "Looks like amateurs can always find a way to keep you busy, Chaim."

"You and I both," Yaniv said. "Of course, the only thing more frustrating than the fakes is when they find authentic artifacts."

"And yet," Graham said, "some of the most important archaeological discoveries have been made by accident or by people who had no idea what they were doing."

"Just so. But have you ever wondered how many finds have never been reported? How many precious treasures have disappeared into the black market? Or worse—think of what treasures were not recognized but were destroyed."

A melancholy smile bent Graham's mouth as he nodded thoughtfully in agreement. "But just think how many things are still waiting to be discovered."

"Like Sinai?" Yaniv asked.

"I'm not sure. But that's what I'm trying to find out. So much of what is said about Jebel al-Lawz is just rumor. What I need are facts, but without actually going there I'm not sure where to start."

Yaniv raised his index finger and held it across his lips, pausing before he spoke. "I think I may know one place we can look."

TWENTY-EIGHT

Back in his office, Yaniv logged onto a law enforcement database, typing as he spoke distractedly.

"If I remember correctly, the way Jebel al-Lawz was identified was by an American who trespassed into Saudi Arabia."

"Yes, Ron Wyatt," Graham said, angling his chair to try to see the screen. "That's really all I remember, though. But why would the Israel Antiquities Authority have files about that?"

"There are two reasons." Yaniv kept his eyes on the monitor as he spoke. "One is that the man who served as the curator of anthropology and archaeology for the IAA while Wyatt was active considered him a fraud and a nuisance. He was quite open about it. Listen to this. It is a quote from a letter that was published where he gave his opinion of Wyatt." He pointed at the screen and moved his finger as he read.

> "Mr. Ron Wyatt is neither an archaeologist nor
> has he ever carried out a legally licensed excava-
> tion in Israel or Jerusalem. In order to excavate,
> one must have at least a BA in archaeology
> which he does not possess despite his claims to the
> contrary. We are aware of his claims, which bor-
> der on the absurd as they have no scientific basis
> whatsoever nor have they ever been published in
> a professional journal. They fall into the category

*of trash which one finds in tabloids such as the
National Enquirer, The Sun, etc. It's amazing
that anyone would believe them. Furthermore,
he has been thoroughly discredited by various
Christian organizations."*

Graham rocked back as if making room for the words.
"Wow. Wonder what he *really* thought about Wyatt."

Yaniv gave a short laugh. "But there is more. And it is relevant to your question. There is a second letter that addresses specific claims."

*"Ron Wyatt has never received a license from the
IAA to excavate here in Jerusalem. If he has, then
let him produce a license for his digs and surveys
in Jerusalem, the Judean Desert, Mount Sinai,
etc. [Regarding] finding a coin at the so-called
Mount Sinai. This shows the total ignorance of
RW and his public who want to believe rather
than to know! Coins were not around at the
times of Moses, even an amateur archaeologist
should know this simple fact! There are so many
so-called Mount Sinais that even the Jews do not
know where it is located. Personally, I believe
that it is simply a literary invention which is
why it will never be found."*

"I didn't know Wyatt claimed to find a coin at Jebel al-Lawz. How bizarre to say it came from the period of the Exodus." Graham looked from the letter to Yaniv. "So what's the second reason you have files on Wyatt?"

"Because when he was caught trespassing, the Saudis thought he was an Israeli spy. The Israelis were able to convince the Saudis that the Wyatts were not spies, but the incident was documented. Unfortunately, there is not much information." Yaniv read aloud, occasionally hesitating, indicating he was summarizing as he read the report.

"In February 1984, Wyatt and his two sons went through the Wadi Araba Crossing from Eilat, Israel to Aqaba, Jordan, but they never went through the Durra Crossing from Jordan into Saudi Arabia. Apparently, when they got near the Durra Crossing, they walked into the wilderness just far enough from the highway to keep from being seen, then simply walked through the desert into Saudi Arabia. They kept clear of the checkpoint, then made their way back to the highway."

"That's insane," Graham interrupted, "on several fronts."

"Just so," Yaniv agreed, then continued. "They were picked up by Bedouin who took them down the coastal highway all the way to Al-Bad'. From there, they made their way inland to al-Lawz. Wyatt theorized it was Sinai on the basis that it is the highest mountain in Midian. He was guided again by Bedouin. When he got to the mountain, he found several things that convinced him it was actually Sinai. He started photographing the area all around it as well as taking home movies. While they were there, soldiers arrived, saw their equipment, and took them into custody."

"If it's so remote, how did the soldiers know he was there?" Graham asked.

"The report does not explain that," Yaniv said, glancing at the papers as if double-checking. "Wyatt and his sons had US passports, of course, but the Saudis were convinced they were spies. The US State Department said they had no idea who Ron Wyatt was. They were in jail in Haql for seventy-five days until Israel was able to finally convince the Saudis he was not working for them."

Graham frowned. "What did Wyatt actually do that upset the Saudis? From what I can tell, there was nothing at that site except some Bedouin camps. Were they upset that he crossed illegally?"

Yaniv raised his hands. "I do not know."

"Is there some military significance to the area?"

Before Yaniv could answer, his office phone rang. Graham silently excused himself back to the reception desk and did a search for Wyatt's arrest. A video of a segment from the CBS Morning News was at the top of the search results. He clicked it and saw it had aired in April 1984, days after his release from Saudi Arabia.

Wyatt wore a trim beard and mustache, and kept his hair pushed back from his face. For some reason, Graham had expected the bombastic claims of a carnival barker. Instead, Wyatt spoke with an almost disinterested factual monotone. Something about him reminded Graham of Patrick McGoohan as he looked when he played Edward I in Braveheart, except Wyatt was in his fifties. He even had the same baritone voice as McGoohan, though Wyatt's was shaped by a southern accent and lacked any kind of theatrical delivery. He seemed like anything but a publicity-seeker and sat uncomfortably in a chair in a Nashville studio as he was interviewed remotely. The Wyatt sons flanked him, looking even more out of place than their dad. Graham thought their long hair and beards made them look more like a southern rock band than legitimate archaeologists.

Graham paused and opened his notes after Wyatt was asked why he thought Sinai was in Saudi Arabia. Wyatt started talking about how he found chariot parts in the Gulf of Aqaba, off the shore of Nuweiba, and that they looked like the ones in King Tut's tomb. He thought it was evidence of where the crossing of the Red Sea took place. He searched a satellite map for the tallest mountain in the region on the other side and found Jebel al-Lawz. And when he saw it had a place for a campsite for the Jews, he was convinced they should check out the location. Graham was impressed at how Wyatt was able to cite scripture from memory, quoting passages describing the things that should be found at Sinai such as twelve pillars, an altar, and pottery. He went on to describe being interrogated by local police, the coastguard, and ministry officials, then said he wouldn't try to go back unless he had proper papers.

When the clip was over, Graham was surprised to find himself conflicted. Wyatt's demeanor was sober, modest, and humble. He did not come across as someone interested in self-promotion, let alone public speaking. Everything about the man made him seem sincere. Graham was convinced that Wyatt truly believed what he said. What Wyatt believed may not be the truth, but Graham didn't think the man was a liar.

Despite that, Wyatt had acquired a number of followers who made pilgrimages to Jebel al-Lawz as well. Graham skimmed several videos and bookmarked a number of sites to investigate further.

"You look perplexed, my friend," Yaniv said, standing in the doorway to his office. "What is wrong?"

"I've been watching interviews with people who found ways to get to Jebel al-Lawz after they heard about Wyatt."

"And have you now crossed it off your list?"

Graham shook his head several times. "No." He looked at Yaniv as if he were apologizing. "No. As much as I don't want to, I think if these people are telling the truth about what they saw, then Jebel al-Lawz would be the best candidate. By far. And if it is not Mount Sinai, then it has everything we'll see at the real Sinai if it is ever discovered."

"I must leave before dawn to go to the Cave of Skulls. I won't be as much help from there. Perhaps you could tell me what you found over an early dinner."

TWENTY-NINE

Graham and Yaniv walked Sultan Suleiman Street, traveling the length of the northern wall of the Old City to the Notre Dame of Jerusalem Center. Like the Rockefeller Museum, the hotel looked like a fortress, as if they were moving from one castle to another. It had been built at the end of the 1800s for pilgrims to the Holy Land. Graham had spent part of his stay there during his expedition a year earlier and discovered the terrace restaurant gave him his favorite view of the Old City, just outside the north wall.

From their table along the balustrade, the domes of the Church of the Holy Sepulchre aligned with the Dome of the Rock against the backdrop of the Mount of Olives. Graham fell into a reverie, contemplating how it compressed so much of Jesus's ministry into one image.

"It must be a sign," Yaniv said, pulling Graham out of his thoughts.

Graham turned to Yaniv and took a handful of nuts from a small bowl on the table between them. "What do you mean?"

Yaniv picked up an almond out of his palm, held it pinched between his thumb and index finger, and chuckled. "It is your mountain. Jebel al-Lawz means *Almond Mountain.*"

The memory of Ravid's comment that he had been offered

items from Almond Mountain—the supposed Sinai—momentarily blinded him. But Yaniv moved on before Graham could mention it.

"And remember Aaron's staff budded with almonds after being laid in the tabernacle overnight. It would make perfect sense if he got the branch that made the staff from there. I am surprised you did not see the blossom yourself at the Topkapi Palace." He paused to laugh at his own joke. "Now, tell me what it is that has changed your opinion of Jebel al-Lawz and of Ron Wyatt."

Graham sighed, ordering his thoughts before he replied. "I still think that Wyatt was terribly mistaken about most of the things he claimed to find. Noah's Ark, the Ark of the Covenant, the blood of Jesus—we can send all of those to the Topkapi Palace. And I admit that in light of those supposed discoveries, it's hard to take this one seriously. But I think he may have actually stumbled onto a legitimate find. Although there are parts of the story that I still don't buy."

"Such as?"

"Wyatt said that when he went to Nuweiba for the first time, he and his sons went scuba diving in the Gulf of Aqaba and found chariot wheels in the growth on the sea floor. They took some pictures and whatever they saw actually does look like chariot wheels."

Yaniv smirked. "How do you know the image is genuine?"

"We're talking about the first half of the 80s," Graham said. "There was no Photoshop."

"Assuming they really are parts of a chariot, what evidence is there to substantiate the claim that they are from the Exodus? Has carbon dating been done? Have any of the wheels been recovered?" Yaniv shrugged. "The statement I read to you from the curator mentioned these so-called chariot wheels. He said they were a hoax."

"True." Graham nodded. "Nothing has been recovered

and no dating has been done. There is no evidence for the claim. As I said, it's one of the crazy parts of the story that makes me want to reject all of it. But he also found an ancient pillar on the shore. It was lying on its side, half in the water. Wyatt thought it looked Phoenician in style and it might have been placed there by King Solomon to mark the crossing point of the Red Sea."

"No small leap," Yaniv said. "Was there an inscription saying such a thing?"

"No," admitted Graham. "Just a pillar. Wyatt noticed that Nuweiba was isolated almost like an island. It was a beach that stuck out into the water with walls of mountains on either side of it. The only way to get there by land was through a very narrow wadi that feeds onto the beach. He realized it would explain why the Hebrews were trapped. If they were being pursued by the Egyptian army through the wadi, then they would have nowhere to go. There was no escape."

Yaniv shook his head. "Surely that is not the only place that fits the description of the Exodus."

"Hang with me," Graham said. "The gulf is only about eight miles wide at that point. You can see Saudi Arabia—Midian—across the water. Wyatt thought that if there was a pillar at Nuweiba then there might be one on the far shore. So that is where he went on the other side after they got a ride from the Bedouin. He claims they found a matching pillar, and this one *did* have an inscription in ancient Hebrew."

"And it said what?"

"He couldn't read it."

Yaniv raised an eyebrow. "At least Wyatt didn't claim to have special glasses that enabled him to decipher it."

Graham was impressed by Yaniv's familiarity with how Joseph Smith claimed to receive the Book of Mormon, but he let it pass without comment.

"Wyatt went south to Al-Bad' and discovered that the

locals have a tradition that it was the home of Moses's father-in-law, Jethro. There is a cave there where they say Jethro was buried. That tradition was also documented by Burton and Philby, as well as a number of others."

"Now that is interesting," admitted Yaniv.

"Wyatt then went inland until he got in the neighborhood of Jebel al-Lawz but didn't know which mountain it was. He asked some Bedouin and they knew immediately what he was looking for. Except they called it Jebel Musa—the mountain of Moses."

Yaniv put his fork down and stopped eating, focusing on Graham.

"When he got to the base of the mountain, he found the remains of twelve huge pillars that had been mostly buried in a landslide. He also found a mound of boulders that looked like they had been placed there deliberately. But what startled him about it was that petroglyphs that looked like cows had been etched into the rocks. And the shape of the cows made them look like the Egyptian god Apis."

"Then again," Yaniv interjected, "Wyatt would not know the difference between Egyptian and Arabic pictograms."

"You may be right," Graham said, "but the bigger problem is that Wyatt seemed to have decided that was the place before he got there, then interpreted everything he found to fit his preconception."

"Confirmation bias."

"Exactly! Wyatt saw just enough to feed the bias. But then soldiers showed up. Wyatt told them about everything he had found, figuring they didn't know about them. He thought they would want to know since Muslims revere Moses as a prophet, just like Christians and Jews. But they didn't believe the story that researching Jebel al-Lawz was his main purpose."

"And that is when they arrested him," Yaniv said, tapping

the table.

"Yes, but while he was being held, he told the representative from the Ministry of Antiquities and Museums about the pillar with the inscription. Apparently, that was news to them. They put Wyatt on a helicopter and had him guide them to it. That was one of the things that convinced them there was some truth to his story. And that was how he was let go the first time."

Yaniv's brow arched again. "The first time?"

Graham nodded. "A few months after Wyatt got home, a Saudi prince flew to Nashville, Tennessee, to meet him. The prince said he was interested in seeing the site and said he would sponsor Wyatt's entry to Saudi Arabia. So Wyatt went back a year after finding al-Lawz. This time when he got to the base of the mountain, he found that a small guardhouse had been erected and a fence had been put up along the base of the mountain. Another was put around the golden calf altar, the place with the petroglyphs. And a sign said it was an archaeological site. Wyatt started taking pictures, but again soldiers arrived, took all the film, and arrested him. This time, though, he was in jail only eight days."

"I thought you said Wyatt was there legally."

"He was. But while they were there, the prince grew more and more agitated and suddenly turned on Wyatt. A few years later, another pair of Americans, a former cop and a commodities trader, met Wyatt's partner from his second trip and used his info to investigate Jebel al-Lawz twice. They found the ruins of what might be an altar. A strange V-shaped structure."

"Why were there no soldiers in the guardhouse monitoring the site?"

"Actually, soldiers did show up and arrest them. Confiscated all their photographs and videos."

Yaniv shook his head. "It is like some legend, like the Bermuda Triangle or UFOs. Many witnesses but no evidence."

"Until the next visitors came, that is," Graham said. "An evangelical American couple working for Aramco, interestingly enough. They lived in Saudi Arabia for twelve years and visited biblical sites in the Middle East on their vacations. One of the trips they took was to Saint Catherine's Monastery. But when they saw what was actually there, they were so convinced it couldn't be the place that they started looking into whether any other mountains had ever been identified as Sinai."

"Apparently, they did not speak with Father Nikolaos," Yaniv said.

"Before his time. Somehow they came across Wyatt's claim and took a trip to Jebel al-Lawz. They were so convinced it was the true Sinai that they went fourteen times during the rest of their time working in Saudi Arabia. They took hundreds of photographs and hours of video, all under the guise of family vacations. They documented the golden calf altar, the V-shaped altar, segments of marble columns, a cave near the peak which they considered Elijah's, and a plateau on the mountain that could have held the seventy elders as they went to meet God."

Yaniv tented his fingers and tapped them together in thought. "That accounts for almost all of the features that would be found at Sinai."

"It gets better." Graham smiled. "They also explored the west side of the mountain, which is the opposite side from the main campsite. In the middle of the wadi there, they discovered a sixty-foot-tall rock that looks like it has been split from bottom to top by hydraulic pressure. They claim it's Rephidim, where Moses split the rock with his staff and brought forth water. And most importantly, they were able to get the pictures and video out of the country without being arrested."

Graham rearranged a few dishes on the table, opened his laptop, and scrolled through several of the pictures he had downloaded from the internet. The cumulative effect of the slideshow dissolved the skeptical look on Yaniv's face.

After the last photograph, Yaniv rested his chin on his hands for a moment before he spoke. "How do you know they did not arrange the rocks into the V-shape to match what Wyatt claimed he saw? How do you know they did not make the inscriptions to match the site? How many other caves are they not showing in the video? They may have simply orchestrated the site to correspond to Wyatt's description."

The idea hadn't occurred to Graham. "Why would they do that?"

"In order to claim the glory of finding the true Sinai. They could be treasure hunters whose treasure is fame."

"I seriously doubt that," Graham said, shaking his head. "I've watched interviews with these people. They could certainly be mistaken about Jebel al-Lawz, but I don't think they are liars or hoaxers. They really don't seem to want anything except to find the historical Sinai. Besides, there have been two more expeditions since the Aramco couple that have shot even more high-quality photos and video."

"Were they oil workers or anesthesiologists?" Yaniv said sarcastically.

"One was a Swedish doctor, and one was a Korean doctor. But the Korean doctor was there because he was the personal physician to the king and one of the princes. He visited al-Lawz something like seventeen times. And he also brought back lots of artifacts from the area."

"Allegedly." Yaniv flicked his palm, as if brushing the claim aside. "As you yourself say, no one trained in archaeology or near eastern studies has ever visited the site, so we still just do not know for sure what is there."

"I did discover that there was an excavation of al-Lawz done by the Saudi Department of Antiquities and Museums in 1996."

Yaniv looked mildly annoyed. "And you are just now telling me this? Does it not settle the question?"

"Unfortunately, no. In fact, it raises more questions than it answers. The report has examinations of most of the same features the amateurs found, but it arrives at completely different conclusions. It never mentions Moses or anything biblical, not even the local traditions. But what is surprising is that many of the features are described or diagrammed incorrectly. And I don't just mean they contradict the stories being passed around. I mean they don't match the photos and videos that have been taken."

"That *is* very strange," Yaniv said, frowning. "But what does it mean? What is it about this place that makes it worth risking jail and possible execution for? What is it that would be worth killing for after 3,500 years?"

Graham's gaze drifted in thought across the Old City, then fixed on Yaniv. "I have been asking myself the very same thing."

THIRTY

The bubbling pulse of "Turn to Stone" by the Electric Light Orchestra woke him before his alarm the next morning. He used a loop of the intro to the song for his ringtone—another archaeological-musical joke told every time he received a call.

"Is this Dr. Eliot?" The woman's voice was clipped and brittle with stress, making Graham instantly alert.

"I need to speak to him, please. It's urgent."

"Yes, this is Graham Eliot. How can I—"

"My name is Sarah McAdams. My nephew, Alexander, is your grad student."

"Alexander is a good—"

"Have you heard from him?"

Graham leaned forward, pulled by the worry in her voice. "No. Not since he left Saint Catherine's. But that was a week ago. He was on his way to England, to Manchest—"

"No, no, no," she said, making it a three-syllable word. "He changed his plan. He called me from Egypt and said he was going to look for Mount Sinai."

"What?" Graham flinched in surprise. "Where, exactly, did he say he was going?"

"I was confused when he told me," she said. "I thought that is where he was already. He said he would explain later. It was hard to hear him. There were announcements in the background, like he was at an airport. But he said he was going to Saudi Arabia."

"But Alexander couldn't just go to Saudi Arabia. It's a closed country."

"That's what I said. But he told me the crown prince had changed its policy and opened it for tourism for the first time ever at the end of 2019. He said he could get a visa online, no problem."

"I hadn't heard about that," Graham said, the news checking his growing anxiety. "So what's—"

"Then I got a voicemail yesterday," she said, cutting across him. "I had my phone turned off while I was at the library, and I forgot to turn it back on. I just saw it a little while ago. I didn't know who to call."

"What did Alexander say?"

"The message was garbled, like it was a bad connection or he was in a strong wind. All I could really make out was that he was in trouble and needed help. He said no one knew he was there."

"I don't understand," Graham said. "You just said he told you where he was going. How could no one know where he was?"

"I don't know," she said desperately. "None of this makes sense. I'm so worried it's hard to think straight."

"Did you call the US consulate in Saudi Arabia?" Graham asked.

"Yes. They said his passport was never scanned in Saudi Arabia. The last activity on it was his entry into Egypt. Like he never left. They said he did apply for a visa, but the application was denied."

"That's strange," Graham said. "Did they say why?"

"Because of his arrest. You know, at Arab Fest?"

"I don't know what you're talking about."

"It was a few years ago. The summer between freshman and sophomore years." Her voice quickened, impatiently telling the story. "Xander decided to go to the big Arab festival they have in Dearborn, where we're from. He wore a shirt that said, 'Ask me about Jesus,' or something like that, hoping to start conversations with Muslims. Instead, a crowd surrounded him, and people became so upset that it caused a commotion. Police officers asked him to leave, but he refused, so he was arrested for disturbing the peace and refusing to obey an officer."

"He hadn't told me about that," Graham said, trying unsuccessfully to picture the mild-mannered Alexander at the center of a controversy getting out of hand.

"So, I'm not sure if the best thing to do is call the authorities in Saudi Arabia. The way Xander talked—I wasn't sure if he was doing something illegal or not, like trying to go there to evangelize the people or something. I assume the Saudi authorities would contact me if he was arrested or hurt. But it's been a day since the message. I wanted to ask you about it before I did anything else since you were the last person with him."

"Ms. McAdams, hold on. I don't understand. Why would the authorities call you? Why not his parents?"

"Because I'm his legal guardian."

Graham knew it wasn't the time to ask for another backstory. "All right. So, what can I do to help you?"

"Find my nephew." Her voice was desperate again. "Please. Find Alexander."

Graham sat back, hoping to calm her by sounding reasonable. "I can't do that. I don't have the authority to do it. And I'm definitely not equipped for it."

"Please, Dr. Eliot. No one has contacted me except him. If the Saudis have arrested Xander since then, they are not saying anything. If they don't have him, then by contacting them I might be exposing him to danger if he made it into the country after they denied him. It would be like turning him in. Then I'm afraid he will be arrested. I have no good options. Except you. I'm begging you. Please help me."

"Ms. McAdams, don't you think Alexander being in custody is better than the possibility of his being injured and needing help?"

"I'm afraid if I bring him to their attention they will look more closely at his background and realize he is a convert from Islam to Christianity. How safe do you think he will be then, in a country that punishes apostasy?"

A wave of conflicting emotions overwhelmed him, making him feel equally impotent and obliged. "But…I'm just one man." Graham struggled for an excuse, grasping the first one he could think of. "I can't do it alone."

"You won't be alone," she said. "I'm calling from London, from Heathrow Airport. I'm on the next flight to Sharm el-Sheik. I'll meet you there and we can try to retrace Xander's steps."

"I'm not in Egypt anymore," he said. "I'm in Jerusalem."

Graham felt like a spectator of his own life as he heard himself give her the address of the Promised Land Hotel. Somehow he had accepted her plea. She was looking at flights and said if she hurried, she could make a connection that would enable her to get to Jerusalem around dinnertime.

He ended the call with as much hope as he could give her.

"I will help you any way I can, but you need to understand that it might not be very much. We do need to figure out what's happened to Alexander. I have a few contacts that might be able to look into it for us. We can talk more when you get here."

"I'm so thankful, Dr. Eliot," she said, her voice quavering with emotion.

"*Graham*, please."

"God bless you, Graham."

THIRTY-ONE

Graham took a table at the far back corner of the Promised Land Hotel's restaurant to give them the most privacy, and waited, sipping a Diet Coke. He had shared the same table multiple times with Daniel Harel as they made their plans the year before. He could hear Daniel's voice joke that since this was the Promised Land Hotel, the buffet should really only have manna. Maybe some quail. Or just goat milk and date honey. The memory unexpectedly reopened the wound he'd felt in Yaniv's office earlier.

He and Daniel had been friends for only a week, but the friendship had been easy, and Graham still felt a deep loss. Being at the table made him realize how much he still struggled with guilt over Daniel's death. It didn't matter that he hadn't killed Daniel, or that the plan creating the circumstances had been made by Daniel himself. It had been Graham's expedition. He was the reason Daniel was there, and that made Graham responsible.

"Graham?"

Hearing his name broke the spell of introspection that had blinded him, making him unaware of the woman who had approached the table. Nothing about Sarah McAdams resembled the image he had formed in his head. Her olive skin, dark brown hair, and large amber eyes looked at home in the Middle East. She was fashionably dressed in a turquoise blouse worn open over a white V-necked top and sand-colored slacks. Graham guessed she was in her early forties, but her most prominent feature was the tax of stress on her face.

"Ms. McAdams?" Graham tried to shake off his thoughts, willing himself present. As he rose to greet her, he banged against the table, rattling the silverware.

"Please, call me Sarah," she said, ignoring his gaffe.

He heard the same Great Lakes accent he detected on the phone as she ordered Arabic coffee with cardamom and thought the sharp o's didn't seem to belong to her.

"Have you heard from Xander?"

"No. The last time he contacted me was a few days ago. But it was just a text with a playlist of David Bowie songs." Graham gave an apologetic shrug. "Can I hear the voicemail?"

"Yes, of course."

"Alexander said you were at USC?" Graham asked as she reached under her chair for her bag.

"I did my graduate work there and ended up staying." She spoke distractedly while fishing out the phone. "Xander and I grew up in Michigan. But my parents immigrated to Dearborn from Syria."

"Quite a culture shock," Graham said.

"It wasn't nearly as big a shock to my parents as when I became a Christian. I was raised a Muslim. Xander wasn't the first in our family."

"How'd they take that?"

A cloud of memory darkened her face at the same time she opened the voicemail.

"I'm sorry," Graham said. "I didn't mean to pry."

"No. It's okay." Sarah put the phone between them, turned on the speaker and hit play.

Heavy breathing scraped across the mic several times before Alexander started to speak, as if he hadn't heard the beep.

He spoke in a harsh whisper, his voice a faint undertone, sounding panicked. The noise of the jostled phone and the static of a poor connection stole random words, redacting as much as they admitted.

"I'm in serious trouble. They're shooting at me. I didn't...don't know what to...truck in Ta...bel al...ash and...No one knows I'm here...the mountain, hiding...so scared. There's nowhere to... no one...need help. Please. Please."

THIRTY-TWO

The fragmented voicemail hung in the air like shards neither of them wanted to touch. Sarah's eyes fixed on Graham's, glazed with tears.

"I need you to send this to me." His deliberate calm only seemed to emphasize how serious the situation was.

"I don't know how to do that. I didn't even know it could do that."

Graham commandeered the phone, clicked the "Send" icon, then texted the audio file to his own phone. Almost instantly, a ding from his own phone announced it had arrived.

"What are you—"

Sarah abandoned her question as Graham touched Yaniv's name in his log of recent calls and held the phone to his ear. He froze in anticipation, listening until he was sent to voicemail. Graham hung up without leaving a message, then opened a new text and quickly typed EMERGENCY—CALL ASAP.

"Chaim Yaniv is at the Israel Antiquities Authority," Graham explained. "He's my best contact here for—" Yaniv's name appeared on the screen of his phone as if summoned. Graham answered and put it on speakerphone.

"Yaniv, thanks for calling back so fast."

"Of course, my friend. You have been on my mind. But

after thinking about what you told me, I do not believe you are in any danger."

"What do you mean? Why not?"

"You said you were attacked in Istanbul as if someone had been waiting for you. But that does not make sense."

Sarah's eyes narrowed in confusion, studying Graham's face as they listened to Yaniv continue.

"If someone knew where to wait, then they also knew where the ostracon was. There would have been no need to wait for you. They would have simply taken it."

"Maybe I was followed," Graham said.

"By whom? How would they know? I highly doubt some rogue monk eavesdropped on your conversation with Father Nikolaos and then pursued you."

"Okay, so who do you think it was?"

"You said there were homeless people taking shelter in the metochion. Wouldn't it make more sense that it was someone protecting their camp?"

"The guy attacked me from behind," Graham said. "He could have yelled at me to get out, but he hit me and then continued to fight."

"Just so. But consider the desperation of someone without a home, who has to beg for food. Graham, my friend, I think you may have taken what happened to you last year when someone really did follow you and attack you, and you have projected it onto this situation. I think you may have merely trespassed and startled a desperate squatter."

"You may be right," Graham said, "but none of that is important right now. I have a real emergency."

"What is it? Are you all right?"

"I'm okay. But my grad student—the one I took to Saint Catherine's—he's gone missing."

"Missing?" Yaniv said, a note of alarm in his voice. "What makes you think that?"

"He was supposed to meet his aunt in England, but he changed his travel plans while he was at the airport. He told her he was going to Saudi Arabia."

"Does this have something to do with Sinai?" Yaniv asked.

Graham locked eyes with Sarah. "He's looking for it."

"That is not such a terrible thing," Yaniv said. "They allow tourism now. Except for Israelis. Although, some people have been denied visas for having Israeli stamps on their passports. But if he has lost his way, report it to the authorities and they will locate him."

"It's not like that, Chaim. His visa was denied, and his passport was never presented for an entry stamp. Officially, he never left Egypt."

"Hmm," Yaniv noised. "That is unusual."

"It gets more unusual," Graham said. "He left a voicemail with his aunt yesterday. Hold on. I'm sending it to you now."

Graham attached the file to a text and hit send.

"And his aunt contacted you?" Yaniv asked.

"Yes, I'm with her now."

"She is in Jerusalem?"

"Yes. She w—"

"Wait. I just received the voicemail."

Graham stared at the phone as he pictured Yaniv listening to the message. He glanced up to find Sarah's eyes fixed on the screen as well. A detachment separated Graham's conscious thought from his action, and the context of the situation receded into the background. No more than two or three seconds elapsed, but it was just enough time to see beneath the mask of worry and fatigue on Sarah's face. Enough time to see the beauty.

"This is very bad." Alarm now seemed to slow Yaniv's voice. "He is clearly in trouble."

"His aunt didn't want to call the Saudi authorities in case he's doing something illegal."

"Regardless of his actions, if he is there at all, it is certainly illegal based on what you told me," Yaniv said as Graham watched Sarah wince at the words. "I assume we are talking about Jebel al-Lawz, yes? What can I do to help you?"

"I need you to ping his cell phone," Graham said. "If it still has any power then we can get a location for him."

"Just what I was thinking," Yaniv said. "Even if he is no longer with the phone, it would give us a place to begin. I will have to use a favor to make it happen, but I can arrange it."

Graham gave him Alexander's number, then hung up after another promise of help from Yaniv.

"You're certain we can trust Yaniv, right?" Sarah asked, more thankful than skeptical now that something was being done.

"We are forever in each other's debt," Graham said.

"Doesn't that cancel each other out?" She squinted slightly as she worked the karmic math.

Graham smiled. "Not this debt. Anyway, he has contacts everywhere. Law enforcement, military, intelligence. And he has access to databases that—"

"What?" Sarah said as he froze mid-sentence. "Did you think of something?"

Graham opened his laptop, then navigated to a login screen.

"Alexander's cloud account. His phone, his laptop, his iPad—they all automatically back up to it. If he made any notes or wrote down his plan or itinerary, then there is a good chance a backup copy would be stored here."

"But wouldn't you have to know his password?"

"Yes," Graham said. "And I think I know a way we could find it. But I need your permission."

"Of course." Sarah nodded emphatically. "This is urgent."

"Good. This is the laptop we use in our scanning project. We all use it. It's supposed to be reserved for just that task so it doesn't get cluttered up. But every once in a while we check our email or do research online. I don't know for sure that he ever signed into his cloud on this machine, but if he did, there might be a way we can figure out the password."

Sarah's eyes filled with scruples. "You mean you can hack it?"

"Not really," Graham said. "But there is a utility that stores all login and passwords. And it might be listed in there."

Graham placed the cursor in the Username field, which contained a prompt for an email address.

"The username for the cloud is his school email address. If he's logged in from here recently, the computer will automatically fill it in if it recognizes it."

Using Calbi University's email naming convention that put the first letter of the last name followed by the complete first name, Graham typed pal. The MacBook filled in the rest: palexander@u.calbi.edu.

"So that means we can get into his cloud drive?" Sarah said hopefully.

"Not unless we can find the password. If he's changed it since he logged in from here, then we'll be out of luck."

Graham typed into the search bar for the entire computer and hit *return*. A spreadsheet appeared, filling the window with several columns of data.

"What's that?"

"The keychain. The login information for everything this computer has accessed."

He typed Alexander's email into the search bar and the columns automatically shrank to list a handful of entries. One was the student portal for the university, and three were social media sites. The only other item was for the cloud. Graham double-clicked the listing, opening a pop-up window. An empty password field ran across the bottom of the window.

"It's not there," Sarah said, looking to Graham's face for his reaction.

"Not yet."

A box to the left of the field was labeled Show Password, and he checked it. Yet another window popped up, this one asking for the password of the computer's administrator. Graham typed in the chapter and verse of his favorite Bible passage, then hit *OK*. The window closed and refreshed the previous window, which now showed Alexander's password.

Graham was startled as Sarah reacted in the way he least expected. She laughed.

THIRTY-THREE

"I should have known!" Sarah said, relief, sentimentality, and anxiety mixing in her voice.

Graham turned back to the screen and typed in the password.

AvraKedavra.

"Xander was heavily into magic growing up. Even into his teens. He called himself Alexander the Great." Sarah used the inside of her wrist to wipe away a tear.

Graham hit enter, then looked back at Sarah as the account logged in.

"He was a great performer," she continued. "A natural in front of an audience. But then he fell in love with guitar and started to focus on that instead. Anyway, I remember when he started to learn biblical languages and I told him that *abracadabra* was derived from Hebrew. That it meant, 'I create by speaking.' He was so excited to see two of his passions connect. It kind of became a catchphrase we used for a while."

"That explains a few things," Graham said. "When we were in Egypt, he told me he wanted to find a souk. He was looking for some coffee cups, the small brass ones they have with no handles. He said it was for a magic trick. I had no idea he was so into it."

"So what's in the backup?" Sarah nodded to the screen

and leaned in. "What is *HANE 30003?*"

Graham looked over the names of the directories. "History of the Ancient Near East III. *AANE 30005* is Archaeology of the Ancient Near East. Then there's Method and Theory, and another for Dissertation. All doctoral stuff. But this one called *Sinai*—"

"Click it," Sarah interrupted.

Graham opened the folder, then clicked on a document called Sinai Criteria and recognized it.

"Those are notes from something I asked him to look into. It's probably what planted the idea in his mind to do whatever it is he's doing now." A pang of guilt rang through him as he said the words.

"What's that one?" Sarah pointed to a folder called *Nuweiba*.

Graham clicked it, revealing almost thirty images of the area. Some were satellite photographs that clearly showed the wadi snaking through the desert mountains before opening onto the beach at Nuweiba. Others showed the pillar found by Wyatt, now erected by the side of one of the main roads. Alexander had also downloaded images of coral formations and other items from the sea floor that were alleged by Wyatt to be the remains of Pharaoh's army.

"What is that place?"

"Some people think it's where Moses parted the Red Sea," Graham said. "On the Gulf of Aqaba."

"Wait. Aqaba?" Sarah glanced at Graham's face, then back to the images. "But that's on the wrong side of the Sinai Peninsula, isn't it? If the Jews crossed there, then they would have ended up in—"

"Saudi Arabia," Graham said, pointing to a satellite image, east of the Gulf of Aqaba. "Which is where Midian is."

"Okay, I'm starting to get it now." Sarah nodded at the screen and pointed to another folder. "What's *Lawz?*"

He opened the folder and found more than a hundred images. Every item he had been reading about earlier in the day was shown from multiple angles. The golden calf altar with close-ups of the petroglyphs, the V-shaped altar, segments of pillars, the cave, the Split Rock of Rephidim—they were all there. Several aerial views showed the area, some including labels pointing to each item's location, including a vast open area at the base of the mountain that could accommodate a camp for two million people. And there were many images of the mountain peak itself, with its mysterious black top.

"What is all that?"

Graham detected an interest in her voice separate from the concern for her nephew. "Well, the Bible describes Mount Sinai as having certain features, some that were part of the mountain and some that were built there. Any mountain that is suggested as being the true Sinai would have to have these things there."

"Even after 3,500 years?"

"Some of them, at least."

"And these pictures are of the things that are supposed to be at the historical Sinai?"

"Some people think so," Graham said, wondering if he was becoming one of those people.

Sarah looked at the images more closely, scrolling through them, occasionally stopping to zoom in to inspect it closer. "What am I missing?" She sat back. "It's really interesting, but I don't get why it's such a problem."

Graham sorted through the possible answers. Glory-seeking treasure hunters. Ignorant amateurs. Suspicious soldiers. But before he could pick one, his phone dinged with a text.

"Yaniv got a ping back from the cell phone."

Sarah's face lit up. "That's great! Where is he?"

"He said we won't like it."

A second text arrived containing a link to Google Maps. Graham pressed the message and watched the map app open on his phone. The northern half of the Red Sea appeared on the screen, and a pin marked a spot near the Gulf of Aqaba.

"He's in Saudi Arabia. Just like we thought."

"Zoom in." She leaned closer to the phone. "Let's see exactly where."

Graham pressed the button several times until the area around the pin filled the screen. As he got closer, a label appeared next to the pin, identifying it as Jebel al-Lawz. He switched to the satellite view and the screen updated to show barren, rugged mountains. Along the ridge near the pin, the mountains turned black, as if ink had been spilled on them.

"It looks just like the satellite photos in his cloud drive," Sarah said. "He made it."

"Yes, but when did he make it?" As he spoke, Graham texted the question to Yaniv.

"Last ping 20 hours ago." The text was followed by several more in succession. "Remember, it does not necessarily mean he is there, only that his phone is. Or was."

Graham read each text aloud as it arrived despite feeling Sarah reading over his shoulder.

"Also called FBI Special Agent Bremmer," continued Yaniv.

"Who's Bremmer?" Sarah interrupted.

"Yaniv and I did some work with him last year. We can trust him. He's a good man. We can count on him to be discreet."

Graham looked back to the texts, which were still coming in, and picked up where he left off.

"He did not find anything about Alexander being in custody but will be on the alert."

Graham quickly texted back a thanks and a promise to keep Yaniv updated. He opened the voicemail and hit play, holding up a finger for quiet as he listened.

"He said, 'went to Ta…' but I couldn't catch the rest of it." Graham studied the area around the map, then pointed. "Tabuk."

"I've never heard of Tabuk," Sarah said. "Why would he go there?"

"Tabuk is the capital city of Tabuk Province," Graham said. "Where Jebel al-Lawz is. Alexander also said something about a truck. He would've had to rent a truck to get to the mountain, and that means he probably got it at the airport. If he was able to get on a plane somehow, it would probably be to fly to Tabuk."

Sarah clicked on the distance tool and drew a straight line from the mountain to Tabuk. "Seventy-five miles."

"As the crow flies," Graham said. "The road goes around the range before you go into the mountains." He traced the general route with his finger. "It's probably double that in drive time. It doesn't really matter, anyway. Even if it were only a mile away, we still couldn't get there."

"Why do you say that?" Sarah said, frowning a rebuke.

"My career has been devoted to developing evidence that corroborates the Bible. You are a Christian convert from Islam. And both of us have multiple Israeli stamps in our passports. I'd say the odds of being granted visas are nil. Alexander might as well be on the moon."

THIRTY-FOUR

Graham moved the map around on the screen, exploring Jebel al-Lawz's surroundings before zooming out to view the whole area, from the coast of the Gulf of Aqaba to Tabuk, a hundred miles inland. The vast region hosted no more than ten towns, mostly along the water.

"There is nothing there," Sarah said. "This place is in the middle of nowhere. Literally."

"I read this afternoon some rabbis think that is actually *why* they were led there," Graham said. "The idea is that since the Torah was given in a place that belonged to no one, there would be no excuse for rejecting it since it had not come from the land belonging to the Jews. The law is for everyone, not just them."

Sarah pointed at Jebel al-Lawz. "And yet if this really is Sinai, the Jews would have a historical, cultural connection to the land."

"Exactly," Graham said. "And the Saudis would never allow the verification of such an important historical event in Judaism. That's already happened in our lifetimes, with Yasir Arafat rewriting Muslim tradition by denying that the Jewish Temple ever stood on the Temple Mount in Jerusalem, even though parts of it are on display there. It's ridiculous." Graham reminded himself the Temple Mount was only several hundred yards from where he was sitting. He self-consciously looked around to see if he had been overheard.

Sarah pivoted the laptop and opened the image showing the area around the east side of the mountain that included labels pointing to each item. "You know what's strange is that the shadow on the mountain is in almost the exact same place in the pictures and on the satellite image." She pointed to the boundary of dark rock around the top of Jebel al-Lawz.

"That's because it's not a shadow."

Sarah zoomed the image as she leaned closer to the screen.

"For some reason, the mountain turns black near the peak," Graham said, studying her reaction as he explained. "Some of the people who have sneaked into the area climbed the mountain to try to figure out what made it black. One guy said he broke several of the rocks open and that they were pink granite on the inside."

"So what made it black on the outside?"

"Well, according to this person, the surface of the rock was obsidian. Melted rock."

"Melted? So it's a volcano?"

"Some scholars have suggested that Sinai was a volcano. But no, Jebel al-Lawz isn't a volcano."

"Okay, so how did they melt?"

"According to some advocates of Jebel al-Lawz, the rocks melted because it was a result of God's presence on the mountain. Remember, God descended onto the mountain in fire. In fact…" Graham opened his phone's Bible app, then selected a verse, switched from a translation to the original Hebrew. "Check this out. Here's what Judges 5:5 says, 'The mountains—'"

"'The mountains trembled before YHWH, the God of Sinai.'" Sarah's voice cut across his, translating aloud.

Graham looked at her in surprise.

"Philologist." Sarah shrugged with a crooked smile. "Did

Xander not mention that?"

Graham chuckled. "Actually, he did. But it had slipped my mind. Now, look how the King James Version renders this verse." He switched to the translation and read the result. "'The mountains melted from before the LORD.' Melted, not trembled. Some take that as more evidence this is Sinai."

"The root words *are* similar," Sarah said, unconvinced. "But *trembled* is the better fit. I assume you showed me KJV because other translations read different ways. Maybe they're just translation shopping, seeing what they want to see."

"Confirmation bias." Graham nodded. "You might be right. Especially because a number of mountains in the region also have dark tops. The rocks are greenstone, which look sort of like coal. But the people who have climbed the mountain swear it's burned granite."

Sarah changed the window so the folder listed the files alphabetically. Alexander had named each of the images, grouping the different features of Jebel al-Lawz together. She moved a finger down the list, then stopped at a cluster of several dozen files that started with the prefix *IMG* followed by a three-digit number.

"What are these?"

"Looks like how the camera names the image," Graham said. "And the date on them is from four days ago. These were probably taken by Alexander and uploaded when the phone backed up automatically."

Graham selected the group and opened them as a slide-show. All the features of Nuweiba and Jebel al-Lawz that were in the other photos were repeated with minor variations in angles and vantage points, but none seemed to add any new information.

"That's interesting," Graham said, pointing to the time stamps on the images. "They're from the same day, but some of the ones of Jebel al-Lawz are from the morning and some are from late afternoon. But the time on the images of the Split Rock are from the middle of the day. Looks to me like he went to the main area of al-Lawz, then to the Split Rock on the other side of the mountain, and then went back to where he started."

"Which means what?" She glanced back and forth from the screen to Graham's face.

"It tracks his movements that day. Don't know how helpful that is, but it's more than we knew before. I wish he would have...Oh my gosh! He *did* tell me what he was going to do!"

"What do you mean?" Sarah said, concern rising in her voice again.

"Remember I told you that he had sent me a Spotify playlist? It was called *Sign Eye*. But I never said it out loud, just read it. I was distracted by other things and didn't recognize the homophone. *Sinai*. Duh."

"I'm so confused. Why would the playlist matter?"

"Look at it." Graham opened the link and the list of songs appeared.

"Fantastic Voyage"
"African Night Flight"
"The Secret Life of Arabia"
"Black Country Rock"
"Law (Earthlings on Fire)"
"Heaven's in Here"

Sarah looked at the playlist, trying to see what Graham saw. "They're all David Bowie except the last one. That's by Tin Machine."

"That was Bowie's band in the late 80s and early 90s. Still counts. But look how Alexander used the order to tell me what he was doing. He was going on a voyage out of Africa to a secret place in Arabia. In fact, one of the lines that gets repeated in 'The Secret Life of Arabia' is 'Never here, never seen.'"

"Okay, but what does 'Black Country Rock'...oh, I get it." Sarah squinted, nodding in understanding.

"Then there is 'Law.' Because it's where Moses received the law."

"But *Lawz* doesn't mean *law*. It's Arabic for *almond*." She looked up, arching her brow. "Philologist."

"Bowie wasn't a philologist. He went to art school. And he didn't have any songs with almonds in the title, so I guess Alexander had to make do. But that one has a sample that runs through it that says, 'I don't want knowledge, I want certainty.' And the last one, 'Heaven's in Here,' must mean it's the spot where God came to dwell on Earth. Jebel al-Lawz is the true God-trodden mountain."

Graham picked up his phone. "I need to give Yaniv an update."

Sarah continued searching the images, as he composed and sent the text.

"So what do we do next? We have to do something to find him. We should go get him."

"Sarah, there is one more thing you should know about Jebel al-Lawz. It is possible that the Muslims may have killed people to keep it from being discovered. Or at least looked into."

"What do you mean? I thought this place could be visited by tourists? We could go there right now if it weren't for our special circumstances."

"True," Graham admitted, "but that is a recent development. And there still may be Muslims in the area who want to protect it from visitors."

"But killing people?" Sarah said dismissively. "That's absurd. Like who?"

"The archaeologist James L. Starkey, for one." Graham

kept his voice level, wanting to guide her through his thinking.

"Starkey? As in, the Lachish Letters?"

"Yes. It's a long story, but I was already looking into the mountain when Alexander disappeared. I feel so guilty that my research inadvertently planted the idea in his head to go there. I didn't tell him what I needed it for, but I guess he had the same ideas I did." He braced himself for rebuke, unsure of what Sarah's reaction would be.

Her gaze darted around the table before fixing again on the screen.

"You couldn't have known Xander was going to go to the mountain. You can't blame yourself."

Graham smiled sadly as he looked into her eyes and nodded his thanks.

"But," she continued, "we do need to go find him."

"Well, we can't do anything tonight. We should try to get some sleep. First thing tomorrow we'll drive to Eilat. It's the Israeli town on the tip of the Gulf of Aqaba, and where we can cross the border to Aqaba, Jordan. We can figure out what to do next from there."

THIRTY-FIVE

Graham stepped into the restaurant again at seven a.m. to find Sarah at the same table from the night before. The top of her maroon USC hoodie draped her back like a monk's cowl. He set his plate of shakshouka on the table as he realized she was halfway through her own helping of the egg and tomato dish.

"Great minds," he said.

"Hope I didn't text too early," she said. "Couldn't sleep. I lie awake most of the night, and by the time I finally fell asleep, the call to prayer woke me up."

"Me too. But I'm glad it did. I wanted some food before we got going. It's a four-hour drive."

On the way out, Graham grabbed a can of Diet Coke, dropped some figs and dates into a to-go cup, and led the way to the car. He loaded their bags in the hatchback of the small Citroën, instantly filling the space behind the front seats.

"I actually asked for something smaller, but this was all they had."

Sarah forced a polite smile, signaling she was not in the mood for the joke.

He drove along the gardens on the backside of the Rockefeller Museum and wound his way onto the Mount of Olives. By 7:30, they exited the Derech Har HaTsofim, the tunnel that channeled traffic through the mountain where Jesus was arrested, and from which He had ascended. After twenty minutes heading east, not far from Jericho, they turned south onto a highway that generally followed the coastline of the Dead Sea. Within minutes, they passed Qumran National Park, where the Dead Sea Scrolls were found.

"Ever been there?" Graham asked, breaking the silence partly to distract her, and partly to get to know her.

"Once. I read that a new cave was found recently. But you probably know more about it than I do."

"I did get to visit the cave with the new finds briefly last year," he said. "Amazing there was anything left since it had been looted before the archaeologists arrived. Makes you wonder just how much is still out there waiting to be discovered."

He stole a glance after getting no response.

"If you don't mind my asking, how did you end up becoming Alexander's guardian?"

Sarah turned back to face the highway and sighed. Graham could see that she suspected the question would come at some point.

"My older sister was his mother. She was a wild child, partied all the way through high school. But she hid it from our parents since they were devout Muslims and were raising us to be like them. Then she left for college and got pregnant during the first semester. Exposed her double life."

Graham gave an ominous moan. "How'd your parents take the news?"

"They totally freaked out. It was World War III at our house for a while. It scandalized the family in our community. My parents ended up disowning her. She was left completely on her own. Xander's father was a loser and she had no intention of marrying him—thank goodness. It was probably the only smart thing she did during that time. But she gave the baby his last name so he wouldn't grow up with an Arabic name. That's why his name is Pearl. The fact that it's Jewish made it even better. It was a slap at my parents—as if there hadn't been enough hurt on both sides already."

"I can't imagine how hard it was for her," Graham said. "Where'd she get the name Alexander?"

"I'm not sure. She used to joke that her family was just Alex-and-her. I'm not sure whether she came up with that before or after he was born."

Graham smiled at the wordplay. "Sounds like something he would say."

"Yeah," Sarah said sadly. "She went from one bad relationship to another. Always moving. Lots of temp jobs and waitressing. I didn't see her very much. She struggled with alcoholism all her life. Had some sober periods, but always fell off the wagon. By the time Xander was in high school, he pretty much took care of himself since he couldn't rely on her."

Graham released a puff of air, as if blowing away the circumstances. "That is a tough situation. Amazing he turned out so well instead of repeating the same mistakes he had modeled for him."

Sarah nodded, then continued. "He was always a good kid. But when he was a sophomore in high school, he got connected with Young Life and became a Christian."

Graham flashed back to his own experience with the group devoted to discipling teens. "I was in Young Life. Great ministry."

"It actually had a huge impact on my sister as well. She was so moved by Xander's transformation that it opened her heart to the gospel. Xander actually led her to Christ."

"Incredible!"

Sarah opened her hands in an expansive gesture. "All of a sudden her alcoholism wasn't a problem anymore. It was like a switch flipped and it was gone. I know it doesn't happen like that for most people, but it did for her."

"I've heard stories like that before," Graham said.

"It was a radical change," Sarah said with a melancholy smile. "Finally looked like she was getting her life together. She had been clean for nine months when she was killed by a drunk driver. The guy ran a red light and T-boned her as she was going through an intersection. It was only ten o'clock in the morning and the guy was twice the legal limit." Sarah paused, apparently negotiating the memory. "By then, my parents had both been put in full-time care facilities. One had Alzheimer's, and the other had Parkinson's. But even if they hadn't been sick, they wouldn't have a relationship with Xander. He was a physical reminder of what they considered their biggest failure. So he came to live with me. Seven years ago, now."

"That was an incredible thing to do," Graham said. But somehow after the story, his response sounded shallow to his own ears, and he intimidated himself into silence.

THIRTY-SIX

An hour later, the Dead Sea was interrupted by Lynch Strait, a land bridge that divided the water into two bodies. But it was a truncated mountain about a mile from the other side of the highway that captured their attention.

"That's Masada," Graham said, pointing across her, out the windshield. "Herod the Great's fortress."

"Looks kind of like a wider version of Devil's Tower."

Graham pictured the iconic projection of rock in Wyoming. "Yeah, it kind of does."

"That was where the Jewish insurrection was finally defeated, right? When the Romans destroyed it?"

"Yes and no. After the siege of Jerusalem, when the Temple was destroyed, the last of the Sicarii—the Jewish zealots—took refuge up there. That's probably also when the Dead Sea Scrolls were hidden in the caves by the Essene community who lived at the foot of the cliffs. Titus marched the Roman army here and when the Sicarii saw how many there were, they knew they could never survive the attack. But rather than die by Roman swords, they burned the fortress down and killed themselves with their own daggers. Almost a thousand people committed suicide up there. When the Romans got to the top, they found seven people alive. Two women and five children."

Sarah stared at the site, watching the sky tram ferry tourists to the ruins at the summit of the plateau.

"There's talk of putting one of those at the traditional Mount Sinai," Graham said, following her eyes.

Sarah responded with a nod, lapsing back into silence.

A few minutes later the southern basin of the Dead Sea appeared on their left. Parallel causeways of dirt segmented the water into a succession of pools. Graham was about to explain they were evaporation pans used to extract the salt, but sensed Sarah wasn't feeling social and chose to stay silent. As they passed a sign marking the lowest point on Earth, he decided it was not the time to joke that there was no place to go but up. After forty-five minutes of silence, a highway sign informed them they were about to pass through Paran, and Graham heard himself speak before he realized what he was doing.

"This is the wilderness the Israelites wandered through on the way to the Promised Land after they left Mount Sinai."

The fact seemed to rouse Sarah from her thoughts and re-animate her. "It's so barren. It's easy to imagine them walking through here, like nothing's changed since then."

"Except the solar farm." Graham gestured to a field of photovoltaic panels that was larger than the tiny village of Paran itself.

Sarah allowed a slight smile, and Graham took the opportunity to pick up the conversation.

"So, how did you convert from Islam to Christianity?"

"Through a dream." She turned to look at Graham. "Do you believe God can speak to us through dreams?"

Graham gave her a sidelong glance and nodded. "God used dreams to lead me back to faith. Two years ago, my daughter, Alyson, died of cancer. She was five. Six months later, my wife drowned in the bathtub."

"I'm so sorry." Sarah's voice was a whisper, barely audible

above the noise of the road.

Graham rarely shared more than what he had just revealed and was surprised to hear himself almost confessing to her.

"I couldn't see how a loving, good, all-powerful, all-knowing God could allow something like that to happen, so I walked away. But a year ago—while I was here working with Yaniv, actually—I had a series of dreams that broke through all my excuses and confusion and grief. And instead of wondering where God had been when I needed Him most, I saw that He had been there all along. I saw that Jesus not only died for my sins, but He also died to take away the evil of cancer and accidental drownings. Alyson is healed, and Olivia is alive, and evil can never touch them again." He hadn't intended to say so much, and he was shocked at the realization that he felt he could tell Sarah something so private. "Sorry. Didn't mean to give a sermon."

The silence that followed grew so long that Graham wondered if he had just alienated her completely. When she finally spoke, he almost felt like he was coming up for air.

"I converted in college. I had a dorm mate who was a Christian. We had lots of talks about who Jesus was, but it never got contentious. You know how some Christians make you feel like a project instead of a person?"

"All too well, unfortunately," Graham nodded with a pained smile.

"She didn't do that. We genuinely liked each other. And I could ask her anything about her faith or challenge her, and she never got offended. One time I came back to the dorm and found her praying. I apologized for interrupting her, but she just smiled and told me she had been praying for me, that she did it every day."

"That would've freaked out my freshman roommate," Graham said. "If there were such a thing as a secular exorcist that expelled all religious belief, he would have phoned him immediately."

"Not me. It made me feel cared for. That night I dreamed a man in a green hoodie was standing by the fountain in the plaza outside the dorms. For some reason—I don't know how—when I saw him in the dream, I knew that the man would tell me about God if I went up to him. When the dream ended, I woke up and couldn't fall asleep again. The next morning, I walked out of the dorm, and there he was. The guy in the green hoodie was standing exactly where I'd seen him in my dream."

"Amazing," Graham said, glancing at her.

"Completely true. I forgot all about going to class. I had no idea what to say, but I kind of timidly walked up. When he saw me, his eyes got really big, and he said, 'It's you!' He was as freaked out as I was. He told me he had had a dream the night before, that a woman in a yellow USC baseball cap—which is what I was wearing since I was too tired to do anything with my hair—would come up to him and ask him to tell her about God. We ended up talking for two hours. He showed me passages of scripture I recognized from my dorm mate, but suddenly it was like they were alive. I understood them. I became a believer right next to the fountain outside the dorms."

Goose bumps rippled across Graham's skin. "That's one of the most incredible things I've ever heard."

"I thought when I told my parents that I had converted, they would disown me like they had my sister. I'm not sure which of us they were more disappointed in. It broke their hearts, but they couldn't bear to lose their other daughter. It was strained for a while, but we got used to avoiding the topic. We lived in a kind of truce."

Graham thought she was about to add to her story, but when she spoke it was only to change the subject.

"How much farther?"

"Almost there. Fifteen or twenty miles."

"What's Timna Park?"

They passed the road sign marking the turnoff, and Graham looked to his right.

"King Solomon's mines. More people than Solomon used it, but he's the one it's known for."

"Gold?"

"Copper. The mine dates back to about the tenth century BC. There's also the remains of a shrine and some Roman inscriptions. And the rock formations are beautiful—natural stone arches and pillars. And they have a full-sized replica of the tabernacle on permanent display."

"Isn't that an oxymoron?" Sarah said. "A permanent tent?"

Graham laughed. "I'm starting to see where Alexander gets his humor."

The outskirts of Eilat emerged from the sand in front of them like an urban oasis. Beyond it, the Gulf of Aqaba began to divide the desert in two. Graham turned left onto the road leading to the Yitzhak Rabin border crossing, then pulled into the parking lot.

"We need to find a place to stay before we cross." Graham opened his phone and did a search for hotels as he explained the stop. "In case they ask. Yaniv said to get a 5-star hotel because they will be less likely to say anything about an unmarried couple." Graham blushed as he heard the implications of his words and began stammering. "I mean, we'll still get separate rooms and everything. But he said Jordanians, they have rules about—"

"It's okay," Sarah interrupted with a laugh. "I get it."

"How about the Double Tree?"

"There's a Double Tree in Aqaba? Sure. Sounds fine."

As they used the browsers on their phones to make reservations through the website, Graham welcomed the silence, hoping it would erase the awkwardness he felt.

"Success." Sarah looked past Graham to the border guards. "I assume we're here officially as tourists. So if they ask what I'm going to do in Jordan, what should I say?"

Graham clicked a link on the hotel's site. "There's an archaeological museum and a Mamluk castle, and Petra is an easy drive away. But most people come here to snorkel or scuba dive. The other thing it's known for is the Wadi Rum Desert. People do jeep tours with Bedouin guides. Tell them you plan on being here a week."

"A week?" Sarah flinched in surprise.

"I don't know how long we'll need, but it sounds like a vacation amount of time."

Less than an hour later, they pulled away from the Wadi Araba checkpoint on the Jordanian side. The Aqaba Special Economic Zone made it easy for tourists to enter the resort city on thirty-day visas.

"That was way less of a hassle than I thought it would be," Sarah said. "It's harder for me to get through the airport. I'm always the one who gets pulled aside and searched by TSA. Xander says it's because I'm the bomb." She put finger-quotes around the last words and gave Graham a look that simultaneously dared and invited him to laugh.

He couldn't help chuckling, but then he saw a veil of tears cover her eyes.

When he turned his attention back to the road, he heard her whisper to herself. "Xander, where are you?"

THIRTY-SEVEN

Cerulean water glistened a quarter mile away, littered with a couple of oil tankers among a dozen yachts. To the right, Eilat spread out in a mirror image of Aqaba, together capping the northern point of the gulf shore. Across the water, the rugged Egyptian terrain looked almost close enough to touch. And on the left side of the water, twelve miles down the coast, lay Saudi Arabia.

"You totally got robbed," Graham said. "My room faces the other side. Incredible view of apartment blocks."

Sarah barely smiled, staring out at the water, lost in thought as she leaned on the balcony rail.

Graham let a beat of silence pass. "You know, I've heard the story of Moses crossing the Red Sea so many times from such an early age that even though I believe it happened, part of me treats it like a legend. I've made a whole career out of finding things that corroborate biblical history. And yet, crossing the Red Sea is one of those things that I still think of as a story told on a felt board. I'm not convinced this is near the place it really happened, but just seeing the land so close on the other side suddenly gives it a reality it's never had for me."

"That's a good way to put it," Sarah said, looking ahead. "Except I grew up with the story in the Qur'an. In that version—" She cut herself off, stepped through the curtains dividing the balcony from the room, and reappeared with a Qur'an. "It was in the drawer of the bedside table," she explained as she flipped through the pages. "Surah 26, verses 60-66.

> *"So they pursued them—the Israelites—at sunrise.*
> *"And when the two hosts saw each other, the companions of Musa said: "'We are sure to be overtaken.'"*
> *Musa said: 'Nay, verily with me is my Lord, He will guide me.'*
> *"Then We inspired Musa, saying: 'Strike the sea with your stick.' And it parted, and each separate part of that sea water became like the huge, firm mass of a mountain.*
> *"Then We brought near the others—the Egyptian army—to that place.*
> *"And We saved Musa and all those with him.*
> *"Then We [Allah] drowned the others."*

She looked up, back to the water. "Not quite as dramatic, but still the same general story."

"It could definitely work on a felt board," Graham said.

She put the Qur'an back in the cloth bag that protected it, set it in the drawer and returned to her place at the balcony railing. "I wonder what that huge flag is."

"That's the flag of the Arab Revolt. You know, Lawrence of Arabia and all that."

Sarah looked at him, brow raised. "I'm impressed."

"Don't be. I read it on a brochure while we were in line at the border crossing."

"So do you have a plan?"

"Not yet. I'm hoping Yaniv can help with that. But if

we're going into Saudi Arabia, we're going to need a couple of things before we do anything else."

"Like what?"

"A wedding ring."

They both looked down at her left hand as it rested on the balcony rail.

"Here it's an act of impropriety for an unmarried couple to travel together. But in Saudi Arabia, it's against the law. At least the religious law. And they have religious police there, the mutaween. The official name is something like, 'The Committee for the Propagation of Virtue and the Prevention of Vice.' Not sure what their authority is now that they allow tourism, but where we're going is rural and probably more conservative. Better not to risk it."

He pulled the ring from the fourth finger on his right hand, where he'd worn it since his wife's death, and slipped it on his wedding finger.

"In that case, I accept your proposal." She gave him a wry smile. "I do."

"The other thing we should get…" He paused, unsure of how she would react to the suggestion.

"Is what?" she asked, cocking her head.

"The other thing we should get is a black abaya." Graham hoped the idea of wearing the traditional full-length covering wouldn't aggravate her. He watched her face darken, but not as much as he thought it might, then finished the suggestion. "And a niqab." Her face darkened another increment, as if drawing an inner veil that illustrated the draconian head covering that left only a slit in the material for the eyes. "Like I said, with tourism, they may not be necessary, but we definitely don't want to be without them if we need them."

She nodded with resignation. "Given my genes, it would probably be better to have them than try to explain why I look Muslim but reject the traditional dress."

The comment reminded Graham that the risks were about to transform from theoretical to plausible, that there could be consequences merely for looking for Alexander.

"I just want to do this as safely as possible," he said, smiling apologetically.

"I understand. It makes perfect sense." Her face was fixed with resolve. "Don't worry about me."

The Electric Light Orchestra's "Turn to Stone" erupted from his phone, jolting her features into confusion.

"Not-so-guilty pleasure," he said, pulling the phone out of his pocket. "Child of the 70s."

He held it up to show her Yaniv's name on the screen, before answering on speakerphone.

"Shalom, Yaniv." He led Sarah off the balcony and back into the room so they could hear better.

"Graham, shalom. I apologize for not being able to answer the phone last night. Reception at the site is not good. I was lucky you received my texts. Where are you now? I will meet you and you can tell me what you have found out."

"Actually, we're in Aqaba."

"Jordan? But what are you doing there?"

"Trying to figure out a way to get to Jebel al-Lawz. We were thinking maybe you could help us with that somehow." Graham raised his brow hopefully, making the face for Sarah. Once again, part of his awareness detached itself from the task he was performing as he looked at her. Standing next to her as they shared the phone suddenly evoked the image of Jimmy Stewart doing the same with Donna Reed in It's a Wonderful Life. The parallel made him feel self-conscious, but Yaniv's refusal to help dissipated the image, pulling Graham back to his mission.

"My friend, I wish I could. But I have confirmed that the Israeli stamps on your passport and the nature of your work make it extremely unlikely you will be allowed entry unless you are sponsored by a Saudi government official. There is nothing I can do. Alexander's aunt may have a better chance, but she will not be admitted on her own. A husband or male family member must be with her to travel in the country."

Graham sighed, heavily. "But we have to find Alexander. Who else is going to do it?"

"Perhaps Bremmer could help." Yaniv didn't sound as if he thought the idea had much merit. "He may have connections. At least he would know someone who does."

Graham considered the suggestion. Bremmer was a special agent for the FBI's Art Crime Unit. It had been Bremmer who informed Graham of his friend Andrew Singer's death and investigated the case since it involved the theft of an ancient scroll found within a mummy mask Singer had been working on.

"He might," Graham said, "but I don't think we have enough time for that. Even if he had contacts, it would take at least a day for Bremmer to arrange it. And it would tip off the government which might make it more dangerous for Alexander. I think we have to do something right now."

"Just so," Yaniv said. "It is a difficult position. I wish I could be of more help to you. But I promise to do everything I can."

"Can I trust you to not do anything with the ostracon until I get back?"

"Of course. It is still in the sack of shards you brought it in, safely locked in my office safe. It really is quite a camouflage."

Graham put his phone back in his pocket, his eyes glazed over with implications as he processed the call.

"Where does that leave us?" Sarah sounded almost lost. "What do we do next?"

He emerged from his thoughts and looked up. "We become *Lawrence of Arabia* in reverse."

"What does that mean?"

"Remember the big line from the movie? *To Aqaba!* He came to Aqaba from the desert. We're going to do the opposite."

THIRTY-EIGHT

Despite how simple the concierge made the directions sound, they managed to take several wrong turns trying to find the souk in Aqaba's labyrinthine layout. Yet with so many unknowns hanging over them, the mere act of physical movement and having a task to perform provided a measure of comfort for Graham, an outlet for his nervous energy.

"Unbelievable," Sarah said, pointing out a Pizza Hut sign just as she had McDonald's, Burger King, KFC, and Popeyes. "Of all the great things America could offer, we give them fast food. Like Columbus bringing European diseases to the New World. There should be a law against the homogenization of culture."

"I was in Moscow a few years ago and thought that exact thing," Graham said. "There is actually a McDonald's right next to Red Square. At first, I was really put out by it. But then it occurred to me that it was far more than a McDonald's. It meant the Soviets had lost the cold war. That's the only way the restaurant could be there. It was a monument to freedom."

"Interesting. Did it make the food taste any better?"

Graham chuckled, thankful for the banter's contrast to the tension. "Actually, any fast food would have tasted good compared to the Russian food I had. But seriously, I think this is one of the ways ideas are spread. The freedom to order what you want on demand isn't part of the heritage of most people in the world. It's not just about the food. It's the idea of it, the philosophy behind it that is important. Besides, if they didn't have these restaurants, they'd probably have some kind of knockoffs. You know, Kentucky Fried Lamb. Or Burqa King. That sort of thing."

"Stop!" Sarah butted her shoulder into his as they walked, stifling a laugh.

After a random turn, they found the souk spread out before them. As they crossed the intersection to get to it, they laughed as they realized they were back on the street they had started from, the same one the hotel was on.

The booths of the souk were mostly full of mass-produced souvenirs for tourists. The concierge had told them the best place to get authentic items handmade by Bedouin was at a souk that was held only on Fridays. But since this was a Sunday, they'd have to settle for the main souk, which usually had a couple of Bedouin stalls hidden among the others. The Bedouin booths were not only distinct for selling local crafts such as glass beads, pottery, silver items, and lanterns, but also because they were staffed by women wearing the traditional clothes Sarah needed.

At one stall they purchased a simple silver ring, which Sarah immediately slipped on her finger and admired how it looked on her as if she were actually making plans for a wedding. A second booth offered the clothes they were looking for. In addition to the black abaya and niqab, she also bought two hijabs, the open-faced head covering worn by many of the local women.

Graham carried the bag of clothes as they left the souk. He noticed Sarah fidgeting with her ring and stealing glances at it. It occurred to him how much like newlyweds they must look, a realization that made him self-conscious, choking conversation. He was thankful to see a rental car office across the street and the distraction it offered.

"Let's see if they have a Jeep we could use."

"What's wrong with the car we have?"

"It has Israeli tags," Graham said. "That's the last thing we want if we're really going to try to get to Saudi Arabia. And we'll need four-wheel-drive to make it to Jebel al-Lawz. There is no paved road there."

Twenty-minutes later, they left with the keys to a Toyota Prado, then followed the directions from the clerk to a camping outfitter around the corner. Graham got them kitted out with backpacks, water bottles, two boxes of meal replacement bars, lanterns, hiking socks, and sun hats. Sarah added a Bushnell monocular to the supplies, small enough to slip into one of the compartments of their cargo pants. As he was paying, he casually looked down into the display case doubling as a counter, saw a handheld Garmin All-Terrain GPS Navigator with a color screen, and put it in with the rest of the equipment.

"I am famished," Sarah said, drawing out the last word.

"If only there was a White Castle around here some-whe—"

Sarah cut him off with a look, squinting daggers at him.

"Just kidding." Graham raised his hands in surrender. "Pick a spot. I'm starving, too."

He followed her into one of the many places offering local fare, a modest restaurant with Middle Eastern pop music bouncing off the Formica tables and linoleum floor. After they both ordered shawarma, Graham picked up the conversation from the trip down as he opened a can of Diet Coke.

"So. Philologist. How did you get into that?"

"Isn't that what every girl grows up wanting to be?" She smiled wryly. "Actually, it was through J.R.R. Tolkien. I read *The Hobbit* and *The Lord of the Rings* as a teen. Twice. And I've reread them since then. I got really into it. The world he created was so rich, so immersive that I preferred it to high school."

"Understandable," Graham said. "I prefer almost anything to high school."

"Well, I was a book nerd, and I fell in love with it. Then I learned that Tolkien had not only invented the whole history of Middle Earth, but he created entire languages for it. Took him years. And he did it because he was a philologist. Did you know he was the translator for the book of Jonah in the Jerusalem Bible?"

Graham gasped in surprise. "I had no idea."

"Anyway, I've always loved words—even read the dictionary front-to-back once—and I speak Arabic because of my parents, so philology put a name to something I seemed to be naturally drawn to. The summer before my senior year in high school, I went on a trip to England with my best friend's family. We went to the British Museum."

"One of my favorite places to visit." Graham was about to launch into his anecdote about handwritten Beatles lyrics but chose not to interrupt.

"Me too. In fact, that's why I was in London. I was doing some research into Linear A—it's this ancient Minoan writing system that's never been deciphered. Anyway, when I went there the first time, I kept going back to the Rosetta Stone."

Graham pictured the famous stele found in Egypt containing an inscription repeated in three different languages.

"I was fascinated by how Champollion was finally able to decode it. I stood there trying to imagine what his thinking was. How he used the Greek and demotic text as a key to finally unlock Egyptian hieroglyphics. I love codes and word games, so when I saw it, I got totally bit by the philology bug. I found I loved learning the history of languages and the cultures they developed in."

A server brought their food, and Graham paused over his

in a silent blessing. He looked up to see Sarah doing the same.

"So…" She paused, punctuating the end of her story. "What's next?"

Graham bobbed his head as he finished his bite of lamb. "Well, the guy who originally connected Jebel al-Lawz to Sinai couldn't get into Saudi Arabia either. He came to Aqaba, then drove down close to the border crossing. But just before he got there, he went off-road into the desert. They found a place to hide the car—he had his two college-aged sons with him—and then they walked through the desert across the border. There's no fence or wall at that point. Once they were in, they got wherever they needed by hitching a ride with Bedouin and hired taxis."

"That sounds too easy." Sarah smirked.

"I know. But it worked. So, I've been looking at the map trying to find a way to recreate their route. Or find a better one."

"And…" Sarah turned her palms up in a question.

"I think I've found a way to get in without hitchhiking. I think I found a path we can drive."

"Thus, the four-by-four," she said, poking a thumb over her shoulder in the general direction of the truck.

"Exactly. Look at this."

Graham opened Google Maps on his phone and waited for it to find his location. As the screen filled in an aerial view of Aqaba, he angled it toward Sarah. He zoomed out until he could fit both Aqaba and the crossing point in the view.

"That's the Durra Border Crossing, about fifteen miles or so south." He zoomed in and pointed to a spot east of the crossing. "This is where the first guy went. The problem with trying to do what he did is that we'd end up on the road that goes right back to the border crossing." Graham scrolled the map inland and downward to show the area they would have to navigate. "Even if we were able to find a place to cross in the truck, then we'd still have to drive to the place we need to avoid. And the way we look—driving a rental from Jordan—we'd probably be conspicuous."

"Okay." Sarah nodded. "That makes sense. But what options do we have?"

Graham continued to scroll the satellite picture to the east. "This highway that runs along the northern border of Saudi Arabia splits off to the southwest about twenty miles inland. Goes to a city called Haql. If we can get to the highway near the split, then we can take the road to Haql, and from there we can get on the highway that takes us close to al-Lawz."

Sarah frowned. "But we still have to find a way to get to the highway."

He zoomed back to Aqaba, then scrolled along the route as he described it. "We could take the Aqaba Highway. It runs east of here and connects to the Desert Highway. If we turn south, then there is another road that branches off and goes into the west side of the Wadi Rum Desert. There's a paved road all the way to this Bedouin camp where tourists can sleep in tents and eat Bedouin food and go on Jeep or camel tours. Now, look at this." Graham zoomed close enough to show an unpaved track leading away from the camp, then scrolled east as he followed it. "This is a trail that leads all the way into the Wadi Rum, which is right along the Saudi border."

The track cut through a narrow passage of rock five miles long, then into an expanse of desert floor the color of red brick.

"Is that the sand?" Sarah leaned closer to the screen. "It looks like someone spilled tomato bisque."

"Yes. That's part of what makes it such a popular tourist attraction." He pointed to a mountain on the southern end of the desert. "That's Jebel Umm ad Dami, the highest mountain in Jordan. And it's only half a mile away from the Saudi border."

The mountain sat in the southeast corner of a large open space. A short chain of smaller mountains formed a wall, closing off the east side of the area. On the other side of the chain, rock formations jutted from the desert floor like a cluster of islands.

"You can see that part of the track actually weaves through these small wadis. Sometimes it doesn't look like a track at all, just the trail of someone who went off-road. But one of them leads to…" The border of Saudi Arabia came into view as he scrolled, along with the highway on the other side. "The highway."

He looked up from the phone and tried to appear optimistic.

"I think we can do it." He nodded, trying to sell the idea. "And we'll have our own car. I'll mark each turn with a waypoint in the GPS so we can retrace our route to get back out. Even if the tracks we're looking at aren't there anymore, I think we should still be able to find our way."

Sarah sighed as if she had been holding her breath.

He thought she might be confronting the reality of what it would really mean to go after Alexander and tried to reassure her. "I can download high resolution maps to the GPS tonight. We'll have a far more detailed image than we're looking at now. I'll download maps for Jebel al-Lawz as well. I can put in waypoints for every place we're going and each place Alexander has been. That way we'll be able to quickly make our way back once we find him."

"If we find him," Sarah said, pointedly.

"Don't say that," Graham said, trying to sound reassuring. "You're the one who came to me looking to share an adventure." When she didn't respond to the allusion to The Hobbit, he became serious. "Think about your own life. About Alexander's. You've been guided through so many difficult things.

I have too. And we didn't need GPS to do it."

Sarah's sad smile only accentuated her look of doubt as she reached across the table and put her hand over Graham's. The gesture was so unexpected that the sensation was heightened, and he realized he had almost forgotten what it felt like to be touched.

THIRTY-NINE

In the moments before dawn, Graham loaded the truck in silence as the call to *Fajr*, the first prayer of the day, blanketed the city. The vague feeling that he was being watched had spread slowly, like a stain, since the metochion in Istanbul. Mostly it lurked in the background of his consciousness, crouching in the shadows just outside his vision. But at night its presence grew as thoughts of the day fell away, making room for it. When the call to prayer began, he was almost thankful and decided to use it as a call to pack. If someone was actually watching him, then loading the gear in the dark would make it harder to figure out what they were planning.

By the time the prayer finished, the gulf was behind them, reflecting light into the rearview mirror as they drove down the street that turned into the Aqaba Highway.

"Sorry." Sarah handed him a protein bar and twisted the cap off a water bottle for him as he drove. "Nothing was open during prayers. It's the only food I could find."

"Not a problem." Graham had resolved to sound as optimistic as possible, hoping it would be infectious. "I take it as a good sign. It means we were prepared. Let's hope we're just as prepared for whatever else is out there."

Just outside Aqaba, the highway forked to the east and entered a pass that zigzagged through a ragged cleft in the range.

Five miles later, they came to the junction with the Desert Highway. Graham pulled to the side of the road to consult the route he had mapped out, then realized the significance of where he was.

"Remember the theory I told you about that said Sinai was a volcano? Charles Beke, the guy who came up with the idea thought that mountain was Sinai." Graham pointed left, toward the base of the mountain the highway skirted around. "That's Jebel al-Baqir."

"Really?" Sarah craned her neck to look through the windshield, up the mountain. "Did he find anything up there?"

"Actually, yes. But not a volcano. He did find some inscriptions, however. And there is a local tradition that the mountain is sacred."

"Interesting," Sarah said. "I'd like to see those inscriptions."

"Me too. But they'll have to wait for another time."

Graham turned right onto the Desert Highway, then drove while glancing at the GPS, knowing the next turn was coming up quickly. After a mile and a half, he turned onto a side road, a ribbon of asphalt wide enough for two lanes, but too narrow for a shoulder. The satellite image on the GPS screen made Graham think of a close-up of the hide of an animal, like an elephant, with calloused rough patches divided by squiggling grooves. Except the callouses belonged to the desert mountains, and the grooves they were wending their way through were canyons. Around them, the mountains glowed to life like embers being warmed as they collected the sun.

Although the road was in better shape than he had expected, he drove unhurriedly, not wanting to disturb the primeval quiet of the landscape. They remained silent, the tension in the air growing more taut, as if they were pulling it tighter the longer they drove. He had just begun to wonder if he'd taken a wrong turn or if the GPS was working incorrectly, when the mountains gave way to a flat, enclosed area, and the Bedouin camp that was his landmark came into view.

Dozens of black tents, some with white horizontal stripes of various widths, stood on the desert floor, clustered in groups like itinerant subdivisions. The shape of the tents reminded Graham of the houses in a game of Monopoly, as if a sore loser had scattered the pieces to the most remote locations on Earth. Several firepits were stationed throughout the camp, each surrounded by long, flat cushions resting on rugs, ready to welcome tourists back from a day of exploration. Four or five Toyota pickups with benches built into the beds to transport campers were parked together, looking like they had accidentally been transported to the ancient past in a time machine.

Graham had grown so accustomed to the silence that the sound of Sarah's voice startled him.

"Amazing how much it looks like Michigan." She kept her face deadpan as Graham chortled.

He studied the GPS and turned off the asphalt onto the track worn into the sand. After stopping to put the Prado into four-wheel-drive, he wove through the camp and found the track leading due east toward the mouth of a wadi, cutting through the sheer walls of the mountains a mile away. A new worry began to stalk his thoughts as he got further away from the camp and discovered that the tracks he saw in the satellite images were far less well-traveled than they had looked. Many were nothing more than soft grooves of sand that would be wiped away by the end of the day, and it made him wonder if they would be able to find the route to the Saudi highway. He decided to distract his own thoughts by distracting hers.

"Speaking of Michigan, how did Alexander get into magic?"

"Dearborn is pretty close to Colon—about two hours

away—which is the magic capital of the world."

Graham laughed, then realized it hadn't been a joke. "I didn't know there was such a thing. And why would it be in Colon, Michigan, instead of somewhere like Las Vegas?"

"I asked the same thing," Sarah said. "It turns out that's where Harry Blackstone, Sr. lived when he wasn't on tour."

"I remember seeing Harry Blackstone, Jr. on TV as a kid," Graham said, emphasizing the junior. "But I didn't know his dad was a magician."

"Big-time. *The Great Blackstone.*" Sarah announced the name with a wave of her hand. "One of the last from the giant magic shows that used to travel all over the world."

"And he was from Colon?" Graham asked.

"I don't think so. Just moved there for some reason. And other magicians followed him. The biggest magic company in the world is based there. Anyway, one of the magicians in the area came to Xander's school in fifth or sixth grade, and he couldn't stop talking about it. It was the first thing he was ever passionate about. He found out the local magic shop had free shows every Sunday afternoon, and he was always there. My sister somehow found a way to pay for some lessons, and it turned out he had a real talent for it. Even though he doesn't keep up with it now like he did, he's still a really good magician. He even goes to the Magic Castle in Hollywood whenever he can. He's taken me a few times."

Graham pictured the Châteauesque mansion one block off Hollywood Boulevard, near the Chinese Theatre. "I've driven past it a thousand times. Always wanted to go in."

The bluffs of the slot canyon pressed in on them so close and with such sheer walls that the passage took on the claustrophobic feel of the deepest parts of Manhattan. But, unlike Manhattan, they felt like the only people on Earth.

The scrub-pocked corridor finished its four-mile-long tear between the mountains and deposited them on the edge of a vast plain of red sand. Islands of rocks broke the surface like peaks of submerged mountains scabbing the landscape. The stark beauty would have awed them into silenced had they been speaking.

Sarah was the first to give voice to the instant enchantment, almost whispering. "The mountains are so much bigger than they look on the satellite images. And they're probably exaggerated by shooting up from the desert floor. Strange looking mountains." Sarah turned in her seat, absorbing the environment. "It's like we landed on some alien planet. Like we're on Mars."

"Actually, you are."

Sarah glanced at Graham as if she expected a punch line.

"This is where quite a few movies have been filmed," Graham said. "Part of one of the *Star Wars* movies was done here. So were *The Martian* and *Lawrence of Arabia*. The real T.E. Lawrence actually lived here at one point. Some people call it the Valley of the Moon."

"I can see why," Sarah said.

The track frayed into improvised routes, leaving Graham to do the same. He had loved the freedom of driving off-road since getting a go-cart for Christmas when he was eleven. But now his purpose made the freedom feel more like a constraint that he would easily trade for a quick and direct route across the sand. He struggled to find the best speed, his anxiety tempting him to go as fast as possible, while his caution kept him from going so fast that he wouldn't be able to avoid the soft sand that could easily ensnare them. Their rush made the journey to the other side of the valley pass by with maddening slowness. The 6,000-foot-tall peak of Jebel Umm ad Dami—his primary reference point—never seemed to get closer despite the fact they were heading toward it, as if to make an illustration of their impossible quest. By the time they were close enough to see change in the perspective, it gave him a small sense of accomplishment. Graham guided them past the mountain, keeping its base on their right as they neared the ridge marking the end of the valley.

"Look on the GPS and help me find that opening we saw leading through that ridge." Graham spoke as if he had no attention to spare, fixing on what was immediately in front of him.

Sarah navigated them along the contours of the dry streambed as it snaked toward the impenetrable looking range. The mountains funneled them into a corner, but a pass—no more than a sliver wide enough for the truck—sliced through to the other side. Graham could feel the wheels work to find traction over patches of loose sand. The sound of each sudden tractionless spin gripped his entire chest, squeezing, making him hold his breath as if his worry suffocated him.

The other side of the pass revealed a terrain crowded with islands of rock, reducing the plain of the desert floor to a system of capillaries to negotiate. The tracks they had seen in the satellite photo had been erased by time and wind, and Graham relied entirely on Sarah's guidance as she stared at the GPS.

"Turn right," she said mechanically.

"I don't think I can. That looks too soft to cross." He nodded sideways at the dry streambed they followed on the right side of the truck. "Let me go down a little farther."

"Okay, but that's where we need to go," she said, pointing to the space opening up outside her window.

Half a mile later, the dry streambed they had been paralleling offered a crossing point. Graham turned into it, then gunned his way up the other side, fishtailing less than he thought he would.

"Nice," Sarah said. "Now, in about a mile this canyon ends and we'll veer left. From there it's less than two miles to the…"

Her voice was instantly muted by a lurching slosh that rocked the truck as it listed to the right. The sound of spinning wheels grew proportionately more furious as their momentum bled away.

"No!" Graham growled, throwing the gear into reverse. "No, no, no!" His protests grew louder as he realized that going the opposite direction only increased the problem. He slammed the truck back into drive and pushed the gas pedal to the floor in frustration until they weren't moving at all. Graham pounded the steering wheel, punctuating his aggravation. "I am such an idiot."

Graham felt Sarah's hand on his shoulder, comforting him as he bent his head to his hand and massaged his temple.

"I'm sure this kind of thing happens all the time," Sarah said. "Maybe we could find some rocks to put under the wheels."

"Okay," he said, raking his fingers through his hair. "Worth a try."

It was easy enough to find rocks to force under the tires, and Graham felt a splinter of optimism work its way into his silent self-recriminations. But when he tried again, the truck still wouldn't move. The only thing that seemed to have changed was the sound the tires made as they slipped across the rocks. He could feel Sarah's eyes on him as he released a sigh that drained him. Then he heard her say the words that he was thinking.

"Now what?"

FORTY

Graham took the GPS from Sarah, contriving calm to mask his panic. He took several measurements, then held the screen between them so they could both see their position in the context of the landscape around them. He glanced between the GPS and the terrain, scanning the area as he deliberated.

"Seems to me we have two options. The first is to get help. We hike back to Jebel Umm ad Dami—six miles away—and find one of the tour groups. The Bedouin have a reputation for being very friendly and helpful. We can get them to pull the truck out. The problem with that is they will wonder what in the world we're doing way over here. Even if they believe we got lost, we'd have to follow them back. We'd lose at least a day, and that makes Alexander even harder to find."

"What's the other option?" Sarah asked, a slight quaver of worry in her voice.

"We walk on. The border is only two miles away, and the highway is another half a mile beyond that. Several of the other explorers who made it to al-Lawz walked across the desert and then hitchhiked rides with Bedouin."

"But that's insane." Sarah frowned. "What if they just got lucky with who picked them up? What if soldiers drive by, or someone from the government? What if they are *mutaween*? They'll have us arrested."

"First, the Bedouin don't care about politics. They just want to be left alone. I've heard of them fighting against other tribes or against the government when it tries to get involved in their business, but they are well-known for their hospitality to strangers. Second, as long as we don't do anything to violate the code of morality, the mutaween won't be a problem. That's one of the reasons we bought you those clothes. Third, if we can hire one to be our driver, then it may end up being the fastest way to get to al-Lawz since there's a chance they know exactly how to get there."

"But how will we get back?" Sarah shrugged. "We can't ask them to wait like some taxi while we search the mountain for Xander."

"We won't have to. Alexander had to have rented a truck in Tabuk. My guess is that the truck is near wherever he is. Or at least where his phone was last. And that was at al-Lawz. Even if we don't find him, we probably won't be stuck."

"Probably?"

"I think it's a fairly strong probably," Graham said. "Strong enough to outweigh waiting until tomorrow to try again. And even then, we might get stuck again. If he really needs our help, do you want to risk that?"

"Is there a door number three?"

"Not that I can see."

Sarah released a heavy sigh, then gave a chivalrous gesture. "Lead the way."

Graham packed the truck that morning wondering if they were over-prepared. Now, as he winnowed the supplies to only what they could carry in backpacks, he wondered if they were prepared enough.

"So, what kind of animals do you think are out here?" Sarah asked as they moved away from the truck.

Graham didn't want to let on that he shared the same fear and mentally edited the list of wildlife he'd read were in the area. *Snakes. Wolves. Hyenas. Rabbits.* "I'm not sure. Maybe some rabbits. If we're lucky we might see some ibexes higher up in the mountains. I think the bigger worry is going to be the heat."

His prediction grew truer by the minute, adding to a burden that began to wring sweat from his body. Forty-five minutes later, the black thread of the highway appeared like a seam in the desert floor.

"Welcome to Saudi Arabia."

Despite the fact that he had never been one to sweat very much, and despite the fact that it was still not quite mid-morning, Graham's internal thermostat was over-whelmed, and he found himself coated in perspiration by the time he stepped onto the road. Sarah was sweating even worse, but he pretended not to notice.

"What city is it we're going to, again?"

"Haql." The air felt hot in his throat as he replied. "It's on the coast, about thirty-miles away. And it's about sixty-five miles from there to Jebel al-Lawz."

Sarah stared down the road toward Haql. "Maybe we could rent a truck there."

"I think they'd want to see a passport and visa. If they took cash, we might be able to—"

The faint sound of an engine eclipsed his thought and turned him around. A truck emerged from the far side of the small mountain behind them. Heat from the highway rip-pled its appearance as if it were being conjured from another world.

Graham felt an initial wave of relief, but it almost instant-ly evaporated in second-guessing as the risk they were taking became real. What if it was a soldier? They'd be done before they even started. Should they hide and try to see who was driving? Then they wouldn't know who was driving until it was too late to get a ride. And if it turned out to be someone willing to give them a ride, how would they know they were not being taken to be turned in? Or they might be mutaween.

"What do we do?" Sarah voiced his own question.

"Better put on your hijab." Then he did the only thing he trusted—he prayed. When he finished his petition for protection and wisdom, he stayed on the road, watching the image of a white SUV become more material as it grew closer in the monocular, slowing down as it approached.

FORTY-ONE

The worn Nissan Patrol sounded more roadworthy than it looked, but to Graham its greatest virtue was that it was not a military vehicle. As the truck slowed to a stop, he studied the details framed by the driver's red and white headscarf. The keffiyeh's twin bands of camel hair rope barely contained a mane of dark, billowing hair, and made his short beard and thin mustache seem like straps holding it on. Lines furrowed the dark face, etched by weather. But it was the driver's eyes that were the most striking feature for Graham; they smiled from the man's face, bright despite being almost black. Graham thought the man could've passed for thirty as easily as sixty.

The driver leaned across the passenger seat of the Patrol and rocked as he used a hand crank to roll down the window, then turned down the traditional music. Graham stepped to the window and noticed the traditional white cotton thobe that covered the man's body to the ankles.

"Assalam alaykum." The driver put his right hand over his heart as he spoke in a surprising high tenor.

Graham recognized the sign of respect and the greeting that wished God's peace upon him.

"Wa alaykum a salaam." He returned the greeting cautiously, hoping he remembered the correct reply while won-

dering what he was getting them into.

"*Hal tahtaj musaeadatan?*"

The syllables rattled out of the man's mouth in a pronunciation Graham found difficult to follow, but he caught enough to know the man was asking if they needed help. But more than the words themselves, Graham heard a friendliness in the voice that told him what he really needed to know.

"*Ana dayie,*" Graham said, confessing that they were lost. "*Sayariti maksurat fi alraml. Bidna naruuH ah Haql law samaHt.*" Our car is broken in the sand. We want to go to Haql, please.

A wide smile pushed the wrinkles to the edges of driver's face like curtains revealing teeth. "You are American?" This time he spoke in heavily accented English, distorted as if reflected in a funhouse mirror.

"Yes, American." Graham smiled back.

The man began nodding, agreeing with his words before he said them. "I go to Haql. Yes. Yes. I give you drive."

"*Shukraan.*" Graham thanked the man and told him how grateful they were.

Graham turned to Sarah—whom the driver had not acknowledged—and tried to give her a look of assurance as he opened the door to the backseat for her. He climbed into the front seat while silently praying two prayers simultaneously—one thankful, the other asking for protection, not quite sure which one was most appropriate.

Almost immediately, Graham prayed for a different kind of protection as their acceleration didn't level out when he expected it to. The driver kept pushing the truck faster as if the speed limit was set by the truck's own capabilities. Of course, that was exactly the case since there were no posted speeds on the highway. More than once, the centrifugal force generated by the turns threatened to roll them off the road. Graham tried to mask his fear behind small talk, a situation that some detached part of him said would make a hilarious story one day—providing he lived through it.

Graham spoke more Arabic than the driver did English, but the man seemed to want practice in English, and between the two languages they spliced the chat together. For some reason, the man bent most of his sentences in an upward inflection that made them sound like questions whether they were or not. Several times he caught sight of Sarah in the side-view mirror, wincing at the bi-lingual mutilation that passed for conversation. He could tell she was frustrated at being constrained by the Saudi culture, unable to speak unless the men she was with were relatives.

The man explained he was a Bedouin who acted as the currier for his tribe, delivering crafts, jewelry, and other trinkets to Haql. One of the shops, as well as a stall in the souk, purchased whatever they made, and it sounded like the only income the tribe had.

Graham realized that he had been so distracted by the mechanics of the conversation that he hadn't learned the driver's name.

He seemed flattered to be asked, and patted his chest, indicating himself. "I am Shu'aib Siddiqui."

Graham couldn't keep from looking to the mirror for Sarah's reaction to see if she picked up on the implication. Her look said she had. *Shu'aib* was the Arabic form of Jethro.

"Shu'aib," Graham repeated, testing the name. "Like the father-in-law of the prophet Musa?"

Another smile parted Shu'aib's face. "Yes, yes! I am name for him. The prophet Musa live near here after he cross sea."

"I thought Jebel Musa was in Egypt." Graham glanced at Sarah again.

"No," Shu'aib said stridently. "Jebel Musa is here in Saudi Arabia. He came to Midian. This is Midian." He gave an expansive gesture to the landscape, letting go of the steering wheel, panicking Graham.

"How do you know this is where Musa came?"

"It is tradition. Everyone here knows." Shu'aib tapped his head. "They remember."

"That's amazing. Will you show us? Can you take us there, be our guide? I will pay you."

A frown uncharacteristically closed his face. "Baksheesh?" He gave one sharp nod to make his point.

"Yes, for baksheesh," Graham said, agreeing to pay for the service. "I want to hire you as a guide."

Shu'aib's face reopened. "Yes. I will take you. Show you many things. But Haql first."

FORTY-TWO

Impossibly, Graham could feel the Patrol accelerate, pushing the engine to a sustained whine that made him picture a rope stretching tighter, certain to snap at any moment. He tried to envision where they were on the map as the highway forked southwest and thought they must be almost halfway to Haql.

At least we're making good time.

A truck appeared on the horizon, occasionally weaving into their lane as the gap quickly closed. Graham held his breath, trying not to appear alarmed as he realized the truck was going at least as fast as they were when they passed. Several more oncoming cars wove in and out of the left lane for no reason that Graham could see, some lingering for an unnervingly long time, as if lanes were merely suggestions. One car was completely stopped in the middle of the road, like a stone in a stream, forcing traffic to flow around it. And although Shu'aib's truck was moving at top speed, they found themselves being passed—sometimes on the right despite the fact that there was no proper shoulder.

Just before noon, they finally slowed to enter Haql. Graham looked at Sarah in the mirror and found her face waiting for him, reflecting his harrowed expression. She blinked several times in a melodramatic flutter of relief.

The deceleration melted the stress as they looped through

roundabouts and onto one of the streets that spoked out from a hub at the center of the town. The plaza forming the hub was like a town square, except it was hexagonal, and instead of a courthouse, the central building was a large mosque. Shu'aib navigated around the mosque to one of the other spokes on the wheel of streets and drove to the far side of the outer rim several blocks away.

Movement in the side mirror caught his eye, and he saw that Sarah had pulled the abaya and niqab from her backpack and was in the process of slipping the robe over her head.

"Good idea," he said softly.

The niqab obscured everything but her eyes and hands. Graham looked apologetically at her. There was something dehumanizing about enshrouding a person like that. He knew some of what he felt could be explained as a cultural difference, but it didn't look like the trappings of modesty to him. It seemed more like a cage of cloth, a denial of the person that left only a wraith. And yet he saw determination in her eyes, the willingness to do what had to be done.

Shu'aib pulled onto a side road off a commercial strip and parked.

"I must deliver." He gestured vaguely to the back of one of the stores. "It will be very little time."

"I can help," Graham said, wanting to step onto solid ground after the drive.

"*Luh!*" Shu'aib said. "No! Not possible. Cannot be alone."

It took Graham a moment to understand they couldn't leave Sarah unaccompanied by a man in public.

"*Ana 'aasif.* I'm sorry. I forgot my place."

Shu'aib hesitated before replying. "Not to worry," he said smiling, apparently pleased at finding the English phrase he wanted.

He went to the back of the truck and unloaded two large plastic tubs and several small rugs. A shopkeeper greeted

Shu'aib at the back door and took the merchandise, scooting it inside. As Shu'aib came back for the second load, the man noticed them but showed no curiosity. Graham took advantage of the delivery to speak to Sarah for the first time since being picked up on the highway.

"You okay back there?"

"Well, I'm alive," she said, a smirk in her voice. "And after *that* drive, that feels like some kind of victory."

"Tell me about it." Graham checked to make sure Shu'aib was still doing business. "I know he's an answer to our prayers, but I kept wishing God would've sent a better driver. Then I saw the *other* drivers and was almost thankful for him."

"And your plan worked," Sarah said. "Actually, it worked better. He's taking us without knowing why we want to go."

Graham could hear hope in her voice for the first time and felt the weight of responsibility grow heavier on him.

Shu'aib climbed back into the truck, turned onto a street at the perimeter of the central hub, and followed it until it fed them onto the highway. Graham steeled himself for another death-ride, but Shu'aib pulled the truck into a gas station on the outskirts of town.

"Need fuel to guide."

Graham took out his wallet and handed him several bills of riyals.

"Luh," he said, shaking his head, handing back most of the money. "No. Too much."

Graham looked up at the sign displaying the price, then used an app to convert riyals into dollars and almost laughed. Gas was about twenty-five cents a gallon.

When Shu'aib had finished, all three walked into the store to use the rest rooms before the drive. The aisles of food made Graham realize how hungry he was. He returned to the truck with a falafel and tahini flatbread sandwich and a Diet Coke.

They had just passed the last of a string of hotels when

Graham felt the truck slow down rather than launch into the desert.

"It is *Zuhr*," Shu'aib said as he pulled the truck into a parking lot. "You wait."

The call to the noon prayer in the distance provided a soundtrack to the scene as Shu'aib produced a rolled-up prayer rug from the back of the truck. He oriented himself toward the *qibla*, the direction of prayer, facing the Kaaba in Mecca, and began the ritual.

Graham took the opportunity to study the route on the GPS, not wanting Shu'aib to see it since it would be hard to explain how they could be lost if they knew exactly where they were. The screen showed Highway 5 running southeast, directly toward Jebel al-Lawz, then angling south down the west side of the range while another highway intersected the 5 and skirted the range to the north. They should be headed inland, but instead, Shu'aib had taken the exit off the 5, onto a road that paralleled the coast. Graham wondered if Shu'aib hadn't wanted to stop on the highway to pray and found a better place. But when Shu'aib finished, they continued down the coastal road.

"Where are we going?" Graham asked, trying to sound conversational.

"I show you where Musa opened the sea." He smiled proudly, then popped a piece of *balasham* into his mouth.

The small pastries looked like miniature churros to Graham, except with coconut sprinkles instead of cinnamon and sugar. Shu'aib had bought a bag of them at the store. Graham's anxiety rose with their acceleration as Shu'aib drove one-handed down the curving road, using the other hand to eat, licking his sticky fingers after each piece.

He tried to distract himself by looking out his window into the Gulf of Aqaba, at Egypt on the other side. *We made it. We're really doing this.* He turned to his right as far as he could, hoping to spot Pharaoh's Island, a tiny mound of land crowned with a Crusader castle on the Egyptian side of the gulf, but it was too far to the north to make out.

Graham faced forward again, and it suddenly struck him where they were headed. They may not be going directly to al-Lawz, but they were following the road to where Wyatt said he had seen the second pillar. Although others had tried to find the pillar, it had been removed after its discovery, leaving a marker mounted on the foundation stone that had once held it. A spark of academic exhilaration in pursuing the location rivaled—just for an instant—the mission of finding Alexander, an excitement he immediately felt guilty for. A road sign read *ras dabr*, confirming they were in the right place. But again, Shu'aib confounded Graham's expectations, and instead of slowing down to visit the spot, he seemed oblivious to it.

"How much farther? Is it near here?" Graham thought the question would trigger the realization they were about to pass it.

"No, no. Longer away. Two times as far."

Graham found Sarah's face in the mirror and gave her a mildly helpless look. He stared across the beach that had possibly welcomed the Israelites to Midian. He could see Nuweiba on the other side of the water and remembered that it was here—maybe—that the Israelites broke into song after the sea drowned the Egyptian army. The event was so important in the formation of Israel that Graham had seen Torah scrolls where the song of Exodus 15 had been formatted differently from the surrounding text.

Instead of the meticulously regulated width that dictated a column of text in the Hebrew Bible, the passage was subdivided so phrases of the song were spaced and alternated to create a brick-like pattern. God had promised to fight for His people. He was their bulwark, and the brick pattern was a picture of it right in the middle of scripture. Graham twisted his body again to look behind him out the window, unwilling to let the promise of Ras Dabr go. He'd prayed to the same God for protection earlier, and he hoped the bulwark would be no less evident.

FORTY-THREE

Graham felt Sarah tap his right shoulder. He had been lost in thought, hypnotized by the Red Sea, and it took him a second to follow her finger pointing through the windshield. The road was leading to a bay of the clearest ocean water he had ever seen. Trucks were scattered on the beach between the road and the water, and he could see people wading in the shallow waves, making their way to what looked like a movie set. A massive oil tanker lay grounded a hundred feet from shore, rocked on its side at a forty-five-degree angle, its back half submerged in the turquoise water.

"Shu'aib, what is that?"

"*Georgios G.* For many years it has been there. Many people swim there. They like to climb on it and jump into the water."

Through the monocular, Graham saw the ship had been there long enough to turn to rust. The road bent to follow the curve of the bay as he tried to decipher squiggles of Arabic graffiti covering it like spray-painted barnacles. There were no buildings in sight to capitalize on the local attraction, just a sign identifying it as Al Mashee Well.

On the other side of the bay, the beach ended as the mountains—which had been nothing more than a jagged tear of rock on the distant horizon—suddenly crowded the coast, the steep bluffs leaving only a sliver of land for the highway to navigate. The road frequently kinked in switchbacks that Shu'aib begrudgingly accommodated with a drop in speed, then furiously compensated for on the straighter passages.

Twenty miles later, Shu'aib pulled to the left side of the road, into the mouth of a severe slot canyon.

"We are here," Shu'aib said proudly.

"We are where?" Graham looked around as if awakening in a different place from where he'd fallen asleep. Several SUVs parked haphazardly in the shade of palm trees at the edge of the bluffs, and multiple tracks led deeper into the canyon.

"Wadi Tayyib Al Ism."

Canyon of the Good Name, Graham translated internally. "I don't understand."

"Where Musa came. This is where Musa closed the water."

Graham stepped out of the car, followed by Sarah, who had slipped her niqab back on. He looked across the water through the monocular and guessed that it was maybe twice as far across as the distance from Nuweiba. The opening of the wadi was—at most—a hundred yards wide, and as it cut deeper into the range, it quickly narrowed to less than half that. And the distance between the water and the beginning of the wadi was less than a hundred feet. There was no room for two million Israelites to gather on the shore and sing. They would have needed to come out of the sea and immediately file into the canyon. This could not be the crossing point.

"Come. I show you." Shu'aib ushered them back into the truck.

They followed the tracks deeper into the wadi as it curved like an S engraved in the mountain. At the point where the wadi became too narrow and rough to drive, a wooden boardwalk enabled tourists to continue down the route. They parked among the other cars and got out, joining the families exploring the area.

"I've never heard of this place," Graham said confidentially as he stood next to Sarah. "Have you?"

"Never," she said softly.

He escorted her onto the decking of the boardwalk as they looked for anything to vouch for the site. Other than the graffiti covering the rocks around them, he saw no clues.

"Either tradition got it wrong or Wyatt got it wrong." He ran through the logic, thinking out loud. "Or maybe they're both wrong, I don't know."

"It must mean something that there's a tradition here at all, don't you think?"

"Normally, I'd agree. But I just don't see how to make this place fit with the description in the Bible. Maybe the beach used to be bigger."

Graham documented the site with his camera phone, then headed back to the Patrol.

"You see? You see?" Shu'aib's enthusiasm for the tradition was untarnished by Graham's merely polite acknowledgement.

"Very helpful. Thank you, Shu'aib. *Shukran.* Where are you taking us now?"

"*Wahah.*" Shu'aib smiled broadly. "Oasis. Very beautiful."

Graham spent the short drive trying to work out how it fit the story of Moses. They entered the tiny coastal village of Maqna, and halfway through town turned onto the junction with the road that led inland. Less than a minute later, a stand of palm trees rose out of the desert off the right side of the highway.

Shu'aib read the road sign aloud at the same time Graham saw it. "Bir al Saidni. Well of Musa. He come here."

They turned into the unpaved lot and parked in a row of cars, several of which were laden with luggage wrapped in tarps. A double row of rectangular stone columns was connected by trunks of palm trees laid horizontally across the tops to form an entry to the oasis. Graham noticed that most of the women in the families visiting the site wore hijabs that left their faces exposed and was thankful Sarah wouldn't have to wear the full covering.

"This way. Come. Come." Shu'aib started down the path into the oasis, twisting himself to talk to them as they followed.

A small pool in the shape of an uneven hourglass—one bulb larger and deeper than the other—opened under a copse of trees. A sloping bank, three feet high and fortified with rocks, rimmed the water, broken only by a few stone steps leading into the shallower bowl. The edges of the basin were sandy mud, but in the middle, water bubbled up from an aquifer and drained into the bigger bowl.

"This is the watering place. Where Musa met Sofayrâ, daughter of Shu'aib."

Graham gave Sarah a questioning look. "I remember the story of Moses watering the flock for Jethro's daughters because shepherds had driven them off. That's in Exodus and the Qur'an."

"Surah Al-Qasas," Sarah said, citing the chapter.

"But what I don't remember is Zipporah—Sofayrâ—being named in the Qur'an."

"She's not. That comes from tradition. Sofayrâ's in the book on the Prophets and their lives."

Graham looked at the families spread around the oasis, watching kids playing in the pockets of water, and wondered how many of them believed the tradition and how many were here because it was the only thing like a park he'd seen since Haql.

He took some pictures of the pool, then noticed the time. Almost three o'clock.

"We need to keep moving if we're going to try to make it to al-Lawz today."

FORTY-FOUR

Shu'aib coaxed them back into the car, smiling proudly. He continued down the road leading inland, toward the mountains.

"Al-Bad'," Shu'aib announced thirty minutes later as another tiny town appeared in the desert. "Home of Shu'aib, father-in-law of Musa."

The road fed into a roundabout decorated with a statue of several chrome-plated dolphins playing with a ball despite the fact that the closest water was fifteen miles away. Shu'aib took the north exit, followed the road for a mile, then turned left at a sign reading *Magha'ir Shu'aib*.

"Caves of Jethro?" Graham asked.

"Yes. Where Shu'aib live."

A modest rectangular box of stone that Graham thought resembled a post office stood on the other side of a parking lot. Two signs hung above the door, each written in Arabic and English. One identified it as the *Al-Bidea Antiquities Office*, the other the *Saudi Commission for Tourism & National Heritage*. Strangely, neither sign indicated what exactly was being preserved. A tall chain-link fence topped with three rows of barbed wire extended from the sides of the building, encompassing the entire area behind and to the sides, lending a prison aesthetic to the welcome center.

The call to Asr, the afternoon prayer, floated from a nearby minaret. Shu'aib parked, excused himself, then left the truck to pray. Graham took the opportunity to study the GPS again.

"How far away is the mountain?" Sarah already had her niqab on, not wanting to draw attention to herself even in the truck.

Graham made a measurement, then looked out the window at the mountains as if to double check his work. "About twenty miles that way." He pointed northwest of the city. "But where we need to get to is on the other side of the peak. We have to go around the range to the north."

Sarah stared at the distant peaks as she whispered her own prayer. "Please, God. Please let him still be there."

After Asr, Shu'aib steered the Patrol to the right of the building and through a double gate. A metal sign—orange with white letters—warned that this was an archaeological area and that trespassing was unlawful by royal decree. The warning was dated 1436 H. Graham converted the Islamic year—the years since the Hijra, when Muhammad and his followers migrated from Mecca to Medina—and was surprised to find the decree was recent, from 2015.

They crossed an expanse a quarter of a mile long and parked with the other cars in the horseshoe-shaped inlet of a large sloping hill. Caves perforated the rock face of the bluffs, and several flights of low, deep stone steps were embedded in the ground to make the climb easier for visitors. Graham thought the steps looked a little like molars, as if he were being given a choice of mouths to be swallowed by.

"Which one is it?" Graham asked as they got out of the car.

"This is it." Shu'aib opened his arms as if to embrace the whole area.

"But which cave did Musa's father-in-law live in?"

227

"They are all his." He looked confused by Graham's confusion.

"Show us, please." Graham didn't know what to expect to find but didn't want to spend any more time looking than he had to. He turned to exchange a questioning look with Sarah, but she faced the opposite direction, fixed on the chain of severe mountains on the other side of Al-Bad'.

"Come. I show you."

Shu'aib walked like he drove, and Graham had to work to keep up, stiff after riding in the car so long.

Although some of the caves looked natural, most of the entrances had been fashioned to make flat walls and rectangular openings. Some featured sculpted facades ornamented with designs. All of them were covered in graffiti inscribed on both sides of the doorways.

"Please." Shu'aib stood to one side and gestured them in like a gracious host.

Graham walked into the cool shade of a square room hewn from the mountain and found himself excited by the archaeological site, but disappointed at how it had been misidentified. This time when he looked at Sarah, he found her eyes already looking for his, asking what he thought.

He shook his head slightly and whispered, "These look more Nabatean to me. Like at Petra. Around the first century AD. And this is a tomb, not a house. If the other caves are like this—and it looks like they are—then either Jethro didn't live here, or the caves he knew were altered to what we see now."

They stepped back into the late afternoon sun where Shu'aib waited for them. Graham swept the area with the monocular, trying to determine if any of the other caves promised something other than what he'd just seen, but saw nothing worth exploring—at least for their current purpose.

"You see?" Shu'aib asked triumphantly.

"Yes, thank you. Very interesting. But I do have a question, Shu'aib."

"Please. You ask," he said, turning serious.

"You took us to the well where Musa met Sofayrâ. But that was very far from here. Why was the well that Jethro used so far away from where he lived?"

"Ah!" Shu'aib's smile instantly returned. "There is well here!"

He turned and started hurrying down the steps. Once they were back in the truck, he drove down a service road toward a guard shack near another gate in the fence, parked in a flat area, and hopped out. He walked several yards off the track, and Graham noticed what looked like a white fire escape ladder disappear into the ground. When he got closer, he saw it was a deep pit, wide enough that stone steps were carved into the side of the wall, spiraling down into what was now filled with litter.

"This is the well of Shu'aib. Very close."

"Yes, this makes more sense to me."

"There is more to see," Shu'aib said. "But the sun is low. Soon it is time for prayer."

"Is there a hotel in al-Bad'?"

"Hotel?" Shu'aib repeated the word, apparently unfamiliar with it.

"*Fanaadiq*," Graham helped.

"Ah, rest house. Yes, yes. We go now."

FORTY-FIVE

Shu'aib retraced the road, passed through the roundabout with the chrome dolphins—which, on second viewing, Graham decided looked like a hood ornament—then continued straight. The town seemed to be broken into three distinct sections set apart from each other. One was on the other side of the dolphins, one was just past the archaeological site, and the third was the main section of Al-Bad', which consisted of three commercial blocks lining one side of the road. Graham guessed that fewer than a thousand people lived in the town, many of them in tents, and wondered what kind of accommodations Shu'aib meant by "rest house."

The Patrol turned into a compound surrounded by a six-foot-tall cement block wall that formed an industrial courtyard. A row of what looked like three self-storage units—complete with wide roll-up metal doors—stood along the other side of the dirt lot. Each also had a narrow door, off-white, decorated with a yellow arabesque design. Rectangular air conditioners extruded from the walls, and satellite dishes topped each module.

"Two rooms," Graham said as he gave Shu'aib some money.

A few minutes later, Shu'aib returned and handed Graham a key. Graham looked at the key and realized his mistake.

"Something is wrong?" Shu'aib asked. A smile suddenly broke across his face as he pulled some riyals from his pocket and set them on top of the key. "Is better?"

Graham used Shu'aib's misinterpretation to avoid what was really bothering him. "Let's unload our bags, then we can get dinner before evening prayers."

Graham opened the door for Sarah, stepped in, then listened until he heard Shu'aib's doors shut.

"Sarah, I am so sorry. He misunderstood me. When I said two rooms, I meant for me and you. I completely forgot he assumes we're married. And now I've put us in an awkward position."

Sarah closed her eyes and smiled. "It's okay. Don't worry about it. It would have been more awkward to explain why you wanted three rooms."

"Maybe," Graham said. He turned the air conditioner on, then looked around the sparse room. "Well, it's cleaner than I thought it would be. And it does have twin beds."

"It will be fine. But we should get some food before this town closes down."

Graham opened the door and found Shu'aib outside about to knock. "Perfect timing. We were just coming to find you."

"Luh." Shu'aib shook his head. "I am sorry. Only you."

"I don't understand."

"There is no place for women in restaurants. Maybe in Jedda or Riyadh. Not here. She must stay. We will bring food."

Graham apologized with a look to Sarah, and she nodded, playing her part.

Shu'aib circled the commercial strip and found what looked like the equivalent of a local diner. Graham ordered two plates of beef shawarma and hummus, while Shu'aib got a wrap of chicken off the spit and rice, something he called *hassan mathar.* Graham used the short drive back to make a plan for tomorrow.

"Is Jebel Musa near here?"

"Yes, yes. I take you there. It is no problem to see."

"I want to do more than see it, Shu'aib. I want to go on it."

"Yes. We drive tomorrow. After morning prayer."

Graham wasn't sure if Shu'aib understood the difference, but as they pulled into the travel house, the call to Maghrib, the sunset prayer, prevented further conversation.

Sarah had shed her abaya and changed clothes, looking glad to be free of the shroud.

"Find anything good?" she asked, looking at the Styrofoam boxes.

"I hope so. Although the menu did have something that looked like fried chicken called *Kentaky Wrap.* No kidding."

Graham said a hushed blessing over the food, conscious of the mutaween's intolerance for any religious expression other than Islam.

"Well, we didn't get as far as I had hoped today, but we got here safely and without arousing any suspicion."

"I just want to go there right now." Sarah tapped the air with her fork to emphasize her words. "I know it's not possible, but the mountain is so close."

"It's about a hundred miles to drive to where Alexander's phone is," Graham said. "We'll leave first thing in the morning. Hopefully we can get there by noon."

"I wonder what he's doing right now. I'm so worried about him. What if he's hurt and needs our help?"

"We're getting there as fast as we can, Sarah. And put yourself in his shoes. Based on what we saw today, all the tradition that is preserved in this region, he might just be the first person with any kind of proper training to explore the mountain. If he is stuck there or even hurt, I'm sure he's also making the exact kind of observations he came to make."

"Do you think we could ask Shu'aib to see if anyone around here has seen Xander?"

"I'm not sure how we'd do that. We don't even know if he came to Al-Bad'. There are no photos of the caves or the well. Maybe when we get close to the mountain there will be Bedouin we can ask."

Sarah sighed. "What about the rock, the one split in half? Isn't that on this side of the mountain?"

"Yes," Graham said. "Actually, I was trying to think of a way to get Shu'aib to take us there. If we find it, maybe he can ask people around *there* if they've seen Alexander. We have a better chance there than here."

Sarah tried to smile, but merely accentuated her concern.

"What we should do now," Graham said, "is pray for his safety. And that God would order our steps to the mountain."

"Just like Moses," Sarah said.

Graham repeated the hope. "Just like Moses."

FORTY-SIX

"Assalam mu alaina wa ala ibad dil lahis sualiheen." *Peace be to us and to the virtuous servants of God.*

"Assalam mu alaikum wa rahmatul lahi wabarakatuh." *Peace be to you all, and the mercy of God and his bounties.*

"Allah hu akbar. La ilaha il lal lah." *God is great. There is no God but Allah.*

Graham could hear Shu'aib recite *Fajr*, the dawn prayer, through the thin walls as he offered his own silent prayer to start the day. He reflected on how similar their prayers were, how he himself could say that same prayer—even the *Allah*—since it was merely the Arabic word for *God*, not God's personal name, and not the exclusive property of Islam. He thought how Jews could pray the same prayer as well. But he reminded himself that the words of the prayer are only as good as the god to whom they are offered. Like Shu'aib, and like Yaniv, Graham believed there was no God but God. Yet each of them believed a different God existed, that the gods of the others did not exist. The one thing they could agree on was that they were not all worshipping the same God, regardless of the similarity of the words they used to do it. Logically, either one of them was right or all of them were wrong.

And now they were headed to what was possibly the actual God-trodden mountain, where the God they disagreed on had revealed Himself to His people, and where He delivered the very first lines of scripture, written in stone by His own finger.

After passing the caves of Jethro, the road joined Highway 5 and they headed north. Shu'aib pushed the truck as hard as he did the day before, but Graham's impatience to see the mountain now made the speed almost feel too slow.

"There." Shu'aib pointed through the top right corner of the windshield. "That is Jebel Musa."

"Which one is Jebel al-Lawz?"

Shu'aib pointed the same direction again. "It is the same. Maps say it is Jebel al-Lawz. People here, Bedouin, we say Jebel Musa."

"Can we get closer?"

"Yes. Little way more. We will stop soon."

Graham looked in the sideview mirror and saw Sarah's eyes remain fixed on the mountain as they paralleled the range. He projected his own thoughts on her expression. *Alexander is somewhere up there. Hopefully.*

A minaret appeared from behind a steep hill as the highway snaked around a bend. Shu'aib slowed and turned off the asphalt onto the open area of dirt next to the mosque. The building was completely isolated, no town to supply worshippers. Graham wondered what kind of infraction an imam had to commit to be sent to this outpost.

"Why is there a mosque here?"

"This is where Musa saw the tree of fire." Shu'aib waved his palm across the area. "When he came to Jebel Musa." He pointed to a peak that looked like a thorn piercing the sky, exposed as they looked down a wide wadi.

"Musa saw the fire *here?*" Graham asked. "How do you know?"

"It is in the Qur'an."

Shu'aib leaned across Graham, opened the glove compartment, and pulled out a small bundle wrapped in a keffiyeh. He carefully unfolded the scarf to reveal a pocket edition of the Qur'an protected by a clear plastic slip case. As he riffled through the pages to the verse he was looking for, he kept the keffiyeh draped over his hands to prevent him from touching the pages with fingers that had not been washed first.

"Surah Al-Qasas, twenty-nine and thirty: 'Then, when Musa had fulfilled the term, and was traveling with his family, he saw a fire in the direction of Tur.'" Shu'aib annotated the text by pointing to Jebel al-Lawz. "He said to his family, 'Wait, I have seen a fire; perhaps I may bring to you from there some information, or a burning firebrand that you may warm yourselves.' So when he reached the fire, he was called from the right side of the valley, in the blessed place from the tree: 'O Musa! Verily! I am Allah, the Lord of all that exists!'"

"Yes," Graham said. "I know that verse, but how do you know it happened here?"

"It is here." Shu'aib nodded at the Qur'an. "Surah Al-Qasas, forty-four. 'And you,' that is Muhammad, 'were not on the *western side*, when We made clear to Musa the commandment, and you were not among those present.' This is the western side of the mountain. This is where Allah appointed Musa to be his prophet."

"But it says, '*not* on the western side.' Wouldn't that mean it was on the *eastern* side?" Graham realized this was as far as Shu'aib had intended to take them and hoped twisting the meaning of the words would steer the conversation to the other side of the mountain.

"No!" Shu'aib said forcefully. "It is here! Do not make words of the prophet say what they do not!"

"I'm sorry. *Ana 'aasif.* I did not mean to be disrespectful. I am embarrassed." Graham saw Shu'aib's confusion at the last word and translated it. "*Xajlaan.*"

Shu'aib responded with a single, cautious nod. "I take you

to Haql now."

"No!" This time the protest came from Sarah. "You can't!"

Shu'aib turned his head sharply and looked directly at Sarah for the first time, not trying to hide his contempt. "The woman does not know her place."

Graham released a heavy sigh, as if shedding their deceit. "Shu'aib, you have been very kind to us. I know you are a good man." He paused, letting the words stall Shu'aib's impulse as Graham tried to find a way to salvage the situation, deciding on full disclosure. "Please forgive her, my friend. She is very worried. Her nephew is lost on that mountain. He might be hurt, and he needs our help. We have come to find him."

"You lie!" Shu'aib spat the words furiously. "You tell me you were lost!"

"That was true." Graham gave a calming gesture. "We were lost. Our truck really did get stuck. But this is where we were trying to come. To rescue her nephew."

"Why did you not tell me this?" The edge in Shu'aib's voice softened a notch, though his scowl remained in place.

"We were scared. We could not come into your country properly. We didn't know if we could trust you. You might have taken us to jail."

"Why could you not come here?"

Graham felt the confrontation subsiding as Shu'aib seemed more interested in understanding what was happening.

"We are American. We live there. But we came to Israel before coming here. I work there sometimes. We have heard that your country does not allow people to enter if they have been to Israel because they could be spies. Even though we are not spies, we did not think we would be believed."

Shu'aib quickly glanced at Sarah and back to Graham. "Why did you not contact the police or the ministry and tell them about the nephew?"

"Because they might have thought *he* was a spy, which he isn't. We thought he would at least be arrested. So we came for him ourselves." As he spoke, Graham opened a picture he had taken of Alexander digitizing a manuscript at Saint Catherine's and held it up.

Shu'aib stared at the image and processed the news silently as Graham felt the tension dissolve. He felt a sympathetic smile form as he reminded himself Shu'aib's anger was—in the context of how devout he was—a rational emotion, consistent with his beliefs.

"He came only to see this mountain?" Shu'aib's normal tone had returned, though with caution.

"Yes," Graham said. "Because he thought this was where Musa had come."

"He is right."

"But most people don't know about it. They think the mountain is in Egypt or somewhere else. We didn't believe it either. But he heard about it and wanted to see it for himself. And we didn't know if anyone here really believed Musa had come here. We didn't think you would know what we were talking about. And if we asked you to take us to a special part of al-Lawz then we really would have sounded like spies. But then you told us about Musa and offered to show us where he'd been. It seemed like the best protection. Again, I am sorry for deceiving you. You have been very good to us."

Shu'aib studied each of them in turn, then craned to look toward the peak of the mountain. "You say he is on Jebel Musa. But what is there to see? The tablets of law are not there now."

"We think he was hoping to find the things that were left behind by the Jews when they camped here." Graham thought through the parallels in the Qur'an in order to avoid appealing to the Hebrew Bible as much as possible. "He thought the altar that held the statue of a calf made from ornaments would still be there. The one that Harun made," he added, using the name given to Aaron in the Qur'an.

"But it is nowhere here." Shu'aib looked at the mountain again as he slipped back into Arabic, speaking faster so that his words could keep pace with his thoughts. "There is no altar here. If the altar was still here, how would you know it was Harun's?"

Graham opened a picture of the bovine petroglyphs on his phone. Shu'aib leaned back in surprise, looked to Graham, then back again in a double take.

"Where did you get this picture?"

"Her nephew took it a few days ago. On the other side of the mountain."

"But that is not right. Why did he not come here, to this side?"

"Actually, he did." Graham scrolled to a picture of the Split Rock. "This is what he found. The rock Musa struck with a stick to make water come out."

"Surah Al-A'raf, one hundred and sixty," Sarah said, demurely.

Shu'aib looked at Sarah, but this time without indignation. He removed the Qur'an again and Shu'aib read aloud.

"And We divided them into twelve tribes as distinct nations. We directed Musa by inspiration, when his people asked him for water, saying: 'Strike the stone with your stick,' and there gushed forth out of it twelve springs: each group knew its own place for water."

Shu'aib looked at Sarah with a hint of respect, then turned to Graham. "You are saying *this* is the rock? That it is here?" Wonder now colored his voice.

"Down that wadi." Graham pointed to the left branch of the passage through the rocks leading toward the mountain.

"How do you know this way?"

Graham removed the GPS from a compartment in the right leg of his cargo pants. He showed him the waypoint on the screen, then pointed to where they were in relation to it.

"Eight and a half miles."

"I will take you there. If the rock is there, as you say, then I will help you find this nephew."

"And if it's not there?"

Shu'aib ignored the question as they started down the dirt track, leaving Graham to wonder what the terms of the wager were.

FORTY-SEVEN

At least a dozen tracks led into the wadi like loose threads unraveled between the rock walls, more traveled than Graham had suspected it would be. The slightly reddish dirt was like a distant geological echo of the Wadi Rum, where they had been a day earlier, though it felt like a year. On the other side of the first bend, the wadi opened up and the collection of threads frayed into capillaries in the rocky terrain.

After passing through another long canyon, they entered a wide expanse at least two miles long, broken by an archipelago of rocky hills. Halfway across, at the base of an island next to the main track, a rectangular white Bedouin tent stood out like a stray trailer home or shipping container.

"Should we ask them about Alexander?" Sarah leaned forward to get a better look through the windshield.

"Doesn't look like anyone is there," Graham said.

Shu'aib tacitly agreed, not slowing down.

Now that the GPS was no longer a secret, Graham tracked their progress, navigating them as he compared their location with their surroundings. The foothills of the range forced them to turn right, into another wide wadi that ran along the edge of the mountains they wanted to be on the other side of. The ninety-degree turn angled them directly at the peak of Jebel al-Lawz, less than ten miles away. But despite being closer to their goal than they had ever been, their attention was absorbed by what lay between it and them.

Even from a mile away, they could see that there was something unusual about the rock formation jutting into the air from the top of a hill of boulders. The tall boxy shape looked as if it had fallen from the sky and embedded in the ground like a missile. Something about it reminded Graham of the iconic monolith in *2001: A Space Odyssey*, despite its slight lean to the right.

"Oh my gosh," Sarah said, her voice just above a whisper. Is that it?

Shu'aib accelerated, giving a physical sensation to the growing excitement in the truck. Graham felt a collective awe bloom in the mix of emotions as the massive scale of the rock became clear. The hill it rose from was itself a hundred feet tall, giving the rock a pedestal that accentuated its towering presence.

Shu'aib guided the Patrol along a track that departed the sandy basin and climbed up the slope as far as he could. He got within five hundred feet, and they got out to hike the rest.

The hill grew steeper as they picked their way around boulders, up the mound to the surreal form. Graham deliberately picked a route that would let him look directly at the wide side that faced Jebel al-Lawz. From this perspective he decided the rock wasn't like the monolith in *2001* at all. It looked more like a long cloven hoof clawing out of the earth and onto the air, trying to escape a terrestrial prison. He estimated the massive rock was sixty feet tall, but the ground sloping down from the peak of the hill made it seem even taller, looming over him.

The split in the rock flared at the top, but was otherwise strangely uniform, making it appear—from a certain angle—like a needle of sky injecting the rock. The first explanation that came to Graham was that it was simply two rocks, improbably standing next to each other in a way that left a channel between them. But as he approached the base of the structure, he could see the division in the rock ended before it submerged beneath the surface. It was clearly one enormous slab of stone. His second theory was that the split was hewn, but when he stepped into the fissure—just wide enough to admit him—he couldn't find any telltale scars left from tools.

"What do you think?"

Graham had been so engrossed that he had almost forgotten he wasn't alone. He turned to answer Sarah, then stuttered when he saw she wasn't wearing any of the traditional clothes, but wore her hiking gear and sun hat instead.

"It's okay," she said, reading his eyes. "I doubt there are any *mutaween* here. Plus, we can see miles in every direction. If we see anyone coming, I'll cover up."

Graham glanced toward Shu'aib to see his reaction, but Shu'aib seemed too spellbound by the rock to notice or care about anything else. He circled the base, holding his palms against its surface, caressing it as he tilted his head up and down to take it all in, every motion slow, as if underwater. Graham could hear him whisper reverently to himself—like a prayer—but he couldn't make out any words.

"So, what do you think?" Sarah asked again.

"It's incredible," Graham said. "So much bigger than I thought it would be."

"Yeah, but what made it? Can you tell?"

"Well, I'm not a geologist, but look how smooth the surface of the rock is all around the base. And look at these furrows that run from here down the mound. Looks like water was here at some point. A lot of water."

"Okay, but where did the water come from?"

"Given that we're standing in a desert where the average annual rainfall is less than half an inch and given that all the signs of water I see lead away from this spot, I'd say it came from here." He kneeled down and touched the space at the bottom of the gap. "It's like this is some ancient geyser that's dried up."

Sarah knelt next to him with a skeptical look. "And happened to have a gigantic rock standing on its end covering its mouth and happened to build up so much pressure that it was powerful enough to cut fifty or sixty feet of granite."

"The naturalistic explanation does seem implausible, to say the least." Graham smirked, conceding her point. "You know, there is a rock at the traditional Sinai that is supposed to be the one Moses struck. And there's another near Petra. I've never been to either because neither of them look like they have a shred of credibility. But this thing...I don't know. If I try to imagine what it would have really looked like, my guess is that it was a lot like this."

"*Iinah rayie. Jamila.*" Shu'aib's voice rasped with wonder. *It is amazing. Beautiful.* "It is just as it says in Surah Al-A'raf. This is the place Musa come! This is why the nephew come?" He turned to look at Graham.

"Yes, but not just here. He mainly came to see the other side of Jebel al-Lawz." Graham looked at the mountain as if he could see through it. "Where Musa received the Law."

"Yes. Yes. We go!"

Shu'aib was now as insistent as they were, and Graham felt suddenly free of the circumstances that had been restraining them. Shu'aib flitted through the rocks, back to the truck before Graham could finish documenting the site with photos and video. Sarah stayed near Graham, staring through the monocular at Jebel al-Lawz, transfixed.

"What if he's not there?" Again, she showed her intuition for what he was thinking, revealing what was bothering her just before he could ask, like a conversation in reverse. "What do we do then? Look at this place. He could be *anywhere*. Lost. Or hurt."

"Sarah. Don't you remember where we are? We're at Massah and Meribah. That's what Moses named this place because the people were testing and arguing with God. After all God had done for them, after the plagues and the Red Sea, the people still doubted. And what was God's answer?" Graham stopped and pointed back to the rock. "You're looking at it. And if He can bring water from a rock, He can protect Alexander."

They continued down the hill in silence, and Graham hoped his words had quelled—or at least diluted—her doubts, that her thoughts weren't trapped in the same void his were when Aly was wasting away with cancer. The void between what God *could* do and what He *would* do.

FORTY-EIGHT

After rattling back through the valley, the asphalt of the highway felt like silk beneath the old Nissan, gliding across the surface as fast as Shu'aib could make it go.

They quickly covered the remainder of the distance to the junction that led east, around the northern end of the range. Fifteen miles later, Graham held the GPS for Shu'aib and pointed to a road about to appear on their right.

"The turn is coming up."

"No." Shu'aib kept shaking his head after the word, as if the sound were not enough to make his point. "Much danger there."

Graham glanced at Sarah then back at Shu'aib. "What danger?"

"Army base on top of the mountain. Many…" He paused as he searched for the word in English but failed and used the Arabic word. "*Sawarikh.*"

"Missiles," Sarah translated.

"What do we do?" Graham asked. "Is there another way?"

"We need gas," Shu'aib said. "There is a station soon. But do not get out of the truck. Be safe."

Graham looked at Sarah and mouthed *abaya*. She nodded quickly, telling him she had already thought of it. As he turned back around, Shu'aib pulled the keffiyeh from his head and handed it to him.

"You wear."

"Shukraan," Graham said. *Thank you.* He fit the scarf on his head and arranged it to cover as much of his face as he could.

Two gas stations appeared, flanking the road, and Shu'aib pulled into the one on the right, choosing the pump farthest from the door. They fueled quickly, needing only half a tank, but Shu'aib stayed inside for more time than it took to pay.

"What's taking so long?" Graham whispered aloud.

"Do you think he's reporting us?"

"I don't think so. He probably would have done it yesterday if that's what he wanted. And he seemed genuinely moved by the Split Rock."

Shu'aib appeared with three bottles of water, handing one to each after he was inside the truck.

"Did you have any problems?" Graham asked.

"I have learned the better way to the mountain. From a Bedouin."

Shu'aib picked up the GPS, his brow furrowing as he moved it back and forth. Graham pressed the button without taking it from him.

"Here." Shu'aib pointed at a wide wadi that opened behind the gas station, a large jag to the south that eventually cut west, back to the range.

Graham found the dirt track he was trying to get to from the military road and saw that it joined up with the route Shu'aib proposed.

"Much better," Shu'aib said, nodding in agreement with himself. "No guards to check."

Shu'aib drove around the back of the gas station, then between two buildings that shared the parking lot. On the other side, a track cut across an open area of desert for half a mile, directly into the mouth of the wadi. They followed the path as it clung to the east side of the canyon, and Graham was surprised at how well-traveled it was. Three large Bedouin camps nested in rocky coves, forming nomadic cul-de-sacs within the first two miles. Several smaller camps strewn along the wadi kept them from feeling completely isolated. After ten slow miles, the wadi bent to the west and Graham found the track from his route T-boned the one they were on.

"Seventeen miles from here," Graham said.

Shu'aib nodded, frowning with concentration. Graham knew he had some capital after the Split Rock, and hoped that if they didn't find Alexander, they would at least find something that would justify their effort to Shu'aib.

The wadi continued several miles through a widening basin, occasionally passing a long black Bedouin tent. Each had several four-by-four trucks and a flock of sheep nearby. They turned into a larger wadi and paralleled its west side, following the rock wall.

Graham wondered why the tracks didn't simply cut straight through the passage. Then he noticed the spindly scars of streambeds that made troughs in the desert floor and assumed that Bedouin had learned from experience that it was quicker and easier to skirt them than cut across them. That was—he remembered—the mistake he had made that got their truck stuck.

Deep hollows in the rock walls sheltered Bedouin tents, some including enclosures for sheep. A number of inlets were scarred with tire tracks disappearing into them. To camps deeper in, Graham assumed. The wadi contracted slowly as they passed through it, and the road grew more rough and wavy. It was as if the mountain sensed their coming and was warning them off while paradoxically enveloping them.

The GPS continued to track their progress, impressively clinging to a signal in the remote canyon. He saw they were coming to the point where the wadi turned south to take them the final six miles.

Two miles after the turn, the wadi opened up to give them their first clear view of Jebel al-Lawz, shooting out of the desert floor, rising 8,000 feet above sea level. Just as in the pictures, the peak of the mountain appeared to be cloaked in shadow despite the cloudless sky. Sarah leaned low onto the console between the front seats, angling the monocular at the peak.

"There it is," Graham said, as if making a note to himself as he pointed.

"No. No," Shu'aib said, pointing to the next peak to the north. "*That* is Jebel al-Lawz." He swept his finger back to the dark mountain, on the same ridge, separated by about two miles. "*That* is Jebel al-Maqla. Black mountain is Maqla."

Graham remembered being confused by the reports he'd read. Some people said al-Lawz had a black peak, others said it had a twin peak that was black, and still others treated them as different mountains altogether. Now that he was looking at it himself, he could see merit in each description. He reconciled it by thinking of Jebel al-Lawz as the proper name of the mountain and that it had a twin peak named Maqla that was the main focus for those who believed this was Sinai.

The wadi shrank to about a hundred yards wide, and the track wove through spurs of rock that clawed out from the mountain, forcing the road to snake around them. They continued to pass Bedouin encampments, some of which were small communities with fenced zones for goats or a crop.

As Shu'aib guided the truck through the narrowest split they'd encountered the entire journey, he skidded to an abrupt stop, blocked by a herd of goats. On the far side of the animals, a Bedouin ushered them away from Jebel al-Lawz with a leisurely wave of his staff.

Shu'aib stepped out of the truck as the goatherd picked his way through the flock.

"Assalam allah alaykum." He offered the greeting, wishing God's peace upon the man as he held his hand over his heart.

"Wa alaykum a salaam." The goatherd returned both the gesture and greeting.

"We are looking for Jebel Musa."

"Jebel Musa huna," the Bedouin answered, saying it was here. He tilted forward and added a phrase Graham couldn't make sense of.

"He said we must be careful," Sarah said softly.

"Careful of what?"

As if in answer to Graham, the man walked Shu'aib to a spot where they could see around the corner, down the wadi. The goatherd pointed to several locations as he explained something, but they had moved beyond hearing range. After the exchange, Shu'aib stole a cautious glance down the direction they had just come from as he walked back to Graham's window.

"He says there is danger here. Soldiers come here, to…" His English failed him, and he fell back into Arabic. *"Bayt alharasa."*

"Guardhouse," Sarah whispered over Graham's shoulder.

"They here much time," Shu'aib finished.

"Why are they here?"

Shu'aib turned away from the truck and repeated the question.

The Bedouin suddenly made a strange hushing noise and waved his hands in front of him as if to wipe away the sound, then touched his ears. The rough purr of a truck engine chewed the silence, distant but growing louder. Shu'aib ran to the driver's side, jumped in, and started the Patrol. The man pointed behind them and to their right, into a branch of the wadi, and Shu'aib took the cue. He swung the truck around the outcrop of rock, and into the Bedouin's camp. Shu'aib pulled as close to the wall as he could and cut the engine.

After they stopped, Graham was surprised to see the Bedouin had run alongside the truck and was standing by the back of the Nissan, bent forward, alert and listening.

Less than a minute later, they heard the engine slow as the unseen truck stopped, blocked by the goats. Impatient honks bruised the air accompanied by angry shouts, creating a cacophony that left the goats unimpressed. Graham extracted a couple of words as they ricocheted off the canyon wall, calling for someone to come get their goats.

The Bedouin feinted forward then stopped himself before finally trotting back to his flock in small steps that made him look like he was moving quickly, but without speed.

"Ana 'aasif. Ana 'aasif."

Graham heard the man apologize and pictured him hustling the goats from the road.

"Min fadlik. 'Afwan. Assalam allah alaykum." Please. Excuse me. God's peace upon you. The engine revved in mechanical annoyance as the truck started moving again, then faded back into the desert.

"Junud." The Bedouin hurried back to the Nissan, combining complaint and explanation into a single word. *Soldiers.* *"When I was a boy, they were not here. They did not bother us."* Now that the Bedouin was close to the truck, Graham was able to better understand his Arabic. *"You go now. They will be back. And they do not—"*

"Have you seen a young man?"

The Bedouin flinched at the sound of Sarah's voice, then took an indignant step back as she got out of the truck.

"American. He was here a few days ago. Please tell me."

The Bedouin continued to stare at her, frozen in judgment.

Graham moved next to Sarah, trying to show solidarity while feeling certain the mission had suddenly failed. He scrambled to invent a reason the man would accept for the impropriety. But if the Bedouin were mutaween, no reason could justify the violation of the code of morality.

Before he could make an appeal, the man's face began to thaw, spreading to the rest of him. Something in her voice—a pleading tone, anxious and pained—must have penetrated the brute boundaries of the law to soften the offense. Graham sensed that the goatherd was a good man.

"*Yes. American. He was here.*" The Bedouin answered uncomfortably.

"*Do you know what happened to him?*" Graham's Arabic was so quick that Graham barely caught it.

"*Soldiers. They took him.*" The man motioned toward Jebel al-Lawz.

Panic detonated in Graham's chest, setting on fire what had been frozen a moment earlier. "When?" He realized he had asked reflexively in English, then asked again in Arabic. "*Mataa?*"

"*Three or four days.*" The Bedouin's expression grew more concerned, mirroring theirs without knowing why. "*He is family?*"

Sarah nodded emphatically. "*Na'am.*"

"*Where did they take him?*" Graham asked.

The goatherd shook his head, then explained he didn't know because he hadn't seen it himself. Someone from their tribe had seen it and had told the others about it, that the soldiers arrested the American. And where they had found him.

Graham tried to hide his reaction to the location. He wasn't sure he had understood correctly when the Bedouin said *where* Alexander had been arrested. "*What is the golden camel?*"

FORTY-NINE

The goatherd shot a look at Shu'aib, incredulous, then frowned at Graham. "It is a very old story. A calf made of gold is buried near the mountain."

Graham mirrored Sarah's face, a mix of excitement and concern. "I thought he said *camel* at first."

"He did," Sarah said, her voice low and calm as she peered down the range. "A calf is the offspring of a camel. It's here. *We're here.* Pray that Xander is still here, too."

After thanking the man and returning to the truck, Shu'aib backed out of the hiding place and angled toward the direction they had come from.

"Shu'aib, what are you doing?" Graham pointed across the cab of the truck. "Other way."

"Did you not hear?" Shu'aib said, hitting the brake to look directly at Graham. "It is too dangerous."

"That is exactly *why* we have to go. Because of her nephew. But I cannot expect you to put yourself at risk." Graham found his wallet and removed a sheaf of riyals. "Here. Baksheesh. For all you have done."

Shu'aib looked at the money without moving.

"It's okay." Graham pushed the cash toward Shu'aib. "We will walk. We're almost there."

"It is too far. There is no place to hide." The voice of the

Bedouin was followed by his appearance on the other side of Shu'aib's open window. "If the soldiers are there, you will be seen."

Shu'aib nodded as he listened, then added another reason. "It will not be right to the soldiers that you are not in a truck." He paused long enough for Graham to wonder again if they had come so far only to fail, thwarted by someone trying to help.

"No." Shu'aib gave a single resolute nod. "I will take you. I will drive close. Then we will hide the truck until you can see what you came for. Take you away safe."

"Thank you, Shu'aib." Graham placed his hand over his heart. "You are a good friend."

The Bedouin left them, repeating the blessing that God's peace be upon them. But as they turned into the wadi and began the final mile and a half, Graham was anything but peaceful.

The unexpected sight of a power line ran down the left side of the wadi, reminding him of running an extension cord from his house to a tent whenever he'd camped in the backyard as a kid. He hadn't noticed it until they were stopped by the goats and assumed it serviced the guard shack.

A small white box about the size of a single-car garage sat on the right side of the valley, a quarter of a mile off the track. The mountain's immense scale dwarfed the structure, making it look like a faulty pixel in a digitally rendered landscape of a barren planet. Tire tracks split off from the path, connecting it to the shed. Even from a distance, he recognized the guard post from the photos. A fifteen-foot-tall chain-link fence topped with strands of razor wire separated the area from the rest of the valley, blocking access to a tributary wadi near the base of the mountain. Looming over the valley was Jebel al-Lawz, the spot where Alexander's phone last touched the outside world. And—possibly—where God Himself once touched the world with a fearful presence.

Graham stared at the shack as they drew closer, watching for soldiers to emerge.

"Think anyone's in there?" Sarah whispered.

"I don't think so," Graham said. "There are no trucks. And I doubt anyone stays there. Too small."

A cluster of buildings—a dozen or so—flanked the road, obscuring the guard post as they passed between them. Some were no larger than garden sheds. The larger ones looked more like warehouses in an industrial park. Two small fields of crops pushed themselves up from the ground, giving the place the feel of an improbable pioneer town.

"None of this was here when Wyatt discovered this place," Graham said. "It was completely deserted." He wondered what the permanent residency meant, given that it was a place no one had lived since the Jews may have camped there three-and-a-half millennia earlier.

"It is not right," Shu'aib said. "There are no people."

"It's like a ghost town," Sarah agreed.

"Or a movie set," Graham added.

"Maybe no one actually lives here." Sarah leaned over the seat, peering ahead. "It could be some agricultural station. An experiment or lab or something like that."

"You might be right. Or maybe the earth opened up and swallowed them like Korah." Graham chuckled, then looked back at Sarah after getting no acknowledgement. "You know, from the book of Numbers. That was God's punishment after Korah rebelled against Moses."

The unnerving atmosphere of abandonment had a kind of empty presence, and Graham realized they may have—after a fashion—followed Korah into the void. After all, with the exception of Yaniv, no one knew where they had gone, to where they had disappeared. But as a Jew who was an official in the Israeli government, Graham doubted the Saudis would pay much attention to Yaniv if he raised the alarm. Even more likely, the missing person report would be treated as a case of espionage, putting them in even more danger. At this point, they were on their own.

"I thought getting here would be the hard part," Graham said, almost to himself. "Now what?"

As they passed the main group of buildings on their right, the chain-link fence became visible again, closing off the half-mile-wide mouth of the wadi that cut into the mountain. For the first time, Graham looked in— the area that—according to believers in the site—still held the altar made by Moses. They referred to it as the Holy Precinct, a name borrowed from descriptions of the inner court of the Temple, where the sacrifices were made.

"Shu'aib, that's where her nephew's cell phone was." Graham pointed into the restricted area. "The other side of the fence. See how close you can get us."

Shu'aib turned off the track to follow a faint impression of tires. The trail led toward a family of hills that formed a spur at the end of the Holy Precinct. After navigating to the southern tip of the hill, Shu'aib parked behind a small bluff that concealed the truck from the track as well as the guardhouse.

They got out of the car and found the fence fifty yards away, at the bottom of a gentle hill that ended at the near side of a dry streambed.

"Look at that!"

Graham spied what Sarah spotted as she said the words. A section of fence lay almost flat on the ground, two of its poles bent inward toward the mountain as if bowing to it.

"Tire marks," Shu'aib said, sounding more intrigued than fearful. "Someone has driven over it."

To their right, less than a quarter of a mile away, Graham studied the guardhouse, hoping his stare wasn't being returned.

Before they left Aqaba, Graham had entered waypoints for each landmark based on the accounts he had read. Now he compared what he was looking at to the GPS to see where they were in relation to what was supposed to be evidence of Mount Sinai. Wyatt and others had said there were boundary markers—evenly spaced piles of stones about four feet high—along the entrance to the Holy Precinct. According to the GPS, one of the markers was on the north end of the hill that shielded them, but was exposed to the guard shack, making it impossible to investigate until they learned whether there were soldiers present.

He scanned to the left, stopping at a waypoint obscured by the foothill of the mountain that formed the south side of the wadi. If the coordinates were correct, he was half a mile from the alleged altar of Moses.

"This is the mountain that turned to dust?" Shu'aib was looking to the top of the black peak, apparently doing the same thing as Graham—trying to reconcile what he had been told with what he saw.

"I don't understand." Graham glanced at Shu'aib then followed his eyes up the side of Maqla.

"Surah 7, verse 143. When Musa came here, he asked to see Allah. Allah said: 'You cannot see Me, but look upon the mountain if it stands still in its place then you shall see Me.' When Allah came down and touched the mountain, it collapsed to dust. Musa collapsed also. When he woke up, he gave praise to Allah and became the first of believers."

"That is when he was given the tablets of the law," Sarah said.

"No," Shu'aib said firmly. "Not *law*."

"The lesson to be drawn from all things and the explanation of all things," Sarah said evenly, using the Qur'an's description of what was on the tablets. "And when he came down from the mountain, he found the people had made the calf."

"Yes, yes," Shu'aib said, satisfied. He looked down into the Holy Precinct, surveying the area. "Where is the rock with the calf?"

Graham twisted around and pointed in the opposite direction. "Over there, behind its own fence. About a half a mile away. We would have gone right to it if we hadn't turned off the main track."

"Where's the spot Xander's phone pinged?" Sarah scanned the mountain again as if expecting to see him through the monocular.

Graham checked the GPS, then pointed to a bluff over-looking the location of the V-shaped altar. From their per-spective, it looked like the top of the mountain, but the satel-lite image revealed it was the edge of a plateau. "Somewhere on the other side of that first rise. Near the top of it. The altar of Musa should be at the—Sarah!"

The name scratched the air, a hoarse scream cast at Sarah's back as he watched her hop through the opening in the fence and cross to the other side. She crouched behind a boulder blocking her from the guardhouse while staying within their line of vision.

"What is it she is doing?" Shu'aib's worried face intensi-fied.

"Saving her nephew," Graham said, detached in thought. Sarah had just run past the boundary markers God placed to keep people off the mountain. And anyone who crossed them and touched the mountain was to be executed. He prayed his theology was correct, that the laws governing the nation of Israel were no longer in force. He gave Shu'aib an apologetic look, glanced at the guardhouse, and ran.

FIFTY

Graham slid to a stop in the loose rock after covering the two-hundred-yard span, Shu'aib close behind. The two men looked at each other, panting in conspiracy.

"Shu'aib, we do not want to make trouble for you." A gulp of air broke Graham's sentence in half. "You do not need to come with us."

"I must see if it is true." Shu'aib held Graham's eyes earnestly. "If Allah wills it."

Graham nodded, then he pulled out the GPS and estimated the sight line of the guardhouse. It had apparently been positioned to detect visitors approaching from the north, the route they had arrived from. The vantage left a blind spot in the part of the wadi containing the western half of the Holy Precinct.

"If we can get down the other side of this hill, we'll be out of sight from the guardhouse," Graham said. "About three hundred yards."

Sarah had been studying the screen at the same time, and again started to the next point before he finished.

Graham checked the guardhouse as he crossed the top of the hill, then slipped down the scree into the dry streambed at the southern edge of the wadi. He clambered up the far side, glanced again to his right to confirm he couldn't see the sentry post, then tried to process what stood in front of him.

Stacked stone walls a foot thick stood waist-high off the ground, conspicuous by their ordered construction. The majority of rocks were the size of bowling balls, and most were the same tan color as the mountain, though dark stones gave it a speckled surface. From his perspective at ground level, the V-shape was not obvious. The structure was in excellent condition for possibly being thirty-five hundred years old and constructed without mortar. Graham was surprised at how much larger it looked in real life compared with the photos. Three long parallel walls created a pair of corridors about twenty feet wide, open at the end nearest him. He stepped into the right channel as Sarah stepped into the other, sharing an expression that was equal parts wonder and analytical.

He counted his strides as he walked the passage, examining the stacked stone. Sixty feet from the end, the walls angled forty-five degrees to the right and ran another sixty feet, forming a chevron shape. He followed it to a narrow wall, on the other side of which the remains of several walls divided the space into irregular chambers.

"What are these round rocks?"

Graham looked back to see Shu'aib standing on the outside of the far end of the chevron, in the middle of what looked like medallions of white stone the size of end tables.

"Those must be the marble pillars." Graham took a picture, documenting the location of the white rocks in relation to the walls, then joined Shu'aib. He knelt next to one of the stones and thought about how to answer as he used his forearm to take measurements. The white marble was unlike anything else they had seen in the area. Each stone was eighteen to twenty-four inches across, but differed in height, the smallest standing eight inches, the tallest just over two feet. They were scattered around the area at the entrance near the V-shape, and several of them were on their sides. He found two or three flat, rectangular rocks almost flush with the ground and wondered if they were foundation stones that once held the pillars. One of the explorers who had written about al-Lawz had counted twelve of them. Wyatt said there were at least ten. After scanning the surroundings, Graham counted only nine.

"What are the pillars?" Shu'aib asked.

"In the Hebrew Bible, after the people entered the covenant with God, Moses—Musa—built an altar and set up twelve standing stones or pillars next to it."

"Why would he do that?"

"No one is sure." Graham shrugged. "Some people think they stand for the twelve tribes of Israel, that Musa sprinkled them with blood when the covenant was made. It was how the people made a promise to God after He called them."

Shu'aib squinted in confusion. "I do not understand."

"God promised to bless them if they kept His law. But if they didn't, then they were cursed to have their blood spilled."

Shu'aib looked at the pillars, as if for confirmation. "Whose blood was it that was used?"

"The blood of young bulls." As he said it, an explanation fell into place, lighting up his face. He pointed back to Sarah, who was standing on the berm at the far side of the chevron, looking into the formation. "Probably killed over there. Come. Let me show you."

Graham led Shu'aib to where Sarah was, giving them a view of the V-shape and the pit where it ended.

Sarah waved a hand over the site. "This is from *al-Jáhili-yya*." She glanced at Graham and saw that he didn't understand. "The Time of Ignorance, before Islam."

"It could be the treasury," Shu'aib said.

"What makes you think it could be a treasury?" Graham wondered what Shu'aib's Bedouin eyes saw that his did not.

"Because of Kárún," Shu'aib said. "The cousin of Musa.

He would need somewhere to keep his gold."

"I'm sorry Shu'aib, but I don't know what you are talking about."

"You do not know the story?" Shu'aib frowned in surprise. "Kárún was very poor. But the sister of the prophet, Kulsum, taught him how to turn metal into gold."

"Alchemy?" Sarah said, brow raised.

"I do not know that word."

"*Kiamya*," she tried again.

"Ah. Yes, *kiamya*," Shu'aib nodded. "It is said the keys to the treasure alone filled the packs of forty mules! His house had doors and a roof of gold!"

"And you think this is the palace?" Graham eyed the stone chevron.

"He had to have a treasury for his gold. Maybe this could be it. Maybe part of it."

"What happened to Kárún?" asked Sarah.

"He became very proud of his riches and he taunted Musa with his wealth. Musa prayed to Allah, and the earth opened up and swallowed Kárún and his family."

Graham realized why Shu'aib hadn't understood his *Korah* reference earlier. "Interesting."

"Yes, yes," Shu'aib said with a quick smile of satisfaction. "Very ancient story. Everyone knows."

Graham found his phone and opened a PDF. "The Saudi Department of Antiquities looked at this place. Their report didn't say anything about a treasury, unfortunately, Shu'aib. They said this building was where workers lived and kept their equipment. There's supposed to be a quarry up on the mountain."

"Makes sense to me," Sarah said. "But I get the feeling you don't buy it. What are you seeing?"

"It's what I'm not seeing that bothers me," Graham said. "This is a very impractical shape for a building that's supposed to house a bunch of workers, don't you think?"

"Now that you say so, yes."

"And there doesn't seem to be any indication the walls went much higher or have any place to support a roof."

"Okay." Sarah drew the word out in anticipation.

Graham traced the halls of the building in the air with his finger. "I think this is a chute that animals were led down to where they were slaughtered."

"How can that be?" Shu'aib looked as confused by the explanation as Graham had been by the treasury theory.

"The V-shape keeps the animal—the ox or the sheep or whatever—from seeing what is about to happen to them. They can be controlled more easily that way."

"I see it now." Sarah nodded. "Some slaughterhouses are built like this even today." She must have noticed the strange look on Graham's face because she went on to explain. "The animal rights activists at USC sometimes have protest posters with pictures from inside a slaughterhouse. And now that you point it out, the idea makes sense. But why is it divided down the middle?"

"I was trying to figure that out," Graham said. "Maybe the animal would be on one side and the priest leading it to the altar would be on the other."

"But there is no altar here." Shu'aib skimmed the area around him to make his point.

"Actually, you're standing on it."

Both Shu'aib and Sarah took a step back, glancing down as if where they stood was suddenly hot.

"Musa made it by stacking rocks that were not cut into shape. It was also near a stream." Graham pointed to the dry bed they had crossed, which ran past the structure. "And it was at the foot of the mountain. All those things are true about this platform." He tapped his foot on the packed dirt held in place by the stone walls.

"But the Jews cannot be trusted." Shu'aib was starting to sound agitated. "The Bible has changed."

Graham didn't want to get into a debate about textual criticism when there were more important things to do. But he couldn't let the comment pass without some sort of correction. "Shu'aib, there are copies of the story that were written down during the time of Isa." He used Jesus's Arabic name to make his point. "During the Time of Ignorance. That is far older than the tradition about the treasury." He looked at Sarah, hoping he used the phrase correctly.

A frown continued to pull at Shu'aib's face as he processed the information.

"And if the story is true and this is the place in Exodus, it doesn't necessarily mean that Islam is false. We are *uhl kitab*, people of the book." Graham tried to keep his debate voice in its cage as he appealed to the distinction Muslims made between those who were Jews and Christians, and those who rejected the idea of God's revealed word altogether. "Musa *is* a prophet in Islam, after all."

"Peace be upon him," Shu'aib said with a bow.

Graham looked back at the Saudi report, then compared it to the area again. The space in front of the alleged altar was divided by a knee-high wall to create two passages.

"The Saudis dug down into the ground in this area," he said, pointing to the left. "Just below the surface they found a deep layer of ash."

"Did the building burn?" Shu'aib's voice had softened, curious again.

"There is no evidence of that anywhere else. Given what this place might be, it's probably where they dumped the ash after making a burnt offering. The report also says they dug into the ground in one of the chutes. It says they found the floor three feet down, and they found some potsherds."

"Really?" Sarah moved next to him and looked at the

phone. "Did they date them?"

"Nabatean era. First century AD."

"But that doesn't make sense if this is the altar of Moses. I mean Musa," Sarah corrected.

"It doesn't have to be one or the other," Graham said. "Just because Musa built it doesn't mean people fifteen hundred years later wouldn't use it for shelter."

"That makes sense."

"What doesn't make sense is that when they found the pottery, they also found a layer of animal waste over a foot thick. If this really was a dormitory—as they say—why would *that* be in the house?"

"Couldn't the remains be Nabatean as well?" Sarah asked.

"I'm not sure they can tell something like that." Graham scrolled the report to a diagram of the building. "Hmmm." He glanced up to the ruins, then down again. "That's strange. The drawing doesn't match what's actually here. It shows the start of the chutes—the place where we entered—as being walled in. In fact, the plan shows thresholds or openings where there are none, and no thresholds where some clearly are." Graham examined the area around him. "And the whole area where we are standing is completely wrong."

"It's like it's intentionally wrong," Sarah said, again looking over his shoulder at the document on the screen. "Makes you wonder about the rest of the report."

"Yes, it does." Graham was lost in thought as he looked at the GPS screen, then looked toward the peak of Jebel al-Maqla. "But what we really need to do is climb up this side of the mountain. That's where Alexander's phone pinged."

FIFTY-ONE

Without the distraction of the archaeological site, the air was suddenly thick with heat. Graham led the way, trying not to kick loose rock onto the others behind. When they reached the top of the first incline, they plopped onto a large rock to catch their breath.

"I'm totally baking." Sarah pinched the front of her shirt, tenting it to vent the hot air trapped in her clothes. "It's like the earth has a fever and I'm the germ it's trying to kill."

Graham gave her a half-smile, then looked out over the Holy Precinct. Even from a third of the way up the first bluff, he was impressed with the scope of the area. It was the way he had expected to feel at the traditional Mount Sinai but hadn't. The area at the base of the mountain was enormous—far bigger than the sense he got from the satellite photo. Graham had no trouble imagining two million people camped on the far side of the Holy Precinct. He looked southeast and tried to make out the mound of rocks that was supposed to be the altar of the golden calf. He borrowed the monocular from Sarah, lifted it to his eye, and found the fence surrounding the mound at the foot of a huge hill. Below him, the V-shape of the altar was now obvious, like an arrowhead impaling the gray streambed. From here, the small stone pillars flecked the ground.

"It's easy to imagine that this was what Moses—Musa—saw as he came down the mountain with the law." Graham handed the monocular back, then documented the view with photos and a few videos.

"I shall turn away from my verses those who behave arrogantly on the earth, without a right, and even if they see all the evidences, they will not believe in them." Shu'aib stared into the basin below as he spoke aloud to himself. "It is what Allah told Musa when he gave the tablets."

"After the mountain collapsed," said Sarah. "Surah Al-A'raf."

"Yes. '*Those who deny our evidences, vain are their deeds.*'"

Graham agreed with the verse silently, though not in the same way Shu'aib did.

"I just wonder if Xander saw this view as well." Worry had returned to Sarah's voice.

"We know he did. The pictures he took prove that."

"How close are we to where the phone pinged?"

"This is right about where the area starts," Graham said. "It's not like it tells the precise point on the earth. The signal was only able to provide about a three-quarter mile area. And we're on the edge of it. It goes to the top of the bluff."

"How are we going to search it?" Sarah sounded as if she were fighting to control her emotions. "We can't just walk up and down the mountain."

"I agree." Graham hoped his calm was reassuring despite thinking the same thing. "But when he climbed the mountain, he probably chose the easiest route in front of him, just as we are doing. That gives us a good chance of following in his steps. Let's just keep going and be on the lookout for the phone. Or anything else that was his."

Sarah bobbed her head nervously, unable to shake the anxiety from her face.

Graham led the way again as they ascended the next third

of the hill, scouring the ground around him as he went. It occurred to him that a little over a week earlier he had been climbing the other Mount Sinai, the pretender. *It may not have been the real location, but at least it had steps.* Graham reminded himself that God ordered the steps that had brought him here as well. Steps that had begun when Nebuchadnezzar sacked Lachish, leaving behind a communiqué on a shard of pottery. Even more improbably, the steps were being shared with a woman he was beginning to suspect could reawaken a part of him that he thought had died with Olivia. He had resolved that if he couldn't have Olivia's light, he would keep the dark she left behind untouched. But now—

"Someone comes!" Shu'aib pointed up the wadi toward where the goats had blocked their way.

Graham squinted with effort to see what had alerted Shu'aib, but his eyes weren't good enough to be sure.

"He's right," Sarah said, aiming the monocular farther away than Graham had been looking. "I can see a pillar of dust being kicked up." She handed the monocular to Graham. "What do we do?"

"Let's just stay here. I doubt they'll notice us unless we move."

"No!" Shu'aib said. "We go now!" He turned away from them and started scurrying down the mountain, apparently assuming they would follow.

"Shu'aib, don't!" Graham said, trying to make a lightning calculation for how far away the white thobe would stand out against the rocks. "They'll see you!"

They were high enough on the slope to watch a truck thread the final switchback and start toward the Holy Precinct. It disappeared behind a foothill that stood between them and the road, then reappeared as it pulled up to the gate near the guardhouse—a utilitarian pickup painted the color of the desert.

"I think it's military," Graham said, looking through the monocular.

He scanned to the right and found the thobe bobbing down the hill, totally exposed to the valley. "Shu'aib, hide! *Iikhfa'! Iikhfa'!*"

He pivoted back to the truck and watched a man in desert fatigues exit the passenger side to open the gate. The man walked the rest of the way to the shack as the truck pulled up and parked next to the building. A shiver of fear passed through Graham, feeling cold despite the heat. "Must be the guards. They're going in."

He handed the monocular to Sarah, then looked down at Shu'aib, who was waiting for Graham to notice him. Shu'aib hooked his arm through the air twice, gesturing for them to join him. Graham shook his head emphatically and held up his palm, trying to warn Shu'aib not to move.

"I wonder if this is what happened to Xander," Sarah whispered. "If those soldiers found him and took him somewhere."

"Maybe. But if they did, I think you would have heard from the embassy."

"He could be in there right now." Sarah poked the air twice in the direction of the shack, in sync with the last two words.

"I was thinking the same thing. We need to wait for them to leave, then see what's in there."

They stared at the guardhouse as if it were the only thing on the landscape and fell into a trance of anticipation that made it difficult to gauge time.

Graham's perspective changed, and he became focused on the view. The valley—like all the hills that formed it—was smeared in tans and browns, treeless and grassless, like a part of the world left unfinished, or even abandoned. Often Graham saw theological truths in the world, like another layer of reality that could be seen only from certain angles. And the view he now had was one of them. Regardless of whether or not this was the true Sinai, the thought of God—whose perfect excellence made Him the source and reference point of beauty itself—descending to one of the most inhospitable and ugly places in His creation was a picture of His love. *Sinai is a picture of me,* Graham thought, *of my heart. Dead and hopeless, but for the grace of God.*

Sarah's voice startled him from his reverie. "When you told me about James L. Starkey, how he might have been killed because he had evidence that led to this place, I confess I didn't believe it. It didn't make sense that the Saudi Arabian government would station soldiers to guard a mountain that might be the site of something so important to the Jews. Yet, here we are." She opened her palm, as if presenting a prize on a game show. "And you think it might even go back to Muhammad himself, that he tried to hide this place?"

"That was my theory. But believe me, I'm just as stunned as you. I could spend the rest of my career investigating this place."

As he spoke, Sarah raised the monocular and pointed it up the wadi.

"There's another cloud of dust." Sarah turned her face toward Graham in alarm. "Someone else is coming!"

Graham looked for Shu'aib, hoping he wasn't moving, but saw he had descended again.

"Shu'aib!" Graham whispered harshly, hoping the Holy Precinct's amphitheater shape didn't carry his voice too far. When Shu'aib turned to face back up the mountain, Graham pointed into the distance. "Truck! Do not move."

"SUV," Sarah said, handing him the monocular. "Doesn't look military, though."

Graham tracked the truck through the wadi and watched it branch off the track toward the guardhouse.

"More soldiers?" Sarah asked.

"Not sure yet," Graham said as the SUV pulled through the gate and stopped next to the pickup.

Two men draped in thobes got out and slid rifles onto their shoulders.

"They don't look military, but they do have guns."

He waited until the men were inside the shack, then stole a look down the slope and saw that Shu'aib hadn't moved. The cold shock of fear had dissipated, and again Graham felt the oppressive temperature. Despite the alarms going off in his head, he felt the drowsiness of heat, like his body was moving in the opposite direction from his racing mind.

"What do you think they're doing in there?"

Sarah's question broke the spell that Graham realized he'd fallen into again—a daze in which seconds, minutes, and hours didn't exist. It surprised him that he wasn't sure how long the men had been inside.

"I don't know, but we have got to get out of the sun soon. There they are." As if on cue, the two thobes reappeared, triggering Graham to snap the monocular in place. "One of them is carrying something. A box. About the size of a milk crate, I think, but not as tall."

He handed her the monocular and she watched until the truck disappeared up the wadi.

"So what was that?" she said, turning to Graham. "I doubt it was Federal Express or somethi—"

Splinters of rock pelted them, instantly followed by a loud crack. Graham jerked toward the sound just as another cloud of pulverized rock puffed from the mountain below them, along with another brittle pop. Close to Shu'aib.

"Get down!" he screamed in a whisper to Sarah, pulling her with him. "They're shooting at us!"

FIFTY-TWO

"What do we do?" Sarah's eyes went wide with panic.

A third shot clapped the air and she flinched reflexively, crouching lower in answer to her own question. "We haven't done anything!"

"Besides trespass after entering the country illegally." Graham scoured the area around them, looking for an escape route or at least a safer place to hide. He pulled out the GPS to see what was above them and how far they were from the crest of the bluff.

"It's too dangerous," Sarah said, guessing what he was thinking. "We should stay here."

"That might be exactly what they want. To keep us here while one of them sneaks around to get a better angle on us so we'll be pinned down. Or maybe they called for other guards to come and are trying to keep us here until then."

Sarah simultaneously shook her head and shrugged. "But where do we go?"

"The top of the bluff is about two hundred yards away. If we can get there, then we can go south to the wadi that comes down the mountain and runs past the altar. It's deep enough to be able to hide us from—"

The rumble of a boulder careening down the mountain came from below. Two shots chased the sound, but this time there was no sign of impact. Graham slowly pushed himself up enough to glimpse Shu'aib and found him staring back, apparently waiting for Graham to chance a look. Shu'aib pointed to his chest, then mimed pushing a rock down the hill. He turned his finger to Graham, then pointed to the top of the hill. Graham nodded in return and slid back down.

"Apparently Shu'aib has the same idea."

"You saw him? He's okay?"

"So far. He pushed a boulder down to draw attention away from us. He's going to push another one down. When he does, we're going to move farther up the mountain while they're distracted. Get ready to run."

"But won't they—"

Another rumble interrupted her.

"Now!" Graham rasped, pulling Sarah from her crouch as he began clambering up the slope.

A rifle coughed almost immediately, followed by two more in quick succession, a pause, then a fourth, like a pattern for a secret knock. Graham kept churning upward, blindly ducking after each shot as he panted with fear and exertion. Each report jolted his nerves, and the detached part of him waited for the pain, wondering what—if anything—it would feel like.

But pain never came. No bursts of dirt exploded with a thump as the mountain absorbed the bullets.

Graham crouched behind an outcrop as soon as the salvo had stopped. "You okay?" he gasped, struggling to form the simple words.

Sarah inhaled audibly before answering. "Yeah. What about Shu'aib?"

A tumbling rock sounded from far down the slope.

"C'mon!"

Graham scrambled up again, following the outcrop that shielded them. When it dropped away, they were near the base of a cliff more than a hundred feet tall. A slap of despair temporarily blinded him to the solution that appeared along with the problem. A lone tree—the only one he had seen on the mountain—stood between two monolithic rocks at the top of the cliff. He recognized the landmark and grasped the significance of where they were. He dropped his eyes to the bottom of the cliff and found what he expected—a trapezoidal void fifteen feet tall and twenty feet wide, directly in front of them.

Another pair of shots sounded. Graham sprang up the escarpment, covering the twenty-five yards to the cave. Again, the anticipation of being hit made the distance seem longer despite his frenzied effort. But like the last few bursts, no bullets landed around them. Sarah slid into the cave and flattened herself next to him on her stomach after pivoting around, positioning herself to see down the mountain.

"The soldiers must think we're running down the hill." Graham huffed as he spoke, awkwardly dividing the words. "I think that's what Shu'aib was trying to make them think."

"But now we're trapped."

"Only if they saw us," Graham said. "I couldn't tell where they were aiming the last few shots."

He felt himself teetering on the edge of another heat-induced reverie and shook away his musings by reaching for the monocular. The soldiers were no longer next to the guardhouse. He swept the area searching for them and spotted the truck moving past the Holy Precinct. Shu'aib appeared in the lens, walking into the open area of the main wadi on the other side of where they had hidden the truck. He held his hands high in the air as he trotted along the track, toward the soldiers.

"The soldiers found Shu'aib. He almost made it back to the truck."

"Is he hurt?" Sarah touched his shoulder.

"Doesn't look like it."

"Are they arresting him?"

"I don't know."

Graham watched quick, angry gestures whip one of the soldier's arms as the other stood behind and to the side with his rifle ready. Shu'aib responded with innocent, apologetic movements Graham could discern without hearing the words that accompanied them. After exchanging several volleys of motion, the soldiers ushered Shu'aib to the Patrol, stabbing the air with their guns to help shepherd him. Shu'aib bent himself into a thankful, obedient posture as he walked backward to the SUV. He pulled out of the hiding place, then drove up the wadi the way they had come. The soldiers followed in their own pickup until both were out of sight.

"How are we going to get out of here now?" Fear knitted Sarah's face, squeezing out the tears pooling in her eyes.

Graham shook his head, not trusting himself to speak. He stood up and looked deeper into the cave. The roof slanted down toward the back, cutting its height in half. Mid-afternoon sun threw a shadow that grew thicker as it collected at the rear, but not enough to steal all details. As Graham's eyes adjusted to the shade, a shape began to emerge—not much more than a dark form entombed in the black. He dug out his flashlight and aimed the beam, squinting in an attempt to extract detail.

A prism refracting light into wavelengths fanned out like a linear rainbow. Except it wasn't made of light. It was the embroidery thread of a patch sewn onto a backpack. The flashlight revealed the iconic cover of Pink Floyd's *Dark Side of the Moon.*

FIFTY-THREE

"That's Xander's! He was here!" Sarah hurled herself across the cave and snatched the backpack off the ground.

"Is there anything in it?" Graham prompted when Sarah paused, the bag locked in her embrace. "Bring it closer to the light."

They sat down near the front of the cave, just able to look over the lip into the valley without fully exposing themselves.

"It's heavier than it looks." Sarah unzipped the main compartment and reached inside. "Binoculars." She handed them to Graham blindly.

"Nice. These are twice as powerful as the monocular." He held them to his eyes, located the V-shaped altar, then slowly swept across the Holy Precinct to the guardhouse. "No sign of Shu'aib or the soldiers."

"Water," Sarah said, then squirted a stream into her mouth.

Graham took the bottle and did the same. "Thank you, Xander."

"Nikon Coolpix." Sarah knitted her brow in surprise. "Never seen this before."

Graham traded the bottle for the camera and turned it in his hand. "One of my other grad students loaned it to him for the trip. It has better optics than his smartphone. And it has an optical zoom." He read the label on the side of the lens. "Wow. Thirty-five times magnification, in fact. And it shoots 4k video."

Graham looked back at Sarah and realized he was talking to himself.

"He's got a few protein bars in here. And…" She drew out her hand dramatically, lifting Alexander's iPhone like a magician producing a lost card.

"This is where it pinged." Graham's face dimmed as fast as it flared.

"Which means we don't know where he is," Sarah said, voicing Graham's thoughts. "It's dead."

Graham took the phone, then rummaged through his own backpack for his portable charger and plugged it in.

"There's something else at the bottom."

She displayed a keyring and dangled it with a bob of her hand, letting the keys clatter. A large tag identified a rental company in Tabuk.

"We have a way out." Sarah's expression showed one less worry.

"Just need to find the truck." Graham hoped it sounded more practical than pessimistic.

"But why is it here?" Sarah said, patting the rock floor. "Why did he climb all the way to the cave?"

"Because this is the Cave of Elijah." Graham backed into the cave. "It's where Elijah came when he ran for his life after defeating the prophets of Ba'al. At least according to those who are convinced this is Sinai."

Sarah followed his eyes, the knowledge a lens that made the hollow space seem suddenly important.

Graham pressed the camera's *on* button, emitting an electronic chirp.

"What are you doing?" Sarah moved next to him to look at the screen.

"The photos we saw in the cloud are from his phone. I'm guessing the pictures on this camera are in the same order, tracing his steps. If so, there may be pictures that fill in the blanks and give us a clue to what happened. Especially the latest ones."

Sarah nodded, giving Graham the impression that she wanted to see the most recent pictures, but was afraid of what they might show.

"More than three hundred images," Graham said, noting the number above the grid of thumbnail images on the camera's tiny screen. He opened the first image—the pillar at Nuweiba. He cycled quickly through the images—the black peak of al-Maqla the V-shaped altar, the golden calf altar, and the cave they were now in, shot with a zoom from the Holy Precinct. After a group of pictures of the Split Rock from the other side of the mountain, another set of images showed the Holy Precinct again.

"They're almost the same as the ones on the cloud," Sarah said. "Just better quality, I guess."

"There are a few videos, too." Graham switched to the list of movies and clicked *play* on the first one. The pillar on the beach at Nuweiba appeared again, jostling as Alexander walked around it to capture it from all angles. A tinny rattle came from the camera, and it took Graham a moment to realize it was the sound of the wind on the beach coming through a minuscule speaker. As the image rotated, the Gulf of Aqaba came into view, and Graham was amazed at how close it was. Several cars obliviously passed on the road between the pillar and the water's edge.

The second video showed the approach to the Holy Precinct shot through the windshield as Alexander drove. The picture was surprisingly good, though it was interrupted several times with violent jerks as the track bounced the truck. But it was the best document he'd seen of what it was like to enter the area, passing the guardhouse, looking into the Holy Precinct itself, then continuing to the fence around the golden calf altar. A third video featured the golden calf altar itself as Alexander walked around it just as he had the pillar. The motion stopped to focus on a large blue metal sign standing next to the fence. Graham had seen it through the monocular but hadn't been able to read the white stenciled lettering. He was surprised to see the Arabic message repeated in English below it. It was the same sign he was skeptical of when he found a similar image online while researching the site.

ARCHAEOLOGICAL AREA
WARNING
IT IS UNLAWFUL TO TRESPASS
VIOLATORS ARE SUBJECT TO PENALTIES
STIPULATED IN THE ANTIQUITIES REGULATIONS
PASSED BY ROTAL DECREE NO. M/26, D 23.6.1392

Graham had seen a blue sign near the guardhouse as they entered the wadi and assumed it contained the same warning. After pausing for enough time to read the sign, the camera moved to the back of the stack of boulders and zoomed in through the mesh of the chain-link fence. The aperture automatically adjusted the picture for the shadows, revealing the petroglyphs. Dozens of stylized cows covered the rocks. Graham was studying the petroglyphs so intently that he was startled when the video ended.

The fourth movie was shot as Alexander walked down one side of the V-shaped altar's chutes, then back out the other. The camera documented the marble pillars, then moved to the location of the altar itself and looked back over the chevron shape, then the rest of the Holy Precinct. Graham hit *play* on the fifth video and the Split Rock appeared in the distance, shot out the windshield as the truck approached it. Alexander kept the video rolling as he got out of the truck and climbed the hill, keeping the rock in view the entire time. The point of view circled the rock, then stepped through it, documenting its immense scale.

Graham hit play on the sixth video, a view of the wadi where the Israelites would have camped taken from somewhere on the slope they had just climbed. Sounds of heavy breathing puffed from the camera, growing slower as the movie progressed, eventually disappearing. The image slid across the screen as it panned the north end of the area to the south, stopping at the golden calf altar and zooming in. The shot widened back out, then tilted down to the V-shaped altar and zoomed in again.

"What's that?" Alexander's mumbled voice sounded as the camera jerked to the left, back to north where the shot began. When the view steadied, it was pointed toward the pass where the goats had been. Alexander made a sharp intake of breath as he zoomed in, as if he had inhaled the distance. An SUV appeared from around the bend, a plume of dust billowing in its wake.

They watched as a scene played out almost identical to the one they had witnessed, like a memory filmed before the event had actually taken place. The truck pulled through the gate in the fence and stopped by the guardhouse. Two men in thobes shouldered rifles as they got out and entered the shack. The camera continued to video despite the fact the action taking place inside the building couldn't be seen.

Graham pressed the *fast forward* button and held it until he saw movement again. One of the men left the building carrying both guns, while the other held a box about the size of a pillow. The second man carefully positioned himself in the passenger seat, protecting the box as if it held something fragile. The camera followed the truck up the wadi, then swung back to the guardhouse as two soldiers exited. They climbed into a military pickup and began to spin around to go out the gate, then jerked to a stop. The passenger door flew open as the soldier burst out and pointed at the camera. Graham could see the face of the man yelling soundlessly, though he couldn't tell if he was alerting the driver or if it was directed at Alexander. The soldier jumped back into the truck as it lurched forward, sharply changing direction, deeper into the Holy Precinct, toward the V-shaped altar and the base of the mountain.

"No, no, no, no," Sarah yelled over his shoulder, growing more emphatic. "The same thing happened. He saw the same thing!"

As she spoke, the image shook violently, then cut off.

"There's one more video."

"Play it!" Sarah demanded unnecessarily as Graham pressed the button.

A dimly lit, extreme close-up of Alexander's face, twisted in fear, filled the tiny screen. A faint glow illuminated the area around his right ear. It took Graham a second to realize Alexander was holding a phone. His eyes darted back and forth between the lens and the left side of the screen.

"C'mon, pick up. Pickuppickuppickup." Alexander's urgent incantation thickened the air in the cave with tension. "Aunt Sarah, Aunt Sa. It's Xander." He started as the phone connected, locking his eyes on the camera. "I'm in serious trouble. They're shooting at me! I didn't think—I thought the guns were just a threat. Didn't even try to ask me anything. I don't know what to do. I don't know how I'm going to get out of here." He panted, trying to decide what to say next. "I rented a truck in Tabuk to get to Jebel al-Lawz. Paid cash and used a stolen license. I did the same at the hotel. No one knows I'm here. I'm on the mountain, hiding in some cave. Halfway up." Xander paused again, breathing heavily onto the camera's microphone. "I'm so scared. There's nowhere to go.

No one knows. I need help. Please. *Please.*"

They stared at the black screen, unmoving, buffering the revelation with silence.

"We have to figure out where they've taken him," Sarah whispered, sounding afraid of her own words.

"Probably to Haql," Graham said. "Or Tabuk. There's no way we're going to get him out of there. Even if he was still here and we found him, how would we get him out? We're trespassers. We can't talk them into releasing him. I don't think either of us are able to take an armed military—"

"But no one's here now," Sarah said, looking down onto the buildings. "The soldiers are gone. And it doesn't look like anyone else is here. We have to look for clues for where they took him at least. There's got to be paperwork or a report or something that says what happened." Sarah gave him a look that continued to plead wordlessly.

"Okay, where do we start? There are a dozen buildings down there."

"The guardhouse, obviously."

FIFTY-FOUR

Graham scooted to the front of the cave, propped himself up on his elbows, and slowly dragged the binocular across the buildings in the valley. "I don't see any movement out there."

"Like a ghost town," Sarah said, mirroring his movements with the monocular.

"We need to get off the mountain, anyway," Graham said. "We don't want to try to climb down at night."

"What do we do if someone comes?" She placed a hand on Graham's arm, apparently rethinking her own suggestion. "They'll see us."

"Not necessarily." He sat up and focused on her eyes, hoping he projected more confidence than he felt. "We're on the east side of the mountain. The afternoon sun is low enough that it will be in the eyes of anyone looking this direction. It also means the slope will be in shadow. As I said, it'll be too dangerous to climb at night. And we'd be completely exposed in the morning. Our best chance is now."

"What do you think happened to Shu'aib?" Sarah said, repacking Alexander's bag. "Think he's okay?"

"I don't know. My guess is that it's a good sign he was escorted out in his own truck. They probably let him go as long as he left. I wish I could thank him. He may have saved our lives by drawing attention away from us." Graham took a swig from the water bottle, then dropped it into the back-pack. "Ready?"

"As I'll ever be."

Graham stepped out of the cave, crouching as if shots were still being fired. They started down the slope along the same trail that had led them there, then angled left, quickly picking their way to the base of the hill that formed the north side of the Holy Precinct. Loose rocks near the base of the mountain slid under the weight of their steps as if parts of it were still molten 3,500 years after God descended on it in fire.

He scanned the area, checking their exposure, and saw that the small hills on the other side of the fence hid their position from most of the buildings. Ahead, on their left, the spur of rock that marked the northeast corner of the area obscured the guardhouse as well.

"We're almost completely out of sight."

"Which means we can't see them either," Sarah said. "Gotta keep moving."

Sarah took the lead without waiting for a response, trotting along the contour of the wadi. Halfway across, Graham remembered this was the area where Wyatt said he found another set of pillars.

"What's wrong?"

Sarah backtracked to where he had stopped.

"Wyatt said he saw pillars around here the first time he came. What was left of them, at least."

"I thought we already found those by Moses's altar."

"These are different," Graham said. "Much bigger. Wyatt said the Bedouin told him it had been an ancient shrine, but that the ruins had been taken to Haql and reused to build a mosque. By the time he came, only the bases remained. He said they were huge. Almost twenty feet in diameter. But they were partially buried by a landslide."

"Well, I don't see anything now," Sarah said, as she started moving again. "And now's not the time to look for them."

At the end of the wadi, they crouched behind a small cluster of boulders and studied the guardhouse a hundred yards away across an expanse that offered no place to hide. The cement block building was about twenty-five feet long and ten feet wide. They faced the short end of the building, a window giving anyone inside a view of their position. The door was on the far long side, hidden from their view.

"Ready?" Graham asked.

"Wait," Sarah said, a hand on his arm. "How do you know it's empty?"

He tried not to react to her touch. "It's barely big enough for two people and yet we've seen four people come out of it. I don't think there's room for anyone else in there. Let's go before someone does show up."

They sprinted in tandem and pressed their backs against the long side of the building, on the opposite side from the gate. He eased his head across the frame of a window, stole a look into the room, then relaxed and stepped fully into the frame.

A rug covered most of the slab floor, leaving a small perimeter of the concrete slab. Half a dozen pillows sat along the walls like a shore containing the carpet. The only other items in the room were cardboard boxes stacked in a corner.

"No one's here," Graham said, despite the fact that Sarah peered in next to him.

"What is this place?"

"I don't know. But whatever it is, they obviously want to keep people away, given their reaction to being seen. My guess is it has to do with whatever's in the boxes."

"Think it's drugs?" Sarah kept her eyes on the stack in the corner as she spoke.

"Let's go find out."

"No!" Sarah grabbed his arm, pulling him back. "It's not important. Xander's not in there."

"Wherever he is, it looks like he's there because he saw some kind of exchange take place. Just like we did. If we knew what was in the boxes, then it might help us if we have to negotiate for Alexander."

Sarah's gaze slid away from his as she considered that. "Okay, I guess."

Graham walked around the guardhouse to the door, glancing toward the cluster of buildings as he moved. He reached for the doorknob in anticipation, moving with his hand out. He rattled it, confirming it was locked. After judging that the door didn't appear very substantial, he rammed his shoulder into it, then looked around guiltily. When no one came out of the other buildings to investigate, he butted it twice more without pausing. As he stood back to rethink the plan, the sound of breaking glass came from the other side of the building. Graham raced around the corner as Sarah emptied a fist-sized rock from her hijab.

"I figured it'd be easier to go in through the window than bang the door down. Plus, a broken door can be seen from the road." She flashed an accusing smile.

He gave her a nod of approval. "I'll give you a boost."

He steadied her foot, then returned to the door as Sarah opened it. Inside the sparse, utilitarian space, a second ramshackle stack of boxes stood in the corner they couldn't see from the window, making about twenty packages in all. The cardboard containers were all different sizes and didn't appear to be organized in any way. Each of the boxes showed wear—unique stains, scrapes, and dents, fortified by tape on top of tape.

Graham took a carton off the top of one of the piles, knelt, and turned it in his hands, inspecting it.

"Not that heavy. Two pounds, maybe." He pulled out

the keys to the car they had abandoned in Jordan. He chose the longest one, jabbed it into the tape, and pulled the teeth across the seam, splitting it open. He pulled up the flaps of the box, revealing a thick blanket of Bubble Wrap cushioning an object that he couldn't make out through the plastic.

Sarah kneeled beside him. "What do you think it is?"

"There's only one way to find out."

FIFTY-FIVE

Graham sliced through tape and unfolded Bubble Wrap to reveal a tablet of white limestone about the size of a smart-phone. Seven columns of text comprised a vertical inscription written in characters formed with long, skinny wedges and no curves.

"Cuneiform," Graham noted aloud. "Some kind of seal. Not exactly what I expected to find in a backwater guard-house."

"It's Akkadian," Sarah said over his shoulder.

"Can you read this?" He carefully passed her the stone. "I could do a rough translation, but it sounds like you might be able to do the job quicker."

Sarah squinted slightly at the ancient grooves, recasting her face into a mask of scholarship. She stayed silent, as if crossing the distance to the time when the message was writ-ten, then translated the words in a halting delivery.

> *"Bilalama, Beloved One of Tishpak, city ruler of Eshnunna. Wussum-beli, son of Lushallim, his servant."*

She looked up and handed the inscription back to Graham. "I'd say it's Babylonian. Probably around 2,000 BC. This should be in a museum. I wonder what it's doing here?"

"It was stolen," Graham answered.

"How do you know?"

"There's an excavation number on the back. Written in grease pencil." He turned the reverse side of the seal toward her and pointed to the identification mark.

"As. 31:492," she recited.

"That will tell us where it's from," Graham said. "What site it's from, what excavation square, and what depth level it was found at. It's an exact address. But that address is nowhere near here."

Graham sliced open another box, this one smaller than the first. He gently removed the Bubble Wrap like a surgeon performing a delicate operation.

"Oh my! That's beautiful." Sarah watched Graham lift a rectangle of amethyst—only an inch wide and half an inch tall—and slowly turn it in the light.

"It's like a tile of purple and pink ice," Graham said. "Another seal. This one has some kind of figure in a gown. Looks like she's holding something. And there's an inscription on either side of it, but my eyes are too bad to make it out."

Graham handed it to Sarah and watched her angle it until the inscription caught the light better.

"There's a head floating above the middle column of text, too. Looks like this piece is from about the same time period as the other. Akkadian." She touched a spot with her index finger. "Looks like she's a goddess. She's dressed very ornately."

"Can you read it?" Graham asked.

"Not all of it. Some of the text is damaged. And the amethyst makes it hard to read something so small." She lifted it closer to her face. "'Mattatum, daughter of…' this part is illegible, 'for her life, for the goddess Kititum, he has presented…' and then the rest of it's damaged." She turned the stone over. "There's a number on this one, too. IS. 34:35."

She flipped it back around to look at the front again as

Graham opened a large square box, two feet on each side and six inches deep. Inside, several different pieces of Bubble Wrap each contained several fragments of an artifact.

"Oh no." Sarah set the amethyst seal back in its box. "That one broke?"

"I think it was already broken when it was discovered," Graham said. "I've seen two different excavation numbers so far. They must have written them before they knew the pieces belonged together. See?" He flipped two shards over and pointed to the grease pencil characters, one cataloged as Kh. III 1207, the other as Kh. III 793.

After removing the rest of the plastic, Graham put the fourteen limestone pieces in the bottom of the box and reassembled them like a puzzle. About a third of it remained missing, but it was enough to recognize they formed a plaque about fifteen inches square. Two figures were depicted, their bodies facing forward, but their heads turned in profile to the left. A faint inscription filled the space between them.

"Looks like there was a square hole in the center." Graham slid the box in front of her so she could study it more closely.

"I think this is older than the others." She bent closer to the fragments. "The inscription is too worn and damaged to read."

Graham opened a fourth box and found a clay seal, two inches wide and an inch tall. The image pressed into the clay showed a bull rearing on its hind legs next to what looked like an elongated spade that Graham interpreted as a stylized tree. "Another seal. The inscription is too small for me to read." He flipped it over and noted the number. AS. 31:627. "See if you can read it."

Sarah's squint intensified. "King," she said almost immediately, then stuttered through isolated syllables. "Shu...tu... rool...King Shuturul."

Graham took out his phone and photographed the front

and back of the seal, then remembered Alexander's camera took higher resolution images. He documented each item, careful to get close-ups of the catalog numbers. After stowing the camera, he sat next to Sarah, looking at the items before them.

"Where do you think these—"

Graham cut her off, abruptly raising his hand, stopping her words in midair. They froze, listening to the sound of a truck in the distance. Alarm bells sounded in his head, breaking the spell, and he burst into action, scrambling to rewrap the pieces and pack them into the boxes.

"What are you doing?" Sarah spit the question out in a frenzied whisper. "We can't just leave these here."

"That's exactly what we have to do," Graham said, without stopping. "We don't know where they're from or why they're here. And if they find us with them, then they will be stolen, and we'll be in jail and we won't be able to find Alexander."

Sarah responded by replacing the boxes, trying to organize them as they found them. Graham didn't waste time taping the Bubble Wrap, and they turned the open flaps of the boxes toward the wall to hide the fact that they had been opened.

"Lock the door!" Graham ordered, as he reached for the backpack.

He pulled the camera back out, ejected the memory card and slipped it into his sock. He found another card in the camera bag, inserted it, then returned it to the backpack.

As he finished, they could hear the crunch of dirt and rocks beneath the wheels of the truck coming close to the shack. Graham pointed emphatically at the window, then webbed his fingers together palms-up and crouched to give her a boost. After she was through, he shoved the backpack out the opening, then dived upward, bent himself over the sash, and wiggled out. He pressed himself against the wall next to Sarah and listened as the door opened.

FIFTY-SIX

The alarmed voices of two soldiers reverberated in the room as Graham and Sarah slid along the wall, away from the window, unheard among the barbs of rapid Arabic. They looked at each other as one of the soldiers barked to check to see if any boxes were missing. In the pause that followed, Graham imagined them inspecting the stacks, anticipating an explosion of words as they discovered several packages had been opened.

"They're all here," one of the soldiers said.

He exhaled a soundless *Thank You* prayer that they had merely counted the inventory. He locked eyes with Sarah again as the guards decided to investigate the ground outside the broken window. At the sound of the door opening, Graham signaled Sarah to move to the front of the building as the soldiers went around the other side to the back.

"What now?" Sarah mouthed, looking trapped.

Graham held an index finger across his lips, then tapped his ear as the voices of the guards spilled around the corner. The words came too fast for Graham to catch them all, but as he tried to fill in the blanks, Sarah did it for him.

"They think whoever did this is probably on the mountain," she whispered. "That he was probably with Shu'aib."

Graham nodded, then scooted to the corner and pulled out his phone. He turned on the front-facing camera, flattened his back against the wall and held his arm fully extended, as if he were taking a selfie. The camera's lens caught the area on the other side of the wall with the broken window. Graham adjusted the angle to catch as much of the Holy Precinct as he could and watched the backs of the soldiers as they jogged around the spur of rock that hid most of the wadi from view.

"C'mon," Graham said, avoiding Sarah's eyes, not wanting to find an expression that would erode the little hope he had. "Through the gate."

He pointed over her shoulder, then followed his own instructions and ran. Twenty yards later, he skidded to a stop, causing Sarah to stop on the other side of him.

"What are you doing?"

"Keep going," Graham whispered. "All the way to the hill." He pointed past her again, to a rocky island on the other side of the fence. "Be right there."

He pulled the gate shut, then grabbed the open padlock on the end of the loose chain he hadn't seen until he was about to run past it. He wrapped the chain around the poles that formed the entrance, slid the lock through the links and snapped it closed.

"That'll at least slow them down a bit if they try to chase us with the truck," he explained, crouching next to Sarah.

"Which way do we go?" Sarah looked up the wadi in the direction they had arrived from. "The way we came in has fewer buildings. That's the way out, but anyone who comes down the road will see us."

"Agreed," Graham said. "And remember: Alexander left his truck around here somewhere. We didn't see it when we drove in, so it must be farther down. Maybe around where we parked, if he was looking at the same things."

Graham took out the GPS and studied the satellite image of the area. "It's about a thousand feet to the closest buildings on the other side of the wadi." He pointed to the screen, orienting her to the aerial perspective. "If we can get there, the buildings will give us places to hide as we move down the valley. The downside is that there might actually be people inside that we haven't seen."

"Okay." Sarah nodded. "Let's do it."

Graham resumed his crouching trot and led them to the other side of the hill, shielding them from the guards in the Holy Precinct, but exposing them to the main track through the wadi. They crossed a dry riverbed, then scrambled to the crest of a smaller hill. Less than a hundred yards away, a line of almond trees formed a break around a vegetable garden next to a long building.

Graham ran outright across the open area, almost slamming into the wall of the building next to the garden. Sarah flattened herself next to him, and they panted together, exchanging reassuring looks. When they got control of their breath, they moved along the building toward the track that ran through the makeshift neighborhood.

At the front corner, Graham stopped and looked more closely at the buildings they had passed through earlier in the afternoon. He saw no signs of life and slid around the corner, stopping again at a window. He hazarded a glance to make sure it was clear before peering inside. The structure contained a single room, about twenty feet square. Like the guardhouse, long cushions lay at the base of the cement walls, and a carpet covered most of the concrete slab.

"If we don't find the truck quickly, we'll have to figure out a way into one of these buildings and stay the night," Graham whispered. "And it's getting dark fast."

"It has to be around here some—"

Sarah's voice was stolen by the appearance of a man in desert fatigues bursting through a door on the other side of the track. A rifle dangled from his right hand as he spit short, sharp words into a walkie-talkie he held with his left. Two other men followed, their movements alert, crisp, and bird-like.

Graham's perception went into overdrive, subdividing time into smaller pieces the faster they unfolded, making them slow down. By the time he told his body to move, he felt he had been frozen for minutes, although less than a second had actually passed. He forced Sarah back around the corner of the building, into the edge of the garden.

"Get down!" he mouthed as he squatted into the shadow, praying it was dark enough to blanket them from a quick glance.

The thorny sound of angry Arabic poked the air from different places, making no secret of the fact that they were looking for trespassers.

A thunk popped from the ground to their left followed by a crack of distant gunfire. As Graham registered the shot, two more reports came. In his frenzied state, Graham spent his first thought trying to work out how the soldiers could shoot around the corner.

"They're behind us!" Sarah exclaimed, abandoning the attempt to hide.

Graham sprang to his feet as he craned his head to look behind them, then realized locating the shooter was less important than getting out of his line of sight. He spun back around, and—for a fraction of a second—stared into the butt of a rifle, tracing its movement before it collided with his forehead. Just before everything went black.

FIFTY-SEVEN

Splinters of undefined sound stabbed the oblivion, making pinholes of consciousness, exhuming Graham in small pieces. Vague sensations slowly accrued into awareness, reacquainting him with his senses by degrees. The smell of concrete pressed into his mind as its smooth hard surface cooled his right cheek. He blinked his eyes open, looking through stuttering vision at long cushions padding the perimeter of a room larger than the one he had seen through the window. No people were there, but he could feel a presence just outside his perception. It wasn't until he tried to move that Graham perceived the awkward position of his body. His torso twisted in the opposite direction from his face, and his arms angled behind his back, handcuffed. He tried to rock himself up but made almost no movement, conspired against by gravity, stiffness, and the vestiges of unconsciousness. The effort spilled pain into his head, blinding him with light, making him wince.

As he struggled to focus, noise knitted itself into voices, though the words remained indistinct. An angry voice—intimidating—forced its way through Graham's daze, making space for the panicked voice of a woman. A different man's voice followed, the sounds evolving into words as he grew alert enough to translate abstractly, as if it were a linguistic exercise.

"Limadha 'ant huna?" First man shouting. *Why are you here?*

"'Ana zayirun. Sayihun." Woman, pleading. *I am a visitor. A tourist.*

The sound of a hard slap burst Graham's abstraction, giving the words sudden context.

"Please, I mean no disrespect to the prophet." The woman's voice sounded between sobs.

Another slap.

"You disrespect the Prophet—peace be upon him—just by being here. Just by mentioning him!"

Sarah. Understanding flooded into Graham like a current that jolted him into another failed attempt to sit up.

"The other one is awake," the second man's voice announced.

Hands grasped under his arms and roughly pulled him into a seated position. Three men—not two—stood in the room. Two of them wore the military fatigues he had noticed earlier, and he assumed they were the ones who entered the guardhouse. One of these two wore a patrol cap in desert camouflage, a full beard and mustache, and a sand-colored vest that hung open. The other was dressed the same, but with a floppy, wide-brimmed boonie hat and a trim beard. Both wore rifles on their shoulders. A third man stood behind them against the wall, holding a rifle across his body, at the ready. Graham recognized him by his keffiyeh as the one who came out of the building with the walkie-talkie. Next to the man's head, a window revealed the opaque black of the desert night. It had been close to sundown when they had been captured, and the absence of daylight left no clues for Graham to gauge how long he had been unconscious.

He glanced to the right and found Sarah sitting cross-legged next to him, hands cuffed behind her back. She turned her face to him, revealing humiliation, terror, and shame. Her left cheek was red, her eyes raw from crying. Tracks of tears streaked through the grime on her face, documenting the fear.

"I said, tell me who you are!"

Graham registered that the question had been repeated, instantly sobering him as he realized it was directed at him. He turned his head with effort and met the accusing eyes of the guards, black with indignation. Cold fear and hot panic mingled as the soldiers focused on him.

"My name is—" Graham's voice was thick, slurring his English words before catching in his throat, broken by a fit of dry coughs.

One of the guards stepped closer and squirted a water bottle into his mouth, offering a frozen gear more than offering aid.

Graham nodded thanks and tried again, this time remembering to use Arabic. *"My name is Graham Eliot."*

"We know your name!" Graham identified the guard as the first voice. The soldier lifted their passports and threw them on the floor contemptuously. *"Why are you here?"*

"I came to see Jebel al-Lawz. I am a—" Graham paused, searching for the word for archaeologist. "Eulim alathar."

"You are a spy!" The charge exploded from the second man.

Graham didn't understand the last word in Arabic, but it was said with such vituperation that not knowing almost made it more threatening. He looked at Sarah again, feeling as distressed as she appeared.

"He said you are a spy."

"Silent!" The first man lunged at Sarah, slapping her again.

"No! No! Not a spy! Eulim alathar," Graham pleaded, trying to take the attention from Sarah.

The second guard kneeled and reached into a backpack Graham recognized as his own. When he straightened up, he held the monocular in his hand and shook it toward Graham.

"This is not a tool for archaeology. It is for spies to see in the dark."

"Please, you do not understand." Graham couldn't keep the desperate tone from his voice and hoped it made him appear more honest than weak. *"It is from Jordan. I bought it in a store in Aqaba."*

The guard extended an index finger from the fist wrapped around the monocular and pointed it at Graham. *"You lie!"* He redirected his finger at Sarah while keeping his eyes on Graham. *"Who is this woman?"*

"She is a professor, too." Graham paused to think of how to explain her work. *"She studies languages. She has come to see the mountain, like me."*

The soldiers glanced at each other, sharing an unspoken question that the first then voiced. *"She is not your wife?"*

A beat passed as Graham deliberated about whether or not to lie, then shook his head sheepishly. *"No, she is not."*

The confession added a new fuel to their outrage, one Graham knew would be justified in their culture.

The first soldier spoke again, apparently so angry that it quieted him, making him more menacing. *"How did you get here?"*

"We hired a Bedouin to bring us here. Our truck got stuck in the sand, in Jordan, near the border."

"You see?" the second guard couldn't help exclaiming. *"He is lying! The Bedouin we chased from the mountain today is who gave them the ride. There is no need to be on the mountain unless they were spying!"*

"No. You do not understand. We told him we thought this might be where the prophet Musa came." Graham examined their faces for any sign that appealing to a prophet from the Qur'an would generate a measure of goodwill. *"We were trying to get a better view of the area and see where he brought*

the people. That is why we were on the mountain. Jebel Musa."
He avoided using the word Jews. "*The Bedouin wanted to see it, too. He had never been here. He took us to many other places. Where Musa crossed the sea, where he met Sofayrâ, and where Shu'aib lived.*" He purposely excluded the Split Rock, not wanting it to become fenced and guarded like this side of the mountain.

"*If what you say is true, why were you hiding?*" the first guard said suspiciously.

"*Because you were cheating us.*" Graham hoped his tone sounded logical.

The two guards turned their backs to them and exchanged whispers. Graham strained the air for words, and although most eluded him, thought he heard *truck, time,* and *meeting.*

After their huddled discussion, the first guard's countenance hardened again, undoing any progress Graham thought he had made. When he spoke, it was almost in a hiss.

"*This is an archaeological site that is protected from trespassers like you. You say you come here to examine it as if you honor it, but what you really do is trample upon it and lie to us.*"

Part of Graham acknowledged he was right, and he had to remind himself that this was not why the soldier was upset. "*I'm sorry.*" The words came quietly. "*I did not mean to make offense.*"

"*Please forgive our ignorance,*" Sarah added, her voice quavering.

Again, the second soldier stepped forward and slapped her, delivering a blow that left her bleeding from her mouth and crying.

"*No more,*" the first soldier announced. "*It is almost time for Isha'a.*"

FIFTY-EIGHT

The soldiers improvised ritual ablutions, using water bottles to wash their faces, hands, and feet. They unrolled prayer rugs and created individual sacred spaces by orienting them toward the Kaaba in Mecca—a direction they called qibla. After positioning themselves on their rugs, the guards stood with their arms at their sides and their eyes closed.

At first, Graham thought they were waiting for something, then saw the lips of one of the guards moving slightly and realized that they were praying silently. Although he knew many Muslims, he had never seen them when they prayed. But he knew the first step was to offer up the intention to pray.

All three lifted their hands above their shoulders, next to their ears with palms facing out, and in unison declared, "Allah hu Akbar." Allah is most great. Each placed their left hand on their chest, then covered it with their right and began to recite aloud:

> "In the name of Allah, the Most Beneficent, the Most Merciful.
> "All the praises and thanks be to Allah, the Lord of all that exists. The Most Beneficent, the Most Merciful.
> "The Only Owner of the Day of Recompense.

You we worship, and You we ask for help.
"Guide us to the straight way.
"The Way of those on whom You have be-
stowed Your grace, not of those who earned Your
anger, nor of those who went astray."

Graham recognized the prayer as the opening words of the
Qur'an. As soon as they finished, they recited another surah.

"Verily, We have granted You Al-Kawthar.

"Therefore turn in prayer to your Lord and sacrifice.

"For he who makes You angry, he will be cut off."

Although both prayers were from the Qur'an, none of the
men used a copy of the book. Graham had always had trouble
memorizing passages from the Bible, and he found himself
admiring their ability to recall the text so effortlessly.

They raised their hands again, proclaimed *"Allah hu Ak-*
bar," then bent forward, putting their hands just above their
knees.

"Glory to Allah.
"Glory to Allah.
"Glory to Allah.
"Free from all defects is my Lord, and with His praise
I bow."

They straightened up and said, "Allah hears the one who
praises Him." Once again, they raised their hands and declared "Allah hu Akbar." The men dropped to their knees and
bent forward until their foreheads touched the floor.

"Glory to Allah.

"Glory to Allah.
"Glory to Allah.
"Free from all defects is my Lord, and with His
praise I adore Him."

The three soldiers sat up on their calves and prayed, *"I ask Allah, my Lord, to cover up my sins and unto Him I turn repentant."* They bowed again and touched their heads to the ground as they repeated the same words as the previous bow. When they finished, they sat back and repeated *"Allah hu Akbar,"* then stood.

"Due to the vigor given by Allah, and because of
the vitality from Him, I rise and stand."

It felt like the night prayer was over, but Graham knew it was only the end of the *raka'at*, and that the entire cycle would be repeated three more times, each quoting different surahs from the Qur'an. And there were other, optional prayers that might be added after that.

As the guards performed the second raka'at, Graham tried to think of a way to escape, but quickly decided the situation would have to present itself, that he couldn't engineer it. But he preferred escape to being taken to Haql or Tabuk and trying to talk his way out of custody. The thought of enduring a seventy-seven-day imprisonment—as Wyatt had—weighed him down with dread. And he couldn't imagine the treatment Sarah would receive. It wasn't merely that he felt responsible for putting her in this position—however inadvertently—it was that he recognized he could develop feelings toward her. He couldn't lose that, not now, not after thinking he didn't have the ability—and certainly not the desire—to connect with anyone the way he had with Olivia. But despite the hint of a future he hoped he had begun to see in her eyes, there was no hope for the present. Only desperation.

Except that here *was* hope. Right in front of him. Prayer. Too often he had fallen into the mistake of treating prayer as a last resort when the truth was that it was his most powerful tool. But his distress at the worsening situation kept him from expressing himself well, from completing his thoughts, even internally. He decided to pray God's own words back to Him. Most of the scripture he had managed to memorize fell from his mind like sand through fingers as soon as he tried to grasp it. He almost felt guilty when he realized that what came to mind were verses he had learned as a child, words he had heard so many times that they had become trite and almost lost their flavor as scripture. But as he tested out the first pair of lines, he found other lines came to him. He knew the prayer was imperfect, missing chunks of text, but he found his soul was given voice and encouragement at the same time.

The LORD is my shepherd,
I lack nothing.
He takes me to lush pastures,
he leads me to refreshing water.
He restores my strength.
He leads me down the right paths
for the sake of his reputation.
Even when I must walk through the darkest valley,
I fear no danger,
for you are with me;
Surely your goodness and faithfulness
will pursue me all my days,
and I will live in the LORD's house for the rest of my life.

After the prayer, Graham opened his eyes and found that

his kneeling position was one of the postures the guards made as they prayed a different prayer to a different god. The realization gave him an unexpected connection.

Elijah.

Elijah had challenged the priests of Ba'al to conjure fire for their sacrifice to prove Ba'al was the one true god. When they failed, Elijah prayed to the God who had revealed Himself to Moses—possibly at this very spot. Fire had fallen from the sky, consuming not only the sacrificed bull, but the wood, stones, dirt, and moat of water that surrounded the altar. The prophets of Ba'al were executed, and Jezebel, wife of Israel's most evil king, Ahab, plotted to kill Elijah. That was why Elijah had come to Sinai and hidden in a cave. God had protected him as he walked through the darkest valley.

"Nar!"

The shout came as the guards were halfway through the fourth raka'at, immediately ending the prayer in confusion. But it wasn't until it was repeated that Graham understood why.

"Nar!" Fire!

The guards shot to their feet and flung themselves out the door, slamming it shut behind them. Graham and Sarah shared a bewildered look.

"Fire?" Sarah whispered the word, as if the guards could overhear her.

Graham fought to grasp the meaning of the word, not because he didn't understand it, but because it arrived like an answered prayer. Had God somehow sent fire like He had for Elijah?

They struggled awkwardly to their feet and looked out the window. An orange tint colored the area outside the window, cast from a fire beyond their view. Graham guessed it was coming from the north side of the building, where they had been captured. He went to the door, felt for the handle behind his back, and tried to turn it.

"Locked. From the outside."

He moved back to the window and watched the shadows and light. As soon as he started trying to think of how to take advantage of the situation, the door burst open. Graham spun around, steeling himself to be punished for moving from his spot.

A slender young man in a white thobe and keffiyeh stood just inside the door as relief, astonishment, and worry collided on his face. "Aunt Sarah!"

Alexander ran to Sarah, embracing her tightly.

"Xander, I thought I'd lost you." Her voice was muffled by the hug and choked with emotion.

"Dr. Eliot." Alexander reached over Sarah to pat his mentor's shoulder. "Thank you so much for coming!"

"Thank you, is more like it," Graham said.

Sarah pulled her head back, looking up at Alexander. "I'm so glad you're okay. What happened to you?"

"Tell you later," Alexander said, serious and urgent. "Right now, we have to get you out of here."

"They'll be looking for us," Graham said.

"You'll have to get in line 'cause they're already looking for me. Besides, they're trying to put out the fire."

"What about our hands?" Sarah twisted around, showing her wrists.

"We'll have to deal with that later. Right now, we have to—" Alexander let the sentence hang as he spotted his backpack near the door. He slid across the room and plunged his hand into the bag and pulled out the car keys. "Excellent! This will make things a lot easier. Let's go. We need to move fast."

He glanced out the door toward the fire while holding up his left hand in a gesture that told them to wait. After scanning both directions, he signed for them to follow as he slipped through the black rectangle.

FIFTY-NINE

Alexander guided them along the sides of two small buildings, holding Sarah's arm. As they scurried across the track to take cover behind a wall on the other side, Graham glanced back at the fire burning the garden where they had been captured, backlighting the building they had just escaped.

"How many soldiers are here?" Graham huffed, fear making him short of breath. "There were three interrogating us."

"I counted five." Alexander held up fingers. "They were all working the fire when I found you."

"If that's all of them, we have a chance," Sarah said.

"The thing is that the way out is on the other side of the fire." Alexander pointed past the flames, then pointed in the opposite direction. "We need to go south to keep from being seen. Plus, my car is down there. If we can reach it, maybe we can find a way out of here."

"All right," Graham said, as Sarah nodded. "Lead the way."

They followed the edge of another, larger garden, then crossed an open area to the wall of a small compound. As Graham followed, he noticed Alexander limping. They reached the south wall of the compound, putting it between them and the fire, and stopped again.

"You're hurt," Graham said.

"Long story." Alexander dismissed the topic without even looking at Graham. "I'll be o—"

"They are gone! Escape!" The shouted Arabic seemed to tear the valley open, making Graham feel suddenly exposed.

Other voices sounded, knotting in confusion over whether to leave the fire to find the fugitives, or put the fire out first. Graham leaned around the corner and saw two flashlight beams already sweeping the area, prodding the darkness like needles searching for something to sting.

"We have to move." Alexander motioned toward shadows in the darkness away from the fire. "We'll keep to the side of the wadi, out of sight as much as we can. Go for that shed."

As soon as Graham located the white building two hundred yards away, Alexander pulled them into the darkness. They angled left, trying to remain obscured by the building as much as they could. The closer Graham got to the shed, the more aware he became that the moonlight that enabled them to see it also enabled them to be seen. By the time they reached shelter on the far side of the tiny structure, they had doubled the distance separating them from the fire without a single gunshot or a shout announcing they had been spotted. Again, Graham looked back up the wadi and saw the lines of light arc aimlessly across the area.

"Where's the truck?" Sarah asked, scanning the darkness. "How much farther?"

"Should be about halfway." Again, Alexander pointed toward indistinct shapes in the distance. "Somewhere over there. The problem is that there's nowhere to hide between here and there. And it'll be a bit of a trick to find. I tried to park it out of sight. I could hit the *unlock* button on the fob to flash the lights, but they might see that."

"In this darkness, they'll definitely see it if they're looking this direction at all," Graham said. "It'll be hard enough to get out of here once we're in the truck."

"We have a monocular," Sarah said. "In the backpack."

"Of course!" Graham said. "Totally forgot about it."

"Why would that help?" Alexander asked.

"It's got night vision."

"No way!" Alexander almost sounded like a kid as he fished the monocular from the bag and scanned the area. "This is amazing!" He fixed on a point and his voice turned serious. "Got it. I see where we need to go."

They darted down the wadi, keeping the craggy wall on their left, moving with their next stop in sight. Clusters of rock materialized out of the void like solid dregs of night. Alexander turned left into a tributary, then quickened toward a spur of rock jutting into the dry bed. As they rounded the point, the back end of a black Toyota Prado emerged from the darkness.

"Yes!" Alexander whispered, eyes closed, head tilted to the sky.

Graham leaned on the five-gallon jerry can of fuel mounted next to the spare tire, catching his breath. "Hope you have some water in the truck."

Alexander answered by holding the key up in show and used it to unlock the door, avoiding the fob and the pulse of light it would have made. After they hopped in, Alexander quickly closed the doors to extinguish the dome light. Alexander found the rental agreement in the glove box, pulled a paperclip off the end, and twisted it into a flared bulb shape.

"Spin around." He twirled an index finger as he looked at Sarah, who had taken the passenger seat. "Let me see if I can get those cuffs off. Dr. E, shine the light on your phone over here."

He pushed the curved wire into the keyhole, turned his wrist to the right, then cranked it to the left. On the third try, the metal jaw clicked open. Sarah pulled her left arm to her front and made circles with her elbow, working her shoulder muscles into their natural position.

"Ha!" Alexander beamed.

"You've still got it," Sarah said, smiling back. "Alexander the Great."

"Where did you learn to do that?" Graham asked as Alexander started to work on the second cuff.

"Houdini was my childhood hero," Alexander said, concentrating. "I got into magic. I wasn't really interested in doing escapes, but I learned how to pick locks like he did when he was a kid. Simple ones, anyway. He used to teach his methods to the Secret Service. Handcuffs like these aren't impossible if you know what to feel for."

On cue, the other cuff fell off, freeing Sarah to hug her nephew.

"You are an answer to prayer," she said. "More than one, actually." She released him as Graham positioned himself so his cuffed wrists lay on the console between the front seats. "Guess all that magic practice was good for something after all, huh?"

Alexander smirked as he prodded the keyhole. "More than you know."

The cuffs opened, leaving the comment unexplained.

"Thank you," Graham said in relief. "Let's get out of here."

"What happens if we go south from here on the main track?" Sarah pointed blindly into the dark. "What's down there?"

Graham had already pulled the GPS from his backpack and turned it on. "If we keep going down this main wadi south to the end of the mountain range, it connects to a highway. One direction goes to Tabuk, the other goes to the coast, and then up to Al-Bad' and Haql." He looked up at Alexander. "Do you need to go back to Tabuk?"

"That's where I rented the truck, but they might have a

place in Haql. Still, the quickest way to get out of here without being seen would be to go east through this wadi." Alexander pointed at the GPS screen. "The satellite map shows tracks that eventually connect to a paved road that connects to the highway to Tabuk. The problem is it's not a very well-worn track as far as I can see, and we don't want to get lost in the desert at night. Or stuck in the sand."

"It's easy enough to get stuck in the sand during the day," Graham said in self-rebuke. "Seems like south would be our best bet."

"Except that they'll be able to see the lights on the truck," Sarah said.

"We can pull the fuses that automatically turn on the running lights." Graham reached for the car's manual from the stack of papers Alexander had taken out of the glove box.

"Then we wouldn't be able to see anything." Sarah threw her hands in the air. "We'd be driving blind."

"Not if we use the monocular," Alexander said, lifting the scope.

Sarah thought a moment. "Think you can hold it with one hand and steer with the other?"

"Not me. I'm not driving." Alexander held the keys out to Graham.

"What do you mean?" Graham looked at the keys without taking them.

"My right ankle is killing me. I can barely move it at this point. It's swelling up again. I sprained it really bad, and think I re-injured it running down here."

"All right. I'll drive."

As Graham and Alexander traded places, Sarah unfastened a panel by her left knee, revealing the fuse box. She studied the legend printed on the inside of it, then pulled the fuses for the headlights and running lights.

By the time she finished, Alexander had situated himself

in the back seat, extending his leg across the bench.

Graham reached for the key, then let go without turning the ignition. "Hold on a second. I'll be right back. I want to make sure the coast is clear before we pull out."

He grabbed the monocular and stepped to the edge of the spur of rocks hiding them from the main track. He lifted the monocular to his eye and swept the wadi to the north. Nothing moved. The glow around the buildings was gone, and Graham assumed the soldiers must have gotten the fire put out. He panned south, wanting to get a sense of the terrain he was about to navigate.

Then he froze. The urgent need to escape instantly vanished.

Inside the circular frame of the monocular—glowing green—an Egyptian bull stood in his way.

SIXTY

The frenzy of escape had extinguished all other thoughts, and he had forgotten what had drawn Alexander here in the first place. Now the altar of the golden calf—at least for a moment—eclipsed the need to escape. Although the rendering was crude, the petroglyph was clearly a cow or calf, made by scraping the dark surface of the rock, allowing the lighter rock underneath to show through. Stylized horns grew from the top of its head and bent at right angles away from each other, like capital *L*s embedded in the skull. The elongated body was subdivided by lines that reminded Graham of a butcher's diagram of meat cuts.

He stepped closer while moving farther to the south face of the monument and found at least a dozen more petroglyphs. Some of the calves had horns like lightning bolts, while others had large hooks protruding forward. One section showed the animals lined up in the same direction on the top half of the rock, then the reverse direction below.

"Amazing, isn't it?"

Alexander's whisper jolted Graham like a shout, twisting him around. "Scared me to death." As his eyes adjusted to the darkness after the monochromatic green, he saw Sarah and handed her the monocular. "You have to see this. It's pretty spectacular."

Sarah moved next to him and aimed the lens at the rocks. "I don't know what to say."

"Look at this area," Graham said, pointing.

She followed his finger, then described what she saw. "Two rows of cattle, facing opposite directions. Like they were turning a corner."

"As in the angled chute of the other altar," Graham said.

"I was thinking the same thing." Sarah scanned the surface near the area. "And there are figures of people around them. Shepherding them, maybe?"

"I've shot footage of it, of this whole place." Alexander swept his hand across the darkness, encompassing what couldn't be seen. "A lot of it is already uploaded."

"We saw." Graham kept his eyes on the pile of boulders despite not being able to see the details without the night vision.

"Let's go," Sarah said. "We have to get out of here."

"One last look?" Alexander took the monocular from Sarah. "Wow, this is so strange in night vision. Green-glowing bulls. Sort of like *The Hound of the Baskervilles*."

"I think you've been alone in the desert too long, Sherlock," Graham said, patting his shoulder. "You heard the lady."

"It's a little ironic isn't it?" Alexander said, not moving. "Moses couldn't wait to get rid of the golden calf altar, and we couldn't wait to find it."

Graham chortled. "That's one way to look at it. Another is to say this is a great example of how God can use bad theology to show the trustworthiness of scripture."

"How's that?" Alexander asked.

"Without the heresy and idolatry of the golden calf, we wouldn't have one of the main things to look for to identify Mount Sinai. It's one of the things that needs to be found at Sinai to show it's the real place and that real things actually happened here. The golden calf altar is the artifact of a myth that proves the biblical story is not a myth."

Sarah nodded in thought. "Like how a shadow is evidence of light."

"Exactly."

SIXTY-ONE

Graham eased the truck to the corner of the fence surrounding the golden calf and checked to see if it was safe to enter the main track. He didn't need night vision to see the pair of headlights probing the wadi from the north, growing brighter as they approached.

"Change of plans," Graham said.

"Kill the engine!" Alexander barked in a whisper, as if they might be overheard.

The black shape pushing the headlights slowly transformed into a desert-colored SUV, faintly illuminated by the ambient light reflected off the ground. Three flashlight beams speared the night, two from the passenger side, the third from the seat behind the driver.

"Do you think they'll be able to see us?" Sarah whispered.

"Hope not," Graham said. "At least the truck is black."

Silence filled the truck, growing thicker as the lights neared. A beam slid across them as it swept over the smaller wadi that intersected the larger one near the altar. It pointed directly at them for less than two seconds, but the needle of light was enough to inject the car with panic. Graham was certain the truck had to have glinted in the dark. The question was whether or not it had been seen. As if in answer, the beam jerked back in their direction, sighting them deliberately.

"They saw us!" Alexander said, full voice. "Go, go, go!"

Graham cranked the ignition and pressed the gas as he twisted the steering wheel to the right, away from the golden calf and the SUV.

"Hang on!" He lifted the monocular to his right eye and realized how difficult navigating would be. "Sarah put the headlight fuses back in."

"I can't," she said, looking into the space in front of her seat. "They just spilled all over the place. Under the seat."

"Never mind," Graham huffed. "It's my eyes. Watch the GPS and tell me what to expect."

Sarah pulled the GPS from the pocket on the right leg of Graham's cargo pants and peered into the tiny screen.

Graham pushed as fast as he could into the jittering green world, struggling to find the balance between the fluid sand that swerved them and the solid rocks that jolted them. He could just make out a faint track and did his best to follow it, vaguely comforted by the fact that someone else had come this way.

"Alexander, let me know when you see them," he said, forcing himself not to look into the rearview mirror. A rock violently unseated them, and as Graham resettled, his eye caught the speedometer. Just over twenty miles per hour—maddeningly slow and recklessly fast at the same time.

"There they are," Alexander said as lights came into view behind them.

Sarah snapped her head around to look out the back window. "And getting closer."

"Any outcroppings we could hide behind coming up?" Graham asked, feeling the pressure pushing them forward increase.

"No. The wadi is really wide here," Sarah said, fixed on the GPS.

"What about another track? I've seen several branch off."

"They don't lead out," Sarah said. "They dead end. But the wadi gets really narrow soon. I'll keep looking for a place to hide. Plus, this track will go to the highway if we follow it far enough."

The headlights behind them bounced into the rearview mirror and grew larger, the light bleeding into the monocular as a green haze. He swatted the mirror to a useless angle and returned the monocular to his eye, restoring clarity to the emerald walls. Graham wondered if the narrowing wadi gave them better protection or made them more trapped.

The answer came as the back window exploded in a hail of glass pebbles that pelted the back of the seats. Sarah shrieked.

"Get down!" Graham yelled. "Both of you!"

Another shot sounded, tearing the air but nothing else.

"We have to do something!" Sarah seemed stuck in a cycle of spinning her head to look behind them, then out the front again.

Graham stole a glance into the back seat and saw Alexander crouching on the floor. "Alexander, look around you. Anything we can use as a weapon?"

He listened to the dragging, sliding sounds of the search, then readjusted the rearview mirror to see into the backseat. He quickly glanced back and forth from the mirror to the monocular, checking the progress as Alexander unlatched the back of one of the seats and folded it flat. He scooted across it, staying as low as possible, shielding himself behind the gate. He blindly reached through the shattered window, searching. Two reports cracked, accompanied by metallic thunks. Alexander recoiled, yanking his arm back into the truck.

"Are you crazy?" Graham barked.

"You're going to get shot!" Sarah said, yelling over Graham.

"It's okay," Alexander said, strangely calm. "I have an

idea."

Before either of them could protest, Alexander thrust his arm out the window again. Three more shots sounded as Graham purposefully wove the truck to upset their aim. After feeling around wildly, Alexander fixed on a point, then drew his arm back, slowed by exertion. He grunted as he dragged the red jerry can of emergency gas over the edge of the gate and into the truck.

"What are you going to do with that?" Sarah worried.

"Open the console and I'll sh_____" he said, catching his breath.

"There's nothing in here. Just a couple bottles of Coke."

"Hand me one."

Sarah passed back the glass bottle, the instantly recogniz-able shape featuring the logo rendered with Arabic letters.

"I found these at a gas station and thought they'd make cool souvenirs." Alexander put his shirt over the cap, twisted it off, then rolled down the side window and poured out the soda. "Where's the folder the rental papers were in?" he asked as it drained.

Sarah found it in the debris littering the space at her feet. He ripped the paper from the folder, twisted the cardboard into a funnel, then stuck the small end into the mouth of the bottle. As he held it in place with one hand, he used the other to guide Sarah's hand to the same spot and replace his.

"Keep holding it like this." He nodded at her confusion until she replaced his hands.

He opened the jerry can, releasing the noxious smell of gasoline into the car.

Graham glanced into the rearview mirror, following the smell. "You can't be serious."

"Alexander Pearl—" The warning tone in Sarah's voice left silence to make the rest of her point.

Alexander ignored them as he carefully tilted the can,

trying not to spill any fuel into the car as it jostled the bottle. A shot rang out as he poured, making him wince, but not enough to interrupt the flow. When the fuel neared the top, he pulled the funnel from the opening.

"Keep holding it." He scrambled to untie his shoes, then peeled off both socks. After twisting one of the socks into a rope, he stuck the end into the bottle, soaking it in gas. When it was saturated, he pulled it out and used a ballpoint pen as a ramrod to stuff the dry end through the opening, giving it a tail. He put the bottle into the drink holder in the console, then grabbed the second bottle and repeated the process.

"Really?" Sarah said, leaning away from the bottles. "Molotov cocktails?"

Graham glanced between the seats. "Very clever. But how are you going to light them?"

"The same way I set the fire earlier." Alexander dug in his pocket and pulled out a plastic butane lighter. "I got a lighter from one of the Bedouin who helped me after I escaped. Almost all of them smoke." He looked out the back, then turned to Graham. "You'll have to slow down. I can't throw it that far."

"I can't believe we're doing this," Graham said under his breath, slowing down quickly, trying to close the gap by surprise.

Light from the approaching headlights skimmed across the wadi, dissolving the night as it grew closer. Graham twisted around to see the front bumper take on definition about thirty feet behind them. Alexander pushed himself out of the window behind Graham, up to his waist, and sparked the lighter. As soon as the flame ignited the sock, he hurled the bottle in a high arc. Graham lost sight of it as it traveled on the other side of the roof for what seemed like minutes.

The truck was twenty feet away when the bottle smashed into the windshield, spreading a sheet of liquid fire, instantly stopping it. Panicked shouts flew from the truck, pulling three soldiers into the desert. Graham stopped and backed up just enough to give Alexander an accurate second throw, as well as time to light the other bottle. He leaned out of the window and watched one of the men form a scoop with his hands and shovel sand onto the blaze. The other two dropped their rifles and joined him. They were too focused on the fire to notice Alexander light another Molotov cocktail. A cry of warning rose above the shouts as fire traced an arc toward them through the night. Just before the windshield burst in flames again, they scattered back as if thrown by the explosion before it occurred. They leaped up to renew their furious shoveling, but immediately froze, stilled by a gunshot.

Sarah stood at the rear of the Prado, her eyes as incandescent as the fire that blazed, holding one of the rifles thrown down by the guards. Graham could see the swirl of rage and confusion on the faces of the guards. He looked past them and saw the right front tire was flat. Sarah's warning shot had been pragmatic as well, crippling the truck.

"Put the fuses back," Sarah ordered, keeping the gun leveled at her former captors. She stepped backward to her door. "Hurry!"

"Got 'em," Graham said, sitting up after frantically sliding his hands across the well of the passenger seat.

As he sorted through the half-dozen fuses, popping them back into place, Sarah shot into the earth at the feet of the nearest guard, warning them to stay put. She jumped into her seat, leaving them startled, the truck already moving as she slammed the door.

The gift of headlights gave Graham the courage to speed—as much as he could—deeper into the wadi without the trepidation that had weighed them down before. And the desire to leave the guards behind added additional momentum as he propelled them away.

"That ought to slow them down a bit," Alexander smirked.

"Yes, but for how long?" Graham was already running through the possible contingencies the guards were considering.

"Aunt Sarah, I always said you are the bomb!"

"Not this time," Sarah said. "That was all you."

"All I know is that I never want to get on the bad side of either of you."

SIXTY-TWO

As Sarah warned that the wadi was about to end, the head-lights began to slide up the wall of rock that formed the base of another range of mountains. Graham turned south, following the track, glancing at their location on the GPS screen in Sarah's hand. When they reached the next geological inter-section, he followed Sarah's direction and started a wide turn to the east, toward the mouth of the narrow wadi that tore through the range.

"Wait. Stop here." Sarah waved her hands, revoking the direction she'd just given. "I have an idea." She positioned the GPS so the other two could see where she pointed on the screen. "If we stick with the plan and take this turn, we go about fifteen miles through this wadi until we hit the paved road. That'll take us south for twenty miles and connects to the highway. That means a couple of hours driving in the wrong direction. And we still have to get back to the Jordani-an border."

"Right," Graham nodded. "I thought we agreed that was safer."

"That was before we set their truck on fire," she said, poking a thumb over her shoulder. "But now that they're stranded, we have another option." Sarah pointed just west of their location marker. "If we turn right here instead of left, it loops around to the track we were just on but avoids the soldiers. From there we can go through the Holy Precinct and take the main track back to the highway we came from. It'll be far faster, and we can do it without having the soldiers on our backs."

"Unless other soldiers came to back them up," Alexander said.

"Way out here in the dead of night to look for a couple of trespassing professors?" Graham inflected his voice in a way that answered the question as he asked it. "Doubtful."

"But there were only three guards in the truck," Alexander reminded them. "I counted five trying to put out the fire."

"Which is what they're probably still doing," Graham said. "Or at least dealing with the damage. Even if the fire's out and there are two guards still at the compound, we could set another fire to distract them."

"And that track we came in on is better than the one we were planning to take," Sarah added. "We'd have less chance of getting stuck."

"Okay, I'm in." Alexander shifted back, wincing as he settled his ankle on the seat again.

"Good thinking." Graham gave Sarah a modest smile, then put the Prado into gear and turned the opposite direction.

Sarah concentrated on the GPS, monitoring their progress around the wedge of hills they were circumnavigating. She guided them to a short slot canyon that opened into the wadi they had been chased through.

Graham turned left onto the track that led back to the golden calf altar and gasped as the headlights unveiled an upside-down SUV. He slammed on the brakes and the vehicle slid to a halt.

"Is that them?" Alexander asked.

"I don't think so," Graham said. "It doesn't look like it was on fire."

"Are we sure this is the right way?"

Sarah held up the GPS. "We're going exactly where—"

"Look!" Graham cut across her. "Someone's still in the truck!"

A tangled body spilled out the passenger window, and from among the knot of limbs, a hand raised laboriously, anchored to an arm that remained immobile. The fingers stretched toward them, as if trying to grasp their attention.

Alexander picked up the rifle and slid cautiously out of the truck. As soon as the gun was clear of the door, he aimed it at the injured man who was squinting against the headlight beams.

"Think it's a trap?" Alexander held the gun in place as he glanced at Graham.

"I was wondering the same thing."

Sarah moved her flashlight beam across the windshield and illuminated the driver's side. The upside-down face of one of the guards appeared, blood streaking up his forehead from a gunshot wound above his right eye.

"Doesn't look like a trap to me," she said, moving the light away as if pulling a sheet of darkness over the dead man.

They walked carefully to the survivor, crossing the sand like it could give way beneath them. Graham stared into the face and recognized him despite the broken nose and trails of blood from a gash in his cheek—it was the soldier who had struck Sarah. But now the hate was absent from his eyes, replaced with pleading. The man tried to speak, and all three of them bent to hear the weak voice.

"*Min fadlak…min fadlak…mustashfaa.*" Please, please, hospital.

Graham silently sentenced the man to suffer what he deserved. He moved the flashlight across the rest of the man's body and winced at the sight of a broken bone protruding from a leg turned at an unnatural angle.

"We have to help this man," Sarah said.

Graham had to stifle his anger at her compassion. "This is the man who hit you. And he was shooting at us."

"He hurt you?" Alexander lifted the gun halfway to his shoulder, preparing to resume his guard.

"It doesn't matter." She seemed as taken aback by their judgment as they were her mercy. "He needs our help."

Shame shot through Graham as he was convicted by her words. "You're right. I'm sorry." He turned to the soldier. "La tuqaliq." Don't worry. "Mustashfaa."

He repositioned himself behind the soldier, reached under the man's arms, and started to drag him toward the truck. The guard let loose a series of short screams, as if the cry of pain was punctuated, stopping Graham.

"Sarah, help me put him in the truck. Alexander, open the back."

Alexander opened the gate and swept as much of the shattered glass from the truck as he could. Graham and Sarah lifted the guard into the truck, placing his leg in a more comfortable angle. The man took short, quick breaths, sweating with pain as they moved him. Sarah handed him a bottle of water from Alexander's supply.

After emptying half the bottle in one draught, the soldier began to mumble, repeating the same word over and over. "Shukran." Thank you.

Graham saw the guard wince as the truck started moving down the wadi. Ten minutes later, the golden calf altar came into view, and he slowed to take one last look before turning right onto the main track.

Alexander pointed at the last building on the left. "Drop him at the same place I found you."

"No." Sarah's tone left no room for discussion. "This man needs a hospital. There is no one here to care for him."

Again, her defense of the man who had beaten her quashed their protests.

"What are you suggesting?" Graham asked, careful not to make it sound like a criticism or accusation.

"We're going through Haql. Surely there is a hospital there."

Graham looked to the left, toward the peak of Jebel al-Lawz, and felt the cross-current of unfinished business as he passed it. He thought about how the Israelites were guided to and from this place by a pillar of cloud during the day that became a pillar of fire by night. He turned back to stare out the windshield, saw the beam of his headlights, and thought about the theological illustration of how he was providing his own column of light, a horizontal one, as if the pillar of fire had fallen.

It took forty-five minutes to cross the fifteen miles of track and reach the paved road, and—except for Sarah's navigation—they remained silent as they drove. After ten miles on the access road, they turned west onto the highway, forty miles from Haql.

Alexander followed his aunt's example, offering a protein bar and sharing more water with the injured man. Both he and the guard sat sideways across the truck, facing toward one another with their injured legs extended, and Alexander distracted him with conversation. Although the guard concentrated his strength on coping with the pain, he shared enough fragments for them to piece together that the driver had been hit by a ricochet or a stray bullet.

The call to Fajr, the morning prayer before sunrise, welcomed them to Haql. Graham followed Sarah's instructions around the hub-and-spoke design of the city and found the hospital on the outer rim.

"What are we going to do when we get there?" Alexander whispered, leaning over the console between the front seats.

"He could have us arrested."

The question made Graham sit up straight. "That's true. I didn't think of that."

"I don't think he'll say anything." Sarah's conviction on the matter once again carried more weight than the opinions of both men. "I think that man is in so much pain he'll be thankful and just let us go. He knows we're not thieves."

"He knows we're not *successful* thieves." Graham couldn't help pressing his point. "Just because he didn't find anything on us doesn't mean he believes why we were really there."

"But he does know that we know he is a thief," Alexander said.

"That's right." Graham glanced at Alexander in agreement. "We can just dump him around the corner from the hospital."

"No." Again, Sarah's voice left no room for negotiation. "No one will see him. He needs help right now. And even if he does turn us in, we'll be long gone by the time they figure out what he's saying."

"We need to pray you're right, Sarah, and that he is more thankful than anything."

She wriggled the abaya over her clothes, then covered her head with the niqab before they pulled into the emergency bay.

As orderlies unloaded the guard, he fixed his eyes on Sarah—standing behind them—and gave her a look of gratitude and contrition.

"Shukran. Shukran."

Before the doors closed behind the guard, Graham pulled out of the hospital, not waiting to be questioned about what happened. He sped across the northern part of the loop to the access road that fed onto the highway, then east, into the desert dawn.

SIXTY-THREE

The only other time Graham had been on this road, he had feared for his life at the speed Shu'aib had driven them. Now he pushed the truck to the same speed, fearing for his life if he didn't go that fast. Driving toward the sunrise added a sense of optimism to their progress, as if the highway before them was a rope extracting them from the darkness.

"Twenty-one miles until this road connects to the one that follows the Jordanian border." Sarah was the first to speak as Haql receded behind them. "Then we go seventeen miles to the spot where we came out of the Wadi Rum."

Sarah craned her neck to speak into the back seat and stared for a moment. "Xander, what in the world were you thinking? Why would you do something like this without telling me?" The rebuke was clearly dulled with relief.

Alexander rummaged through his backpack for his usual clothes, then changed out of the thobe as he spoke.

"Well, on the bus to Sharm el-Sheik, the whole Sinai thing really started to bug me. Saint Catherine's is obviously not at the actual place. And even though Wyatt's claims sounded a little crazy at first, there was something about them that wouldn't let me go. I thought I might never get the chance to look into it again. I mean, I was already next door to Saudi Arabia. And I have way more training than anyone who has made it to al-Lawz. When I got to the airport, I decided to take a later flight and took the bus to Nuweiba instead, just to look around. It fits the description in Exodus perfectly. The Hebrews would have been totally trapped there. And the pillar is bizarre. I couldn't think of any reason why a single ancient pillar like that should be there. There are no ruins of a temple or anything like that there for it to come from. I got lots of pictures to show you."

"We saw them," Sarah said. "All the pictures you uploaded—the golden calf altar, the Split Rock—everything."

"Yeah, you said that before. But how?"

"When you went missing, we hacked into your cloud account to see if we could find clues for where you went," Graham explained.

"Avrakedavra," Sarah said, with a magical gesture. "I know you better than you think."

"Busted." Alexander laughed. "So, finding the pillar made me think there really might be something to this theory. At the hotel, I was looking stuff up about al-Lawz and found out Saudi Arabia had opened for tourism. You can even get an e-visa in like fifteen minutes. Then I saw there was a flight from Sharm to Tabuk. The next day, I went back to Sharm. That's when I called you, Aunt Sarah. After we talked, I filled out the form for an e-visa, but I got rejected. Remember when I got arrested at that Arab Fest?"

Sarah nodded. "I called the consulate when I didn't hear from you. They told me you got denied. So how did you get to Saudi Arabia?"

"I had a thobe and a keffiyeh I got at a souk in Nuweiba as souvenirs. And it gave me an idea. I put them on and went to the mosque in the airport. I figured there'd be lots of people going in and out for the daily prayers and offering prayers for safe travel. I thought I'd see if anyone went in that looked kind of like me. I guess I was thinking about trying to get a passport, but I didn't really have a plan."

Sarah turned to send a reproachful look into the back seat, but Alexander kept talking.

"When the call to prayer started, I saw this guy go in who was about my build and height. I thought I might be able to pass for him. I waited for a couple other people to go in, then went in and looked for him. It took me a minute because he'd taken his thobe off and set it next to him. He was wearing this kind of thobe that only went to about his knees, like a coat unbuttoned all the way down the front. I found in the back row, right behind him. And then I saw the edge of his passport sticking out of the pocket in his coat. It was like the door just sort of opened, you know, Dr. Eliot, like how you sometimes talk about how you can see your steps being ordered?"

Graham smirked into the rearview mirror at Alexander. "Sounds more like you were ordering your own. God's steps don't require larceny."

"Whatever," Alexander said, skipping past more details. "So I used that passport to get on a flight to Tabuk. It was completely surreal. I got a room at the Hilton, rented this truck, and spent the rest of the day getting supplies and figuring out the best route. I left at dawn the next day. Once I got off the paved road, I got totally lost, but some Bedouin pointed me in the right direction. I knew I was close cause they kept correcting me when I said *Jebel al-Lawz* and told me it was *Jebel Musa*. When I finally got there, I was stunned. It was absolutely perfect. The place has everything the true Sinai should have. Everything that could still be there after thirty-five hundred years is there. Well, you saw it too. It felt—I don't know—holy, somehow."

"I felt the same way." Graham nodded.

"I tried to document as much as I could—took as many photos and videos as I could—but I didn't have lots of time. I didn't want to spend the night in the desert, and I wanted to find the Split Rock as well. So, I drove around to the other side of the mountain and found that a couple hours later. That thing is massive. Way bigger than it looks in the pictures."

"We know." Sarah arched her brow as she closed her eyes, envisioning it. "We went there, as well."

"You guys did some serious detective work!" Alexander sounded impressed. "On the way back to Tabuk, I decided to take a closer look at the petroglyphs. I parked the truck and took a bunch of pictures, trying to get close-ups of as many of them as I could. I decided to walk back to Moses's altar and get some more pictures. Then I realized I needed pictures of the whole valley for context, so I started climbing the hill. I wasn't planning to go very far—just enough to get all the sites in one shot that showed the relationship between them and the scale of the place. I got about halfway up to the cave, which I really wanted to explore but didn't think I had time for. After I got the images, I switched the camera to video. I was panning over the wadi when I heard a truck coming and followed it until it stopped at the shack."

"We saw the video, too." Graham glanced into the mirror. "It's a great piece of evidence."

"It was still on? I thought I hit pause. So, you saw them go in the shack and come back out with a box?"

"It's all on video. Including when they see you."

"I totally freaked. I didn't know what to do. I heard them shout for me to stop. I don't know what happened, but I just ran. I thought I could hide from them and started trying to get up the mountain as fast as I could. I thought I lost them and kept moving behind boulders. I realized I was pretty close to that cave. I thought I was getting away, but now I think they were just being patient. They saw where I was going. Right when I got in the cave, they shot a couple of times. Every once in a while, another shot would zing past. Looking back, I think they were trying to keep me there while they climbed up. That's when I called you, Aunt Sarah. Did you get the message?"

"Sort of," she said. "It was pretty garbled. I couldn't make out all of it."

"I was shocked I had any cell connection at all there," Alexander said. "So after I called, I put the backpack in the rear of the cave. I didn't want to lose all the stuff I shot, and I wanted whoever found the backpack to know what happened. Except the guards or whoever they were. I didn't want them to find it. When they got to the cave, I didn't try to resist or anything. They tried to question me, but they didn't believe I was here to look around the mountain. They were really angry, like, way more than they should be at a trespasser. I was terrified. They walked me back down the mountain at gunpoint and took me to the same place they took you guys. By that time the sun was going down. They went into the next room for prayers and it gave me time to think. I was sitting there in handcuffs and all of a sudden I thought of Houdini."

"I thought the way Houdini got out of handcuffs was that his wife would pass the key into his mouth when she kissed him right before the escape." Graham felt a tinge of pride at knowing the trivia, even though it was the extent of his knowledge of magic technique.

"Yes," Alexander said, "but not every time. I had shoved the stolen passport down the back of my pants before they got to the cave. I remembered the entry forms were paper clipped to the cover. So I found the paper clip with my fingers and pulled it off. I could hear them praying in the room next door. I didn't know how much time I had, so I immediately started trying to pick the lock."

"You're lucky they left you alone," Graham said. "They didn't leave the room for prayers when they were questioning us."

"Maybe 'cause I escaped," Alexander said. "The real trick was picking the lock behind my back, without looking. It took a little jostling and I lost track of where they were in the prayers. But I popped one open and just barely squeezed through a window to get out 'cause the door was locked from the outside."

"Houdini would be proud," Sarah said.

"Maybe, but getting out of the cuffs didn't mean I was safe. I ran across the wadi to the golden calf altar and got to the truck before I realized the keys were still in the backpack in the cave. So, I started going back across the wadi and that's when they discovered I was gone. I could hear them shouting. I started to run as fast as I could for the base of the mountain, then thought I'd never find the cave in the dark. I'd have to wait until morning."

"Which also means they would be able to see *you* better," Graham pointed out.

"I admit I wasn't exactly thinking clearly," Alexander said. "So, I turned around and started running back toward the truck. But then I realized I didn't want them to find that either or I'd have no way back. I ran past it, onto the hill right next to the altar, and climbed to the top, hoping I could get high enough to watch the search. That way I'd know when it was safe enough to go up to the cave and get my backpack. I picked out a spot just over the crest but when I sat down, the rock rolled backward and threw me with it. I did, like, back somersaults down the hill, and I guess I got knocked out."

SIXTY-FOUR

"Hold on a second." Sarah turned to Graham. "You're about to hit the junction." She looked back at Alexander and touched his knee. "Sorry. Go ahead."

"The next thing I remember, I opened my eyes, and I was inside a Bedouin tent. I don't know how long I was out. I had a massive headache that got worse when I tried to stand up. Plus, it gave me vertigo. And I couldn't put any weight on my right ankle. I guess I twisted it when I fell. The Bedouin were incredibly kind. Treated me like a guest. They fed me and gave me tea. And a couple of them spoke pretty good English."

"Didn't they wonder what you were doing there?" Graham asked.

"Actually, no," Alexander said. "I think they thought it would be rude to ask. But I told them I was looking for Jebel Musa, and they all knew what I was talking about. They kept saying, 'Yes, Jebel Musa here. Here Jebel Musa.' They took great care of me for several days. But then I accidentally upset them."

"What happened?" Sarah asked.

"I'm still not really sure. I had been there three nights, I guess. I was having tea and some of the kids were sitting with me. So, I thought it would be fun to do a couple of magic

336

tricks for them. I took three of the teacups, really small ones with no handles, almost exactly what I used when I used to do the cups and balls trick. Remember that one?"

"The one where you set three cups mouth down, each covering a ball?" Sarah asked.

"Exactly. And when I tip each cup over, the ball is either gone or there is more than one ball. Well, I did that with the teacups and some almonds. Before I even got through it, the kids started screaming like they had seen a ghost. A couple of the men ran in and asked what had happened. I told them I had no idea, that I was just doing a trick to entertain the kids. One of them said, 'What do you mean a *trick*?' I picked up the routine where I left off, stacked the cups, and made each almond travel through the cups, one at a time, until they were all under the bottom cup. They had no idea what was going on and were saying things like *'What is this that you have done? What are these powers?'* I mean, it would have been funny except that it really rocked their world. So much so that they made me leave. They thought it was real magic!"

"Did you not know magic was illegal in Saudi Arabia?" Graham asked flatly.

"You're kidding," Alexander said, not sure if it was meant as a joke.

"No, I'm serious," Graham said. "It was, anyway. Even if it's legal, this place is too rural for that kind of stuff. They didn't even have movies here until they opened for tourism."

"But I'm not doing any sorcery. This is just entertainment."

"For these people that is probably a distinction without a difference."

"Whatever it was, they made me leave. My ankle was killing me, but it started loosening up as I walked. I was able to make it to the truck and was trying to figure out if I could make it up the mountain when I heard shots. At first, I thought they had seen me, that they were shooting at me. But I didn't see any bullets hitting around me. I realized they were shooting in the opposite direction, into the mountain."

"They were shooting at us!" Sarah completed the timeline.

"But I didn't know that," Alexander said. "I thought that when they came off the mountain they would be distracted and I could get my bag. I waited until they came down and that's when I recognized you. So, I made my way up the wadi and had to figure out a way to get you out of there."

"And that's when you saw the fire," Graham said.

"Well, it is where Moses saw the Burning Bush, right?"

SIXTY-FIVE

The road became a jagged series of switchbacks that took them up and over the pass of a small mountain.

"Two more miles," Sarah reported as the highway straightened up on the other side.

"So, Dr. E, how are we going to find a truck you left abandoned in the middle of the desert?"

"I put a waypoint on the GPS so we can go right to it," Graham said. "Unfortunately, I don't have anything as precise as, say…oh, a playlist of David Bowie songs or something like that."

Alexander laughed. "Hey, I thought that was pretty clever. I wanted you to know exactly where I'd gone without being specific because I didn't want to get you in trouble. Come to think of it, I might need to add 'Ashes to Ashes' as the last song."

"One of my favorites songs ever," Graham said. "Why that one?"

"Think of all the fire at Sinai. The Burning Bush. The pillar of fire. God's immediate presence on the top of the mountain. The burnt sacrifices. The destruction of the golden calf. But we didn't find a single flame—except the one I set, of course. All we found were the remains, the ashes. Like a shadow after the light has gone."

"Hmm." Graham nodded with a thoughtful smile.

"Hate to break up your little rock-n-roll fraternity meeting, but this is where we get off." Sarah looked up from the screen, reconciling the satellite image with the view on the ground.

Graham pulled to a stop and studied the area they had to cross. "How far to the truck?"

"Two-and-a-half miles. Look." Sarah pointed to parallel grooves weaving through the sand in the direction they needed to go. "Tracks."

"All right," Graham said. "Fingers crossed."

He guided the truck onto the tracks, following them around a dune. It continued on the other side, skirting the bank of a dry bed that looked too sandy to cross. Within a mile, the track faded into the desert, leaving Graham to his instincts. He stayed to the right of the dry bed until the wadi opened into an expanse.

"Almost there." Sarah pointed directly in front of them. "Half-a-mile more."

"How close are we to Jordan?" Alexander looked around, as if for a sign announcing it.

"You're here," Sarah said, turning to look back at him. "You're not in Saudi Arabia anymore."

The dry bed pinched to a narrow, shallow bend, and Graham traversed it without losing traction. He aimed toward a pass in the low mountains ahead of them and discovered another set of tracks, joining them across the flat sand that grew redder as they crossed it. The track became more defined as they turned around an outcrop of rock and into the pass.

"There it is!" Sarah put a hand over her heart and released a heavy sigh of relief.

As Graham closed the distance, he was surprised to see that the truck looked more abandoned than stuck. He had pictured the tires sunk deeper into the sand than they actually were.

"Doesn't look too bad." Alexander stuck his head out of the window as they pulled up beside it. "Maybe we could nudge it with this truck."

"That's what I was thinking as well." Graham got out and walked a circle around the other Prado, joining Sarah and Alexander standing next to the truck as he completed the loop. "If the sand is too soft for it to go forward, let's try to push it back. Sarah? Want to do the honors?"

She took the keys he was holding out, then hopped behind the wheel. A moment later, the engine came to life.

"Great! Put it in reverse, but don't hit the gas until I start to push you back."

Alexander stood to the side of the gap between the bumpers, holding his palms straight up before him to show the distance left before the trucks touched. Graham slowly kissed the other bumper, then pressed the gas.

"Now!"

Graham's truck powered forward, inching in sluggish progress that made him think he was merely embedding the other truck deeper into the sand. But just as he'd decided to let off the gas, Sarah's truck lurched backward.

"Yes!" Alexander raised his arms in victory.

Graham reversed his truck, thankful to find it hadn't become stuck during the rescue. He put it in park and jumped out, joining the others.

"Great work, Sarah! Let's get out of here."

Sarah shook her head, erasing her smile. "We're not done yet."

"What do you mean?"

"We can't just leave Xander's truck here. Especially not in another country."

"It's okay," Alexander said. "I used that guy's ID to get the truck. And I paid cash."

"It's still not right to leave it here," Sarah said. "We need to drive both trucks back to the highway and leave Xander's there. We know the way, now. The tracks will still be there."

"But we can't get that truck across." Graham gestured to the sand where the truck had been stuck. "That was the problem in the first place."

"What about over there?" Alexander pointed to a shallow spot upstream in the dry bed.

Sarah raised her brow in a way Graham took to mean the correct answer was to trust and follow her.

"Okay." Graham nodded. "Give it a shot. Once you're across, follow me back to the highway."

Alexander joined Sarah, and Graham sighed with relief as he watched them cross the dry bed without any trouble, happy to have his doubts proven wrong. He glanced repeatedly in the rearview mirror as they made their way back across the border, both to check on them and to remind himself he was not alone—an unnerving feeling that had surprised him by growing in intensity the longer they drove.

After abandoning Alexander's truck on the Saudi highway, they retraced the path, following it through the slot canyon into the basin in front of Jebel Umm ad Dami.

"This place is incredible!" Awe hushed Alexander's voice as he alternated between windows, trying to absorb the brutal beauty surrounding them. "Absolutely amazing!"

Graham tore across the sea of red sand as Sarah guided them to the wadi on the other side. They slipped between the mountains and followed the channel. Midway through, the sight of approaching traffic made Graham tense up. But as they got closer, he realized they were Bedouin pickups, outfitted with benches in the bed that held tourists. The wadi released them outside the Bedouin camp, where the tourists had started from. On the other side of the camp, Graham pulled onto the paved road and thought there was a symbolic quality to it, having left the turbulence behind.

By the time they reached the hotel where they had left the car they'd rented in Israel, it was mid-afternoon. After transferring their gear, Graham left Sarah and Alexander as he returned the Prado. Half an hour later, they headed for the crossing point from Aqaba to Eilat, into Israel.

"What are you doing?" Sarah grew more agitated as signs for the border led them out of town. "Xander doesn't have a passport stamp from Jordan. He can't get out. We need to make a plan."

"It's okay. We have one." Graham glanced at Sarah, re-inforcing his words with a look of confidence. "I spoke with Yaniv and he has arranged everything. They are expecting us. Alexander, stick your passport under the seat or somewhere like that. The Jordanians have been told you are a tourist who was injured on a hike and that you lost your passport. Your injury is not so bad that it needs hospitalization, so we are taking you back to Jerusalem."

Graham listened to his own words and hoped it would really go as smoothly as Yaniv promised. He pulled into the last gas station before the checkpoint, and as he filled the tank, he threw the stolen passport away, along with the monocular since it had seemed suspicious to the guards at al-Lawz.

"What about the camera?" Alexander asked, seeing what Graham was doing.

"I took the card with all the images out and put in the other that was in the bag. They can confiscate it if they want. We'll still have everything."

Graham spent the short wait in line at the crossing trying to will himself calm. "Pray that this works," he said as the guard waved their car forward. After repeating the words Yaniv had given him to account for the missing passport, the guard gave them a scrutinizing squint, then left them sitting as he retreated to the office. Waves of fatigue threatened to drown Graham in sleep, the heat of the late afternoon not helping at all. When the guard finally returned twenty minutes later—to their shock—he waved them through, already studying the next car in line.

"That's it?" Alexander said, baffled and tentative, sounding like he didn't want to jinx their luck. "You gotta be kidding."

"Thank God for Yaniv," Sarah said with a heavy sigh.

"Thank God for Yaniv," Graham repeated. "Guys, I have to stop. We haven't slept in over twenty-four hours. I've just been running on adrenaline. Now that we're safe, all the stress is draining out of me. I have to sleep."

"You'll get no argument from me." Sarah sounded relieved at the suggestion.

"I haven't slept in a bed in days," Alexander said as if he'd just realized it. "Plus, I gotta stink. I need a long hot shower."

Graham turned south onto the highway and headed for the resort hotels towering over the coast.

SIXTY-SIX

"I do not know what to say." Yaniv leaned back in his chair, fingers steepled, balancing his chin in thought.

Graham, Sarah, and Alexander squeezed into the space in front of Yaniv's desk. Alexander had appropriated a chair from the outer office but had to leave the communicating door cracked to make room for it. Graham set aside his need for personal space, happy to have had an unusually long sleep, two marathon showers, and some food before the drive back to Jerusalem.

"You came here to see if there was any evidence that Mount Sinai is in Saudi Arabia," Yaniv recited, restating the facts, fixing them in place. "And you suspected that the Saudis may also believe it is there, but do not want anybody to know it. And you also thought there were some Muslims who might kill to keep that knowledge secret."

"Correct." Graham nodded.

"And then your graduate student here decided to look for it on his own and got himself in trouble. So, you crossed into the country illegally to find him. Not only did you find him, but you discovered there was something secret hidden at this place. And that some Muslims there actually *would* kill for that."

"Yes, that's right."

"In fact, you were even attacked in Istanbul when you—" Yaniv cut himself off, not wanting to mention the ostracon before the others.

"It's okay. I told them about Starkey. They deserved to know so they could understand what was happening." Graham tipped his head toward the others, then fixed on Alexander. "And, no, as far as I know, he was not related to Ringo."

Alexander shrugged. "Richard *Starkey*. Had to ask."

Yaniv ignored the side comment and picked up where he left off. "—when you began searching for clues. But now you think the attack was mere happenstance, the act of a transient you accidentally disturbed. Regardless, you still say some people would kill to protect this secret, but it has nothing to do with whether it is Mount Sinai or not."

"It sounds crazy, I know." Graham shrugged apologetically.

"Just so. It is like a puzzle that you were expecting to make a certain picture, but when it is assembled reveals an entirely different picture."

"That's a good way to put it," Graham said.

"So tell me, what is the picture it makes now?"

Graham pulled out his laptop and opened the images of the items from the boxes in the guardhouse. "These are the things we found."

"Looks like they are Babylonian." Sarah's voice took on an academic authority.

Yaniv glanced at her, then looked at the screen. "Yes, these are not the kinds of things I would expect to find in Saudi Arabia. I agree Babylon is more likely. Iraq. Which gives me an idea."

Yaniv adjusted his keyboard, typed in several bursts of taps, then pivoted his monitor so they could all see it. A browser window displayed a rudimental website designed more for function than form. The unadorned title across the top read *Lost Treasures from Iraq*.

"This is a database of items missing from the Iraq Museum in Baghdad," Yaniv said. "As you know, it was looted in the spring of 2003, during the US invasion."

"Fifteen thousand artifacts were stolen." Graham sat up as Yaniv's theory dawned on him. "Most of them are still missing."

"Let us see if we can find any of the items you discovered among the list of lost artifacts."

They watched the cursor on the screen as Yaniv clicked on the option "Principle Object Type," then chose the category "Materials." A grid of images appeared, each labeled with a different material—bone, bronze, clay, gold, ivory, shell, and stone. Yaniv clicked "Stone," and the grid was replaced with another, categorized into forms such as vessels, inlays, beads, seals. Yaniv selected "Reliefs," and the grid changed to an array of topics. Yaniv scrolled the page down, past animals, boats, combat, gods, and clicked on "Inscriptions."

The page refreshed, leaving only one image. Yaniv clicked the black and white thumbnail and opened a larger image showing a square stone with two figures in profile facing left with an inscription between them. The stone had been broken and was missing a number of pieces, but it had been reassembled for the photograph.

Sarah pointed at the screen. "That's it! It's a match!"

"Exactly." Graham stared at the old photograph that mirrored the color image on his laptop. "I got a shot of the backs of the fragments that show the excavation number." He opened the image and read the grease pencil markings aloud. "Kh. III 1207 and Kh. III 793."

"It is the same." Yaniv pointed to the catalog information to the right of the image. "That is what the database shows. Incredible."

"It's from 2400 BC." Sarah read aloud additional information from the screen. "Found at Khafaje. That's close to Baghdad, if I remember correctly."

"Do the next one," Alexander said impatiently.

Graham opened the next image on his laptop, an inscription of seven columns of text. Yaniv studied the picture briefly, then clicked "Materials" to start the new search. They watched the cursor click "Stone," then "Cylinder Seal," followed by "Inscription." A grid of sixteen black and white thumbnails appeared, and they all leaned forward to get a better look.

"Top row, on the right," Alexander said.

"This is the one you were able to read, Sarah." Graham watched the larger version appear on the screen.

"From 2000–1800 BC," Yaniv read. "Found in Tell Asmar. Sumerian. These items really are priceless."

Graham opened the next image. The amethyst tablet with five columns of text and the relief of a goddess between the second and third columns appeared.

"Magnificent," Yaniv said, nodding his appreciation. He hit the back button, reloading the set of thumbnails.

"There it is." Graham tapped the monitor. "Third row, second image."

"Babylonian," Sarah said.

"Yes," Yaniv agreed. "Old Babylonian. Dated 1800–1700 BC. Found in Ishchali. That's close to where the previous item was found."

Graham called up a fourth image. "Here's the last one."

Yaniv looked at the misshapen disc of clay with an inscription next to the image of a bull on its hind legs. He selected "Materials," then "Clay," "Sealing," and "Inscription." Only one image was returned, and it matched Graham's photograph.

"Akkadian." Alexander read the catalog data aloud. "2300–2200 BC."

"Another find from Tell Asmar." Yaniv looked at Graham seriously. "My friend, it appears you have discovered a black-market store of sorts, dealing in some of the most sought-after items in the world."

"The Saudi government is selling artifacts stolen from the Iraq Museum?" Alexander said it as if repeating a secret.

"Someone is." Graham shrugged. "My guess is that it is not the Saudi government. But it looks like some soldiers are being used as go-betweens."

Sarah alternated looks between Graham and Yaniv. "Surely this can't be the only place they use."

"Undoubtedly not," Yaniv agreed. "And if they are wise, they would not use this place anymore. You have done important work by discovering this scheme. I know it is not what you wanted to find, but it is incredibly important, nonetheless. It brings us one step closer to recovering artifacts that help us understand the world of Abraham and Moses, which was, after all, your intention in wanting to find Sinai in the first place. I hope you do not think of your expedition as a failure."

"On the contrary," Graham said. "I am almost convinced that Jebel al-Lawz really is Sinai. And if it is not, then the true Sinai must look very much like that place. It's hard to imagine a site that would better match all of the criteria."

Yaniv gave him a sad smile. "And yet we may never know for sure. Between the 3,500 years that have passed and the political quagmire that surrounds it, it is doubtful it will ever be properly investigated. Like the Ark, and like the Temple, God seems to think it best to hide it from us for a reason only known to Him."

"Maybe so." Graham mirrored Yaniv's smile. "But I'm thankful there is still so much He sees fit for us to discover. So much left to find."

Yaniv bowed in appreciation. "Just so."

SIXTY-SEVEN

Graham joined the current of tourists pressing their way through the door of the Church of the Holy Sepulchre. Even though it was 7:30 p.m., and would close in half an hour, the church was still as full of visitors as it was at midday. But despite his fascination with the site, he was too exhausted—physically and emotionally—to appreciate it.

He had planned on being asleep by now in his room at the Promised Land Hotel, where he'd gone directly after being debriefed by Yaniv. He had made it as far as sitting on top of the bedspread and laying back, fully dressed, sampling the rest that was to come while knowing he would have to rally himself in a few minutes to get ready for bed in earnest. But as his head hit the pillow, an electronic ding announced a text as if he'd triggered a bell. A groan of protest rattled his throat and he had waited until it stopped before twisting to look at the phone without sitting up. He held the screen in front of his face, then reluctantly opened his eyes to read the preview of the message on the home screen.

COME TO THE CHAPEL OF HELENA

He had expected the meeting the next day, but the summons had given him the shot of adrenaline he needed to rouse himself into action and make the mile-long walk through the Old City. Inside the entrance of the church, most of the visitors veered left, heading for the rotunda that housed the Edicule, the structure protecting the tomb of Jesus. Graham slipped through the people clustered around the stone of anointing and turned right, into a corridor. He passed the entrance to Golgotha, and found the stairs along the right wall, leading down.

The stone steps were smooth with wear, and dirty streaks ran down both sides of the stone walls, smears left by pilgrims who brushed against them. Dozens of crosses were etched in the stone walls, graffiti left by Crusaders after converting the quarry cavern to a chapel. The floor at the bottom was paved in an ornate mosaic commemorating Helena. Four large pillars merged in arches that supported a dome with windows along its base. A chain drooped between the two pillars nearest the bottom of the stairs, preventing tourists from walking on the mosaic. On the far side of the design, a low black iron rood screen separated the nave—where Graham stood—from the chancel of the chapel. The air between the mosaic and dome was festooned with gaudy brass lanterns orbiting an electric chandelier. Along the right wall, another set of stairs led deeper into the former quarry, to where Helena claimed to have found the very cross used at the crucifixion of Jesus.

"Dr. Eliot, I am so pleased you could come on such short notice."

Graham followed the voice and turned to his left to see the slender form of Father Nikolaos rise from a stone bench against the back wall, his black habit draping him like a physical shadow.

"Father Nikolaos. It's good to see you again. Thank you for coming all this way."

"The pleasure is mine, Dr. Eliot. It is not every day that I receive a letter from twenty-five hundred years in the past."

The monk looked down at the shopping bag Graham was carrying. "Is that it?"

Graham lifted the bag, pulling it open so the librarian could look inside. He watched as confusion wrinkled Father Nikolaos's face. The priest reached into the bag and gently sifted the shards of pottery. The brittle scratching sound of hardened clay scraping together stopped, and the monk broke into a subdued smile as he drew out the lost ostracon.

"Very clever, the broken pot." Father Nikolaos's eyes smiled more than his lips, conveying both admiration and gratitude. "Very clever. Thank you for recovering it. Even more importantly, thank you for being a man of your word."

"Thank you for entrusting me with it," Graham said, bowing his head. "What will you do with it?"

"I think I will try to carry on the tradition of Saint Catherine's and leave it for someone else to find after you and I are gone. The monastery has been a source of many treasures in the church, and the ostracon will no doubt be another important find discovered there. But I think now is not the time for it to come to light. Too much trouble could possibly result. It will be safe, and one day it will be found. Hopefully, at a time when it can be appreciated in a way that does not cause danger."

Graham sighed, both agreeing and disagreeing as he acquiesced. "As much as I'd like to publish on that letter, I think you're probably right. Your secret will be safe with me. Yaniv may be another story."

"I am sure we can come to an agreement," Father Nikolaos said. "The monastery is forever in your debt."

"Father—" Graham hesitated, speaking before he could compose words for the delicate news he needed to share, not wanting to spoil the goodwill. "You also need to know that I may be publishing something with my graduate student about the location of Sinai. We have made some discoveries that call the historical claim of the monastery into question. Please understand that I mean no disrespect to you or the order or the monastery."

Father Nikolaos seemed unfazed. "I understand. But you can have your plot of land. No matter how big that mountain is, it could never outweigh tradition."

Graham smiled thankfully. "It's a goat, even if it flies."

Father Nikolaos raised his brow in surprise as his eyes lit up in amusement. "I see you know the fable. Yes. We shall each tend our own goats. And I do hope we will see each other again. You are always welcome at the monastery—goats notwithstanding."

SIXTY-EIGHT

Graham left Father Nikolaos and mixed in with the tourists reluctantly leaving the empty tomb, victims of closing time. He slowly dodged a path through the plaza without noticing what he was doing, emotionally dazed by the last week. He turned left onto Saint Helena Street and wondered what would have happened if Constantine's mother had done better research on the actual location of Sinai, if she had identified Jebel al-Lawz instead. Would the golden calf altar and V-shaped altar still be there? Would the Split Rock still be standing? Would mosques be built on top of them, converted from Crusader structures that modified chapels built by Constantine? Or would war, vandalism, and Islamic iconoclasm have left nothing for the monuments to protect, marking only where the sites used to stand—like the tomb of Jesus.

Graham turned left onto Beit HaBad Street, toward the Damascus gate, wandering more than navigating the surroundings that normally enchanted him. The sound of his own name startled him from his reverie.

"Lost in thought?" Sarah smiled, seeming both amused and concerned as he collected himself.

"Yeah, I guess you could say that." He realized he had almost run into her without noticing he was about to collide with someone, let alone who that someone was. "What are you doing here?"

She looked up and to the left, searching the buildings. "I went to a restaurant on the roof of a hotel around here once. It had a fabulous view. Alexander fell asleep, so I texted you a little while ago to see if you wanted to join me, but I didn't get any reply."

"Really?" He pulled out his phone and was embarrassed to find the unread message alert on his lock screen. *Dinner?* "I'm so sorry. Reception is spotty in some of these old streets. I had to…run an errand." He wasn't sure why he didn't tell her about Father Nikolaos, then decided he did the right thing, keeping the number of people who knew what happened to the ostracon to a minimum.

"Well, if you're done with your errand the offer is still good. Care to join me?"

Fatigue instantly disappeared from Graham, replaced with a feeling he had suppressed the last few days, a feeling that had been missing since Olivia died. A feeling he had been certain he would never have again. He allowed his renewed sight to fully admit how beautiful Sarah was, a beauty he now believed reflected her heart.

"Absolutely. I'd like that. I'm starving. And I know the restaurant with the best view of the city."

He led the way back through the Christian quarter of the Old City, to the New Gate and the Notre Dame of Jerusalem Center Hotel on the other side of the street. A table had just opened up along the balustrade of the terrace restaurant, silencing them with the view.

"Spectacular," Sarah said. "This is the best view of the Old City I've ever seen. Jerusalem's like a jewel that becomes duller in daylight."

Graham watched her dark eyes slide across the lights of the Old City until they landed on his.

"Thank you for helping me find Xander. I don't know

what I would have done without you." As she spoke, she reached across the table and placed a hand on his. "He's the only family I have left."

Graham trained his expression into what he hoped was a thoughtful smile, and—with effort—removed his hand and scratched his nose, pretending an itch, then draped his arm onto the balustrade railing. The touch of her hand electrified him, but it reverberated in a pang of guilt, as if he were being unfaithful to Olivia. "I only did what had to be done. anyone else would do."

"That's not true." She drew her hand back, his action not affecting the look of appreciation on her face. "And I want you to know I am profoundly in your debt. I'm so thankful God blessed us with you."

"Blessed you?" Graham studied her face for irony and found none. "You know I'm the one who planted the idea in Alexander's head in the first place. I'm more responsible for him being lost than found."

Sarah smiled, shaking her head gently. "Not at all." She paused, weighing her words. "I've been thinking about what happened with your wife and daughter. I'm so sorry. You must be a man of great faith to bear it."

Graham glanced out at the domes of the Holy Sepulchre with the Temple Mount aligned behind them, then down at the table before him. "No, not really," he sighed. "It's odd to think of such emptiness as a burden. But nothing has ever weighed on me more than their absence." He looked up, not knowing what else to say, wondering if he'd shared too much already.

"I can't pretend to know what that is like," she said, "but the way you describe it touches on the way I feel about my family. But in your case, you know they have the promise of eternal life. They are in the presence of our Heavenly Father. There is no other hope."

Graham offered a sad smile. "A year ago, I wasn't able to recognize that truth. I almost didn't make it out of the darkness that fell on me. It's like they left behind their shadows. And then I became one myself. A living shadow." He paused, as if illustrating his own absence. "But God patiently pursued me and kept reminding me of His goodness. I couldn't taste it at first. Like anesthetic wearing off after you get a filling at the dentist. Eventually, I not only felt His touch again, but I craved it. I couldn't resist it." He put his hands back on the table and folded them in front of him, wishing he could undo his earlier recoil.

When the waiters began their rituals of closing for the night, both were surprised to discover they were the last table left in the restaurant, oblivious to the time that had passed. After insisting on paying, Graham rummaged through his pockets for coins to include in the tip, trying to rid himself of as much change as possible, since he wouldn't be able to use it at home. He sorted through the money and saw that one of the coins was an Egyptian piaster.

The sight of it—of the word *piaster*—evoked the lyric of a song that had always intrigued him. He could even remember looking up piaster as a teen as he read the words while listening to the album. Then he remembered the lines that came before it, something about how the singer's life began again with the unexpected arrival of a woman.

"What is it?"

Graham could feel her eyes study his expression, trying to read his thoughts, but he ignored the question, instead letting it be answered by the voice of Donald Fagan as Steely Dan broke into "Doctor Wu" on his internal jukebox. He pocketed the coin and borrowed a line from the song. "Are you with me, doctor?" He took her hand and together they guided each other through the New Gate.

AFTERWORD

Although the story that threads these archaeological locations and finds together is purely my invention, the places and items themselves are portrayed as accurately as I am able. No history or legend was harmed in the writing of this book—at least intentionally—with one exception.

On January 10, 1938, James L. Starkey was murdered by Arab bandits while traveling from the dig he supervised at Lachish to the opening ceremony of the Rockefeller Museum in Jerusalem. The question of why he was killed is still fodder for conversation among some archaeologists. However, it was certainly not because he had discovered an ostracon in addition to the eighteen others he had already recovered. The nineteenth ostracon is the only fictional archaeological find in the book. Three more ostraca were found in the months following Starkey's death. Today the twenty-one letters are on display in the Rockefeller Museum, Israel Museum, and the British Museum.

Saint Catherine's Monastery is the oldest continuously inhabited monastery in the world and became the focus of much attention after Constantin von Tischendorf's controversial discovery of Codex Sinaiticus. The monastery still claims the Bible is rightfully theirs, but it remains on display at the British Museum. The 1975 discovery of twelve missing leaves from Sinaiticus—along with 1,200 other manuscripts and fragments of 50,000 others—in the ruins of a fire several years earlier demonstrates the wealth of material at the library there. Only the Vatican Library has a larger collection of ancient biblical manuscripts.

I am grateful to Father Justin, the librarian at Saint Catherine's Monastery for graciously answering my inquiries about the Ashtiname and Nectarius's *Epitome*, a history which includes the story of Helena's identification of the site. Also, some of the dialogue of Father Nikolaos, my librarian, was lifted from *The Ladder of Divine Ascent*, a medieval spiritual classic by John Climacus, abbot of Saint Catherine's in the seventh century.

The description and text of Tischendorf's promissory note comes from Dr. Daniel Wallace, who was shown a digital copy of it while working at the monastery. His account was given in a lecture, and he was kind enough to supplement my understanding of it through email. It is Dr. Wallace's work through the Center for the Study of New Testament Manuscripts that is the inspiration for the digitization performed at the beginning of the book. You can learn more about—and support—their fascinating and important work at http://www.csntm.org.

The traditional location of Mount Sinai in Egypt was not examined critically until the birth of archaeology, when an interest developed in investigating biblical history. Many people who have visited the mountain have had difficulty reconciling it with the features described in the Bible. But no other proposed site for Sinai—and there are many challengers—seems to fare any better. Except for Jebel al-Lawz.

Although Beke, Burton, Doughty, Philby, and Musil all proposed sites for Sinai in the northwest corner of Saudi Arabia before Ron Wyatt, Wyatt was the only one to take the time (besides Beke, a hundred years earlier) to actually go investigate his candidate closely. Wyatt's surreptitious 1984 trip into Saudi Arabia became national news upon his release after he spent over two months in jail for being an Israeli spy, and he was interviewed on the CBS Morning News. What he found at Jebel al-Lawz has been ridiculed as the act of an over-zealous amateur who saw only what he wanted to see. His claims to have also found Noah's Ark and the Ark of the Covenant have made him a cult hero in pseudo-archaeology, and a pariah to scholars. And yet, something about Jebel al-Lawz can't be easily dismissed.

Part of the mystique comes from the sudden appearance of the security fences and guardhouse, erected before Wyatt's second visit, apparently in response to the first. Clearly, the Saudis believe something of archaeological import is there, even if it is not the biblical Sinai. Another part of the mystique comes from the claim that his photos and video were confiscated by soldiers both times. Several years later, explorers Bob Cornuke and Larry Williams followed Wyatt's example and illegally made their way to the site before having their documentation taken from them. Although there is a missile base several miles away on the top of another part of the chain that includes al-Lawz, the presence of guards who didn't allow photographs at this particular location seemed very suspicious.

It took the ingenuity of Jim and Penny Caldwell to finally find a way to get images of the site out to the world. During their tenure with Aramco, they took fourteen family camping trips to the site, one of which led to the discovery of the Split Rock. The vacations gave them an excellent excuse for the images. I am thankful to Penny for sharing several high-resolution images with me and for taking the time to trade emails about the site. Since the Caldwells, the site has been photographed by Lennart Möller (a Swedish medical doctor), Aaron Sen (one of the people who accompanied Möller), and—most extensively—by Sung Hak Kim (a Korean doctor who was a personal physician to one of the Saudi princes).

There are a number of scholars who have argued against Jebel al-Lawz based on the known facts, not because Wyatt and those who followed him are not properly trained archaeologists. Joe Zias, the curator of archaeology and anthropology at the Israel Antiquities Authority during the period of Wyatt's work, officially commented on Wyatt in two different emails that have been published online. His remarks are quoted in this book verbatim.

The only investigation of the site by archaeologists was done in 1996 by Saudi Arabia's Ministry of Antiquities and Museums, and produced a report entitled *Al-Bad' History and Archaeology*. According to published interviews conducted with the Caldwells, there are a number of inaccuracies in the report, and drawings of the V-shaped structure contradict what is shown in photographs.

All of this adds up to just enough evidence to arm both advocates and detractors, but not enough to prove or disprove either side. Some Bibles now include Jebel al-Lawz on maps of the area as an alternate location for Sinai.

The abandoned mansion of the Metochion of Sinai can still be seen in Istanbul, apparently sinking below the surface of the street. I am indebted to my good friend Ladd Lesh for indulging me on an excursion to find it during a long layover.

The Siloam Inscription is kept at the Istanbul Archaeological Museum at the Topkapi Palace, despite being found in Hezekiah's Tunnel in Jerusalem. The biblical and Islamic treasures of the Topkapi Palace are faithfully described.

As for the fate of the original manuscript of the Ashtiname, I am indebted to the kindness of Islamic scholar Dr. John Andrew Morrow. He shared the knowledge that the document was last renewed in 1904, and that it was last seen by a non-Muslim about a hundred years ago. Dr. Morrow also shared that the archives are a mess. His work, *The Covenant of the Prophet Muhammad with the Christians of the World*, is an invaluable resource for understanding how Christians and Muslims can peacefully coexist. The English translation of the "Ashtiname" is by Anton F. Haddad and found in his book, *The Oath of the Prophet Mohammed to the Followers of the Nazarene*.

The stories of Lady Stanhope, both Philbys, Masada, Timna, the Moabite Stone, the Holy Sepulchre, the twelfth Dead Sea Scroll cave, and the Cave of Skulls are told without embellishment. The mask described in the archive of fakes that purports to be from Jebel al-Lawz is real, as is the likely-mistranslated inscription. Any inaccuracies in the stories as they are retold are failures of mine.

The legends passed on in the book come from anecdotes in travelogues. In particular, the story of Moses's cousin, Kárún, comes from Richard Burton's, *The Land of Midian*, volume 1. The legend of the Golden Camel is found in Larry Williams's book, *The Mountain of Moses*.

The Oriental Institute at the University of Chicago does host a database for the artifacts that went missing from the Iraq Museum after it was looted in 2003. How accurately it is maintained is unknown.

The archive of archaeological fakes kept by Yaniv at the Rockefeller Museum does not exist. (Or if it does, it is an accident of creative license).

All quotes from the Qur'an were taken from *The Noble Qur'an in the English Language*, translated by Muhammad Taqi al-Din al-Hilali and Muhammad Muhsin Khan. The authors include parenthetical remarks in the text for clarity, but I have either removed or incorporated them without the parentheses to make it more readable. It was my intention to convey the Qur'anic text as faithfully as possible, but those familiar with the Qur'an may find subtle changes made to preserve the meaning without having to resort to explanation that would slow down the narrative. In the interest of full disclosure, I have listed the changes.

When surah 28:30 is cited, I translate the word *'Alamin* to read *all that exists* in order to help the flow of the text by not having to define the word. The translation is the parenthetical one supplied by the translators.

In surah 7:146-7, I substituted *verses* for *ayat* in the first instance, and *evidences* in the second two. All are suggested parenthetically in the English translation and were changed to avoid having to explain the Arabic word.

The quote of surah 1 during the prayers of the guards was changed from the translation only to conform to proper English capitalization rules.

Alexander's criminal record was inspired by my friends Nabeel Qureshi (a classmate of mine at Biola) and David Wood, both passionate and talented Christian apologists. They were arrested for disturbing the peace at the 2010 Arab Fest in Dearborn, Michigan, but were eventually found not guilty. It is with David's permission that I appropriated their experience. Nabeel, sadly, was taken by cancer in 2017.

ACKNOWLEDGMENTS

Although there is no shut-up music to much me. I have rambled too long in thanks and gratitude, I must express my profound appreciation to a number of people. (I'll leave the musical cue to wrap-up to you.)

Without the WhiteFire team, none of this would be possible. David and Roseanna have been a well of encouragement, and Roseanna's gift for excellent covers is once again on full display. Janelle Leonard's thoughtful editing ironed out all the wrinkles and removed more than a few warts.

Dan Lynch remains the only person in the world who has passed the time in lines at DisneyWorld by reading my manuscripts on his phone. If he ever discovers the Lightning Lanes, I may have to find a new agent.

Many thanks to Rick Altizer, Jamie Brandenburg, Bob Cooper, Mark Haggard, Jay Hollis, Cyndy McRae, and Eric Smith for their thoughts and suggestions on early drafts. The book is better because of you all.

Most of all, thank you to my wife, Jennifer, who graciously allowed me the time to play in my sandbox of words.

PICTURE GUIDE

St. Catherine's Monastery at the foot of the traditional Mount Sinai. It is the oldest continuously operating monastery and oldest continuously operating library in the world.

Constantine von Tischendorf, discoverer of Codex Sinaiticus.

James L. Starkey in 1935.

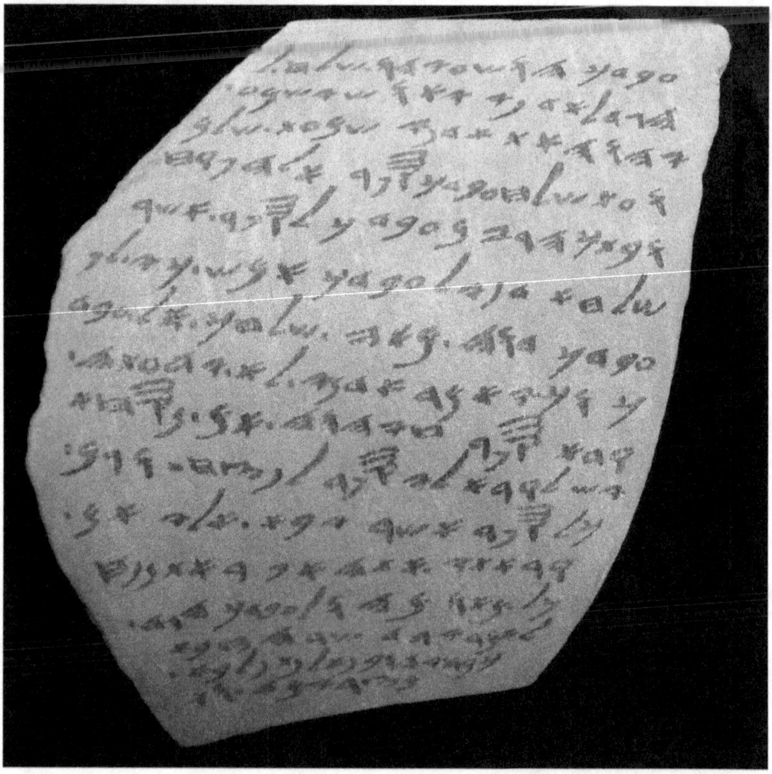

One of the Lachish letters discovered by James L. Starkey in 1938.

The copy of the Ashtiname at Saint Catherine's Monastery.

The Metochion of Sinai as it appeared in 2019. (Photo: Doug Powell)

Rear of the Metochion of Sinai in 2019 (Photo: Doug Powell)

Entrance to the Ecumenical Patriarchate (Photo: Doug Powell).

Entrances to the Topkapi Palace and its Chamber of Sacred Relics
(Photo: Doug Powell).

Rockefeller Museum, Jerusalem (Photo: Doug Powell).

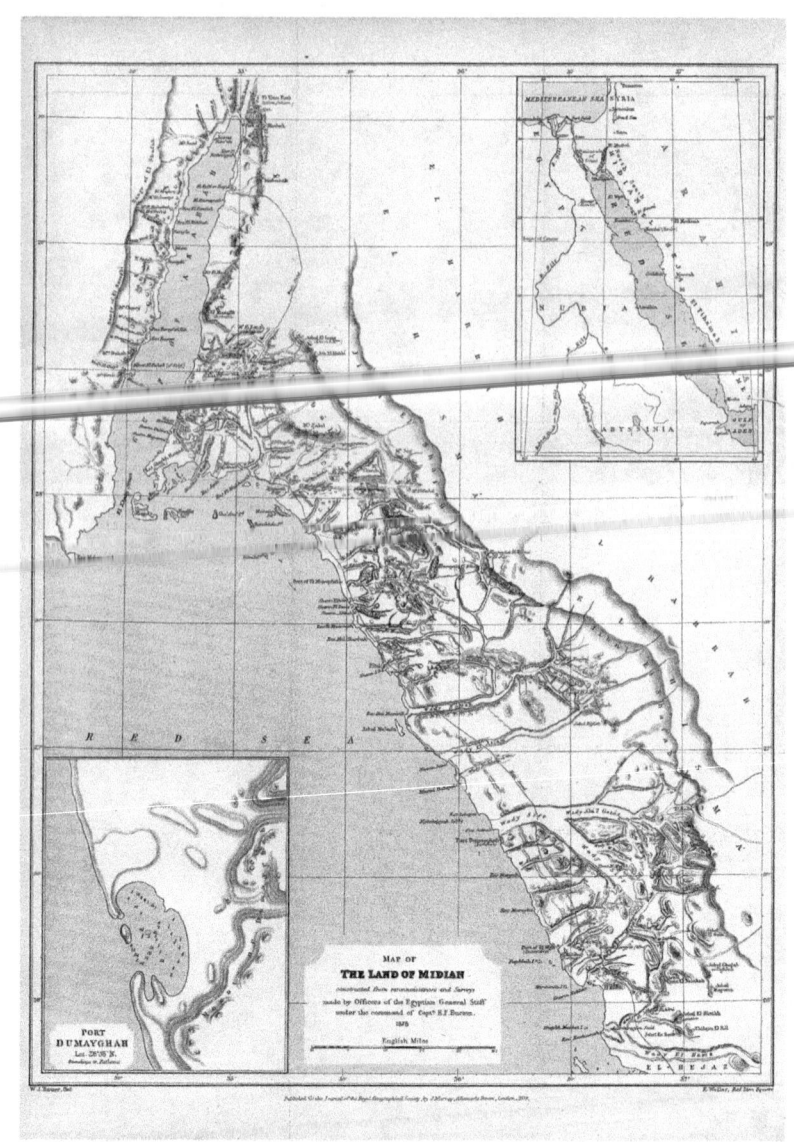

Richard Burton's Map of Midian.

Satellite image of Nuweiba showing the winding canyon route to the beach. (Photo: Earth Science and Remote Sensing Unit, Lyndon B. Johnson Space Center

The pillar discovered Ron Wyatt on the beach, now erected on the outskirts of Nuweiba (Photo: Africa / Alamy Stock Photo).

Traditional Tomb of Jethro near al 'Bad
(Photo: by Khawaja Umer Farooq/Shutterstock).

Possible Split Rock of Horeb
(Photo: by Khawaja Umer Farooq/Shutterstock).

Possible Golden Calf altar
(Photo: by Khawaja Umer Farooq/Shutterstock).

One of the bovine petroglyphs on the alleged Golden Calf altar.
(Photo: by Khawaja Umer Farooq/Shutterstock).

The black peak of Jebel al Lawz, called Jebel Maqla seen from the Golden Calf altar. The "holy precinct" is at the foot of the mountain. The expanse between is large enough for the Hebrew slaves from Egypt to camp. (Photo: by Khawaja Umer Farooq/Shutterstock).

See these and more images in the online photoguide at:

grahameliotseries.com

Follow the latest Doug Powell news at:

dougpowell.com